MARK H BARTON

The Wrenkle

First edition

ISBN: 979-8-9997183-0-3

Editing by Dan Hanks
Editing by Laura Joyce
Editing by Lucy Littlejohns
Cover art by Adam Fyda

This book was professionally typeset on Reedsy.
Find out more at reedsy.com

To my dear daughter Samantha, for forcing me to tell you this story and strongly encouraging me to write it. Without you, this series would remain hidden in the shadows of my mind.

Acknowledgments

I am very grateful to my editors, who's keen eyes, thoughtful insights, and unwavering support helped shape this story into its final form. Your patience and precision brought clarity where there was once only chaos, and your encouragement meant more than I can say.

To my illustrator — thank you for helping bring my book to life in a way that words alone could not. Your talent captured the soul of the story and gave it a face.

To my family that helped review and provide feedback, I cannot thank you enough. Your support means a great deal to me.

This book is stronger because of each of you. Thank you.

1

The House-sitter

The abrupt chirp from the nightstand jolted Sarah's attention away from the magazine she was flipping through. She felt a chill, slightly nervous at hearing a sound that she hadn't heard before. She was house-sitting, deep in the Virginia forest, and she hadn't yet got used to the strangeness of the place.

She glanced toward the source of the noise, but she couldn't see what was causing it. She listened intently, then turned back to her magazine, only for the chirp to come again, seemingly louder this time.

"Well, that's going to be annoying!" she said, aloud, tossing the magazine aside and abandoning the open bag of chips beside her. "All right, all right, I'm coming!" Keeping up a stream of bright chatter helped her to feel less unnerved by the unusual sound.

Standing now, she scanned the room for the source of the noise. It didn't sound like her phone or anything she recognized. The chirping was faint, as if obscured by something. She held still and listened, her body tensing.

After a minute of this, realizing how silly she looked, she relaxed into a sheepish grin and loosened her body. She looked around the dim room searching for a clue.

The odd episode made the silence feel deeper, and she considered how isolated she was out here. The darkening room cast long shadows in this house, in the forest. The vacation spot was a stark contrast to her life in her bustling city apartment and her busy college schedule. She'd seen these expansive forests on television but she never considered the thought that she'd be out in them alone. It was only the encouragement from her relatives and the constant nagging from her friend that finally forced her to commit to this trip. Now that she was on her own in this dark cabin, she wondered if she should have held her ground and stayed at home. A chill crept up her back and goosebumps prickled her arms. She turned her focus towards the open doorway, where darkness loomed just beyond the door frame. Her imagination ran wild with thoughts of horror movie monsters lurking just out of sight.

A fresh noise broke the silence, suddenly.

"Eek!" She spun around to see where it was coming from. Relief washed over her as she recognized it was just her phone. She laughed and shook her head. "Very adult, Sarah... A promising psych major indeed... Oh my gosh."

She let out a single sigh, and in a single stride, leaped back onto the bed, grabbing her vibrating phone. As she answered the video call, Gwen's weary face appeared on the screen.

"Hey Monkey! How's it going?"

Sarah laughed at the nickname. Gwen had lovingly coined it in grade school after an embarrassing incident on the monkey bars. *Leave it to Gwen to get the entire class to call me that for the rest of the year.*

"Hey Gwen! Things are great… Wait, are you still at home?" Sarah saw her own puzzled expression on her phone screen. "I thought you'd be on the road by now. Did something happen?"

Gwen sighed. "Before you get angry, let me explain."

Sarah tuned into the details of the call – she could hear a background hubbub of sound, and she saw people walking behind Gwen, onscreen.

"I know you planned on me arriving tonight, and I really want to be there, but I'm still stuck on this lousy essay. I need to finish it to pass my English Lit class, or my grade is going to be no bueno. The professor said he'd bump my grade up if I rewrote it."

A loud bang came from behind her followed by laughter. Her expression shifted to one of irritation as she turned away. Sarah could hear her shouting off-screen. "What did you break now Kevin?! Come on guys, keep it down please, I'm on a call over here!"

Sarah rolled onto her back and brushed her brown hair from her face. "Gwen, I totally understand… I'm just excited to see you… It's been forever. But yeah, you gotta pass that class."

"Thank you for understanding, I'm really sorry… I didn't realize I was failing the class until this afternoon. Ever forgive me?"

"Maybe," Sarah said, with a grin. "Just promise you'll be done in time to get here tomorrow, and we'll talk about it."

Sarah saw Gwen grin, an echo of her own smile onscreen. Gwen's posture straightened as she used her index finger to draw an invisible 'X' on her chest. "I promise, cross my heart

3

and hope to have to date Brad."

Both girls giggled.

"Hey!" From behind Gwen, a surprised young man could be seen; his head poking just round the door.

"Oh hey Brad... I wasn't talking about you. I was talking about another... Brad that I know." Gwen turned back to Sarah and grinned. She whispered, "Totally him."

They both snickered quietly.

"Oh Monkey. I'm so excited for this trip! I really do need a break from this place. These people here are driving me bananas lately." She motioned over her shoulder. "So what's it like? The house and the area... Is it as nice as you thought it would be?"

Sarah looked up from the phone, surveying her surroundings. "Well, it's definitely nicer than anything I'm used to, that's for sure. How do I explain it? It's sort of a cabin, type of thing, yet huge... Sort of backwoods – very secluded and dark. I haven't explored the entire house, but I think my aunt and uncle must be loaded because from what I've seen tonight, it seems pretty posh."

Sarah turned her phone's camera to pan across the room and then she returned to the call, showing her face. "Oh and Gwen, don't bother bringing any food. On the last call I had with my aunt, she insisted they'd treat us to all the food we'd want. I didn't get a great look but I think she has the fridge fully stocked for us. We're going to have the best time getting fat while we're here!"

"Cool!" Gwen patted her belly. "Wait Sarah... Did you say it's up in the mountains? Sorta creepy, like a scary movie mountains? Man, I'd hate to be alone up there."

"Hey! Shut up, it's exactly like that here. I might die tonight

THE HOUSE-SITTER

and be on the front page of the podunk newspaper here. Give these folks something to read about." Sarah said, smiling wryly.

Sarah watched as Gwen began typing. "You know, if I get this paper knocked out soon, I could drive through the night and get there by morning."

"No Gwen. You don't want to do that. You'd never find the place. Seriously, these trees are pretty dense, and the roads are mostly unpaved. I barely found the place myself. And on top of that, we don't need you falling asleep at the wheel and becoming a statistic."

Chirp chirp! The strange sound came again. Sarah thought it might be from the corner of the room. She turned to look but still couldn't trace the origin. She was distracted by the loudness of the noise on the video call. She looked back at the screen and saw several people walking into Gwen's tiny dorm room. Gwen rolled her eyes and stopped typing.

"Hey monkey girl, I'd better go... I need to get this paper done!" she yelled, emphasizing the last two words while glaring at the intruders. "I'll see you tomorrow night okay? Love you, girl... Watch out for anyone carrying an axe!" Gwen gave Sarah a quick smile and a wink before someone bumped into her laptop and the video disconnected. A text came through shortly after. **Jerks in my room. Cya tomorrow.**

Sarah responded and then tossed the phone onto the pillow. She turned to look again at the corner where the sound seemed to have come from. She let out a loud sigh, got out of bed, and leaned down to check under an old lamp shade. Feeling around, she turned on the light and looked at the assorted detritus on the nightstand. There was a hardback book lying open, its pages mashed and creased. She moved

5

it aside to uncover an illuminated iPad showing a picture of her aunt and uncle on its home screen. Several pieces of paper fell from inside the book and onto the floor. She leaned over and collected the papers, stacking them neatly and then putting them back into the book. She read the name 'Black Coast Insurance' in bold font on several of the papers. Just then, a new message popped up on the iPad, accompanied by the familiar chirp.

"Ah so you're the culprit. Found you."

Unplugging the charging cable, she picked up the tablet and quickly brought it back to the safety of the bed. Propping up a few pillows, she sat up, leaning against the headboard to take a closer look at the iPad. The screen showed several alerts. She tapped the top message, and the screen changed to reveal an application with the caption 'CV Pro.' Below it were nine boxes, each displaying different images. It was the video security system for the home.

She zoomed in on the top-left box which showed a gravel road and her small white car. The adjacent box displayed a large tree and part of a rustic-looking pavilion. *These must be in the backyard*. The images were live video feeds from cameras around the property, providing full coverage of the front, side, and back of the yard and house.

Paranoid much? she thought, smirking. Why would her aunt and uncle need so many cameras so far from civilization? It was more usual in the city where theft was more common, but out here it seemed a little excessive.

As she scanned the feeds, she noticed movement in one of the boxes. The creature, by the pavilion, was small and brown with erratic movements; it was some kind of animal. On closer inspection, she decided it must be a raccoon or something similar, rummaging on the ground. "I think I've solved it," she said to herself, with a grin. She concluded, triumphantly, that her relatives must enjoy watching the wildlife from a safe distance and these cameras allowed them that.

As she continued to look at the other video feeds, another one caught her eye. It showed a large rustic building, possibly a shed or maybe a workshop. It had one wood-framed window and two barn-style doors. The building looked like something from a painting but seeing it on the oddly colored video feed was a little unsettling. The image had an eerie quality. She noted the feed was labeled 'Shop View.' Directly adjacent to this feed was another labeled 'Shop View 2.' Sarah thought this feed might be from inside the shop because the light coming through the window matched what she'd seen in the other feed.

Suddenly feeling tired, she checked her phone. It read '10:32 p.m.' She dropped the iPad and stretched. "Time for bed," she said, letting out a loud yawn.

The iPad chirped again. She reached out to silence it. Just then, another alert. She saw a notification bell icon in the upper right corner of the screen with the number '382' beside it. A strange feeling arose in her chest. She wasn't sure if it was the thought of that many animals moving about the yard or something else. She considered the feeling for a moment... It almost felt like an intuition but she quickly pushed the thought out of her mind. *Every thought and feeling has a logical reason,* she thought, quoting her favorite professor. Clicking the icon brought up a new screen labeled 'Events' showing a list of camera names and times. She selected the top event - 'Backyard – 10:33 p.m.' - and saw a picture of the animal, now highlighted with a red box. The program had identified what had caused the motion alert with the red outline. She zoomed in to confirm what the animal was. *Yep, a raccoon. Dang, I am good.* Then she closed the picture and scrolled through the rest of the events. As she did, she noticed one labeled 'Shop View 2 – 7:05 p.m.' This event stood out from the others and made her pause. *What could possibly be moving inside the building?*

Selecting it, she revealed a static photo of the shop's interior, which was still dim, but she could see a little more clearly. The most prominent objects in the shop were a large workbench and a wall of tools. On the ceiling was a black square that looked like some sort of attic access. The shape was framed with a red outline, signifying movement. Sarah drew in a sharp breath and tilted her head. She used her fingers to zoom into the shape, but it was too dark to make anything out. After a minute of effort and consideration, she concluded it must be a glitch in the software. She'd seen this same anomaly in her grandfather's remarkably similar system. She yawned again and put the iPad back in its place on the nightstand, trying to shake off the reoccurring feeling that something might be wrong.

After preparing for bed, she turned off the light and noticed the beautiful night sky through the window. It was brighter outside than in her room and she'd never seen a sky like it. However, there was something oddly familiar about it and it brought her comfort as she made her way through the dark room. She crawled onto the bed marveling at the starlit canvas above. Kneeling, she looked down from the second story room and recognized the yard, including the pavilion and the shop. The moonlight made the large building look less eerie now. To her surprise, she noticed the small window was slightly open. This was enough to give her further pause. *Hadn't the window been closed in the video feed?* She considered double-checking the iPad, but something caught her eye. Through the window, she could see a slow, red, blinking light. It reminded her of an old digital alarm clock that had reset after a power loss. Her grandfather had one of these old relics and it was also Sarah that had to reset the time after one of their typical brown-outs.

She yawned again and then scanned the sky and backyard one last time. The strange feeling returned again. She'd seen this before from somewhere. *Had they sent me a picture of this place?* she thought as she continued to take in the scene. When her eyes returned to the shop window, she was shocked to see the red blinking light she'd just seen was no longer visible. Not only that, but something also seemed to be blocking her view. She rubbed her eyes and looked again. She was seeing clearly but there was something wrong. It appeared as though a dark shape, tall and slender, was standing inside the shop, staring back at her.

She gulped, horror-struck, then quickly ducked down, hitting her head on the wooden headboard. Pain shot through her forehead as she touched the developing bruise. Too scared to scream, she bit her lip. Tears rolled down her cheeks as she tried to stay still, and her heart seemed to thrum in beat with the throbs of pain. The overwhelming unease she'd felt before overcame her, now accompanied by deep fear. She felt alone and very vulnerable. She wiped at the tears, but a fresh batch trickled down her face. The stinging pain and fear mingled together and settled into her stomach. She held very still for a few minutes, breathing deeply in an attempt to calm herself. Once things finally eased, and her shaking subsided, she decided to face her fear. Slowly, she raised her head back up above the headboard.

She peeked out the window and saw the yard and the top of the shop roof. All looked normal. Very slowly, she continued to straighten her body until more and more of the shop came into view. Just before seeing the window, she drew in a deep breath and held it. To her surprise, the red blinking light, and the workbench, were both visible again.

She exhaled, unsure if she had seen what she thought she had. *Was my mind playing tricks on me? I mean I only looked for a moment.* After a few minutes, she decided to try not to think about it more tonight. She took one last look and then quickly dove into bed, pulling the covers up to her chin, and stared into the dark of the room. The thoughts returned unbidden and troubled her. She really wasn't sure she'd seen what she thought she had, and it was difficult to jettison the image from her mind. It had happened so fast, but she was almost certain she'd seen a dark silhouette inside the shop. In her imagination, the shape took on different forms, many more horrifying than the last. It would be a while before she could sleep, and the thought of what might be in the shop left her restless throughout the night. The last thing that floated through her mind as she was overcome by sleep was whether she had remembered to lock the front door to the house.

2

Alexander

12 March 1705

He leaned the pitchfork against the door frame and set the slop bucket down with a dull thud. The sky had long since darkened, and the air carried a chill. He hesitated; he was late, which would likely lead to his father's displeasure. Drawing in a breath, Alexander pulled the metal latch, which was cold to his touch. The door creaked open, and as he stepped inside the familiar warmth of the hearth reached his chilled nose. Carefully, he wiped his boots on the worn mat, every movement deliberate, as though he could somehow delay the inevitable.

"Alexander, a word." His father's voice came from the parlor – calm, but firm.

"Aye, Father. I'll be with you shortly." He winced as he lowered himself onto the stool near the front door. He braced himself, tugging off his boots, each action dragging on, trying to prepare for whatever was coming next.

He straightened his shoulders and breathed deeply, before

entering the parlor.

His father sat in his customary high-backed chair, the firelight flickering across his face, pipe smoke curling lazily around his spectacles. His feet were propped on the ottoman, a letter spread across his lap. It was a picture of calm that filled Alexander with a cautious hope. Perhaps his father was in a forgiving mood tonight.

"Would you care to explain?" His father's tone was conversational, his eyes still on the letter. But Alexander knew better than to be lulled into complacency by the calm demeanor.

"I was delayed, and it took longer to finish my chores because…" He hesitated, searching for the right words, knowing that careful honesty was his only path forward. "I made a friend on the way back from school, and we decided to fish by the lake."

The silence that followed seemed to stretch, only the sound of the crackling fire filling the space. Alexander felt his pulse quicken as he waited for judgment.

His father finally set the letter aside, regarding him with an unreadable expression through the haze of pipe smoke. "Fishing, was it?"

"Aye, Father."

"And tell me, does that sound like the decision of a responsible young man?"

"No, Father. Chores first, distractions later, as you have always counseled."

His father narrowed his eyes, considering. "That is correct." He paused, staring at his son for what felt like an eternity before continuing, his voice formal. "The usual punishment for such an infraction is to send you to bed without supper. However, I'm sure your mother left you something by the stove. You will need your strength for the morning's work."

Relief washed over Alexander, and despite his best effort to stay serious, he felt a smile twitch at the corners of his mouth. "Thank you, Father."

His father's face remained stern, but there was a twinkle of amusement behind his spectacles. "Do not mistake my leniency for approval. This must not happen again. Now, off with you."

"Aye, Father. Thank you."

Without another word, he quickly made his way to the kitchen, his stomach gurgling in anticipation. The faint scent of meat and potatoes still lingered in the air, reminding him of how long it had been since his last meal.

"Is that you, Alex?" his mother's voice called out before he even rounded the corner. The warmth of the kitchen greeted him, along with the comforting remnants of supper.

"Good evening, Mother." He stepped forward to give her a quick, appreciative kiss on the cheek.

"There you are! I thought I'd have to send your brothers out to search for you before long. And what's this I hear about you meeting a new friend?" She was already at the hearth, filling a small plate with what was left of dinner.

"Must you listen in on every conversation I have with Father?"

"That's my right as your mother." She dropped the plate down in front of him with a gentle thud. "Now, do not avoid the question. Who had the honor of your company today?"

He hesitated, considering his words. He had no habit of lying to his parents, but the idea of his older brothers discovering that he'd spent the afternoon with a girl was enough to make him break some rules.

"Her name is Margaret," he finally admitted, trying to sound as casual as possible. "She's good at fishing. Better than me at catching them, too."

His mother raised an eyebrow but continued scraping the last bits of food into a dish for the family dog. "Margaret, you say… Would she happen to be from the Vikar family over the hill?"

"I don't know, Mother. I didn't inquire. She's just smart and pleasant to be around, that's all. I hope I get to see her again soon."

His mother smiled, her eyes softening. She tousled his hair in a way that only mothers can. "Well, be sure your chores are done first next time. Friends, smart or not, can wait."

"Aye, Mother," Alexander mumbled through a mouthful of food. He knew she would be pleased about the prospect of him making a new friend. She always had a way of making conversations easy.

"Good, then finish up and get to bed. Your father will need all his sons out in the field bright and early tomorrow. We cannot have the youngest falling ill for lack of sleep." She planted a soft kiss on his forehead before leaving the kitchen.

He quickly polished off his supper and set about cleaning his plate and fork in the basin. His fingers were numbed by the chilly water, but he dried everything carefully with his mother's cloth, just as she liked. Once done, he hurried upstairs, eager to capture his thoughts before the day slipped away.

Inside his small bedroom, he sat at his simple wooden desk, the flickering candle casting shadows on the pages of his journal. He considered doing his Bible study first but quickly pushed it aside. This felt more important. With ink and quill

14

in hand, he began to write:

Alexander's Journal

This evening I write to speak of my new, wondrous friend. This day, whilst others toiled in school, I passed the hours with her. I fear I did commit a small sin in omitting this to Father, yet I hope God will forgive me. When she asked if I might join her at my favorite fishing spot, my heart leaped, and I could scarcely contain my excitement.

Ne'er have I seen hair so dark, as black as the deepest night. My heart did cease its beating when she first spoke "hello" and smiled upon me. I was struck dumb, standing there with my mouth agape, unable to find my words. At this, she laughed – oh, the sound of it! Though I felt shame, she reached out and touched my hand, and I knew then that she was no ordinary girl.

Her name is Margaret. She invited me to visit her family home tomorrow, but alas, I am bound to work with Father, preparing the wheat for the season. Still, I hope with all my heart that I might see her again soon.

Satisfied, he closed the journal, feeling a soft smile touch his lips. He could still hear Margaret's laugh echoing in his mind as he blew out the candle and climbed into bed, eager to replay his day with her in his mind.

3

The Visitor

Sarah woke to sunlight reflecting off the wall, casting a warm glow across the room. She felt sweat bead on her forehead as she shifted to her back and stared at the ceiling – dust particles floated lazily in the air, catching the light.

Last night was now a fuzzy memory, and the room, once shadowy and foreboding, now appeared bright and inviting. Large wooden beams crisscrossed overhead, supporting pine-colored planks, and across the once-dark walls, she could see the cheerful artwork hung there. She suspected that her aunt, Melissa, was behind the decor. She'd gathered that her aunt was artistic from their various correspondences. Aunt Melissa seemed to also be into the finer things and talked excitedly about them.

Freeing her arms from the tight cocoon of the blanket, Sarah stretched. She felt relief as her muscles unwound from the twisted position she'd slept in. She glanced around, searching for a clock, but found none.

Sitting up, she rifled through the blankets, searching for her phone, but it was nowhere to be found. She kicked her legs free from the covers and got out of bed. Her feet were sore for some reason, and she flexed her toes while stretching her back. She discovered a throbbing pain on her forehead that reminded her of the knock she'd given herself last night. She gingerly touched the spot, wondering if it had left a bruise.

Walking to the foot of the bed, she shook the blankets, hoping her phone would appear. On the second tug, items from the bed tumbled to the floor with a thud followed by a series of clattering noises. She sighed, discovering a spilled bag of corn chips scattered across the beautiful planks. "Sarah, is it possible for you to be any more of a klutz?" she muttered to herself, staring at the mess.

Rolling her eyes, she knelt and scooped up the chips and the crumpled metallic bag. Crawling on her hands and knees, she swept the remaining crumbs into the bag the best she could and tossed it into a small wooden wastebasket. Glancing at the nightstand, she noticed something she hadn't seen the night before. There was a vase with a single flower and a framed photo of her aunt and uncle on a ski slope. This made her smile. She could see a resemblance between her aunt and herself – something about the eyes.

Returning to the search for her phone, she finally spotted it under the bed, near some stray chips. Lying flat on her stomach, she reached out and grabbed the device with her fingertips. The chips, on the other hand, were just out of reach and she decided to leave them for when she could find a broom.

As she stood, her eyes were drawn out of the window to the shop. The fear she'd felt the night before started to creep back in, making her pause. Facing her fear, she slowly edged toward the window and peered out. The shop doors, which she had thought were previously closed, now appeared slightly ajar. *Hold on, maybe it was too dark to see the doors completely closed?* The logical part of her mind told her there must be an explanation and she shook it off.

With a long sigh, she tore her gaze away from the building. Determined to shake off the silly notion, she focused instead on unpacking her bag and making the bed. She selected her clothing, which included her favorite green tee shirt, and headed to the bathroom for a shower.

After getting herself ready, she opened the master bedroom door, stepping out of the room for the first time since the previous night. The hallway, once dark and dingy, was now bathed in the golden sunlight streaming through the skylight above. The house, a mixture of rustic and luxury, was decorated with heavy wooden beams and richly paneled walls. It felt like a cabin yet had an undeniable elegance. It was warm and inviting. This was a stark contrast to the previous night when the empty house had felt dark, cold, and almost uninviting.

She explored the house, finding two bedrooms on the same floor as hers, each with its own bathroom. The stairs down led to an open area that included the grand front door as well as a small library with walls covered in green wallpaper and bookshelves. Directly above the library the second story hallway could be seen nestled behind a beautiful wood railing. It gave the front interior of the home a large and open feeling. A large window and skylight allowed golden rays to illuminate the room. Sarah's attention was drawn to several pictures that hung down the stairway. All of the them appeared to be family photos, several from an earlier era, and a few more contemporary. She made a mental note to take a closer look at them later. Beyond the library, an archway led to a spacious family room and connected kitchen. She'd sort of seen this area the prior night, but it had been dark, and she hadn't really taken the time to explore and appreciate it. However, in the light of day, the kitchen looked amazing. It bore large opulent cabinets, a commercial-grade refrigerator and large twin gas stoves that would make Gordon Ramsay proud. This was a chef's culinary dream.

Continuing her exploration, she found an office, a guest bedroom, a main-floor bathroom, and a small deck that opened from the family room. It offered a view of the pavilion in the backyard as well as a partial view of the shop.

Deciding it was time for breakfast, she opened the fridge, remembering the abundance of food and snacks she'd briefly seen the night before. *I definitely underestimated the food.* She stood marveling – it looked like enough to feed a family of six, not just two nineteen-year-old college students. She pulled out a small container of fruit and a quart of milk, then located some cereal in the well-stocked pantry. As she sat at the long bar, she noticed a brown paper bag filled with even more food. Near it was a small envelope with her name on it. Opening it, she found a letter and four one-hundred-dollar bills. The letter read:

Hello Sarah!
   We're so excited and grateful that you're able to house-sit for us! Please make yourself at home.
   I wasn't sure what kinds of food you and your friend liked, so I bought a little of everything. I hope you can

find something you enjoy.

I've written the Wi-Fi password, our email, where to find the hidden key, in case the code doesn't work, and our cell numbers on the back of this paper. If you need anything, please email us, and we'll call as soon as we have connectivity. We'll be at sea for most of the time but should have phone access near ports.

As we discussed, you'll need to feed Ralph. If you haven't seen him yet, he's probably hiding in the garage. His food is in a cabinet by the garage stairs.

Thanks so much and enjoy your stay!

Love, Aunt Melissa

Sarah smiled at the letter, touched by her aunt's thoughtfulness. She hadn't known her aunt and uncle before she had met them at her grandfather's funeral, but they had become a great source of support over the past few months. Her grandfather had essentially served as her father, and the regular phone calls, texts, and emails from her newly acquainted relatives had really been a blessing in her life.

Mental note: get aunt and uncle a thank you gift.

She turned over the letter. On the back, she saw the letterhead for the company, 'Black Coast Insurance.' Here, her aunt's additional instructions were written. Sarah folded the letter back up then looked around the room, wondering where Ralph might be hiding. In the adjoining garage, she found a small silver bowl with his name inscribed on it. She poured some food into the bowl, hoping the cat would appear. "Here, Ralph… Come here, kitty!" There was no sign of him.

Shrugging it off, she returned to the kitchen, cleaned up

her breakfast dishes, and put away the extra groceries. She briefly considered pulling out her laptop to work on a paper but her lazy side prevailed. Instead, she flopped down on the white sofa, pulling out her phone to check her messages.

There was one unread text from Gwen: **Hey Sarah. Tried to call and got voicemail. Finished my paper this morning and OMW! See you tonight.**

Sarah smiled and replied: **Awesome! Give me a call when you're close. See you soon! Love ya!**

Doing some quick mental math, she estimated Gwen's arrival time and frowned, realizing it would be near or after dark before she would show up. The thought of being alone at night again made her uneasy. Despite spending a lot of time alone in the city, being alone here in the country was different; it was almost too quiet for her. She shook off the feeling. *I'm a tough city girl.* She grabbed her phone charger and searched for a power outlet.

Just then, a low rumbling sound outside caught her attention. It grew louder, and she quickly realized it was a vehicle of some type. She placed her charging phone on the side table and moved cautiously toward the front of the house. There was no way Gwen could have arrived this fast. *I mean, she's a fast driver but even she can't get away with speeding through Baltimore and D.C. unnoticed.*

Peering through the front window coverings, Sarah saw a yellowish, rusty pickup truck idling near the property's entrance. The cab was far away, and she couldn't make out the driver. The vehicle lingered for a moment before slowly rolling past the house and then out of view.

She listened until the noise of the truck faded into the distance. "Hmph, guess I'm not getting any visitors after all." Her introverted side really didn't want to see anyone up here anyways, especially while she was in such a rural and unfamiliar setting. She let out a long sigh and looked around, suddenly unsure how to keep herself busy.

Grabbing her backpack, she moved to the office at the end of the hall, setting up her laptop on the desk. As she plugged in the power adapter, she glanced out the window and saw the shop again. Just as before, the doors were slightly ajar, confirming her earlier suspicion. She gazed at the large window and envisioned the thing she thought she had seen the night before standing there. That familiar chill ran down her spine. The thought of someone – or some large animal – moving around the property while she was alone was unnerving.

The hours passed quickly as she fiddled with her computer, watched a movie, and worked on her paper a bit. The house had become eerily quiet, the silence only broken by the occasional creak or settling sound, normal in a house of this age. Lost in her work, she barely noticed the fading light until her stomach growled, reminding her she hadn't eaten since breakfast. *What time is it?* She scanned the room, but she couldn't see a clock. There was something strange about the office that she hadn't noticed before. It was clean, unused, almost sterile. There were no papers, open notepads, or scribbles of any kind. Even the insides of the various drawers looked to be carefully arranged and untouched. It reminded her of a set from a TV show. Her stomach clenched again, a second reminder of her hunger. Instead of pushing the virtual snooze, she decided to get something to eat. *Lunch er dinner... linner?*

As she walked into the dimness of the kitchen, she flipped

on the lights. Seeing the garage door off the family room, she remembered Ralph and decided to check on him. There was no sign of the cat but the bowl was empty, so she filled it again. She paused and wondered how much food a cat should really eat. *Well, I guess you're on vacation too Ralph.* "Enjoy!" she said with a shrug, and she went back inside.

Back in the family room, she picked up her phone and saw two missed calls and several texts from Gwen. She had completely forgotten to check her phone earlier. A sense of panic settled over her as she listened to the voicemails.

"Hey Sarah. Hope your phone isn't dead. I'm about an hour away. Call me back when you can."

"Hey, it's me again. I think I'm on the right track, but I'm having trouble with the directions. Call me back when you get this."

Sarah's heart sank. The time stamp on the first voicemail read 6:05 p.m. It was now 7:33 p.m. "Shoot!" She quickly dialed Gwen's number, but the call went straight to voicemail. After a brief moment of panic, she tried again, but there was no answer. She read through the texts, and they said the same thing. Her friend was probably lost, and she'd missed the opportunity to talk to her.

She stared at her phone, chewing her lip, hoping it would somehow tell her what she should do. Suddenly, a loud knock at the front door startled her. It was a knock so forceful that it reverberated through the house.

She tossed her phone down and ran toward the noise. *She*

made it here on her own. Happy to greet her friend, she yanked hard on the large metal handle. "Gwen!" she began to yell but stopped.

Instead of her friend, a large, bearded man stood near the doorway. His gaze was intense as he stared down at her.

"Yes? Can I... help you?" she stammered and her grip tightened on the door handle.

The man stared at her for a moment longer and then looked into the house and then back at her.

"I'm lookin' for Steve. He around?"

She blinked, her mind racing. This man was too much to take in. His appearance was a muddled mix of hair, scars, and wrinkles. He wore what looked like a sailor's cap and one of those corn cob pipes in his mouth. "I'm sorry, they're, he's, not here, they are away... right now. Can I help you with something?"

The man frowned slightly; his expression unreadable. He again looked past her into the house. "You're alone," he said as his gaze returned to her. The sentence sounded like it should have been a question, but it wasn't.

"What?" This wasn't what she had meant to say. She wanted to ask him what gave the old sea dog the nerve, but by the time she regained her faculties, it was too late. The old man let out a grunt and was already heading back up the driveway.

She watched, dumbfounded, as he walked the long distance and climbed into his truck, the same rusted pickup she'd seen earlier. As it drove off, she slowly closed the door and engaged both of its locks for good measure.

She stood there for a moment, her heart still pounding. What had the man wanted with her uncle? And why in the heck did she tell him they were gone! She looked at the ceiling in exasperation and then she looked out of the window.

She kept her eyes on the driveway. Her mind kept imagining the truck pulling back up and when that didn't happen, she was then finally able to think of Gwen again and how to help her.

4

Margaret

16 May 1707

Alexander removed his hat and bowed low before Mrs. Delaney Vikar, Margaret's mother. He could feel her eyes on him, sharp and unwavering, and it gave him a nervous feeling in his stomach. The room he was standing in had a dark and eerie quality to it. He could see no further into the house; a large curtain blocked his view.

"It is a pleasure to make your acquaintance," Delaney said, her words precise. Though she spoke politely, her tone lacked the warmth he had hoped for. Her eyes, steely gray, were cold, and her mouth remained a thin line. From the corner of the room, a pair of young girls, Margaret's sisters, giggled behind their hands. A quick glance from Margaret silenced them and they went back to their game.

The tension was thick in the air, making Alexander's fingers twitch nervously. His cheeks burned. He hadn't really been taught and wasn't well-practiced in formal greetings, and now he felt the weight of his own awkwardness. "Thank you... madam." He fumbled around, unsure of where to look, his hat still dangling from his hand like a foreign object he didn't know how to use. One of the girls snickered again.

Delaney's eyes lingered on him, unblinking. "Do not concern yourself with them. The youngest is Alice and her sister next to her is Madilyn." She pointed them out one by one, her long finger not moving from the chair. "They are unaccustomed to visitors, especially those of the male persuasion. And please, there is no need to stand on ceremony here, Alexander. We are not so formal in this house."

Her words were meant to reassure, but they did little to calm the nervous fluttering in his chest. There was also a subtle tension that hovered between her and Margaret, who shifted on her feet as though awaiting unspoken instructions.

"Margaret, why don't you offer our guest a seat."

"Yes, Mother." There was something tentative in Margaret's voice, and she seemed reluctant as she glanced at Alexander. "I had thought to show Alexander about the house."

Her mother's expression didn't change. She stared at Margaret with an intensity that made the room feel even smaller. It was as though they communicated without words, a silent battle of wills. After a long pause, Delaney finally spoke, her voice crisp but quiet. "I should like a word with Alexander first. A brief word."

Margaret gestured weakly to the high-backed chair beside him. "Will you sit, Alexander?"

He awkwardly shuffled to the chair, sitting quickly, his body stiff as he settled in. Margaret followed him, quietly taking a seat across the room as if Delaney had already decided where she ought to be.

"Well then, Alexander," Delaney began, her voice deceptively calm but her eyes piercing as they studied him. "Where do you claim as home? You and Margaret have known one another for a while, I think it's high time I get to know you as well, don't you?"

"Yes, ma'am. I live just beyond the hill. We farm the land for Lord North, as we have for as long as my family has lived near Otterburn. And I beg your pardon for not coming to introduce myself before now. The fault was mine. We are much engaged during this season of the year."

"Yes. I believe I have met your mother, Mrs. Martha McGregor, is that not correct?"

"Yes, ma'am, that is indeed my mother. Do you know her well, ma'am?"

"I met her but once. I encountered her on her way to church not long ago. A kind woman." She paused, eyes narrowing slightly as she added, "Your family, are you all of the Catholic faith, Alexander?"

Margaret tensed, her face flushing as she shot her mother a look. "Mother, not this again..."

"It is a perfectly harmless query, Margaret." As she spoke, her gaze never left him for even a moment. Her voice remained calm, but there was an undercurrent of tension that made him shift uncomfortably in his seat.

"Mm, yes ma'am. We attend church each week... Save for during the harvest." He felt his head begin to spin slightly, and his stomach churned as her eyes seemed to bore deeper into him. "We miss a few weeks during that time of year." He then felt his eyes glaze over. He tried blinking them but was unable. He struggled internally as he stared deeply into her gray eyes.

"And your father, what is his occupation? Does he also toil upon the land alongside you?"

As she said this, her long finger began moving, drawing a circle in the air.

"My father… Um yes we assist him in working the land," he responded. He could hear his own voice, but it sounded monotonous, almost mechanical.

"Yes and what of your mother? I assume she helps him in his labors? I assume you have brothers and sisters?"

"My… mother? She… well… She helps around the estate…" He could feel the words coming out of his mouth, but they didn't seem to be his own. Alexander felt his mind drifting in and out of consciousness almost like the moment before he fell asleep.

Margaret stood suddenly; her face flushed with frustration. "Alexander, let us go outside." She quickly pulled him to his feet.

"I have… two brothers… and a sister… ma'am…"

"What is the haste, Margaret? We were but getting to know one another," said Delaney, her gaze still locked on him and a small smile on her lips.

The room seemed to tilt under his feet making him stumble sideways a step. Margaret stepped in between them and immediately he began blinking and looking around the room.

"Mmm… It was a pleasure to meet you, ma'am."

Delaney tilted her head slightly, her smile widening. "The pleasure was all mine, Alexander." She reached out and offered him her hand.

Alexander, dazed, reached out but before he could respond to the gesture, Margaret tugged him firmly, pulling him through the house and out the front door, leaving Delaney's hand dangling in the air. Delaney let out a low chuckle and snapped her fingers.

The front door slammed shut behind them with a loud thud. The sound seemed to further shake Alexander out of the strange trance he had fallen into. He continued to blink rapidly.

"Are you well?" Margaret asked, her forehead creased with concern as she peered at him.

"I am well... I think. In truth, I feel exceedingly well." His voice was oddly flat. "Why do you inquire?" His words came out still almost mechanically, as if he wasn't fully aware of his own response. A moment passed before he blinked again, as if waking from a long sleep. "Wait... how did we get out here?"

Margaret's face tightened. She closed her eyes for a brief second and then cast an angry glance back toward the large windows of the house. In the dimly lit room, she could just make out her mother's silhouette standing by the window. Her face was still showing the broad grin that she had when they left. She then nodded to Margaret, almost like a sign of approval. Margaret rolled her eyes in response and tugged on his arm again.

"Come, Alexander. Allow me to walk you home."

He nodded and put his arm out, the daze still on his face. He sounded almost drunk as he spoke. "I should be the one to walk you home, Margaret. My little Raven."

She sighed and then let out a small giggle and shook her head. "Come, let us return you home." She put an arm in his and they began the long journey.

As they walked, his strides became more surefooted, and he felt his mind coming back to him. "Margaret, can you tell me what transpired at your home?"

"I do not believe you would fully comprehend." Her eyes flickered to him for a brief moment. He continued to watch her, expecting an answer. "My mother does delight in making others uncomfortable. It's her way of…" She paused for a few moments, trying to choose her words. "Measuring people. She sizes them up, one might say."

"Yes, but why did my interaction with her feel like a dream? I can scarcely recall but vague fragments of our meeting. Was it perhaps some sort of trickery?"

"Yes, you might say as much," she said, but she gave a look that signified that there was more to it. She stopped walking and turned toward him. She wore a serious expression that held a tentative edge. "Alexander, there are matters I must reveal to you regarding my family. Matters that I ought to have disclosed before now, but I fear this is not the proper time nor place." Her face flushed and she looked down, her eyes only looking at him briefly, to judge his reaction.

He considered pressing the matter but then relented. He grabbed her hand and lifted her face to meet his. "My pretty Raven, I'm feeling myself again. Allow me to escort you home. My father always taught me to be a gentleman. I should feel the sting of his belt were he to witness you walking home with me." He offered her his other arm and a kind smile.

"Raven." She mused at the nickname. She put her arm in his and they began the journey back. "So, do you really believe me to be pretty?"

5

The Lost

Sarah's car sped down the dirt road, the gravel spitting up behind her as she drove much faster than she should. Her nerves were shot, and anxiety gnawed at her, concern for Gwen gripping her lower abdomen. Glancing at the phone beside her, she saw the time: 8:45 p.m. It was dark now, the narrow beams of her headlights cutting through the blackness ahead.

She had only driven this route once, but she felt confident that if Gwen was nearby, she'd find her. She hoped that as she drove, the cell reception would also improve, allowing her to call Gwen. She tossed the phone back onto the passenger seat and muttered a curse. The man who had turned up at the house unannounced had unnerved her. He'd shown up at the worst time and his behavior had been unsettling. She shook her head. There was something else that bothered her as well. She really hadn't given it much thought but despite the strangeness, there was a familiarity about him she couldn't place. She knew him from somewhere. A thought crept into her mind. *What if I'd seen him on one of those serial killer documentaries?* A loud expletive slipped from her mouth, and she pressed down on the throttle, pushing her car faster down the dirt road.

A familiar noise snapped her out of her thoughts, and she slammed on the brakes. The white coupe skidded to a stop; her little phone buzzing next to her. Snatching it up, she answered. "Hello?! Gwen?!"

"Sarah?" Gwen's voice was faint and breaking up. "Can you hear me?"

"Yes! Where are you? I'm so worried! Did you drive back to town or are you still nearby?"

The words 'I,' 'think,' and 'close' were the only things Sarah could understand before the connection fizzled out, dropping the call. She cursed again as she tried to call her back, but it went straight to voicemail.

At least it sounded like Gwen was still searching for the cabin.

On Sarah's drive up the canyon yesterday, she had noticed several roads branching off the main one. Perhaps Gwen had taken one of them and gotten lost? Continuing on, she slowed down where the road grew bumpier and twisted around sharp corners. The farther she drove, the more surprised she was that the two cars hadn't crossed paths.

Finally, she reached an intersection. The road here was paved – she recognized it instantly. This was the highway she had taken the night before. The contrast between the dirt road and the pavement was unmistakable. Frustrated, she turned the car around, then brought it to a stop and tried to call Gwen again. Voicemail. "Hey, Gwen. I'm at the main turn-off. I'm heading back up the mountain. I'll try to catch you on the way back."

After many more minutes of driving, Sarah was fairly certain Gwen had either taken one of the forks off the main road or hadn't found the correct turn-off from the highway. Both scenarios were dangerous at this hour. She considered her options: head back to the cabin and call for help or explore one of the side roads herself. The thought of getting lost, or worse, getting a flat tire on an unmaintained road, made her dizzy with worry. She flexed each hand individually and made a conscious effort to stop clenching the steering wheel. "So, this is what they mean by 'white knuckle driving,'" she said aloud. Tears pricked her eyes as the road steepened ahead. She remembered this stretch from earlier – it was the last long hill before the road flattened out near the cabin. The road shoulders narrowed here, almost too tight for two cars to pass each other. Then she saw it: a faint glow coming from the drop-off on the left. Her heart leaped, and she pulled the car to the left side of the road to get a better look.

As she neared, the vague light separated into two distinct beams. It was a car already parked on a road she hadn't noticed before. Sarah pulled as close as she could to the edge on the road's shoulder, killing the engine and flipping on her brights. She stepped out and inched closer to the edge. Peering through the trees, she saw the car below, maybe a few hundred feet down, though the darkness made it hard to tell the true distance.

She yelled her friend's name, but the sound seemed to get lost in the trees. She tried again, with no response. She leaned into her car and pressed the horn. In the distance, an answering honk responded back, but it was faint. *Was it an echo?*

She considered hiking down the hill. She weighed her other

option which was to find a way to drive to the car, but that felt like a gamble. What if she got lost? What if Gwen drove by while she was off on a side road? No, the only real choice was to go down on foot. *I hate both plans actually.*

She pulled out her phone and activated the rear light. The trees near her were lit only by her car's headlights which cast long shadows into the forest. She drew in a deep breath and then took her first step off the trail and started down, holding the phone out to guide her. The descent wasn't too difficult at first – the trees were spaced out, and there weren't many obstacles in her way. Soon the terrain grew steeper, and wet leaves made her slip before regaining her balance. Steadying herself, she continued the descent.

Surprised at how far she had come, she found a spot to take a break and sat on a fallen pine tree. Mud caked her shoes, and she began picking at it with a small branch. As she did, she looked up at her car, considering its distance from her. It was much farther than she had previously thought. She didn't relish the idea of hiking back up but knew that she and Gwen would be able to drive back up together. A sense of pride actually started percolating inside her – she had never done anything like this before. *I mean, I've spent a good deal of time alone in the city but nothing like this.* She tossed the stick aside and got ready to keep going. Then, she heard it: a low rumble from the vehicle below. Her heart sank immediately. That wasn't Gwen's small car. It was a truck – and not just any truck. The sound was unmistakable. It had to be the man she'd encountered earlier. The pride she'd felt immediately evaporated. "You have got to be kidding me!" she yelled at the truck below.

Sighing, she flipped her legs over the log and stood up. The climb back would take twice as long. "The next time I see that old man, I'm going to give him a piece of my mind!" She shook a fist in the truck's general direction and then began to leave. Behind her, the truck engine changed pitch. She turned and watched in disbelief as it reversed out of its spot and slowly drove away from Sarah, up the dirt road, eventually disappearing around a bend. Silence fell, except for her own steady breathing. What little light there was had gone.

The path ahead was nearly pitch black. She stared into the darkness for several moments before letting out a long drawn out sigh. She finally pulled out her phone, its small light barely cutting through the night. She was angry but in the silence of the night, her feeling was slowly replaced by a creeping fear. Alone in the dark forest, she now felt vulnerable. She pointed her light around, trying to get her bearings. Her headlights above were just visible, pinpricks in the dark but a distant beacon in the night.

As she inched forward, she marveled at how quiet the forest had become. Every motion she made was amplified. Every step and every breath. She walked on, stomping loudly as she went. Above those noises, she heard it – a branch snapping far behind her. She froze, holding her breath, listening. Another snap, closer this time. She turned, her light flickering off the nearest trees, but she couldn't see anything beyond them. Her mind raced. Had she imagined it? *Ears could play tricks on you, couldn't they?* But then came a louder snap, followed by the sound of something pushing through the underbrush. It was close. *Way too close.*

Fear gripped her. She moved faster, her footsteps now urgent. Her care for making noise was diminished. A loud scraping sound echoed behind her, more deliberate and human than before. Her heart pounded as she pushed herself harder, her shirt now soaked with sweat, her lungs burning.

She stopped again, leaning against a tree, gasping for air but trying to be quiet. A loud snap came from behind, followed by the unmistakable sound of footsteps on rocks. Whatever was behind her was no animal – it was following her like a person would.

Panic surged, releasing her primal side. She turned and sprinted up the hill, her movements clumsy and desperate. Rocks and branches tripped her up, but she kept going, every sound behind her driving her faster. Her phone light whipped wildly in the dark, illuminating trees, rocks, and nothingness as she scrambled forward.

The footsteps behind her quickened. Whatever it was, it was right on her heels. Her legs burned, her lungs screamed, but she didn't stop. She couldn't imagine it.

Eventually, her strength gave out. Her legs buckled, and she tumbled to the ground, rolling to her side and cracking her head on something hard. She lay there, gasping, tears streaming down her face. She curled into a ball, covering her head with her arms, waiting for the inevitable attack.

But nothing happened.

The forest was silent again, the only sound, her own labored breathing and her desperate weeping. She opened her eyes slowly, wiping them with her shirt. The sky above was dark, but she could see light filtering through the trees. Trembling, she looked around, but the forest was still.

She lay there, shaking uncontrollably, her body cold and numb. Something was wrong. The cold sensation crept up her legs, into her chest, and she felt it: a black shape loomed above her, blocking out the sky. It was close. Cold air brushed her face, and a foul odor filled her nostrils. She opened her mouth to scream, but only a whimper escaped. Her strength drained away, her eyes rolling back as she started to slip into unconsciousness.

In the distance, she thought she heard a car's brakes squeaking, and faintly, the music of a flute. Then, darkness.

6

Raven

16 December 1707

Alexander sat down after supper and prepared for bed as he typically did. He thought about the next day and the chores he'd need to finish, and he hoped he'd have an opportunity to steal Margaret away from her family for a few hours. He paused and pondered her odd family and the strange things he'd seen while at their home. They'd seemed to have grown accustomed to his presence and, though he'd come to feel welcome, he never quite felt comfortable with their traditions. He reached up and felt the back of his hair and could feel the notch where some was missing.

After reading a few verses in John, he closed his Bible and pulled out his journal to write what was on his mind.

Alexander's Journal
I have made a firm resolve to limit my ventures to the Vikar home. All my former visits there have been quite strange, and I

have ever departed with a sense of unease and discomfort.

During my last visit, but yesterday, Margaret's elder sister did invite me to sit within a great circle upon the floor of her chamber. Though Margaret had suggested otherwise, I did comply. Her sister, Claire, then proceeded to sever a large lock of my hair from my head. When I did protest, she merely laughed and did tuck it away in a pocket of her petticoat. She did then proceed to recite some poem, the meaning whereof I could not comprehend. Margaret did take this foolishness far harder than I. This among other things that I shan't write, have been a true oddity.

I have now come to the conclusion that her family is too strange to bear as a whole. Henceforth, I shall continue my acquaintance with Margaret and limit my time with the Vikars.

I do believe that Margaret and I have become more than mere friends, and I do pray that I may begin courting her when the time is fitting. I have come to care for her a great deal. I find her intelligent, amiable, and most fair to behold. Her fair skin is rivaled only by her pitch-black hair. She is my best friend; she is my Raven.

He pushed the book aside and yawned. He blew out the candle and dropped into bed, falling asleep almost immediately.

Later that night, a sharp tapping against the window stirred him from sleep. He blinked, groggy, as the sound came again, louder this time. Pushing himself up, he peered out the window to see Margaret standing below, tossing another pebble. It made another pinging noise off the glass. With a wave, he slowly opened the window.

"Come down," she mouthed, her voice a whisper in the night.

He stared back with tired eyes and shook his head. The last time he'd left the house during the night to meet his friends, his father had punished him. However, something in her demeanor was troubling, the shadows of night making her appear more fragile. Her silence was unnerving. After a long pause, he lowered his head. "One moment." He knew full well that the belt awaited him for this disobedience, but he needed to know if she was okay.

Quietly, he changed out of his nightshirt, pulling on his work trousers and shirt. He rushed back to the window, pushing it open farther. With a glance over his shoulder, he slipped one leg over the sill, then the next, and gingerly climbed onto the roof. He shimmied down the post, his feet landing softly on a barrel below.

"Pray, what was all the trouble for?" But before the words fully left his mouth, Margaret had thrown her arms around him, burying her face in his chest.

"Margaret?" His arms hovered awkwardly above her. A soft sob escaped her, muffled beneath the veil of her dark hair. "What troubles you? What is it?"

He could feel her tremble in his arms, and after a few moments, she finally pulled away. Her tear-streaked face, her swollen eyes – it was clear she had been crying for hours. Instead of replying, she grasped his hand, tugging him insistently toward the grove of trees they often visited.

"Wait... allow me my boots!"

But she kept pulling him through the field. Barefoot and stumbling, he followed, the wet grass and sharp stones licking and biting into his feet.

They reached the small grove, both panting from the long run. She led him to a fallen log, where they often sat, side by side in the quiet of the night.

"Now, pray tell, what has caused you such grief?"

Margaret turned to him, her eyes still glistening but with an odd glimmer of hope now. "Alexander..."

"Yes, Raven?"

She paused, staring into his eyes for several moments before speaking again. "Have you ever wondered what it would be like if you were to run away? Leave everything behind – your family, your troubles?"

"Whatever do you mean?"

Her eyes grew desperate again, wide with emotion. "What if I should leave? What if I should go far from here?"

"Margaret?"

She gripped his arm tightly, her voice breaking as tears welled up once more. "Would you come with me? Pray, say you would come with me tonight."

"Margaret!" He stood abruptly, his voice louder than intended. He turned to face her, his eyes wide and confused. "Surely you jest. This is no time for such play. You wake me up for this... game?" He began to walk away but she only grabbed his hand and pulled him back. There was a seriousness in her eyes.

"Very well. Where would we go? Where would we live? We aren't even betrothed."

"That doesn't matter. I have no time remaining." Her eyes now stared at the ground. She seemed to be battling with some inner problem that she was trying to solve. "My mother has informed me today that I have come of age." She shook her head, as if in disbelief. "The time is right."

"I cannot even begin to comprehend. But whatever the trouble, we will resolve it together."

"Alexander. There are things that I needed to tell you before now... but there isn't time. Please come with me. Let us depart now. I need to leave, and I wish you to accompany me!"

"Margaret, whatever it may be, we can mend it, together. I will never leave your side." He held her hands, pulling her close to him. "But I cannot leave with you now. Not in this manner."

Suddenly, she stiffened, her posture becoming rigid. Her tear-filled eyes closed as she whispered, "I no longer have time. We should have flown when we had the chance."

"Raven, I do not understand..."

"She speaks of leaving before her time to become awake." There was a familiar voice from several yards behind them.

Startled, Alexander whipped around, his eyes wide at the dark figure emerging through the grove. "Claire?"

"Good evening, Alexander." She moved closer, her face becoming visible in the moonlight. "She speaks of her time to join our company... our coven, one might say." Her smirk widened as she reached them. "Margaret, Mother is troubled. It took me some time to find you." Her tone dripped with mock concern as she stared at her sister. "Thanks to Alexander, it was not too difficult." She patted something in her pocket.

"Pray what do you mean by that?" Alexander said.

"Very well. I will come. Only give me a moment. Please, Claire." Margaret's voice was small and thick with resignation.

Claire exhaled loudly and rolled her eyes before nodding.

"You need not go." Alexander whispered, urgently. "You may stay here if you wish. We can explain this to my..."

43

Before he could finish, Margaret leaned in and pressed her lips to his, silencing his words. It was his first kiss, and it felt desperate as she pulled him tightly to her. This startled him, and before he understood what had happened it was over.

When she pulled back, her eyes locked with his, filled with unspoken words. Then, without another glance, she walked away.

"Good evening!" Claire's voice was as playful as ever. She waved, holding up the lock of hair she'd taken from him days before. Even in the dark, he could see the wink she had sent him.

He stood, staring after them as they walked away into the black of the night. A mixture of emotions swirled inside him, confusion, anger, and love, bundled together. He slowly walked back to his house, resolved to straighten things out in the morning.

7

The Found

Sarah sprinted through the dream-like forest, trees whipping past as she splashed through mud and scrambled over rocks. She'd never been much of a trail runner, and she was surprised by how fast she could run. *This has got to be a dream*, she thought, but she continued forward regardless. The path ahead twisted and turned, rising over hills and dipping into ravines. Thin fog curled through the trees in every direction, lending an eerie quality to the landscape. Her legs felt heavy, like they were made of lead, but she continued to move at a great pace.

A stream emerged from the fog ahead. Without breaking stride, she planted her foot and leaped over it gracefully, her landing as smooth as if she were a deer.

Faint plodding noises echoed from far behind her. They didn't sound threatening, more like the skittering of a small animal across a wooden floor. She pressed on, faster than before, driven by a need to keep moving, though she had no clear destination in mind.

A creaking noise sliced through the forest's tranquility,

snapping her out of her rhythm. *That doesn't sound like something you hear in a forest*, she thought, glancing at a patch of wildflowers she passed. She tried to refocus on her run, finding unexpected joy in the movement despite the strangeness around her. She kept her legs and feet in sync which required more concentration now.

Another louder, creaking noise shattered her focus. It was close now, so close that she stumbled over a small rock she hadn't noticed. *This is the strangest forest I've ever been in. Not that I've been in many, but I don't recall any creaking noises in those nature documentaries that Mr. Vargas forced us to watch in Biology class.* She snickered at the thought and then looked down. She had stopped running altogether. *Wait, what was I doing again?*

Sunlight filtered through the thickening mist, its beams fragmented and pale. Exhaustion washed over her, sapping the strength from her legs and making her feel impossibly drowsy. She squinted, searching for a place to rest, but the mist had become thick, and she found it hard to see. *No, wait, there's a spot!*

Through a small break in the fog, she spotted a patch of grass, lush and inviting, reminiscent of the park where she and her grandfather used to picnic.

Sweat dripped down her face, and she trudged toward the spot, her limbs growing heavier with every step until she was barely shuffling. Looking down, she realized her feet were buried up to her ankles in mud. *Where are my shoes?* She winced as the moist dirt filled the spaces between her toes. Each step was a struggle as she pulled her feet free from the muck, the mud slapping back to the ground with each effort.

Finally, she reached the grassy spot and collapsed onto it.

The ground was soft, warm, and surprisingly comfortable, providing a perfect place to rest her head. There was a strangeness to it, like she was being cradled in firm but soft arms. She considered sitting up to remove her muddy shoes, but at that moment, she felt them leave her feet. Then there was pain as something invisible touched the side of her head. *Ouch!* she tried to say but the words wouldn't come. Then the pain was gone, and she began feeling drowsy again.

Just as her eyes began to close, a loud crunching noise broke the silence. The fog had thickened so that she could no longer see the forest around her. Another crunch, then another – something about the sound was off. It didn't match the expected noises of leaves or bark underfoot; it was more like someone munching on a bag of potato chips. She tried to look in the direction the noise seemed to be coming from but was unable. Stranger still, the sound wasn't coming from the trail; it was much closer, almost as if it were beneath her.

This has got to be the oddest place I've ever been.

Another crunch startled her. This time, fear spiked through her, sharp and clear. The sound shouldn't have been so frightening, but it set off alarm bells in her head.

She lay still, hoping to go unnoticed by whatever was making the noise. The tinkle of bells sounded. Then a loud thump nearby, igniting a desperate urge to run. She tried to move, but her body felt like it was encased in a heavy, numbing cement. It was like the aftermath of a Novocain injection – she could feel her limbs, but they were distant, sluggish, and unresponsive.

The mist had thickened into an almost tangible mush, and she could feel it closing in, warm and humid against her skin. Sweat beaded on her forehead and under her arms. Then, something pressed against her right leg – a poke, a scratch, followed by a firm pressure that sent her heart racing. She tried to turn her head to see what it was, but she couldn't move. The fog darkened, and as the last of the light dimmed, all she could do was close her eyes.

This has got to be the strangest forest I've ever been in… The thought returned, unbidden, but she cut it off, disturbed by its persistence. It felt like her mind was stuck, repeating the same thought over and over.

This has got to be…

Then a sliver of fog separated and in the distance, she saw a woman with pitch black hair, coming out of the forest line. She walked slowly but deliberately towards Sarah. A new sound interrupted her. It was so out of place that her eyes snapped open. The fog was gone, replaced by darkness. The mist, which had seemed so real, now flitted away going behind her eyes and dissolving like it had never existed. The last thing she saw fade away was the woman and her dark eyes. Then she heard the sound again – soft, familiar. A cat's meow.

Her mind crawled back to consciousness, and she realized she had been dreaming. Not only that but a familiar dream, one that she'd had before. The forest, the running, the mud, the grass, the woman – all of it faded away as she inhaled deeply and sighed with relief. Her heart raced, and she felt drenched in sweat. She brought her hands to her sides, realizing she was in a soft bed, layered in blankets that now felt stiflingly warm. As she tried to free herself from the blankets, sharp pains flared across her body – scrapes, bruises, and a throbbing headache. She reached up and felt something soft wrapped around her forehead. A bandage.

Apparently the pain is real.

She considered getting up and grabbing her pen and pad to record the dream but before she could, something moved against her leg, and she froze. Memories flooded back: searching for Gwen in the forest, the reckless hike down the hill, the terror of whatever had stood over her in the dark, and the oddly familiar dream she had just had. It all layered together, mingling one with another in a disorganized manner.

The presence in the bed shifted again.

She wanted to leap up and confront whatever had followed her from the dreamy forest, but her body screamed for her to move slowly.

With cautious determination, she pushed the blankets aside and peered into the darkness. The room was pitch black, and her eyes struggled to adjust. The cool air was a welcome relief, and she slowly reached toward the movement by her leg. Her hand found a familiar shape, and she exhaled in relief. It was Ralph, the family cat, nestled against her.

"Ralph! You scared me half to death. Was that you making all that noise?" she murmured, stroking his fur as he purred softly in response.

"Did you find those chips I left for you? I heard crunching all through my dreams," she added with a weary smile.

As she shifted to sit up, pain shot through her bruised legs. She gingerly moved her right leg out from under the covers, wincing as her body protested. Pulling herself into a sitting position, dizziness washed over her, forcing her to close her eyes and steady herself. She couldn't remember how she'd gotten home, but she needed to know if Gwen was safe and perhaps have her fill in the gaps in her memory.

The last clear memory she had was of the dark figure looming over her. Everything after that was a blur, a confusing tangle of sensations and half-formed thoughts. Pushing herself to her feet, she waited to see if her body could support her weight. The room swayed as she inched toward where she thought the door might be. Her hand met the wall, and she followed it to the light switch. She reached instead for the doorknob and pulled it open, revealing a soft blue glow from the hallway and beyond. Even that dim light stung her eyes.

Leaning heavily on the railing, she slowly descended the stairs, each step sending jolts of pain through her scraped and bruised knees. The light led her to the family room, where she found new evidence that someone had been there – luggage on the floor and a half-eaten meal on the counter. Rounding the corner, she saw the muted glow of the television playing an old movie.

On the couch, Gwen lay curled under a blanket, fast asleep. Relief surged through Sarah, so powerful that she had to cover her mouth to keep from crying out. She had seen Gwen only weeks ago, but it felt like months had passed since then.

"MEOW!" Ralph had followed her down the stairs and was now announcing his presence.

"Quiet, Ralph," Sarah whispered. Gwen stirred, her eyes opening to scan the room before finally seeing Sarah.

"Hey! Monk!" Gwen's voice was groggy. "What are you doing up?" She quickly moved to Sarah's side, wrapping an arm around her and guiding her to the couch. "You need to stay in bed. Do you need anything? More painkillers?"

"Hi, Gwen. What time is it?"

"Um, it's after three…" Gwen checked her watch and then

the family room window. "…in the morning. Did you need something?"

Sarah opened her mouth, but no words came. She struggled to gather her thoughts. "I… I just had the strangest dream. A forest and a fog, and—"

"You were running through the forest?" Gwen rubbed her eyes and shook her head. She was obviously still very tired.

"Yes. How did you know?"

"Because you wouldn't stop talking about it the entire time we carried you back here. You kept saying you had to keep running, that you couldn't let 'it' find you."

"Wait, what do you mean when you say *we* carried you?"

"We've already been over this, little Monkey. McGregor, the man you met earlier, he helped bring you back, helped rescue you. Still don't remember talking to both of us?" Her face was pensive. "You really hit your head hard, kiddo. Let's talk about this when you're back to yourself mmkay?"

A sick feeling bubbled up from Sarah's stomach as she considered the man McGregor and the events that had taken place but she couldn't recall. She opened her mouth to ask more, but before she could speak, exhaustion overcame her, and she dropped her head onto Gwen's shoulder. The room spun and then went dark.

8

Caged

02 March 1708

Against his mother's recommendation, Alexander headed down the long dirt road toward the Vikar house. He had waited long enough. There had been several visits to their house, but none had yielded any success. It seemed that all the family were now in league against him. The excuse was that she wasn't home or that she couldn't have visitors. Even Margaret's two little sisters had sent him away without an explanation. He was going to put an end to this once and for all.

His anger grew the closer he got to their home, and he resolved that he would not leave without being given a reason for her sudden absence. He'd talk directly to Delaney if needed. He shuddered at the thought, but he was committed to confronting Margaret.

Reaching their property, he marched up to the door of the dark house, its heavy silence seeming to scream *go away*, despite his resilience. A cold wind rustled some old leaves, as if the house itself was cautioning him to keep his distance. He tugged the leather hat off his head, revealing the sweat and dirt from the day's toil in the fields. As he raised his hand to knock, his breath caught, a strange foreboding settling in his gut. Something was wrong. Still, he ran his hand through his hair and knocked firmly.

"Looking for Margaret?" a familiar voice drawled from behind him. Alexander spun around startled. His heart sank as he recognized Claire approaching, a basket of food slung over her arm. Her unnerving smile stretched wide, and, for a moment, he remembered that chilling night two months earlier.

"Hello, Claire." His voice cracked, exposing his uneasiness. In the daylight, she didn't seem as menacing, but there was something in her tone that unsettled him. "Do you know where I might find her?"

"I assume you mean Margaret?"

"Claire, I need to speak with her. It's of great importance."

"Oh? And what could possibly be so urgent at your young age?" Her voice became playful, dripping with mockery. But he wasn't in the mood for her games.

"Are you going to tell me or not? If you aren't in the mood to be of assistance to me, I can wait here all day if necessary." He leaned on the railing next to the steps trying to show confidence, but it felt awkward.

Her smile somehow grew even broader, and she raised an eyebrow, clearly enjoying his discomfort. She opened her mouth to continue the taunt but was cut off.

"That will do, Claire."

Margaret's voice was soft but firm as the door opened, revealing just her face. Alexander's eyes widened, his heart pounding as he saw her for the first time in months.

"Well, it appears she is home after all." Claire smirked as she pushed past him and then past Margaret into the house. "You always spoil my fun."

Margaret stepped into view, and he felt his breath catch in his throat. She looked nothing like the girl he remembered. Her hair, once so long and smooth, was now thick and tangled, and her eyes, surrounded by dark circles, seemed hollow. Her clothes hung limply, wrinkled and unkempt, as though she hadn't changed them in days.

He took a step toward her, but she held up a hand, shaking her head slightly, stopping him in his tracks. She looked over her shoulder back into the dark house and then back to him.

"Margaret, I've been worried about you. I haven't seen you for months. I've sent messages – have you not gotten them?"

Her expression remained unphased, her eyes distant. "Alexander... I can't talk at the moment." There was a flicker of emotion that briefly crossed her face. "I... I haven't been feeling well. You should probably go back to your home."

Without thinking, he reached out, grabbing her shoulders, and pulled her through the door onto the steps, his voice rising with emotion. "Margaret! I've been concerned about your safety! You came to my house in the middle of the night, you told me things I still don't understand, and then you all but vanish! No messages, no word. Your family won't disclose anything about you! And this is all you have to say for yourself?"

She said nothing.

He opened his mouth to speak but she gave him a look and reached back and pulled the door closed behind her.

"Alexander... That night." Her chin trembled. "It was

a misunderstanding between us. I was wrong to come to your house, and I apologize. I was… not in my right mind." Her head swiveled and she quickly looked through the front window of the house and then back to him.

"Margaret… Raven, please… I care for you. Do you not see that? Tell me what I must do."

The door behind her creaked open once more, and a familiar voice echoed from the shadows. "Margaret, it is time to retire. Say farewell to your friend."

"Yes, Mother." Her voice was flat, drained of all emotion. She began to back away, retreating into the house. He grabbed her arm, his eyes pleading as he searched her face for any sign of the young woman he'd known, but she pulled away from him. "Please do not return, Alexander." The words hit him like a punch to the face and he stared, dumbfounded. And with that, she slipped from his grasp and disappeared into the dark house, the door slamming shut behind her.

He continued to stand frozen at the threshold, his hand outstretched. The air around him felt colder now, an unnatural chill creeping from his back. Something was very wrong in the Vikar house. He could feel it in the pit of his stomach and there seemed to be some unseen force encouraging him to leave. As her silhouette vanished behind the door, he couldn't shake the haunting feeling that this might be the last time he would ever see her.

He stared at the front door and windows for a few minutes and then reluctantly backed down the stairs. His mind tried to retrace the night she'd left. She was so desperate that he should understand something. What was it? Claire had said something about awakening and about a coven. None of it made sense to him and each step towards home added more pain and confusion. Above that, his resolve that he'd had was now gone.

9

The Better Day

Sarah woke up in a bright, beautiful room, the sunlight streaming through the windows in amber rays. The warmth on her face was comforting, but there was a faint sense of unease clinging to the edges of her mind, like the remnants of a bad dream that hadn't quite let go. She stretched out luxuriously, her body sinking into the softness of the bed, and gazed around at her aunt's perfectly decorated room. *I really need to tell Aunt Melissa how much I love her entire house.* She smiled, her eyes tracing the arrangement of the furniture, each piece perfectly placed as if it had always belonged there.

For a moment, she considered rolling over and going back to sleep. But her bladder had other plans. With a reluctant sigh, she pushed the blankets off and let the warmth of the sun envelop her legs. She stretched again, a full body stretch that made her feel more alive, more awake.

After finishing in the bathroom, she found herself in front of the mirror, staring at the reflection of someone who looked both familiar and strange. Her hair was a tangled mess. She smiled at herself. "That's some serious bedhead, Sarah." She grabbed her brush and worked through the snarls. As it tugged at her hair, she winced, feeling a sharp discomfort on the side of her head. Her hand instinctively reached up, fingers brushing against a tender spot. Pushing her hair aside, she froze.

A bruise, dark and angry, stretched across the side of her head. *Wait, wasn't I wearing a bandage?* The thought came suddenly, cutting through the fog of sleep. She backed up, staring at her reflection, her hands beginning to probe other parts of her body. Scrapes and bruises adorned her skin, but the pain was distant, dulled by the long night's rest. Still, they were there – evidence of something she couldn't fully remember. Her knees and elbows bore similar marks. She felt faint echoes of discomfort as she flexed them.

The haze continued as she made the bed and dressed in fresh clothes. As she pulled on her socks, she tried to remember how she'd ended up in the bed last night. The last clear memory was a frustrating conversation with Gwen on the couch, and she was almost certain she'd fallen asleep there. But everything after that was a blur, like trying to grasp smoke.

Downstairs, she found the kitchen sparkling clean, the remnants of human activity neatly tidied away. The family room was in similar order, with cushions perfectly placed, no sign of a blanket, and the TV remote nestled neatly in its caddy on the coffee table. This didn't concern her. Gwen was an early riser and a neat freak. *Good old Gwen,* she thought, with a smile. *Her perfection makes me want to strangle her sometimes.*

She walked down the long hallway, expecting to find Gwen

in one of the rooms, maybe nosing through a family album or looking for her Uncle Steve's tax documents. If nothing else, her friend adored snooping and nothing ever seemed to be off limits. But as she rounded the corner to the office, her smile faded. The room was as empty and sterile as before. In fact, there was no sign of Gwen or her belongings. Confused, she walked back up the hallway and into the library. Looking out the front window, she expected to see Gwen's little green car, but instead, her own car sat parked in the same spot she'd left it the day before.

A frown creased Sarah's forehead. *Where would she go? Maybe to run an errand?* The feeling of concern receded the moment it entered her mind. She knew Gwen very well and this was actually very normal for her friend. As long as she'd known her, Gwen couldn't ever sit still and would certainly turn up. Just then Sarah's stomach growled loudly, pulling her thoughts back to the present. It was difficult to recall the last time she'd eaten, or what she'd had. Shrugging off the oddity of Gwen's disappearance, she made herself a large turkey sandwich, a small bag of chips, and a couple of servings of yogurt.

After eating and cleaning up, she filled Ralph's bowl with cat food and flopped down on the couch to call or text Gwen. Reaching for her phone, she realized it was missing. Pausing, she tried to trace her steps, but the night before was still a blurry mixture of memories and dreams, each intermingling with the other until she couldn't tell what was real. Her phone's last whereabouts were lost in the fog.

Just as she was about to search for it upstairs, a noise came from the back door. Through the glass, she saw a figure. The door flung open.

"Hey, sleepy! Is it after noon already?" Gwen's voice was bright, her smile wide as she entered, a wrench in one hand and something metal in the other. She kicked the door shut behind her. "Did you get the beauty rest you needed?" She did a quick mock survey. "Nope!"

"I've been searching all over for you. Where'd you go?"

"Oh, I've been here and there. Had a very productive day, actually."

"But... where's your car? I couldn't find it. Did you drive mine back last night?"

"I have it parked on the side drive." Gwen wiped the metal object in her hand with a paper towel. "My trunk is doing that thing again – gets stuck open sometimes. My dad told me how to fix it, so I thought I'd give it a try. Hope I didn't wake you with all my loud swearing and banging."

Sarah shook her head, still trying to piece together her fragmented memories. "No, I didn't hear anything."

"Good. I'm glad you're awake. How ya feelin'?" Gwen's gaze was appraising.

"I'm feeling okay, actually. I slept well and I just finished eating like a pig." Sarah patted her stomach with a grin. "A big fat hog. I think my goal is to gain ten pounds while we're here, and I'm not giving up until I succeed."

"Well, good! I'm starting to get a little oinkish myself. I think I saw some Oreos earlier. Oh and hey, your aunt really hooked us up didn't she. You weren't joking about that."

"Indeed, I formally invite you to join my weight gain goal. You know you wanna..."

Gwen put down the wrench and the car part and sat beside her. "It's really good to see you up. You really scared me last night you green-eyed monkey. You were really out of it. I mean, I've never seen you like that, like ever."

"Let's not jinx it." Sarah reached over then knocked on the table. "I'm up now, and glad you're here and ready to roll. I'm game for anything. Need help destroying your car?"

"Hey! I'm handy. You should be proud of me. I got up early this morning, checked on you, then decided to go for a hike. I made it all the way to your car and even brought it back, I'll have you know. That's the farthest I've walked all year." Gwen's pride was evident. "And I've borrowed some tools from that shop and here I am fixing stuff."

Sarah's mind snagged on the detail about the shop.

"You went into the shop? Umm... what... did you see... anything in there?" She tried to sound casual, but her heart sped in her chest.

Gwen gave her a puzzled look. "Shop stuff... You okay?" She grinned suddenly. "What, you still think there's a monster out there?"

Sarah smiled back, feeling embarrassed. "I saw something in there... Wait, how did you know that?"

"You told me all about it last night, but don't worry." Gwen's expression grew more serious. "I did see something odd out there."

Sarah's breath caught, and she waited to hear what Gwen had seen, expectantly.

"Yeah... I think an animal's been living there. There were droppings all over the place from something small. Like a racoon or rabbit."

Sarah's thoughts raced back to the first night, to the shadow she thought she saw standing inside the shop. *Could it have been an animal?* Maybe the raccoon she'd seen on the camera? She smiled, trying to brush off her evident fear. "Yeah, I guess that could explain it. The door was open after all. A family of raccoons could easily have made their home there."

Gwen nodded in agreement. "Anyway, let me finish putting the trunk lock back together, and we can do something. Okay?"

Sarah gestured a thumbs up. "I'm game! I'm going to take a quick shower, and I'll meet you back here." She paused then, looking at Gwen. "I'm really happy you're here. Thank you for everything – like saving my life and stuff. I feel really foolish for going into that forest alone at night. It was stupid."

"Well, you are a monkey after all. What are friends for anyway? And don't worry about it. We're together, no homework, no parents – time to party!" Gwen hugged her and kissed her forehead. As she headed for the back door, she grinned over her shoulder pinching her nose. "Yep, you definitely need that shower. You even smell like a monkey."

Sarah watched her go, then checked to see if Ralph had visited his food before heading upstairs. The shower was a welcome relief, washing away not just the grime but some of the tension that had settled into her shoulders. Gwen hadn't been entirely kidding – there was a ripe odor that needed to be scrubbed away.

As always, shower time meant reflection to Sarah and she often found peace. This time was an exception to the norm and she continued to wrestle with various thoughts and feelings that she couldn't quite put her finger on. Overall she couldn't explain all that had happened the night before and she wondered what her reaction should be. She'd always prided herself on being very logical and could always explain strange phenomena that typically troubled others. In fact, she typically made light the various claims she'd heard others make and in a way it made her feel superior. Now, she didn't know what to think. All she could do was mentally shelve the event on the hill and file it as unknown. She didn't like this feeling.

After rinsing her hair of the conditioner she had used, there was another strange thought that occurred to her. *No, not a thought, a feeling.* It was the oddest sensation, one that made no sense as, she had certainly never been in these mountains nor many forests in her past. Despite this, she couldn't shake the undeniable feeling of familiarity... As if she'd been here before. Déjà vu? No, it was more than that. She tried to shake the feeling and put it aside, shelving it like the other anomalies. *This is supposed to be a vacation, Sarah, don't screw it up.*

After getting ready, she did a thorough search of the house for her phone but came up empty-handed. Even her car was a dead end. Walking around the side yard, she found Gwen sitting in her car with the door open, a cookie in her mouth and a manual in her lap.

"Not what I was expecting. I thought you were going to be wrist deep in greasy parts."

"Who me? Nah, this is easy work," Gwen said with a smirk, turning a page. "Well... Not really. But I've got this figured out, I think."

Sarah walked around the car, surveying Gwen's handiwork. The trunk was held open with an old broomstick handle. She leaned against the car, arms crossed. "You're really going to fix it? Do you even have the parts?"

"I'm good." Gwen's voice was determined. "Dad told me what I need to do – there's a trick to getting the catch to reset."

"And the broomstick? What's that for?"

"Keeping the trunk from decapitating this gorgeous head." Gwen paused, looked up, and blew a strand of blonde hair from her face. "Hey, I was thinking. After this, how about we do something easy – like a movie marathon? I think we've both earned it."

"Deal," Sarah agreed, and felt a small surge of relief. She felt good but didn't want to push it. "That sounds perfect. I'll grab some blankets and the junk food."

10

Coven

23 March 1708

Alexander removed his gloves, one finger at a time, the rough fabric scraping against his calloused skin before he stowed them in his pocket. Despite the gloves, his hands bore fresh blisters and cuts, raw from a long day's labor. He plunged them into the basin of tepid water, wincing as the cool liquid stung his wounds, then he scrubbed them with the rose soap perched at the edge of the basin. Its floral scent was sharp against the stale air.

"Is that you, my son?" came his father's voice from the dining table. "Just in time for supper."

"I shall be in directly." Weeks had passed since Margaret had commanded him to depart and never return. He had heard nothing from her since, and no amount of the labor that his father had prescribed had been sufficient to erase her from his thoughts. Work kept his hands occupied, yet his mind still wandered to her as night fell.

He removed his hat and hung it upon the hook, then joined

his family at the table. "I beg your pardon for my tardiness, Father. I wished to ensure all the wood was secured in the barn before the morrow."

"Pray, think nothing of it. You are just in time. We have just completed saying grace."

He slid into his chair slowly, avoiding the gazes of his parents and siblings. He felt their eyes upon him, the heaviness of their concern seemed to sit at the table with them. The familiar knot in his stomach twisted again – a reminder of the sadness that had taken residence within him, no matter how hard he endeavored to push it aside.

The silence at the table stretched on until his mother's soft voice finally broke it. "Alexander, I observed you cleared most of the grove today."

His eyes flickered up for a moment, and he offered her a weak smile and a nod.

"That is most helpful. I very much thank you for that." She glanced at her husband and shot him a look.

"As your mother said, you've put in a great deal of work. Thank you, son."

His parents had sought to cheer him for weeks now, but they had exhausted their efforts and ideas. He kept assuring them he was well – that he merely required time. Yet the truth was, he didn't know if he would be well. Not until he could remove her from his thoughts.

A wave of nausea washed over him as he forced himself to chew a piece of bread. It felt akin to sawdust in his mouth, and he had to fight the urge to gag. Still, he swallowed it down. It wasn't that his mother's food wasn't good, he'd just lost his desire to eat, and it had been that way for weeks.

"That was delightful, Mother." His voice was flat, and his

words felt hollow. He stacked his utensils on his plate and stood. "Father, may I be excused? I wish to rise early. I want to get the wagon loaded before sunrise."

"But you have scarcely eaten, Alex."

"I am not feeling too well, Mother. I wish to retire early."

"But Alex—"

"Let him go, Martha. Go ahead, son."

As Alexander ascended the creaky wooden stairs to his attic room, the muffled argument between his parents followed him upward. His mother's voice rose in concern, lamenting how thin he had become, while his father's steady voice insisted that he was now a man and could make his own decisions. Their words, once sharp, faded into the background as he reached his small room.

Pale moonlight streamed through the narrow window, casting silvery beams across his bed and desk. He reached for the tinderbox to light a candle but paused, deciding against it. He was too weary – his body heavy with fatigue. He kicked off his dirt-caked shoes and peeled off his work-stained shirt, collapsing onto the bed with a long, tired sigh.

After a moment, guilt tugged at him, and he rolled off the bed, dropping to his knees to pray. After praying for forgiveness for not being totally honest with his parents, he got into bed, his eyes fixed on the faint patterns of moonlight dancing upon the ceiling. His mind buzzed, the silence of the room doing little to soothe his racing thoughts. Sleep was very slow to come.

But when it did, it was light and restless. It had been this way for weeks, with him waking several times each night. This night proved no different with one exception. His eyes fluttered open at the sound of a faint thud, followed by a soft scraping noise. He rubbed his eyes, trying to shake off the haze of slumber. The moonlight seemed to flicker, yet when he focused on the ceiling, nothing had changed.

Another sound, a creaking noise, followed by the distinct groan of the window hinge.

He sat up abruptly, pushing himself back until he was against his headboard. His heart raced in his chest as he blinked through the darkness, trying to comprehend the shadowy figure crawling through the window and onto his bed. The moonlight illuminated the figure as it moved.

"Margaret?"

She didn't respond but instead, crawled toward him, leaping into his lap, her arms wrapping tightly around his chest, her breath quick and uneven. The dampness of her tears soaked into his shoulder as she pressed her face against him, her body trembling.

His mind swirled with conflicting emotions, confusion, anger, joy – all crashing together. Yet in the quiet of the moment, he made a choice. He exhaled deeply, his own tension melting away as he gently enfolded his arms around her.

Deep sobs escaped from beneath her hair, soaking his chest as he gently stroked her long, dark strands and patted her back. He struggled to find words, his mind racing with confusion and concern.

"All is well, Margaret. Everything is fine."

After several minutes, she slowly lifted her head, her face obscured in the shadows of the dim room. "May I remain here with you?" There was a rawness in her voice.

"Forever. Or at least until daylight, whichever should come first."

She pulled away, kneeling near the edge of the bed, her hands trembling in her lap. "Alexander, I am so very sorry for how I've treated you. There are matters... I mean there are things that are exceedingly complicated in my life, and I wanted to set things straight with you."

He looked at her for a moment and then pushed his way out from under the blanket and stood. After several attempts, he managed to light the candle on his nightstand. The soft glow illuminated her face, and he felt his breath catch. She appeared even more beautiful than before – fragile, yet strong. He set the candle down and pulled a chair closer to sit beside her.

"Margaret..." He watched her for a moment and tried to choose the correct words. He wanted now more than ever to have the whole truth, not the cloaked riddles he was used to. "I must know what is transpiring. I want to aid you – I wish to be with you – but I cannot do so unless you reveal the truth of what is happening with you and your family."

She nodded, her eyes remaining downcast, avoiding his gaze. He reached out, gently lifting her chin to meet his eyes. "Whatever it may be, I will understand."

A weak smile flickered across her face as she let out a small, nervous laugh. "You shall not understand but as you say, I feel you must know. Though I fear it may cause you to banish me henceforth." A shiver seemed to go through her, and she repositioned herself where he had been lying and pulled the blanket over herself. "I'm not certain where to start my tale. I dwell within what is termed a coven. I don't believe there is another term like it, nor do I have anything to compare it with."

"I recall your sister mentioning that. But what does it

signify? Is it a religious sect?"

"You could call it a religion but I'm afraid it's not the best comparison. Instead, it is a gathering of women. Women with... special talents and abilities."

"Abilities? What manner of abilities?"

"Those like none that any regular person has ever seen. Some are those that we are born with, and others are ones we learn and become skilled at performing."

He stared at her, his face holding a puzzled expression. He opened his mouth to ask a follow-up question, but nothing came.

"Some might label it witchcraft. The women of the Vikar family are part of a witch coven."

"You are a witch?" he asked, slowly.

She nodded, tentatively.

He leaned back in his chair, feeling a mixture of surprise and skepticism. "Is that all? That is what all this is about? Because your family believes themselves to be witches?" A smile started to form on his lips as he stared at her in wonder.

"Yes, my mother, my four sisters, and me. We are all witches, and we are part of a larger coven of witches in this region."

"Raven, I presumed it to be something of greater gravity – such as your family's disapproval of me. Or that my love for you had become unrequited. I spent many hours trying to understand what it could have been, and I could have spent a hundred more and would have never guessed it."

Her eyelids fluttered at each word as if they were poking at her heart. She reached out and grabbed his hand. "I would never want to be away from you. I only asked you to leave to spare you a life that most find... unnatural or abnormal. But it's nothing like that..."

70

He grinned wide and moved to sit beside her on the bed. "Raven. For weeks, I've been trying to put you out of my mind, thinking the worst. Why did you not just convey it was merely this?"

"Do you mean... you do not mind? I do not believe you comprehend what I'm trying to convey. We do not merely play but are in fact the genuine article."

He let out a quiet chuckle and put his arms around her. "You never cease to amaze me. All this time apart and it was merely a family pastime."

"Alexander... It is not merely a pastime or some hobby – it's real and it's no game."

"Raven, you can name it whatever you wish but I simply don't believe in witchcraft nor witches. I know many in England believe otherwise and it's caused a great deal of tension, but we reside in a modern age now. Such notions are but antiquated superstitions and most of us pass these things off as mere whimsy – fanciful beliefs that are harmless."

She pushed away slightly, the candlelight exposing her serious expression. "Alexander, you asked for the truth, and I've given it to you. What we are is no simple caprice but a real practice. It is sometimes even dangerous."

He smiled, dismissively, and pulled her close to him again. "Very well. Perhaps it would be better if we discussed this in the light of the morning. I am tired, and we can untangle this matter then."

She gave a small nod, though her eyes retained a trace of doubt and frustration at his casual attitude. She lay down beside him, closing her eyes as she whispered, "I missed you with all my heart, Alexander. I never want to leave your side again."

Before he could respond, she pulled a hand out of the blanket and snapped her fingers – the candle beside the bed extinguished instantly, plunging the room into darkness.

11

The Intruder

Sarah woke abruptly, startled by a sound that seemed to echo in the darkness. Her heart pounded hard in her chest as she took a deep breath, trying to calm the residual tension from a dream she couldn't quite remember. She exhaled slowly, attempting to convince herself it was nothing. As she began to drift back into sleep, a soft, melodic tune reached her ears – faint, like music played from a flute. Sarah's eyes fluttered open again, but the melody quickly faded, allowing her to drift back into unconsciousness.

"Sarah…"

A sharp whisper cut through the silence, jolting her awake. Her eyes snapped open, scanning the dark room, but there was nothing – only shadows. Was it just another figment of her imagination? She rolled onto her back, staring up at the ceiling, when a dim light caught her attention. It was a faint glow, like the light from a phone receiving a late-night message. *My phone!* The realization hit her, excitement momentarily overcoming her unease. She'd been so distracted by the day's events that she forgot to ask Gwen if she'd seen it.

Sarah turned towards the light, squinting through the darkness. She let out a bloodcurdling scream.

Inches from her face, a shadowy figure crouched on the floor beside her bed. Panic surged through her, and Sarah rolled off the opposite side of the bed, hitting the floor hard. The figure moved quickly, scrambling around the mattress, towards her on all fours. Sarah crawled across the floor to flee but before she could scream again, hands clamped over her mouth, muffling the sound.

"Shhh!" The figure whispered loudly. "It's me! It's Gwen. Be quiet!"

Sarah's breath was ragged against Gwen's hand, her body trembling uncontrollably. Gwen held her hand firmly over Sarah's mouth, her own breathing harsh in the silence.

"Sarah... Listen to me. You need to be quiet." Gwen's voice was barely audible, a desperate whisper.

Sarah nodded slowly, and Gwen's hand cautiously released her mouth. She grabbed Sarah's hand, pulling her up with surprising strength. Moving silently, Gwen led Sarah back to the bed. She then pulled Sarah down to the floor again, her actions deliberate and precise.

"Wait here..." Gwen's voice was a breath in the darkness before she disappeared around the bed. Sarah stared after her, trying to process what was happening. The familiar dizziness from the previous night began to return, disorienting her further. Moments later, Gwen reappeared, holding something emitting a low light. She sat next to Sarah, her back against the bed, her face barely visible in the faint glow. Gwen had always been fearless, the one who faced challenges head-on, but now her eyes were wide with fear. She motioned for

Sarah to look at what she was holding – an iPad, its screen dimly illuminated. Just then, a loud chirp filled the air, cutting it like a knife. Gwen grabbed Sarah's hand and both of them froze as if to undo the noise.

Gwen pointed to something on the screen. Sarah recognized the interface immediately – it was the same surveillance software she'd seen the first night. Confusion washed over her. *What was Gwen doing with the iPad?*

Gwen responded as if she could read her mind. "This thing has been chirping like crazy. I came in to see what it was and found this." She pointed to a specific video feed and pressed play. The screen showed a night vision view of Gwen's car, bugs flitting around the vehicle under the eerie green tint.

"Yeah? What of it?"

"Just look!" Gwen's rasped, her frustration palpable as she pointed and poked at the screen. A figure appeared at the bottom of the camera view, walking close to the house. As the person moved closer, the man's body became distorted in the camera before disappearing off the right side of the screen. Gwen's gaze bore into Sarah, her expression intense. She quickly switched to another video feed, showing a man wearing what looked like a sailor's cap, walking past the backyard camera near the shop.

Gwen mouthed a single word, articulating each syllable clearly. "Mc. Greg. Or."

Sarah's blood ran cold, her heart skipping a beat. She mirrored Gwen's expression, their shared terror bonding them in that moment.

"Look…" Gwen's voice trembled as she tapped the screen, opening multiple views that showed the man wandering around the yard.

"What the heck is he doing?"

Gwen put a finger to her lips, motioning for silence. She closed the last video and pulled down a menu labeled 'Zones,' selecting 'Internal Realtime.'

Sarah's confusion deepened. *Internal? Cameras inside the house?* She hadn't noticed any when she arrived. Gwen seemed to know exactly what she was looking for, scrolling through each feed until she found one labeled 'Family Room.' Gwen's hands shook as she pointed at the screen, her breath hitching.

Sarah squinted, trying to make out what Gwen was so terrified of. Then she saw it – McGregor standing at the family room window, his hands cupped around his eyes, face pressed against the glass as he peered inside. Sarah's breath caught in her throat as the figure remained motionless, staring into the dark room.

"He's been back to that window a few times…"

"Are we sure it's McGregor?"

"It's him. I saw his face clearly when he was at the front door. He's been circling the yard, always coming back to this window."

"Told you this guy was a creep! I got bad vibes from him…" Sarah's eyes were glued to the screen, her anxiety spiking.

"Wait, what's he doing? Is he… No…" Gwen trailed off, her eyes widening in horror. She turned her head, straining to listen. A distant sound reached their ears, and they both looked at each other, wide-eyed. On the screen, McGregor at the window moved to the door, turning the handle. The man was now inside the family room, the camera capturing his slow, deliberate movements.

"Crap! I must not have locked the back door when I came

in!" Gwen whispered loudly. She jumped to her feet, rushing to the door. Sarah sat frozen, watching the man move out of the family room and into the kitchen. She fumbled with the program controls, desperate to switch views. A loud click echoed from across the room – Gwen had locked the door to the hallway.

"Come on, come on…" Gwen tugged on Sarah's arm, pulling her to the other side of the room. Panic gripped Sarah as she struggled to keep up. They stumbled into a large walk-in closet, shoes and clothes tripping them up as they searched for safety. Gwen hurriedly closed the closet door behind them.

"Sarah! Where are you?" Gwen's whispered voice was frantic, almost a hiss.

"Back here. Keep coming." Sarah's heart raced as she heard Gwen crawling toward her in the dark. Gwen's hand found her knee, and she pushed aside some shoes to sit beside her. The two girls huddled in the darkness, their breathing heavy as they tried to stay silent.

"Did you lock the bedroom door?"

"Yeah," Gwen whispered back, still trying to calm herself. "I tried to wedge the chair under the knob, but it wouldn't stay."

"Gwen. Hey, it's going to be fine. We're safe." She tried to sound reassuring even though she didn't believe it.

She flipped the iPad over; the screen having shut off in the chaos. Her fingers fumbled to find the power button, and the screen flickered back to life, casting a faint glow over their terrified faces. They both worked silently, bringing up the video feeds, scanning each one desperately. McGregor was nowhere to be seen.

"There's got to be something in here we can use to defend ourselves." Sarah crawled across the floor, the screen illuminating the closet's interior. She reached out, her hand brushing against something cold and metallic – golf clubs and a bag.

"What are you doing, Sarah?" Gwen's voice was strained, barely keeping panic at bay.

"Hold on, I think I found something. Here, take this." She handed the iPad to Gwen, who grabbed it with shaking hands. Sarah slid a large club from the bag and gripped it tightly, awkwardly testing its weight. "If he comes in here, he's going to regret it." She was trying to sound confident but the fear in her voice was evident.

"Sarah. You need to see this." Gwen's voice cut through the dark, too loud. Sarah turned, annoyed, but Gwen thrust the iPad at her, pointing at the screen. McGregor was at the bottom of the stairs, staring up toward the hallway.

"Is that a knife or something else?" Sarah's whisper was strained. In his hand, what looked like a knife glinted faintly in the camera's night vision. Gwen quickly snatched the iPad back. "Knife? No, he's not holding anything."

"I know what I saw!" Sarah said almost too loudly, leaning over to look at the screen again. Just then they saw him put one foot on the bottom stair.

The girls sat frozen, the tension almost unbearable. Sarah still felt a deep fear inside her, but beneath it was a growing anger. This man had invaded their space, their safety, and she wasn't going to let him get away with it. He remained at the base of the stairs motionless. It was difficult to make out the image, but it seemed that he was staring at something on the wall. Then, slowly, he turned and started back toward the kitchen. *He's leaving!*

Just then, a loud clatter came from the side of the closet as the remaining golf clubs slid down the wall and slammed on the floor. They froze, both held petrified grimaces on their faces. On the screen, McGregor paused for a moment in indecision.

Gwen let out a whispered curse and the pair of them exchanged a look of confusion and cautious relief as they watched him continue on. Gwen's hand hovered over the screen, unsure whether to follow him on the cameras.

What's he doing? Why isn't he coming up? Sarah's thoughts raced as the girls sat, barely daring to breathe.

McGregor paused in the kitchen, his body language tense as he seemed to reconsider. But instead of turning back, he continued walking toward the back door. He hesitated for a moment, his hand on the doorknob. Then, with a final glance around the room, he stepped outside, closing the door softly behind him.

The girls watched in disbelief as he crossed the yard, his figure growing smaller and smaller until he disappeared into the darkness.

"Is he... gone?" Gwen whispered, her voice trembling with a mixture of fear and relief.

Sarah nodded slowly, not trusting herself to speak. They sat in the closet for a long time, the silence pressing in around them, waiting to be sure that the nightmare was over. Finally, Sarah exhaled deeply, releasing the tension she'd been holding in.

"I think he's really gone," she whispered, still holding the golf club tightly.

Gwen let out a shaky breath, the tears she'd been holding

back finally spilling over.

Sarah reached out, pulling her into a tight embrace, both of them trembling with the aftermath of fear and adrenaline.

"Come on... Let's get out of here," Sarah said, softly, helping Gwen to her feet. They stepped cautiously out of the closet, the weight of the night heavy on their shoulders. Moving quietly, they unlocked the bedroom door, peering out into the hallway. It was empty, the house eerily silent. The girls walked through the house, checking each room systematically to ensure he was truly gone.

Finally, they stood at the back door, staring out into the dark yard to where they thought McGregor had vanished. The night was still; the only sound their own breathing.

"Do you think he'll come back?"

Sarah tightened her grip on the golf club, her resolve hardening. "If he does, we'll be ready."

They locked the door, barricading it as best they could, before retreating to the safety of the bedroom. As they sat on the bed, neither able to sleep, the first light of dawn began to creep through the windows, chasing away the shadows of the night.

"We're going to be alright."

Gwen nodded, her head resting on Sarah's shoulder as they both closed their eyes, fear finally giving way to the relief of survival.

"Gwen, in the morning we really need to have that conversation about the other night. I need details."

Gwen said nothing but Sarah felt her head nod again. Sarah turned and stared through the back window; the dark silhouette of the shop roof stared right back.

12

Elizabeth

05 September 1708

Alexander's Journal

Things have at last mended between the Vikar and McGregor families. My mother, who has long disapproved of my rekindled attachment to Margaret, did express her fears of my heart's undoing once more. She was, I confess, quite vocal in her sentiments, not only with me but also with Margaret and her mother. Yet, today, in a most welcome turn of events, my mother has declared her happiness for us and even wishes all the best for our future. She has gone so far as to extend an invitation for supper to the Vikar family, and though the differences between our households are plain to see, I find the Vikar kin to be more amiable than I first thought.

Mr. Vikar, though sparing of words, is ever kind to me. And Delaney, despite her colder nature, hath shown kindness on occasion, especially of late. As for my beloved Margaret – my Raven – we are as happy as any two souls might be.

As for the matter of the Vikar family's peculiar traits, including those that Margaret undeniably possesses, we have chosen not to reveal them to my own family. This decision, though painful, seems the wisest course. Though I do not agree with their practices, Margaret and I have sworn that such things shall have no place in our household once we are wed.

I must confess, the sudden awakening to the truth of magick hath left me sorely discomposed. When my dear Margaret did make manifest its power, and did wield it with such troubling ease, I found myself in doubt of much that I had heretofore held as certain. 'Tis my earnest hope she might yet forsake the practice, and that it become not a canker upon the life we strive to share.

Alexander set his quill back in the ink jar, then pushed his journal aside to dry. The sounds of conversation filtered upstairs from below. His mother had informed everyone earlier that the Wrenkles, a new family in the community, would be joining them for supper. Apparently, she and Mrs. Wrenkle had become good friends.

He closed the journal and made his way down the stairs to the parlor. Their usual dining table had been turned sideways to fit the kitchen table beside it; both were now set with extra place settings. He surveyed the crowded room, noting the new faces filling the space. The larger table was already occupied, and a few guests stood waiting to sit.

"And this is my youngest son, Alexander." His mother introduced him with a pointed glance his way, clearly reminding him that he should have helped more with the preparations.

"Good evening, Alexander," Mr. Wrenkle greeted him, offering a firm handshake. He then introduced his four daughters, beginning with the eldest and ending with the youngest, Elizabeth. Alexander's breath caught as he took in the group. Three of the daughters had golden hair, with the youngest a striking red hair. All were beautiful, but what truly made them unique were their eyes – each had the deepest, most vibrant green eyes he had ever seen.

He barely heard the rest of the introductions, his attention lingering on Elizabeth. This made her blush.

"Hello, Alexander. It is a pleasure to meet you."

Before he could stop himself, Alexander blurted, "Your eyes are the greenest I have ever beheld."

His oldest brother, John, shot him a disapproving look from across the room. "Refrain from rudeness, Alexander."

Alexander's face flushed with embarrassment. "I beg your pardon."

Mrs. Wrenkle laughed gently; her voice warm. "Pray, think nothing of it, Alexander. We are quite accustomed to remarks upon our eyes. It's an oddity that runs in my family in the woman. It's a pleasure to make your acquaintance. You may call me Amelia."

For a moment, Alexander was entranced by her gaze, struggling not to stare too long. The intensity of the eyes of the Wrenkle women was mesmerizing, almost hypnotic.

His mother, sensing the awkwardness, jumped in to break the tension. "Alexander, I have set you a place at this table. Come help me finish setting out the food."

Relieved by the distraction, he followed her to the kitchen.

"May I assist, Mrs. McGregor?" Elizabeth offered, stepping forward from behind Alexander.

"Thank you, dear," Martha replied, handing her a large pan. "Could you take this to the main table?"

As Elizabeth obliged and left the room, Martha gave

Alexander a queer glance. "She is a lovely young lady, is she not?" She casually handed him a hot plate. "Only a year younger than you as well."

"I suppose," he responded, matching her casual manner.

Martha smiled to herself, placing a few more items in his hands. "You should sit by her, get to know her a little."

"I know what you are about, Mother."

"Oh? I only wish you to make new acquaintances, my dear son." She wore a coy expression as she put the last of the food on a plate.

"As you wish, Mother. I'll sit by her. Perhaps I'll teach her the foul quip Benjamin taught me just yesterday."

"You would not dare, Alex," she called after him, her casual manner all but a memory.

Nodding with a wink, he carried the dishes back to the parlor, his eyes instinctively searching for Elizabeth. She had already taken a seat, leaving the chair beside her empty. He hesitated a moment, crossed the room to distribute the food, and then sat beside her.

Each of the Wrenkle girls smiled warmly at him as he joined the table. His cheeks flushed at the intensity of their gazes – those striking green eyes seemed to pin him in place. He returned a simper of a smile and felt awkward under their attention.

Fortunately, Mr. Wrenkle broke the tension with his loud booming voice. "I would be pleased to offer a word of grace," he said in response to Mr. McGregor's request. Alexander bowed his head and closed his eyes, using the moment to steady his nerves, breathing in deeply. But just as it had begun the prayer was already over, and he immediately felt the scrutiny of the girls again.

"So, Alexander," began the eldest Wrenkle daughter, sitting directly across from him, her voice gentle but inquisitive "Your mother tells us that your family works this land. Do you assist with that?"

Grateful for the shift away from the silence, he nodded, reaching for the plate of food. "I do. I help in the field, care for the animals, and my brothers and I sell crops in town for the landowner." He passed the plate to Elizabeth, who had been listening closely.

"And your mother tells us you keep sheep, did we hear that correctly?" Elizabeth asked suddenly, her voice soft yet full of interest.

"Aye, we do. Sheep, pigs, a few chickens, and oxen also." He caught her smile – an unguarded, genuine expression – and his heart skipped. *She is truly beautiful*, he thought, his face flushing. The thought must have shown, as Elizabeth's cheeks reddened in response.

He tried to cover his embarrassment. "And, um, horses." He glanced at the others at the table, who exchanged little glances and subtle smiles.

Elizabeth seemed determined to hold his attention. "We keep no animals," she said lightly, her gaze fixed on him. "My mother and I work with fabrics. She is a seamstress. My father is a tailor." Elizabeth leaned in slightly, her green eyes catching the candlelight. "If you shear the sheep, I could fashion you a woolen shirt. I am quite skilled at knitting."

The offer was unexpected, and for a moment, he didn't know what to say. He swallowed, feeling the weight of her gaze on him. "That... That would be very kind of you."

Elizabeth smiled softly, clearly pleased with his response.

"We have some wool to spare, Elizabeth," Martha called

from the other table. "I shall find you a bolt as soon as I can." Her delight at the unfolding situation was evident, and Alexander couldn't help but feel a twinge of annoyance. *Must she listen in on all of my conversations?*

He paused then, his mind flashing to Margaret. He felt a tinge of sudden guilt knotting in his stomach. Would she approve of this friendship? The thought lingered –Margaret was his one and only, and he wanted to keep it so. He began to feel mild panic as he sat next to her. He wondered again what Margaret would make of the new acquaintance and hastily made a decision.

"My elder brother often labors in the cold mornings. Perhaps you could make him a woolen shirt rather than me."

A flicker of injured embarrassment crossed Elizabeth's face, and she looked down at her plate, her excitement visibly deflating. She nodded and smiled meekly.

Martha shot Alexander a sharp look before chiming in. "I am certain both my sons would appreciate a knitted shirt, my darling. I shall assist you with it." Her eyes flickered to Alexander again, unmistakable disappointment in her expression.

As they finished their meal and moved on to dessert, many had left the small table to help clean up the place settings. Elizabeth, however, remained seated next to him, seemingly determined to win his attention. Despite his attempts to deflect her interest with short answers and an averted gaze, she seemed undeterred.

After a few moments of silence, she spoke up quietly. "Have I done something to offend you or cause you displeasure?"

The question caught him by surprise. He drew in a deep breath, searching for the right words. "I beg your pardon,

Elizabeth. It's not my intention to be unkind." He paused, meeting her gaze. "I have something of an understanding with another, and I am uncertain how she would feel about our friendship."

A smile broke across her face, a dimple appearing on her cheek. "I desire nothing more than to be friends with you, Alexander." She touched his arm, sending a warm sensation up his spine. "Yet, should my friendship with you cause her any sorrow, I would cease at once."

The shame he felt was immediate and he placed his hand on hers. "I must apologize. Perhaps I did overreact. Please accept my apology. I would like nothing more than to be friends with you."

Her grin widened, her deep green eyes sparkling once again. "Then friends we shall be!" she declared, leaning forward to peck him on the cheek before standing. "Perhaps when I return, you can teach me the quip your brother taught you?" Her smile was as wide as ever, and she giggled loudly before quickly leaving the room.

He sat in silence, his heart racing, a warm feeling rising in his chest. The brief touch of her lips lingered on his skin, and he couldn't help but smile at her playful humor. His thoughts swirled with ideas, each one more elaborate than the last, as he wondered what he could say upon her return. He was determined to impress her, to show her that he could also be quick-witted.

His thoughts were interrupted by his brother John's voice. "Help me move this."

"I beg your pardon – aye, of course." He stood and helped his brother move the table back into the kitchen, setting it near the stove where it belonged.

When Alexander returned to the parlor, the others had arranged themselves in a semi-circle, seated and waiting expectantly. In the center of the room, Elizabeth stood, holding a violin.

Curious, he edged closer, choosing to remain at the back of the gathering. As the families settled, murmurs quieted in anticipation. Elizabeth's gaze scanned the room, and when she found him, her eyes locked onto his. A gentle smile played across her lips. Her gesture made him quickly look away.

Then, she began to play.

The haunting, lilting melody of the violin filled the room, weaving through the air like a soft breeze. The music was beautiful, mesmerizing in its simplicity, and drew his gaze back to her. Her eyes remained fixed on him; her expression serene yet filled with something deeper – an unspoken connection that passed between them as she moved the bow skillfully across the strings.

Each set of notes seemed to resonate within him, the sound echoing in the small space, and for a brief moment it felt as though the rest of the room had faded away. His heart beat faster. He was unsure if it was the music or the way she looked at him, but he couldn't tear his eyes from hers.

As the song came to an end, the final notes lingered in the air before gently dissipating. She lowered the violin, her eyes still on him, as if waiting for a response. He swallowed, his pulse still racing, but he couldn't find any words. All he could do was smile back and clap, caught in the spell she had cast with her music.

13

The Next Day

Sarah watched the man as he took notes. He was handsome, and, despite being in uniform, looked a little young to be a police officer. He continued to scribble in his notebook before looking back at Sarah, smiling pleasantly.

"You sure you don't want another cookie, officer?" Gwen called from the adjoining kitchen, finishing up her cleaning routine.

"Oh no, thank you, that was delicious." He shot Gwen a quick smile. "I think I'm all finished up here. Any questions for me, Miss... umm... Jensen?" He glanced at his report, then back at Sarah.

"Can you give us anything concrete? He broke into our house last night with a knife – how are we supposed to feel safe here?"

The officer's smile faltered slightly. "McGregor... Liam, is sort of a landmark around here. He's been around a long time, long before many of us actually. This isn't the first run-in we've had with him but it's never escalated like this before."

He hesitated. "We're going to hold him in town overnight. You shouldn't have any problems with him tonight."

"And tomorrow night?" Sarah pressed; her voice tight. "Can we get a restraining order or something?"

Officer Lambert's expression softened, but his answer was firm. "These things take time. It's not a simple process."

Gwen joined them, her tone lighter than Sarah thought appropriate. "We're going to be here for a while... at least two weeks. What do you suggest we do if we see him again?"

"I don't think I can handle another encounter with him. Two weeks might be a stretch," Sarah interrupted.

The officer's voice remained calm, though his expression grew more serious. "If you don't feel safe, do what you feel is necessary. I can't guarantee he won't come back. We've had complaints about him before, enough to hold him for questioning after what you've just told me... especially since there was potentially a knife involved."

"Oh, there was definitely a knife – I just couldn't get the software to show you!" Sarah snapped. She felt her face flush with frustration. She'd tried to show the officer but each time she tried to play back the videos, a password prompt would show up, denying them access. It had flustered her and she was now angry and felt defensive.

"I believe you," the officer said, raising his hands. "But without recordings, we can't hold him on that." He paused, considering his next words carefully. "In all the years he's been around, we have no record of him harming anyone. But I understand your concern." Sarah began to argue, but he held up a finger. "I can't guarantee anything, but I do patrol this area. I'll check in on you. And..." He flipped over a sheet on his clipboard, revealing a card. "Here's my direct number.

Call me if you need anything." He handed it to Sarah.

"Thank you. We don't mean to be a burden, officer…" Sarah glanced at the card to remind herself of his name, catching Gwen's playful expression from behind him.

"Lambert. Officer Lambert, ma'am. And don't worry, it's no trouble. I pass by McGregor's place often. I'll make sure to keep an eye on things and soon, it will be like he never bothered you."

"That's very kind of you," Sarah said, her voice a mix of gratitude and lingering doubt.

"Lambert, you ready?" A voice called from the other room. Sarah turned to see another officer enter the kitchen, a cat cradled in his arms. Gwen waved at him, and he nodded in return. "Is this your cat? Came right up to me, seems friendly."

"Oh, yeah, that's Ralph. He belongs to my aunt and uncle."

"Well, nice to meet you both. We'll file this report and have a chat with Liam on the way back. Hopefully, this was all just a misunderstanding." Lambert placed his hat on his head and then walked out of the kitchen, followed by the other officer, who was munching on the cookie Gwen had given him.

"Thanks, officers!" Gwen called after them, waving energetically. "Wow, he was cute!" she exclaimed, eyes wide. "You've got your own little bodyguard now."

"Oh, shush! Give it a rest, Gwen. I bet he's married anyway."

"I'll ask him for you. Maybe I'll write him a letter in your handwriting."

"You're the worst!" Sarah yelled with an embarrassed smile, tossing a pillow at Gwen, which missed entirely.

"So, do I get to pick what we're doing today? I've got a good one!"

Sarah's smile faded as she stared at Gwen. "Gwen... Have you already forgotten about last night?"

Gwen's expression grew serious as she sat next to Sarah. "Listen, I get it. Last night was terrifying. If you want to cut our trip short, I'll understand."

"A man we don't know broke into our house in the middle of the night with a knife! Does that not freak you out?"

Gwen sighed. "I get it, Sarah. But did you hear Officer Lambert? He doesn't seem to think Liam's a threat. Maybe this was just a freak incident... a misunderstanding. We don't even really know if there was a knife..." Sarah began to protest but Gwen stopped her by nodding and putting her hands up before continuing. "Yes, I know... And they're holding him for at least a day. Let's just wait to see what the police tell us."

Sarah leaned back into the sofa, still a little shaken and frustrated. The last two nights' events haunted her, and even Gwen's reassurances didn't ease her fear. The thought of Liam McGregor carrying her to bed, as Gwen had described this morning, sent a fresh shiver through her body.

Gwen had recounted the night and had given Liam all the credit for finding Sarah. She had said that if it hadn't been for his truck blocking the road, she wouldn't have stopped and would have driven right by. She also filled in gaps in Sarah's memory, recounting again the stories Sarah told both her and Liam... Stories about a dark figure in the forest and other wildly imaginative things. Gwen also mentioned that other than being a quiet man, Liam had been very instrumental in carrying Sarah up the stairs to bed. "I thought he was a good guy... almost a gentleman," she had said.

"I don't know, Gwen. These last few days have been rough.

What do we do if the creepy old sailor comes back? What if he gets into the room next time? Not the smartest move."

Gwen cuddled up to Sarah, her tone softening. "I'm not asking you to commit to the full twelve days. Let's just calm down, relax, and wait to see what the authorities say. If we're not comfortable, we'll leave."

Sarah glanced at Gwen, a small, shaky smile forming. "You always get your way, don't you?"

"Hey, I'm not the one who got Officer Friendly's number!" Gwen teased. "You'll probably have a new boyfriend after all this."

Sarah's mood lightened and while she didn't feel entirely at ease, Gwen's carefree spirit was hard to ignore.

Sarah paused for a few moments and then shook her head in resignation. "So, you mentioned activities... Wait, haven't all our activities been your ideas this trip... let alone our entire friendship?" Sarah mock retorted, folding her arms. "And no, they aren't always good ones."

Gwen moved back into the kitchen and pressed a button on the dishwasher, the noise of the gushing water filling the room. She turned back to Sarah with a huge smile. "That's more like it! Okay, here's the plan: I found a cool little trail on my hike yesterday. Let's check it out – it's not far from here."

Sarah hesitated. "Okay, but think we could look for my phone also? I think I dropped it that night somewhere in that area."

"Absolutely! I didn't see it, but it was dark, and we were pretty focused on getting you up the hill. Are you sure it's not here somewhere?"

Sarah shook her head. "I had it on the trail – I remember

93

using it as a flashlight until… well, I know I had it. It's lost."

"No worries. The trail I found might lead us in that direction anyway. We'll get you some fresh air and potentially find your phone. And if we don't find it, can't we use your laptop to locate it?"

This made Sarah smile, and she nodded thoughtfully at the notion. *Gwen, always the optimist.* "Sounds like a plan. Let's go!"

They changed clothes, grabbed packs, packed lunches, and locked the house before heading out. Gwen led the way, and they quickly found the well-marked trail not far inside the forest. It was wide and flat, winding through patches of wildflowers and over small bridges crossing streams. The scenery was beautiful, but Sarah couldn't shake a growing unease as they ventured deeper into the woods. There was something familiar about the area, the trees.

Gwen, ever the optimist, twirled around, arms outstretched, soaking in the sunshine. Her long ponytails whipped around as she spun. "Oh my gosh, Sarah, this weather is perfect!" Her voice carried loudly through the forest. "Look at those flowers, can you believe it?"

Sarah forced a smile, trying to bury her anxiety.

The trail began to climb, winding up the mountainside in switchbacks until they reached a wide dirt road. Gwen studied it, nodding. "I think I've driven this road. It might lead to a small house I saw."

"Really? Did you see anyone home?"

"Nope. It was too small to be your relatives, so I didn't knock. Come to think of it, I saw a few homes in the area, they all looked abandoned to me."

Sarah scanned the horizon, again feeling an odd familiarity.

94

She wasn't sure if it was from travels that night or something else. "This looks like the road I saw that truck on. I mean it was dark and far away, but this looks like the road I saw it drive up. I guess that means the main road is likely over there?" she said, pointing. "I bet we can cut across this field to reach it."

Gwen cheerfully nodded, and they crossed the field with no issue and reached the opposite dirt road. Gwen pointed. "See that slope? I think that's near where I found your car parked."

They followed the road until they found tire tracks, and Sarah quickly located the little trail leading down the embankment. It wasn't long before Gwen let out a triumphant yell as she bent down and picked something up. "Bingo!"

Sarah let out a sigh of relief and reached for the small device.

"But... Yikes, your poor phone has seen much better days."

Sarah's ease faded as she examined the cracked screen and scratched and bulged plastic. "How did this happen? It looks like it was hit by a hammer repeatedly... From the inside." There were odd, raised bumps on the back of the phone. "Gwen, what do you think caused this?" Sarah felt chilled by the mutilation of her phone. It was almost as though someone, or something, had done it deliberately.

"Maybe the battery exploded or something? I've never seen that before and I've destroyed many a cellphone."

"Okay but this doesn't look like any of the phones you've broken. I mean look at it... Does acid do this?"

Gwen shrugged. "I'll try that next time."

Sarah tried to power the phone on, but there was no sign of life. Sighing, she shoved it into her backpack, deciding to examine it more later.

They decided to descend back to find the trail, the terrain familiar to her despite it being daytime. How had she climbed this in the dark? The thought sent a shiver down her spine as she recounted the experience and as they walked, she saw broken branches and long muddy foot prints from her prior journey.

As luck would have it, they found what looked like the main trail crossing their path and they decided to follow it. Eventually, the forest thinned, and they reached a clearing. Gwen eyed the dark clouds overhead. "We might get wet. If we're lucky, this trail loops right back to the cabin, and you know what that means... Ice cream!"

Sarah smiled and they made their way across the clearing. As they started to go back into the trees, Gwen slowed, looking back. "Hey, we've got some company."

Sarah turned to see a figure emerging from the trees behind them. The hiker was distant, but something about their slow, deliberate gait felt off. Sarah squinted, trying to make out more details. "Hmm... What are they wearing?"

"I was wondering the same thing," Gwen said, frowning. "What's on their head? Oddly flowing shape, isn't it? And is that a dress?"

The figure's appearance, a dark shape from this distance, was odd but in other ways featureless. Sarah didn't have a real reason, but she hadn't wanted to see anyone out here while they were on the trail. The sight of this person didn't change her mind in any way.

"Gwen, that person is kind of creeping me out. Doesn't it seem a little strange?"

"Oh, come on. They're probably just a lone hiker out here

enjoying this gorgeous day." Gwen looked back again and began cheerfully forward up the trail.

Her carefree demeanor was encouraging to Sarah, but the uneasy and familiar feeling continued to gnaw at her. As they reached a fork in the trail, before Sarah knew it, Gwen had made a quick decision. "Let's go left – it should take us back towards the cabin more quickly."

Sarah didn't argue; she wanted to keep moving. The trail wound back south, climbing a more prominent hill. Sarah's legs burned and sweat dripped down her face. She had almost forgotten about the person but glanced back; her heart skipped a beat when she saw the figure had chosen the same path. "Gwen, that person..."

Gwen turned and waved cheerfully. "Hello!!!"

"What are you doing?" Sarah hissed.

"Just being friendly. Stop being so antisocial."

They continued until the trail leveled out on a high plain. Gwen, panting, sat on a stump and stared off into the distance. "Hey, is that the cabin down there?" she said after swallowing water from a container.

Sarah squinted, looking past the row of trees in the distance. "Yeah, I think so. Oh... yep. I see your car on the side of the house. Wow, that's pretty far away..."

Sarah surveyed the trail and wondered if they'd taken the wrong way. They were obviously high on the hillside above the cabin now. They'd probably need to double back. She looked back down the trail where they'd come and then back at the cabin.

As if reading Sarah's mind, Gwen rolled her eyes. "Seriously? You need to relax, Sarah. I promise, it's just a hiker! If we need to circle back, we will... No big deal."

Sarah just nodded. In her mind she knew what Gwen was saying was true and she felt silly for being frightened but something wasn't right, and she couldn't shake the feeling. She tried to appear calm but even she knew she wasn't fooling anyone.

Gwen stared at Sarah for a moment and then sighed with an obvious hint of frustration. "Fine, stay here with my pack. I'll go ask for directions and prove to you that there's nothing to be afraid of, okay…"

"Gwen, come on, I'm not afraid. I'm just concerned, that's all."

"Seriously, Sarah, what is up with you? You've been freaking out about every little thing today."

Sarah looked at her feet, unable to answer the question. Instead, she began to feel defensive. "You mean like the time you thought Billy Parsen was following you at school?"

Gwen shook her head and dropped her backpack at Sarah's feet and shoved the water container into her hands. "I'll be right back."

Sarah's eyes widened. "Gwen, wait, I didn't mean it. Let me come with you – don't go alone!" But Gwen, who had started jogging, was already out of earshot.

Sarah watched her friend disappear down the trail, the uneasy, shameful feeling growing stronger. She sat on a rock, leaning against a tree, trying to calm herself. After several minutes had passed, she noticed the wind had picked up, rustling the leaves around her. It was at this moment, she heard it – a whisper, carried on the breeze. It was low, but it almost sounded like a voice, and Sarah was sure that it said her name. Then in her mind, she saw it. It was terrifying, a woman's face – the one from her dream.

Her blood ran cold. Her eyes fluttered as she whipped around, but other than the wind, the forest was silent, and the vision of the woman was gone. "Gwen? Is that you?" Her voice trembled, barely a whisper. She forced herself to stand, heart pounding harder than normal in her chest. "Gwen!" she called out, louder this time, but the response was only more silence.

She walked around the trees and peered through them. Panic gripped her as she realized Gwen was nowhere in sight. Walking out of the small grove she was in, she began to make her way back down the trail. Behind her, she heard an odd noise. She turned back to the trail, eyes widening in horror. The woman's face flickered again in her mind and the dark figure was there, emerging from the trees where she had just been. It paused, staring at her, then after a moment slowly raised a long arm to wave. She could see wisps of smoke emanating from it, then disappearing in the daylight.

Sarah's breath caught in her throat as she shakily waved back. The figure then began to beckon her to come. Sarah gulped and then shook her head in disbelief, terror flooding her senses. The figure nodded slowly and beckoned again, its movements eerily slow, deliberate.

"Sarah." The voice was clearer now, as if whispered right in her ear. She felt a familiar cold sensation in her legs. "Come, Sarah." Without thinking, she turned and ran.

"Gwen!" she screamed, the word tearing from her throat as she sprinted down the trail, tears streaming down her face. She barely noticed when one of the packs slipped from her shoulder, her only focus was getting away from the dark figure behind her. "Gwen!"

14

Twin

23 February 1709

Alexander knelt behind a large beech tree. He had to remain absolutely still to keep from being caught by his pursuer. Noises came from the other side of the hedge and he quickly held his breath. A bead of sweat formed on his forehead as he held his entire body still.

"Found you!" Margaret squealed from behind him, tapping him on the shoulder. He flinched, his whole body jolting at the surprise. He whipped around with a playful gleam in his eye. Without a moment's hesitation, he gave chase. By the time he caught her, Margaret was laughing so hard she could barely breathe, both collapsing onto the grass, he tickled her mercilessly.

"That will do, you two," Claire remarked, rolling her eyes theatrically. "Now it is Alexander's turn."

"Very well," he replied, casting a wink toward Margaret. "I shall find you first this time, I assure you."

"I wish you success with that!" Margaret teased, springing

to her feet. "But close your eyes – no peeking!" she called over her shoulder, her giggles trailing behind her as she ran.

"As you wish!" Alexander pressed his face against the bark of a tree, covering his eyes as he counted aloud. Claire and her sisters scattered in all directions, each moving with the utmost silence.

"Twenty-three, twenty-four, twenty-five! Here I come!" he declared, his eyes scanning the scene for the easiest target. He soon spotted young Alice, perched in the low branches of a nearby tree, her expression souring at his discovery.

"No fair! I am always found first!" Alice protested, scrambling down after being tagged.

"It was indeed a clever hiding place, Alice," Alexander said, kindly. "I have keen eyesight."

With Alice now tagged, he turned his attention back toward the hedge maze, which he was familiar with from all his visits to the garden. He dashed through each dead end, systematically eliminating potential hiding spots. To his dismay, the maze was empty. Frowning, he returned to the entrance, squinting into the distance. A pair of feet at the base of a nearby tree, caught his eye.

Why would someone hide so obviously? he wondered, feeling a grin tugging at the corner of his lips. With quiet steps, he crept toward the tree, preparing to surprise the hidden individual. He held his breath and then jumped out.

"Found you!" he proclaimed triumphantly, tapping Claire on the shoulder.

But the reaction he received was far from what he had anticipated. Claire stared at him darkly, her eyes narrowing, and her dark brows furrowed deeply.

"What precisely are you doing, you addle-pated fool?" she

demanded, rising abruptly, her voice as cold as ice.

Alexander blinked, taken aback. "Doing? Merely playing our game – there is no cause for such anger—"

"Anger?" Claire's tone dripped with disdain. "You do not yet understand the meaning of the word!"

The breeze that swept through the garden turned cold, sharp and unnatural, biting into his skin. The air grew heavy, pressing down upon him as if an unseen weight were present, robbing him of breath. The world seemed to warp and twist under the force of Claire's will, the garden itself shrinking, as though it were alive with her fury. His legs buckled beneath him, and he crumpled to the ground, struggling to regain his breath. She pointed at him, her finger turning, making a small circle in the air.

"Stop this, Sister!" A voice cut through the suffocating haze, commanding and sharp. Footsteps echoed in the thickened air, and as Alexander blinked, he saw, to his horror, two Claires standing before him. He rubbed his eyes, but the double vision didn't relent.

The oppressive force lifted, but not before he heard a low, unsettling laugh from one of them.

"He is my friend, Agatha! We were merely at play," Margaret shouted, stepping protectively in front of Alexander, her voice trembling slightly. "He meant no harm!"

Agatha's expression softened in an instant, her cold fury dissipating as if it had never been. A disarming smile graced her lips, unsettling Alexander further. "I was not aware." Her tone was almost playful. "He did but leap out and strike my arm, after all. I was merely returning the favor."

The abrupt shift in her demeanor left Alexander uneasy, his stomach churning. Her movements were fluid but carried an unsettling quality, and the way her eyes flickered about, as if listening to something only she could perceive, made him apprehensive.

"Well then," she continued, her voice now light and almost songlike, "I trust you may accept my apology?" She stepped closer, her eyes gleaming mischievously, offering a smile that failed to reach her eyes. "I am Agatha Vikar – Claire's far more charming and beautiful twin sister." She offered a long white hand.

Her grin widened, a dangerous glint dancing in her eyes as if she toyed with something beyond mere jest.

Alexander grabbed her hand, and she tugged him with surprising strength to his feet. He then stood, momentarily speechless, glancing between the two sisters. *There are two of them?* His thoughts whirled in confusion. Agatha seemed to read his bewilderment, and her smile deepened into something more sinister.

"Margaret, you failed to report that he was so handsome," Agatha purred, a wicked smile tugging at her lips. "Had I known, I would have returned sooner to claim him for myself. Perhaps I still shall."

Margaret shot her a sharp look and quickly grasped Alexander's hand, holding it tightly. But Agatha's playful grin persisted, and there was something lurking in her gaze – something wild, unstable, waiting just beneath the surface.

"I jest, of course," Agatha then added, her voice light and teasing. "A pleasure to make your acquaintance, Alexander." She curtsied formally and bowed her head with a grace that even a noblewoman might envy. "Now, if you would all excuse me, I must greet Mother. I am just back, and she would never forgive me if I failed to say hello." With that, she turned and strode off toward where Delaney sat far off beneath another tree.

"And you believed *me* to be troublesome," Claire whispered in Alexander's ear before darting off with a laugh.

Alexander stood, brushing the dust from his trousers, his movements stiff with irritation. "I believe it's time I take my leave," he muttered, barely meeting anyone's gaze. He had endured quite enough of the Vikar family's peculiarities for one day, and Agatha's sudden appearance, and her easy display of power, had pushed him beyond his limit. The cold tension still lingered in his muscles, a reminder of the oppressive force that had pinned him down moments before.

"Already? One more game!" Alice exclaimed, her voice bright as she dashed off, oblivious to the undercurrent of frustration in his tone.

"Indeed, I must," Alexander replied, forcing a strained smile that he knew did not quite reach his eyes.

Margaret faced him, concern etched upon her brow. "She meant no harm – you just startled her. And she was only jesting." Her hand slipped into his, trying to anchor him, but her touch felt lighter than usual, as if she too sensed the widening rift between them. "There is no need for you to leave."

"I pray I'm not around when she decides she isn't jesting." He glanced down at their clasped hands, then back up at her, the frustration coiling tighter in his chest. "I'm sorry, Margaret, but I believe I have had my fill for today." The words felt heavier than he intended, but he could not bring himself to soften them. He placed a quick kiss upon her cheek, more out of obligation than affection, and turned away briskly, attempting to mask the anger simmering within.

Behind him, he could feel Margaret's eyes on his back. For a moment, he thought about going back, but continued apace. He was far too angry.

15

The Dubious

Gwen hastily followed Sarah, who shoved the front door open with more force than necessary. The wood groaned as the door lurched against the doorstop, but Sarah didn't care.

"Sarah, please wait!" Gwen grabbed Sarah's arm. She jerked it free, her movement sharp, knocking a picture off the wall. The frame hit the floor with a sharp crack, but Sarah didn't even glance back as she stomped up the stairs, her footsteps echoing in the large cabin. Moments later, the sound of a door slamming shut reverberated through the house.

Gwen stood at the base of the stairs, frozen in place, unsure of what to do. Her shoulders sagged as she stared down at her feet, hoping – foolishly – that Sarah might turn around, apologize, or at least explain what the heck was going on. Gwen would apologize too, if she could just figure out why everything had spiraled out of control like this.

She sighed, her mind spinning. Sarah had always been the steady and logical one – the rock that grounded them both. So why was her friend acting like this? Sarah's behavior lately had been very strange and unpredictable. She couldn't shake the feeling that something deeper was happening, something she couldn't see. She was worried about her friend's mental health.

After a moment, a flicker of anger shot through her. She clenched her fists. *I should be the one who's angry!* she thought, the resentment simmering. The first night, she found that Sarah had gone into the dark alone and had been hurt. She had to be brought back here, and she had been babbling an insane story about a... a monster in the dark, something trying to possess her. *What was she even talking about?* Gwen hadn't pressed the issue too hard, but the whole thing had been ridiculous.

And then there was the old man wandering into the house. *Okay, that had been super creepy.* But hadn't Sarah overreacted after the officers explained that Liam was harmless? Gwen huffed. *I mean, did she really see that he had a knife or was it something else? Okay, maybe she was within her rights on that one.* But then there was the hike. A beautiful trail, a perfect morning, and the second she saw another human out there, she flipped out. *Heck, I even go to introduce us to the hiker and the moment we get separated for ten minutes, I find her running like a lunatic down the path, screaming. And I'm the one that's in trouble because I don't believe in monsters.*

Gwen sighed loudly, and her shoulders slumped as she remembered the other thing Sarah had told her. She winced. "My pack!" she blurted out suddenly, eyes closed, as she recalled the backpack Sarah had left behind in the chaos. Her phone and keys were still in it. "Great!" She rubbed her temples, feeling a small headache forming. She'd have to go find it.

Her eyes fell on the picture that had been knocked off the wall. The medium-sized frame was lying face down on the bottom step. With a frustrated sigh, she bent down to pick it up. Luckily, the glass hadn't shattered, and the frame was intact. As she turned it over, she noticed something odd about the photo inside. The image was old – probably early 1900s – showing a woman dressed in a high-necked gown. But the strangest part was the center of the photo; it had been burned. Only parts of the woman's face were easily visible, the rest was charred beyond recognition.

What an odd picture to have on such a nice wall, Gwen thought with a frown. She shook her head and carried the frame with her into the kitchen.

"I'm going to have some of that ice cream, want some?!" she yelled up the stairs, but there was no reply. "More for me..." she muttered under her breath, a small defiant smile tugging at the corner of her lips.

She pulled a pint of ice cream from the freezer, grabbed a spoon, and plopped down at the kitchen bar. The frame, still in her hand, found its place propped up on the counter, facing her as she dug into the ice cream. There was something oddly captivating about it, though. Gwen found herself staring at the damaged image longer than she intended.

Why is the burn so perfect? she wondered, her spoon pausing mid-air. There was no indication that the rest of the photo had been touched by flames, and the edges of the burn were almost too clean, too deliberate. *Was it in a fire? Or was this done intentionally using some other method?*

Her curiosity getting the better of her, Gwen turned the frame over, inspecting the back. She carefully unlatched the frame, pulling out the photograph. The back of the picture was clean – no signs of smoke or fire. In the upper left-hand corner, a neat handwritten inscription caught her eye: 'Elizabeth Wrenkle McGregor –1905.'

Her brow furrowed as she flipped the picture over again, squinting at the faint remnants of the woman's face. Despite the burn damage, she could now see that the woman's eyes were striking; haunting in their intensity.

After finishing her treat, she put the picture back together and placed it back on the wall by the stairs, glancing at the other framed photos nearby. Nearly all of them were old. Probably photographs of Sarah's relatives and ancestors. The picture directly next to Elizabeth's was a more modern photo. Gwen was astonished; the woman in this photo also had the same gorgeous eyes as those in the burned image - bright green in the color photo, and stunning. Gwen found herself wondering about the history of the place, of these people. *I guess this is where Sarah gets her green eyes from.*

Her thoughts were interrupted by a loud, hard knock on the front door. Gwen's heart skipped a beat, her body tensing involuntarily. She glanced toward the window and saw the familiar sight of a police cruiser parked outside.

Relief washed over her as she opened the door. "Officer Friendly!" she greeted him with a cheerful tone.

Officer Lambert raised an eyebrow, then smiled. "Well, hello, Miss?…"

"You can call me Gwen."

"Gwen, then. Good to see you again." He tipped his hat. "Just stopping by like I said I would. Is Miss Jensen around?"

Gwen hesitated, looked over her shoulder and then forced a smile. "She's… not available at the moment, but we're fine, really." She hoped her lie was convincing.

The officer nodded, though he seemed to pick up on her unease. "Glad to hear it. Need anything before I head out for the night?"

Gwen laughed softly. "Unless you have a police chopper and want to drop me off up that hill?" She pointed over his shoulder to show him where.

Officer Lambert smiled. "I don't have a helicopter, but I can offer you a ride to the trailhead. Save you some time."

Gwen hesitated. She wasn't one to get into cars with strangers, even if they were police officers. But Lambert had been kind so far, and it would cut her trip down considerably.

He's a cop. What could go wrong?

"Alright, Officer Friendly, you've got yourself a deal."

Lambert chuckled as they headed toward his cruiser. "You might want to let your friend know you're heading out," he said, motioning toward the house.

Gwen waved him off. "She's asleep. I'll be back before she even notices I'm gone."

Lambert shrugged, and they got into the car. As he started the engine, he glanced over. "By the way, you can call me Clark. No need to keep calling me Officer Friendly."

Gwen smiled playfully. "But where's the fun in that?"

Clark smiled and shifted the car into gear. Gwen felt mild relief at the prospect of a ride. The walk back to the trailhead would have been long and more tiring, but with his help, she'd get there and back much faster.

Before she could fully settle into her thoughts, the car rolled to a stop at the familiar location. Gwen peered around and confirmed this to be where Sarah and she had come from the trail to the main road earlier.

"Thank you so much," Gwen said, her smile genuine, the

stress of the day momentarily easing.

"Don't even mention it," Clark replied, returning her smile. Then, after a brief pause, his voice softened. "Quick question, if you don't mind. I noticed a bit of tension between you and Miss Jensen. Everything okay?"

Gwen felt her cheeks flush but managed a half-smile. She hesitated, not sure how much to reveal. "She's just had a rough week."

Clark remained silent, as if waiting for more. His expression was calm, patient.

Gwen sighed. *Might as well tell him something.* "Okay, truth is, Sarah's been acting really strange lately."

"Strange?" Clark tilted his head, his tone gentle but curious. "Like, she might need a doctor? Or maybe just some rest?"

Gwen bit her lip, feeling the weight of her own confusion. "Really strange." She paused, before deciding to spill. "Like earlier, when I told you she was asleep... she's not. She's actually in her room because she's angry with me."

Clark looked mildly confused. "And this makes her strange?"

"Well, no, not exactly. She's upset because I don't believe what she says she saw up on the hill earlier."

At this, Clark's smile dimmed slightly, replaced by something more serious. "Really? What did she say she saw?" His eyes sharpened, though his smile returned, masking the intensity.

"You're going to think it's silly. I don't want to make her seem... ridiculous."

"I promise I won't think it's silly," Clark said, his voice still calm but firmer now. "As a peacekeeper around here, I'm interested. Especially if there's anything unusual."

Gwen hesitated again, then sighed, giving in. "Okay... she said she saw a dark figure. Something like a monster, and that it chased her. She even said it called out her name – put strange things in her mind."

She cringed inwardly as the words left her mouth, bracing for the inevitable chuckle. *Why did I tell him that? It's time to get out of the car.*

But instead of amusement, Clark's face darkened. The warmth in his expression drained away, leaving something colder, harder. "Did it... say anything else to her?" he asked, his voice now measured, the playful tone long gone.

Gwen blinked, taken aback by his sudden change. "Um..."

The silence in the car lingered before Clark let out a laugh, breaking the tension. "Just messing with you!" His grin returned, though it felt off this time, too quick, too forced. "Gwen, she probably just needs some rest – some time alone. I bet by tomorrow, she'll be right as rain."

Relief flooded Gwen, and she laughed awkwardly, nodding as she opened the door. "Yeah, thanks. I'll keep that in mind."

She stepped out of the car and closed the door behind her. Clark rolled down the window, leaning over the passenger seat.

"Gwen, it's going to be dark in a few hours. Maybe I should come up with you."

"Oh, it's fine. I just need to grab my pack – it's not too far up the trail."

"You sure? It's no trouble and it's easy to get lost up here."

"I'm sure. I'll be up and down in less than an hour. Piece of cake, Officer Friendly."

Clark grinned and then shrugged. "Suit yourself. Here, take this." He offered her a bottle of water. "Stay hydrated."

"Thank you. And I appreciate the ride."

"Oh, I almost forgot," Clark added with a snap of his finger. "I wanted to let you know we had to release Liam earlier today."

Gwen froze. "Wait, what? Really?" She was shocked. *Liam, out? Already?*

Clark nodded; his expression unreadable. "Yeah. Turns out we didn't have enough evidence to keep him. I wanted to tell Sarah personally in case you saw him – but don't worry," he added quickly, "we had a good conversation with him. It was all just a misunderstanding... He said he was hunting a small animal, said it's caused him a lot of issues, and thought he saw it go into the house."

Gwen's mind raced. *A misunderstanding? Small animal?* She thought about asking more questions, but something in Clark's tone made her hesitate.

"Just steer clear of him," Clark continued. "He shouldn't bother you again. And if he does, go ahead and call us. I can be here within minutes."

Gwen nodded, though doubt lingered at the back of her mind. "Alright... I will."

Clark smiled once more, tipping his hat slightly before pulling away. Gwen watched as the cruiser disappeared down the dirt road, a sinking feeling settling into her chest.

She turned, looking thoughtfully up the hill. "Man, what am I going to tell Sarah?" She bit her lip and started up the trail.

16

Gift

24 February 1709

Two soft knocks echoed through his room. Alexander, engrossed in the Bible, looked up.

The door creaked open, and his mother stepped into view. "Good evening, my son. Might I interrupt your study for a moment?"

"Of course, Mother." He closed the book and set it aside. Rising, he offered her his chair, seating himself on the edge of the bed.

She sat down gracefully, her brow slightly furrowed, as though weighing her words. "Son, I've got a very morose-looking girl waiting for you in the parlor... I trust all is well between you and Margaret?"

He nodded slowly, biting his lip. His mother's intuition had always been sharp, and he hesitated over how much to reveal. "Aye, all is well." He paused, considering his words. "We had a slight misunderstanding, but I expect matters will soon be mended. There are things her and I need to discuss."

She inclined her head, her expression patient yet probing. "I noticed you returned home sooner than expected yesterday. Your father and I were under the impression you'd be with them the day through."

"That was my intent, indeed, but it is her family, Mother," he began, hesitantly. "They possess certain... peculiarities, which sometimes make our time together... trying."

His mother's eyes softened, her hand resting on his knee. "Son, you do know that we are here, should you require counsel or aid in any matter, do you not?"

"I do, Mother. Thank you."

She eyed him for a moment. "Very well then." She then rose to her feet. "Perhaps you can go down and lift her spirits."

"Of course, Mother." He responded with a smile. She put her hand on his cheek and returned the smile before making her way to his door.

"Oh, and I believe she's accompanied by one of her sisters. I never can tell those Vikars apart... All of them quite beautiful mind you. This one is a bit peculiar..." she said with wink before leaving. This made him snicker.

Alexander made his way slowly down the stairs, running a small comb through his hair as he descended. His eyes narrowed as they fell upon the two figures seated in the parlor.

Margaret stood as he approached, her expression anxious. She forced a smile, but it was evident she had been very distressed since their last meeting.

He approached the two, not sure which twin was with her. "Good day Margaret and..." Alexander began to greet them, but Agatha interrupted.

"Agatha." Her tone was less casual than before, her de-

115

meanor gentler. He swallowed hard, disappointed by her presence. He wondered if he'd ever be able to tell them apart. Truthfully, he had wished he'd never see the sisters again. The two had done enough to sour his affection for the Vikar name.

"And Agatha," he repeated, forcing a smile while suppressing the lingering embers of anger. He bowed slightly to both. "To what do I owe this visit?"

Margaret hesitated before sitting down, her movements awkward without his usual kiss of greeting. She glanced at Agatha, then back at Alexander. "I... We were all concerned for you when you left so suddenly yesterday. I wished to be certain all was well between us."

Alexander sighed softly, taking his seat opposite them. His gaze lingered on Margaret. He loved her, undeniably, but the growing weight of the witchcraft – the secrecy he was expected to maintain – gnawed at him. He had been wrestling with his conscience for weeks now. The very beliefs he had been taught and held close were now at odds with the strange and unsettling practices of this family. Until the Vikars, Alexander had rarely lied and would not so much as hurt a flea. Now, he felt as if he had to omit the truth to almost everyone he cared about.

"Thank you both for coming," he said, at last, though his voice was guarded. "I am... well, but I must confess that there are things which have unsettled me, things I do not fully agree with."

Margaret opened her mouth to speak, but it was Agatha who replied, her gaze sharp. "Would you be referring to our practices, perhaps?" She looked past him, toward the kitchen where his mother was, then back at him.

Alexander met her gaze coolly. "Indeed. I find certain aspects rather peculiar, and they do not sit well with my religious nor civic principles."

Agatha's eyes flickered with irritation, but she masked it quickly. "Perhaps, if you were to learn more, you might grow more accustomed to our ways."

Alexander set his jaw. "I believe I have seen more than enough to know where I stand on the matter."

Agatha leaned forward, a small grin on her face, a rebuttal ready, but Margaret quickly placed a hand on her arm. The two exchanged a silent look before Agatha relented with a smirk.

"We did not come here to speak of that," Margaret said, her voice tight with frustration. "We came to apologize, Alexander. And as Agatha is not often inclined to such things, I thought it best to ensure she conveyed her remorse properly."

Agatha threw Margaret a sideways glance, clearly unamused, but then turned to Alexander. "It is true. Apologies are not my strength, but for my actions yesterday, I do offer my regrets. I am... sorry for frightening you."

Alexander raised an eyebrow but chose to accept the apology, nonetheless. "Think nothing more of it. I too apologize if I startled you."

"You are most graciously forgiven," Agatha said with a mocking bow of her head.

For the first time, Alexander studied her closely, realizing that he could now discern the difference between her and Claire. There was something distinct in that ever-present smile... a peculiar shape set her apart from her twin.

"See, sister," Agatha said to Margaret, "we are fast friends now, just as I said."

"Not so hasty," Margaret replied, her tone serious. "There is one more thing."

Agatha paused, clearly reluctant, but under Margaret's firm gaze, she sighed and pulled a small velvet pouch from her pocket. "I have brought you something, if you desire it. Just a trifle item that you might not appreciate."

"Agatha!" Margaret snapped.

Agatha relented, a mildly resentful expression settling in her eyes. She bowed her head and held the bag out.

Alexander politely accepted the pouch, his brow furrowing in curiosity. "Thank you, Agatha," he said slowly, untying the ribbon. From the pouch, he pulled a pocket watch attached to a long, elegant chain.

"It is a most thoughtful gift. You need not have—"

"Oh, but I did," Agatha purred, her playful tone returning. "Mother and Margaret insisted. Let us call it a token of my goodwill – perhaps an engagement gift, for when I steal you from my dear sister." She winked as Margaret jabbed her with an elbow.

"Alexander, we shall trouble you no longer this evening," Margaret said, standing and placing a rolled piece of parchment in his hand. She kissed his cheek softly. "I do hope you will join us for supper later this week."

"I shall put forth my best effort, Margaret. Thank you both for the visit."

As the sisters departed, Alexander unfurled the parchment and began to read.

Alexander, my dearest,

The watch you now hold is more than just a simple timepiece. It bears an enchantment, one that will shield you from certain magics – especially those of mine and my sisters. It will go far in diminishing the advantage she holds over you. The cost to us was no small one as it was a gift from my father and required some sacrifice on both my sisters' behalf. Please, I beg of you, forgive us for the folly of yesterday. Agatha will trouble you no more. Wear it well, always.

Yours eternally, Margaret

Alexander stared at the shiny brass watch, pondering its mysterious nature. He didn't particularly like the thought of the sisters conducting some sort of dark incantation on the device deep in the Vikar home. He awkwardly let the timepiece fall and dangle by its chain for a few moments before sliding it begrudgingly into his vest pocket.

"Alex. May I inquire as to what that was all about?"

"Must you always listen in on my conversations, Mother?"

"'Tis my right, son," she said, poking her head around the kitchen wall. "That one, Agatha, seems to be a mite peculiar. Would you not agree?"

"That is most assuredly one way of putting it. But I only made her acquaintance yesterday, and perhaps I ought to extend her the benefit of the doubt."

At this his mother smiled and nodded before disappearing behind the corner.

"I think I'll retire back to my room and finish my Bible study, Mother. I'll be back down to help prepare dinner shortly."

"That would be most kind of you. Perhaps at dinner, we can

discuss the practices that you two were discussing as well."

17

The Impostor

Sarah's eyes fluttered open, crusted with the remnants of dried tears. The familiar dream of that malicious-looking woman faded, and she recognized the dark room. The memories of the day came flooding back – swirling in her mind like water from a broken dam. The terror she had felt on the hill, the thing she had seen. And the bitter sting of Gwen's disbelief; an ache far deeper than the fear. She felt alone, afraid, and betrayed.

Her eyes drifted toward the partially open door of her bedroom, where she had holed up in anger. She considered finding Gwen, an apology at the edge of her mind, but the knot of pride kept her rooted in place. She had spent nearly the entire day and night here, only leaving once to feed Ralph. Gwen hadn't been around then, probably in her room, avoiding her too.

Despite her pride, what she wanted more than anything now was to make things right. Gwen had always been her anchor. That's what made the disbelief so painful, so personal.

Sarah's gaze lingered on the door, moonlight filtering through it and casting faint shadows on the hallway beyond. *Should I go?* She hesitated, unsure if it was too early to wake Gwen. *What time is it anyway?* She remembered her broken phone and sighed.

Reaching over to her uncle's nightstand, she fumbled for the iPad. Its glow stung her eyes, harsh in the darkness; 3:01 a.m. She replaced it, the brightness still imprinted on her vision; a ghostly afterimage.

It's early. Maybe she should wait until morning. She rolled onto her back, staring at the ceiling, her mind circling the same thoughts.

Then, *chirp chirp!* A notification pinged from the tablet, startling her. She'd heard it a few times before in the last couple of days. Nothing important.

Just then, a crunching sound came from directly under the bed.

Sarah smiled to herself. *Ralph.* He must have come back to reclaim more of the spilled chips. "Hey, Ralph," she called softly, still half-drowsy. "Bring me a few of those, would you?"

She waited, expecting the cat to leap onto the bed. Company, even from that rascal, would be welcome right now.

"Ralph?" She leaned over slightly, offering her hand to coax him up. *Come on, kitty.* But nothing happened.

Instead, a chill crept up her arm, the room suddenly feeling colder. It wasn't the absence of Ralph that set her on edge – it was something else. Something she'd felt before.

Her heart lurched. That cold... that same creeping cold that had brushed her skin on the hill and in the forest that night. *No.* The thought of that nightmarish thing finding its way into the safety of this home sent a shiver through her. Sarah pulled her arm back to herself, drawing her legs close, instinctively making herself smaller.

The cold slowly seeped through the mattress, rising from beneath, and her pulse quickened, pounding in her ears. Her eyes darted around the room, looking for something, anything, but they landed on the dark corner where a strange fog – black, twisting – began to rise like smoke against the wall. Her other senses seemed to follow suit and one by one alerted her to the new presence in the room. The odor hit her nostrils like a smack to the face. Her breath caught in her throat.

It's here.

The wisps curled around the mattress, spiraling upward. Sarah froze, every muscle in her body locked, her heart hammering so fast she thought it might burst. Her breath came out in ragged, shallow gasps. She could faintly hear it, the noises of something crawling below. The bone-on-bone sound and crunching of the chips, smashing into powder at each movement.

At the foot of the bed, the dark fog shifted, pulling itself together into something more tangible – a solid shape rising, blotting out the moonlight on the far wall. It grew, taller and taller, a towering mass that loomed over her.

Sarah's mind reeled, her vision blurring at the edges. Her body felt like it was shutting down, paralyzed; her limbs heavy and useless. Despair was inevitable. But even as the world darkened, a sound filtered through – the soft trill of notifications again, and... *music?*

A melody, faint at first, like a flute playing a distant, eerie tune. It tugged at the corners of her mind, familiar somehow.

I've heard that before. The fog shape jerked and twisted at the sound, moving erratically as the music grew louder.

Suddenly, Sarah's senses snapped back into place, her mind clearing as if someone had thrown open a window in her head. The music was closer now, unmistakable, and the thing at the foot of the bed shifted again, as if agitated.

Without thinking, Sarah sprang up, the word tearing from her throat in a ragged scream. "*Gwen!*"

She was already moving before she knew what was happening, feet hitting the floor as she bolted numbly toward the hallway, her right shoulder ramming directly into the door as she ran past it. She tumbled several feet into the open hallway, the sharp smack of her face against the wooden floor jolting through her. Pain flared across her cheek, but there was no time to process it.

"Gwen!" she cried again, though this time the words came out weak, strangled in her airless lungs. *Wake up, Gwen!* The thought echoed in her mind, desperate and panicked. She waited for the door leading to Gwen's room to open but it never did. She needed her friend. Needed her to witness this... needed her to help her face this demon that seemed to target only Sarah. She let out one more plea for help, a whimpering sob that seemed to get lost in the dark.

A sound rose behind her, something so alien, so guttural, it twisted her stomach. It reverberated through the walls – crackly, yet with a horrible fluidity, as if the air itself was being shredded.

Her eyes widened. The noise moved closer, each step slow and deliberate. Sarah rolled to her back, instinct taking over as she pushed herself to her elbows. She had to see it.

Through the doorway, moonlight poured in, casting an

eerie glow. The creature's silhouette filled the space, crouching now, its body low to the ground like a predator ready to pounce. Wisps of smoke swirled around it, outlining limbs that seemed too long, too distorted. The beams of light slashed through its form, but the shadows clung to it, alive and writhing. In her mind's eye, the face of that woman flashed unbidden.

"What... what do you want?" Sarah's voice cracked, hysteria creeping in. Her chest heaved as she tried to breathe, to think. But the creature didn't answer. Instead, it began to crawl toward her, its movements fluid yet jerky, each twitch sending ripples through the darkness surrounding it.

Sarah scrambled backward, her hands slipping on the cold, slick floor. The air felt heavy, thick, as if it was pressing down on her. The chill clung to her skin; a biting cold that seemed to seep from the creature itself.

Then, far below, the flute again. It floated up through the house like a lifeline. As before, the sound agitated the creature, and it recoiled, retreating a few feet. Its elongated arms shot up to its head, clutching as though the music was splitting its mind.

What are you? she screamed internally as she watched the thing writhing in agony. She forced herself to her feet, her body trembling, adrenaline surging through her veins.

"What do you want?!" she screamed again, this time her voice piercing the still air.

But then, the music stopped. Silence fell, thick and suffocating. Sarah's eyes flicked downward toward the stairs, but before she could move, the creature shifted. In an instant, it closed in on her, closing the distance between them so quickly that she had no time to react.

"You…" it rasped, its voice wretched, as if dragged from the depths of some unspeakable place.

A force slammed into her, and she flew through the air. The world spun wildly around her, the walls and ceiling blurring together. The hallway floor vanished beneath her feet, and then – impact. The rug at the bottom of the stairs rushed up to meet her with a thud, knocking the breath from her chest. She couldn't even scream. Her body convulsed, gasping, fighting for air, but none came.

Seconds seemed to stretch into eternity as she lay there, her chest heaving, her vision swimming.

Above, there was the sound of wrenching wood. Then a crack, loud and violent, followed by a heavy thud on the floor nearby. Sarah's head lolled to the side, eyes barely focusing. The creature had leaped over the railing above, landing hard on the floor below, and continued coming for her from the library, its presence filling the room with that awful cracking sound – its movements scraping against the quiet, each slow step deliberate.

From behind her, there was another sound – different this time. The creak of a latch, then the front door swung open.

Sarah lay still, paralyzed by pain and terror. But through the haze, a figure stepped over her body, casting a shadow against the dim light. She couldn't see who it was, her vision blurred and her head swimming with disorientation, but she heard it – the soft music again.

The sound seemed to fill the room, much closer now, and the effect was immediate. The creature, still in the library, let out a horrible shriek, crashing into the bookcases and furniture in its retreat.

The figure above Sarah continued to play, stepping toward

the creature with deliberate calm. Wherever the music followed, the creature recoiled, slamming against the walls as though the melody itself was a weapon.

The cacophony of crashing furniture grew more frantic until, with a final loud *crack*, the sound of breaking glass filled the air. The music continued to play, and she could hear it slowly retreating into the night until the house was silent once more.

Sarah lay still. Her heart continued to thrum desperately in her ears and pulsate up her neck. Her eyelids flickered wildly as she attempted to comprehend what had happened.

In the far distance she thought she heard the faint sound of the music. She lay there gasping for air. She could hear nothing but her ragged breathing. The house was quiet again and she wondered what would happen next. Would she find her body too damaged to move, or would the creature return and finish what it started? Her eyes continued to circle in their sockets, searching for something, anything that might bring her peace. They finally landed on the long line of pictures hanging along the stair wall. There was little light and she could only make out a couple of the images. This seemed to bring her mild comfort as she waited silently in the dark.

18

Away

17 April 1709

The spring breeze danced through the wildflowers as the fishnet hammock swung carelessly in the wind. Margaret's head lay on Alexander's chest, her eyes closed. In the distance, birds chirped in the large trees. His horse stood nearby, tied to an oak.

A gust of wind blew her hair up, covering his face. He exhaled and blew the black strands from his mouth. She pulled her hair back and tucked it under her head. "Why is it that you have never brought me here before?" she asked, a content smile on her face.

"My first time as well my Raven. I oft begged my father to stop here during our long travels each month, yet he ne'er allowed us the time."

"Well, it is beautiful. Other than our lake, 'tis my second favorite place in the world." She stared up at the clouds slowly rolling by for a moment. She then rolled over and repositioned herself to face him. The hammock swayed back and forth at her movements. "What are you thinking of?"

"Nothing."

"You are a poor liar, Alexander." She reached up and tapped his nose with her index finger.

He looked at her, his eyes more serious now. "Tell me again, why do you need to leave?"

She nodded, a knowing look on her face. "I promise it will not be long. I did commit to my mother I would attend. It's a long family tradition after all."

"And what manner of school is it? Remind me, I pray."

"It's a special school." She laid her head on his chest again, her gaze drifting into the distance. "Truth be told, I know not what to expect. And even if I did, I told you already, I am not meant to tell... others about it. I am not even sure my father knows all."

Alexander nodded with a smile and pondered in silence. He put his arms around her and pulled her tight. "You cannot fault me for trying."

"Will you wait for me?" she asked, her voice wavering slightly. He felt her heart quicken against his chest. She waited for several seconds. "Alexander?" Her head popped up. He still bore the grin on his face and let out a low chuckle. His eyes were closed, a look of relaxation on his face. She gave him a sharp punch to his stomach and he let out a loud laugh.

"My Raven, I shall wait forever if need be."

"That is the proper answer I was in search of."

"When you have returned, I have a question for you... and I do hope your answer is yes." He opened his eyes after a few moments to see her eyes wet with tears.

She threw her arms around him and gave him a long kiss.

"If I must answer only when I return, then I must make haste, mustn't I?" She beamed. "It shall pass faster than you think. Then we shall be together."

"Forever... I promise." He said in a low whisper before kissing her again.

21 June 1709

Alexander's Journal

To my utmost displeasure, my sweet Raven departed last month. She hath journeyed abroad to a school known solely to the Vikar family, the same institution which all women of their line attend when the time is deemed proper. I made my objections known, yet Margaret assured me that this is the only path whereby we might secure our future freedom. In my reluctance to see her leave for so many months, I broached the subject of marriage upon her return. This filled us both with much joy, and we have resolved to enter into an engagement at that time. I shall offer my daily prayers for her safety whilst she is away, and that she shall return to me with her sweet nature unchanged.

In the midst of my solitude, I have busied myself at the mill, both to occupy my thoughts and to earn extra money and means for Margaret and me to wed upon her return. Yet, even with this, there are days of darkness. Thankfully, my dear friend Elizabeth hath offered me companionship in my loneliest hours, and I, in turn, have been a comfort to her in times of need.

Moreover, I have made it a point to visit Mistress Vikar and her family from time to time. They have been most kind to me and do occasionally provide company, yet I must confess that the oddity of their home still casts a shadow over my visits. I do hope that, in time, this discomfort shall pass. One thing is for certain, I do not take a liking to Agatha but, despite my reservations, I carry the gift she gave me wherever I go.

2 August 1709

Alexander's Journal

I'm writing for the first time since the passing of my dear father. The illness took him much faster than any of us thought. Mother seems to be taking it well, but we do our best to comfort her. We buried him by the old ash tree near the field. Mother said he would have wanted to be here to rest with us. I will continue to miss him. Benjamin will be helping around the farm for the time being and has already proven his worth to the landowner, securing our commission for several more seasons.

19

The Ancestors

Sarah wrinkled her nose, squinting at the pages of the book in front of her. The words were legible, but they jumbled together, making no sense. Frustrated, she let the book slip from her fingers, and it landed with a loud thud on a glass-topped table. The sound echoed unnervingly through the room.

She realized, for the first time, how many people were in the large hall. Heads turned toward her from all sides. Their eyes fixed on her with annoyed, judgmental stares. Sarah's heart raced as she quickly scanned the room, trying to avoid their gazes.

"Sorry... I'm sorry," she muttered, repeatedly, sinking deeper into her seat.

She could see that she was in a large auditorium that was arranged like a classroom with rows of sleek, modern desks that sloped downward to a stage at the front. It looked like a lecture theater in a prestigious university, yet the people seated around her didn't fit the place. Their clothing spanned centuries, as if each one had walked out of a different time period.

Sarah stifled a nervous laugh. *How did I get signed up for this class?* she thought, eyeing the woman seated closest to the stage. The woman's outfit looked like something out of the 1700s – a pilgrim's bonnet and simple dress, but foreign.

As Sarah's gaze traveled upward through the rows, she noticed the strange progression of time through the clothing – each person appeared more modern than the last. By the time her gaze reached the people in her row, the fashion had advanced to the 1960s. She glanced at the woman sitting in front of her, who was dressed in full flower-child regalia: a tie-dye top, bell bottoms, and a large ginger afro.

The juxtaposition was so absurd, Sarah couldn't help but chuckle again.

"Shhh!" The flower child spun around, her brow furrowed, and finger pressed to her lips in disapproval. "You need to be quiet now, Sarah."

"Sorry..." Sarah mumbled, stifling her laughter, but it escaped as a nervous giggle. The woman narrowed her eyes and then placed a finger over her mouth before turning back to the front of the room.

Sarah's face burned with embarrassment. She looked at others sitting near her and noticed some that looked close to her age, all with worried expressions on their faces. Sarah leaned forward to look far to her right, a small girl of maybe ten years of age and large glasses sat, her eyes buried in her book.

This has got to be a dream, Sarah thought as she continued to look around her. *Yes, this is certainly a dream and it's not the first time I've had it.* The room, the women, they were all familiar to her. She wondered why she hadn't recalled this dream until now. This was more than déjà vu; this was a vivid memory, and these women were people she knew – or should have known – from somewhere.

Her thought was interrupted. The lecturer's voice came from the front of the room. She was a dark-haired woman in a gray overcoat. Sarah could barely make out the words she was saying. The tone was familiar, yet the language was gibberish, like hearing her own voice distorted through an untuned radio.

Intrigued now, Sarah focused on the front and the two peculiar figures standing on each side of the professor. To her left sat a woman slumped in a chair, her wild, frizzy hair covering her face. Her dress was tattered and dirty, as if she'd crawled out of a nightmare. To the right stood a man, hands bound behind his back, his face twisted in agony. Every few moments, his mouth would open wide, as if screaming, yet no sound escaped. On a whiteboard behind them, the words 'McGregor and Wrenkle' were written behind the respective figures in green marker. Each name was circled in green, and the words were connected by a line. Both circles also had lines that Sarah followed to a third circle, but she couldn't pronounce the name that was written there.

Then Sarah saw it. On the floor, sitting in front of the lecturer, a pitch black creature sat. It appeared to be chained up and it rocked back and forth inside a large circular shape etched into the floor. Sarah cringed at the sight. *How did I miss that before? It's massive and hideous!* It seemed to be looking for a way to escape.

Then the voice boomed through the room. "Are you listening?" The words cut through the dissonance. Sarah's attention snapped back to the professor, who was now staring directly at her.

"Me?" Sarah pointed at herself, confused.

The room had fallen silent. Every pair of eyes – belonging to the women and girls – were locked onto her.

Her pulse quickened. The collective gaze felt suffocating. Sarah's throat tightened, panic rising, as all the women continued to stare at her, judging her.

From the corner of her eye, she saw the figure with the frizzy hair slowly raising a hand – pointing directly at Sarah. The creature on the floor also now noticed her and began yanking on its bindings. She made to scream but a sharp gust of air hit her back, jolting her. She leaned back in her chair and the large room seemed to start shrinking. She felt a cold sensation on her back that traveled through her body. A loud whistling sound hit her ears and she awoke.

Her eyelids fluttered as the remnants of the dark dream slipped away, leaving nothing but a faint unease. She blinked rapidly, bringing the room into focus. Scattered across the floor, books lay in chaotic disarray, tossed from the shelves as if by a violent hand.

Memories rushed back, crashing over her like a wave. She glanced toward the stairs she had been hurled over just hours earlier, every moment replaying in vivid detail: the towering, smoke-wreathed creature, its unnatural movements, its voice rasping in her mind – *You.* The exhaustion that settled in her bones now numbed her to the terror she'd felt. Too drained to cry, too empty to feel, Sarah simply wanted to find Gwen.

She gingerly rolled onto her back, probing her limbs for injuries. Scrapes and bruises flared to life, but miraculously, nothing seemed broken. She pushed herself upright, wincing as a throbbing headache pulsed behind her eyes. The front door hung ajar, a thin stream of chilly morning air creeping in, numbing her body.

She dragged herself to the door, shutting and locking it before turning to face the staircase. Her thoughts shifted to Gwen again – how had she slept through all this chaos? She pulled herself to her feet. Anxiety gnawed at her as she clumsily made her way up the stairs, each step sharp with dread. Gwen's room was neat, as always, but empty.

Panic prickled in Sarah's gut. She checked the other rooms, her pace quickening. Nothing. No Gwen.

The guilt from their last exchange twisted inside her, growing heavier with each empty room. As she rounded the corner into the family room, her eyes caught something out of place – a door. Where there should have been a solid wall beside the garage entry, there was now an open passage.

A hidden door.

Sarah's breath caught in her throat. Slowly, she approached it, peering down into a stairwell that disappeared into darkness. Her mind reeled with questions: *Why was this hidden?* She wondered if this was it just another of Aunt Melissa's eccentric decorative ideas or something else.

"Gwen?" she asked the darkness.

A part of her hoped Gwen had stumbled on the door and decided to explore, but the eerie silence only deepened her unease. She shuddered, backing away from the gaping void below.

A loud crunching noise came from her heel. *Broken glass.*

The back door leading to the yard was broken, shards glittering like ice on the floor. It hung slightly off its frame, swaying with the breeze.

"Gwen?" Her voice grew more urgent, rising with the fear

now crawling up her spine. She looked back toward the mystery door.

Her mind spiraled with terrible possibilities. *What if Gwen had gone down there and never come back. What if she was hurt... or worse.* Each of her senses screamed at her to close the door and walk away but her concern for her best friend prodded her forward.

Sarah hesitated at the threshold for a few minutes before she reached inside for a light switch. To her relief, she found one quickly and flipped it on. The soft hum of electricity filled the air as light spilled down the staircase, revealing a plush brown carpet below. She took a breath and descended carefully; each step slower and seemingly louder than the last.

The basement wasn't at all what she expected. Like the rest of the house, it was elegantly furnished, reflecting her aunt's meticulous taste. The decor was warm, even inviting, but something about the room felt wrong. It was too empty. The absence of sufficient furniture in such a large, otherwise well-decorated space felt unsettling, like a stage set before something awful unfolding.

"Gwen?" she called out again, though her voice faltered. She didn't expect an answer now.

She scanned the room, moving along the walls, checking doors methodically. Most opened into barren, unused spaces, save for one, which was already ajar. The slight opening tugged at her curiosity. She stepped toward it, noticing the door's spring-loaded hinge – a feature designed to keep it closed.

She opened it fully and was greeted by the sight of a furnished room and chilly air. Unlike the emptiness of the others, this room was in use. She saw a desk, papers strewn across its surface, and shelves crammed with books. It felt lived in, worked in – far more personal than any other space she had seen.

The walls caught her eye next. They were lined with large, intricate diagrams – no, not diagrams, family trees. They seemed to cover every inch of the large room. She moved closer to one that had red notes scattered across it, her gaze tracing the names and pictures that adorned each branch. One tree in particular grabbed her attention, and her heart skipped a beat. At the top, among the names and photos, she found her own picture, the very one she had sent to her aunt and uncle recently. Despite the gnawing fear in her gut, there was something oddly comforting in seeing it there.

A sharp gust of wind cut through the room, startling her. Sarah turned toward a smaller door she had assumed was a closet. But wind? She approached it cautiously, finding the same spring-loaded hinges as the room entrance. Slowly, she pulled the door farther open, her heart pounding harder as a blast of air hit her face.

Beyond the door was not a closet but a long, narrow hallway. She fumbled for the light switch and when the bulb flickered to life, her eyes widened in surprise. The hallway stretched toward a ladder at the far end. It didn't take her long to realize where it led. "The shop," she whispered, her thoughts racing. That had to be it – the ladder must lead to the inside of her uncle's shop outside. But why? A secret passage leading out of the house? *Why would they need this?*

She stood at the entrance to the passage, torn. Her mind swirled with confusion and worry. Gwen wasn't here, but where was she? Had she gone outside? Or worse, had something forced her out? Sarah's pulse quickened, fear coiling tighter around her chest.

Without another word, she slammed the door shut, locking it behind her. She needed to get out of here. Gwen wasn't in the basement, and Sarah couldn't shake the dread curling inside her. There was no more time to waste – she had to find Gwen, figure out what had happened, and leave this place.

Determined now, Sarah whirled around, ready to get out of the house. As she passed through the office, something familiar caught her eye – a picture on the wall. She paused, staring at it, but couldn't quite place where she'd seen it before. Another twinge of unease crept into her chest, but she shook it off. *There's no time for this.*

She hurried toward the kitchen, feeding Ralph quickly, before setting her sights on finding her keys. *What's the plan?* she thought, gripping the counter as her mind scrambled. All she knew was that she needed to leave – and fast.

Keys in hand, she stepped outside, the cool mountain air brushing against her skin. She slid into the car and pulled away from her aunt and uncle's house, her heart racing, unsure where she was going but certain she had to escape.

As the road twisted beneath her, a sudden realization hit her like a punch to the gut – the picture. Her mind raced back to the office, to that image she couldn't place before. Now, it was painfully clear.

The flower child.

20

Changed

16 September 1709

Alexander dismounted from his horse, inspecting one of its hooves. "As I suspected – she's thrown a shoe."

"Indeed," Benjamin replied, wiping sweat and dirt from his brow as he approached. "Best unhitch her now, lest we worsen the damage. She'll need new shoes before tomorrow's labor."

Alexander nodded, setting to work unfastening the plow. As he reached to loosen the girth of her bridle, something distant caught his eye – a solitary figure, dark against the sunlit field, making their way toward them. He squinted and shielded his eyes from the sun. "Can you finish here brother?" Alexander said with a new hint of excitement in his voice.

Benjamin looked beyond the horse to what Alexander was staring at and grinned. "Aye, leave it to me." And then slapped him on the back. "Please give her my regards."

Without another word, Alexander dropped the reins, ducked beneath the horse's neck, and sprinted across the field. His heart racing at her sight – it was Margaret, returned at last. He reached her and embraced her tightly, picking her up off the ground and spinning her around. They both laughed excitedly.

After a moment, he put her down and stepped back. His eyes widened, surprise mingling with concern as he took in her face. Though she was still the Margaret he loved, something had changed. Her features were sharper, her once-soft face was now gaunt, and in her eyes – still beautiful – there was a newfound gravity, something that reminded him uncomfortably of her mother. He lowered his gaze and stepped back, giving her space.

"Forgive me, Margaret," he said softly, apologetic. "I had not meant to soil your gown with the dust of the field."

"Think nothing of it," she replied, her smile still wide. Something about it reminded him now of her older sisters. "I only returned today, and my first thought was to come see you."

"Well, I'm more the grateful for it. I missed you more than I have words. Have you been home yet? I would be honored to escort you there."

"I have and in fact, visited with my family and have just come from your home. Your mother was kind enough to send me here, but I suppose it is now time to head back. I would be glad for your company on the way if you have the time."

"For you I have all the time in the world." He smiled and took her hand, leading her through the field and onto the road. As they walked, he glanced at her with a look of deep affection. "You cannot know the joy it brings me to have you home again."

"I feel much the same," she replied, though her voice held a subtle distance. "Being back feels almost like a dream. It is as though I have been away for years, though it has been but a few months."

"And I long to hear all about it. Perhaps we could spend tomorrow at the lake, where you might recount your time abroad."

"I would enjoy the lake," she finally replied, with a slight smile. Yet, there was still something in her eyes, something distant and troubled that did not sit well with him.

"And perhaps," he began hesitantly, "we could speak of our future?"

At that, Margaret stopped abruptly, turning to meet his gaze. Her expression was grave, and there was a flicker of fear in her eyes. "Alexander... There is much I wish to speak of. Indeed, we must. But not before I tell you all that transpired while I was away."

"My dearest Raven. Whatever it may be, we shall weather it together." He took her hand once more, and they continued their walk in silence.

A faint smile appeared on Margaret's lips as she glanced at him with hopeful eyes.

They walked quietly for a time before Margaret broke the stillness, her voice soft yet hesitant. "Alexander, might I ask – who is this Elizabeth? When I called upon your home earlier, I found her in company with your mother. It appeared they were engaged in some knitting or the like."

He gave a nod. "Aye, I believe I have spoken of the Wrenkles before. Their family is held in great esteem by ours, and we have become fast friends."

Margaret nodded, but her brow furrowed slightly. "When

I saw her, there seemed to be some understanding between you two. When she laid eyes on me, I sensed that she was less than pleased with my return." Her words were slow and measured.

"Aye," Alexander replied, with a smile. "Elizabeth has, indeed, become a trusted friend of mine."

Margaret's gaze grew sharp, her voice edged with concern. "More than friendship, perhaps?"

He let out a soft chuckle. "Margaret, I did not know you were given to jealousy."

She gave him a playful push, though her own smile was faint. "I merely seek to know where your affections lie."

"No other, Margaret. None could ever take your place, nor ever shall."

"That, sir, is the proper answer I was searching for." Her eyes flicked up to his hat before she knocked it off his head. "Jealousy indeed! But can she run as swiftly as I?"

With a burst of laughter, she sprinted down the road. He paused only long enough to scoop up his hat, a grin spreading across his face as he gave chase.

21

The Pit

Gwen strained against the ropes, her left leg outstretched, toes just inches from the knife on the table. Pain surged from her wrists as the rough rope bit into her skin, a dull throb mixing with the sharper aches in her shoulders and hips. She let out a sigh of deep frustration, her leg dropping to the floor. Her right hip screamed in protest from the repeated failed attempts to reach the knife. Her hike had turned into an experience of utter terror. She had encountered Liam, and now he held her prisoner.

The old man hadn't just tied her tightly – he'd anchored the chair to the wall, securing her like an exhibit on display. A bitter curse escaped her mouth as she kicked futilely at the air, her body trembling from the effort.

"Ow!" Gwen yelped as her right toe slammed into something solid beneath the table. The whole thing jostled, knocking a few items to the floor. Tears stung her eyes as she winced, pulling her foot back. *Great.* Was it broken? Pain pulsed through her boot with each heartbeat.

Resigned, she slumped back into the chair and scanned

the room. The cabin was rough –logs for walls and barred wooden shutters over the windows. The flickering lanterns cast jittery shadows, making every corner feel threatening. A large, stone fireplace dominated the far wall, its mantle adorned with an antique rifle. The smell of woodsmoke clung to everything, mingling with something dank and earthy.

She let out another loud sigh in frustration. She continued to scan the room and wondered why he'd plucked her off that front porch the moment he'd seen her. She felt her heart race as she briefly recounted the event. One moment, she was asking for directions, the next, she was inside this cabin, like a fly in a web. *I can only think of one or two reasons why that old man would do such a thing and neither of them are good.* She shoved the unimaginable thoughts from her mind and tried to focus on the one positive; he had left the house, giving her an opportunity to escape.

Looking back at the table, something caught her eye – the knife was missing and had fallen to the floor. She felt her heart thud loudly in her chest with sudden exhilaration. She must've knocked it down during her tantrum. *Finally,* she thought, exasperated. She'd been trying to get the knife for over thirty minutes.

She didn't hesitate. Swiveling her body as far as the ropes would allow, Gwen stretched her leg and began nudging the knife closer with her heel. The thick rug slowed its movement, but eventually, the knife slid off onto the wooden floor, easier to drag now. A breathless laugh escaped her lips. *Phase one, done.*

Leaning back, she eyed the knife. *Phase two.* She slipped off her boots carefully, wiggling her toes free and bracing her feet on the floor. With delicate precision, she pressed down on the sheath with one foot, tugging at the handle with the other. The knife came loose after a few awkward tugs, and she kicked the sheath away. She could see the blade gleaming in the dim light.

Now came the tricky part – phase three. Carefully, Gwen clamped the knife between her toes, lifting it toward her lap, her heart thudding in her ears. If it slipped now, she might not have any time to recover.

The knife dropped into her lap, blade-first but safely angled. She exhaled sharply. *Thank goodness for all that yoga.* She thought with a small fearful grin. Rocking side to side, she was able to wedged the blade between her side and the chairs arm rest. Biting her lip in concentration, she leaned to the side and reached with her hand. Despite being tied, she was able to grab the knife and pulled it behind her. Immediately, she started sawing, awkwardly rubbing the blade against the rope. Each cut took too long, each motion too slow, but at least it was progress. She continued the cut, bit by bit, only resting when her fingers became stiff.

In the distance, the low rumble of a truck engine startled her. "No!" She screamed. Her heart raced as the sound grew louder and then eventually stopped. Gwen's breath caught.

She sawed faster, her movements frantic, the rope resisting her shaky grip. "Come on, come on," she muttered under her breath, sweat beading on her forehead. The sound of a truck door slamming shut reached her, followed by the crunch of boots on the gravel path. He was getting closer.

Gwen's hands shook, her fingers fumbling with the knife as the panic surged. Footsteps echoed outside, growing louder with each second. She dropped the knife onto the chair seat, too terrified to keep cutting. It was useless now. Liam was here… The spider was going to get its meal.

The rattle of metal keys scraped at the lock; the clinking unnervingly slow. Gwen held her breath as the door creaked open. Liam paused at the threshold, scanning the room before his boots thudded across the wooden floor.

"Get away from me!"

Rough hands grabbed her shoulders, wrenching the knife from behind her. "What were you gonna do with this, huh?" He brandished the knife in front of her face, close enough to make her flinch.

He leaned over, grabbing the sheath from the floor, and stabbed the knife into the coffee table with a loud thud. "Were ya planning on sticking me with it?"

Gwen glared at him, biting back her anger, frustration burning through her veins. His timing couldn't have been worse.

Liam scowled down at her, his face twisted in irritation for a moment and then shook his head and turned away, muttering something under his breath.

Gwen's eyes followed him as he moved through the cabin, rifling through wooden boxes and cabinets, tossing objects into a satchel. "What do you want with me?" she demanded. "Liam!"

After gathering what he needed, he swung the satchel over his shoulder and finally glanced back at her. He hesitated, eyes flickering toward the gag lying on the table, considering something. But instead of replacing it, he left it there.

With unsettling speed, he pulled the knife from the coffee table and stepped toward her. Gwen tensed, but he merely leaned down and sliced through her bindings.

He paused, staring at her before turning to leave. "There's

bread n' milk in the fridge." His voice was distant and cold as he walked to the door, locking it behind him with the same unnerving clinks of metal as before.

Gwen stared at the door, rubbing her wrists, the fading warmth of Liam's hands still on her shoulders. She heard the familiar rumble of Liam's truck as it drove away. *What now?*

It only took moments for Gwen to be on her feet, rushing to the wooden door. Her hands fumbled against the solid wood, desperately searching for any weakness, but as expected, it didn't budge. She pressed her shoulder into it, putting every ounce of strength behind her push. Nothing.

Gritting her teeth, she gave up and moved systematically to the windows, tugging at each one with trembling hands, praying Liam had left one unlocked. No luck. Each window was barred or tightly shut. The frustration built inside her, feeding the panic that gnawed at her gut.

"This guy is seriously twisted," she muttered to herself. *What the heck is his game? Does he bring women here often?* Her skin crawled at the implication. She yanked at the next window with renewed fury, rattling the frame. "Who the heck has locks on the outside of their house?"

The horrible thought injected itself back into her mind – how she ended up here and how Liam had so easily trapped her. The trail had been much longer than she thought and when she finally found her backpack, the sun was just getting ready to set. She let out a loud sigh when she recalled the decision she had made to continue down the trail rather than double back. That had really been when she had sealed her fate. *That was a stupid move, Gwen. You get lost on that trail and even came right up to Liam's house.* She shook her head and continued to check the house for ways out.

In the kitchen, her eyes caught on something – a locked door different from the others. Hope surged inside her as she spotted an old key hanging nearby. She grabbed it and tried it in the lock, her hands shaking. After a quick twist, the bolt retracted with a satisfying click. She swung the door open, revealing a set of narrow stairs leading downward.

A cold, damp smell wafted up from below. Gwen's breath hitched as she peered down into the murky gloom, her mind racing with terrible possibilities. The stairs creaked under her weight as she descended, each step sounding like a warning.

At the bottom, she stopped, blinking as her eyes adjusted. It wasn't a simple dirt-floor cellar as she expected. Instead, it was more like a small, poorly furnished basement – old concrete floors, a threadbare chair, a small bed, and a wood stove in the corner. The room was eerily tidy, but that only made it worse. Gwen's stomach twisted as her imagination conjured horrific images of what this room had been used for.

How many women had Liam trapped down here? What had he done to them? She wanted to scream but bit it back, steeling herself. She had to find a way out.

Her eyes darted around the room, searching for anything she could use. An axe, a crowbar – anything. She yanked open a rusted toolbox, but it was empty, its contents long gone. Frustration burned in her chest as she rummaged through cabinets and crates, each one more useless than the last.

Then, as she turned toward the far corner of the room, her heart nearly stopped. Gwen staggered back, almost tripping over her own feet. There, hidden by shadows, was a deep, gaping hole in the floor. Her boot brushed against a short stone wall surrounding the pit, stopping her from tumbling headfirst into the abyss.

She crouched, heart hammering in her chest, staring into the dark void. A thin cord dangled from the ceiling above the hole, barely visible in the dim light. Gwen reached up, her fingers trembling, and gave it a tug. A weak bulb flickered to life, casting a faint yellowish glow over the pit.

It wasn't just a hole – it was an old well. The circular shaft extended about fifteen feet down, the bottom barely visible under the dirt and debris that had collected over time. Gwen's breath caught in her throat, and a sickening thought wormed its way into her mind.

Had he ever thrown someone down there? The thought hung in the air, the nausea in her stomach became unbearable. She pressed a hand to her mouth, backing away from the hole.

She leaned over the edge trying to get a better view, half-expecting to see something – or someone – staring back up at her. But there was nothing, just the cold earth and some random items. She backed away quickly, her skin crawling, as her eyes flicked to the two large, worn slabs of wood leaning against the wall nearby. It didn't take long to realize they were once the cover for the hole.

Something else caught her eye – a faint stain, smeared on the wall near the floor. Blood. Old, dried, but unmistakably blood. Gwen's legs buckled for a second, and she stumbled backward, almost tripping over the wooden stool behind her. *I've got to get out of here.*

She turned, shaking, and fled up the stairs, her body trembling uncontrollably. Each step felt like it stretched on forever, the walls of the stairwell closing in on her. Back on the main floor, she gasped for breath, her thoughts spiraling into a frenzy. There had to be something she missed.

Something to get her out of this nightmare.

She grabbed a cast-iron skillet from the kitchen counter, weighing it in her hands. It was heavy enough to smash a window, but past the heavy wooden and barred shutters? What was her next move? She couldn't stop thinking about the basement, about the horrors that might've happened down there. She hefted the skillet again and considered its other uses. *I've got to get out of here*, she thought again as she continued to search the house.

22

Broken

17 September 1709

Alexander watched as Claire stooped to pluck a small, flat gray stone from the shore. She cast Alexander a sly grin. "Observe, and you shall be astonished," she declared with a mischievous twinkle in her eye. She bit her lip in concentration before hurling the stone low across the expanse of the lake. The stone flew a fair distance before plummeting unceremoniously into the water with a great splash. Claire stamped her foot in frustration, muttering a soft curse under her breath.

Alexander's laughter rang out, full and hearty. He doubled over, clutching his sides. "Astonished? Perhaps not as much as you would wish," he joked, his voice echoing across the water. From behind them came a stifled giggle, drawing a sharp glance from Claire. Margaret quickly pressed her lips together, striving to keep her composure, but her eyes betrayed her amusement as they flicked toward Alexander.

"Might you give it a go, Margaret?" Claire shot back, her

brow furrowing with mock indignation.

"No, Claire, I shall leave the skipping to you and Alexander."

"Well then," Alexander interjected with a playful gleam in his eye, "allow me to astonish you in her stead." He turned to Margaret, his gaze lingering on her for a moment longer than necessary, sending a strange, unsettling thrill through her.

Margaret's face warmed under his gaze. She sat upon a fallen log, her parasol shading her from the abnormally bright sun, yet his look alone made her feel as though she were exposed. "Go on then," she urged softly, "astonish us both, if you are able."

"If I must." He selected a stone and sent it skimming over the lake's surface. It skipped once before sinking with a splash, meeting the same fate as Claire's.

Claire burst into laughter, and soon the three of them were consumed by it. "Are you astonished now?" Alexander called as he chased Claire along the shoreline.

When the laughter subsided, he returned to Margaret's side, taking a seat next to her. "Are you enjoying the day, my Raven?"

"Aye," she replied with a soft smile. "I had forgotten how pleasant these visits to the lake can be. I would spend every day here, were it possible."

"Then you shall have it. We could build a cottage here if you please."

"Alexander," she began hesitantly, "I have told you of the school, and all I have learned there…"

"Yes, you have told me, my love. I found it very peculiar but… interesting. What troubles you? Speak freely – there is nothing you could say that would mar this day."

Claire, sensing the shift in tone, rose to her feet. "Allow me to find more stones and prove my skill," she declared with mock pride, striding off along the shore, leaving them to their private moment.

Margaret's hand trembled slightly as she clasped Alexander's. "It is not merely the school, but the… expectations laid upon me. My family holds fast to their ways, and I am torn."

"Do you speak of the coven? We've long discussed this, Margaret, and I thought we had reached an accord. Has something changed?"

"I care for you dearly, but I am also bound to my family. I feel myself being drawn in two directions, and I know not which way to turn."

"Do you not wish to be with me, Margaret? Is there something that holds you back?"

"No, there is nothing I want more!" Her voice broke as tears welled in her eyes. "But…"

"Then surely your family, who also claim to love you, will understand," he murmured, cradling her now against his chest as her sobs wracked her slender frame.

She buried her face in his chest, her words muffled. "What if, like my family, I also love it? What if, like my sisters, I want to learn more and master it?"

He paused for a few moments, taking in what she had said. "Do you mean to say that you have no plans to omit the practice? Is this what you mean to say, Raven?"

"What I mean to say is that I believe there is room for it in our life together."

Her confession struck him like a blow, and for a moment, he could not speak. His mind reeled as he tried to make sense of her words. Could he bear to share her, not only with her

154

family but with this... this dark power that went against all he held dear?

"I thought we had settled the matter, Margaret. I was under the impression that we would raise our family under a religious roof, that we'd teach them to be God-fearing and righteous. Is this not the case any longer?"

She turned away and slightly shook her head. "Is one fanciful practice greater or truer than another? At least we've seen evidence of my family's power."

"Margaret," he began, his voice hoarse, "from where do you believe this power, this witchcraft comes from? Is it not from a dark place?"

"It is not as you think, Alexander. You believe it to be evil, but it is not. You do not understand. No one does. It comes from another place, a peaceful one."

His eyes, usually warm, were cold now, and his face had grown pale. The pain in his heart spread, dull and persistent, like a sickness that could not be cured. He exhaled slowly; his voice drained of all emotion. At that moment, he knew that they would never be free of the Vikar family tradition. She had had a taste of it, and he didn't believe she would ever be able to be free of it. "As you say, Margaret. Perhaps it was unfair of me to expect otherwise."

"Alexander, I beg you, try to understand. I hold faith that our beliefs may yet coexist, and I still believe we can make this work."

Alexander's head dropped slightly, and he stared off into the distance. "No, my Raven. Some things are not meant to work together and are destined to be broken." He responded, giving her a resigned smile.

They sat in silence, the lake before them serene, while the

storm within them raged.

Claire returned, her arms full of stones, her spirits undampened. "Are you ready to be astonished?"

Alexander forced a wider grin and rose to his feet, though his heart weighed heavy in his chest. "Aye, let the contest resume." He gently pulled his hand from Margaret's grasp, though she clung to him.

He hurried down the shoreline, collecting stones for the game. "Prepare yourself, Claire, you shall be truly amazed," he called, his laughter hollow. Inside, his heart lay broken, and the joy of the day seemed but a distant memory. He glanced once more at Margaret, who sat staring at her feet, tears streaming down her nose.

23

The Town

Sarah stood in the small, cramped office, her nerves on edge. The old sign behind the counter read 'County Police Department,' but there was no one in sight. She anxiously tapped her foot, casting nervous glances around the space. The room smelled faintly of stale coffee and old paper.

As she poked her head around the corner, trying to glimpse someone, anyone, from the back rooms, she chewed the inside of her cheek, her mind racing. Should she try to call Officer Lambert? But she'd left his number behind in her mad dash from the cabin. *Stupid. So stupid,* she scolded herself. At least she'd sent a quick email to her Aunt Melissa and left a note for Gwen, hoping her friend would remember how to get inside without a key.

Sarah had driven two long hours to get here, the twisting roads through the mountains blurring together in her panic. She had two choices: keep driving through the woods, hoping to stumble upon Gwen – or get help. And in part, she needed to get away from the cabin. There was no way she wanted to be found again by that thing.

But now, standing in the near-empty station, doubt gnawed at her. *Did I make a mistake coming here?*

The door behind her creaked open, and Sarah whirled around to see a short, stocky woman in uniform. She'd barely even heard the door open.

"Oh!" Sarah gasped, her voice cracking. "I didn't see you."

The officer's smile was polite, but there was a sharp edge of impatience in her eyes.

"Clearly. You looked like you were a million miles away," she said, stepping behind the counter and settling into a worn-out chair. "What can I do for you?"

Sarah could see the officer eyeing her less-than-presentable appearance and hesitated, fumbling with her words. "I – I need to report a missing person. It's an emergency."

The officer arched an eyebrow, her hand moving slowly to pull out a pad and pen from the drawer. "Okay. Name?"

Sarah's heart pounded. Why did this feel so... routine? *Did she not hear me say emergency?* She was barely able to suppress her frustration as the officer asked more questions.

"How long has your friend been missing?"

The words caught Sarah be surprise. *How long?* Guilt washed over her as she recalled the last time she'd seen Gwen – storming out, too angry to even look back. "About... twenty hours, I think."

"Okay and is there any reason to believe your friend might be in danger?"

Sarah blinked, thrown off by the question. *Danger? Of course, she's in danger.* But as she struggled to articulate what had happened, her spotty story sounded absurd, even to her. *A monster in the woods? How am I supposed to explain or even bring that up with this lady?*

The officer was listening, but her eyes were glassy, like she was going through the motions. When Sarah loudly mentioned the earlier encounter with Liam McGregor, the officer's pen finally stopped. She had detected the escalating tone in Sarah's voice.

"Ma'am, I'm going to need you to calm down. You mentioned an intruder. Did you file a report for that?"

"Yes. It was Officer Lambert who came out a few days ago. They brought Liam in for questioning or something."

"You said Officer Lambert handled this?" She paused then yelled over her shoulder. "Hey, Mike, is Lambert back in the office yet?"

A middle-aged man stepped out of a nearby office, a phone to his ear. He shook his head at the officer's question. The officer quickly typed on a keyboard and then shook her head.

"Miss Jensen, I have no record of this. No report, no booking, and no one by the name of Liam McGregor has been brought in recently."

The room seemed to tilt as the officer's words sank in. *No report? No record?* "There... there has to be a mistake... Officer Lambert... can we call him?"

The officer's eyes hardened, losing all semblance of patience. "There's no mistake ma'am. And Officer Lambert is actually on leave for three weeks. It's highly unlikely that you have the right officer. Do you have another name?"

Sarah stared at the woman in disbelief. "Another name?" she said, feeling her face flush. Her mind spun as she searched for a suitable answer. Her body felt numb, very likely from a combination of a lack of sleep and her recent traumatic experiences. Her mind went blank and she merely stared back at the officer.

"Yes, another officer perhaps?" the officer asked but was already pushing the keyboard under the monitor.

The wave of frustration and helplessness that washed over Sarah was unbearable. Her throat felt tight, her skin prickling with heat. How could this be happening? Why wasn't anyone helping her?

She opened her mouth to argue, but the officer was already turning away, gesturing to a pile of paperwork on the desk. "Now, if there's nothing else, I have work to do. Come back when your friend has been missing for seventy-two hours, and we'll chat mmkay? In the meantime, please fill in the rest of this form."

Sarah stumbled out of the station, her vision swimming with tears she refused to let fall. *No one believes me.* Sarah barely registered, opening the car door before collapsing into the driver's seat. She stared blankly ahead, her body heavy with defeat. *None of it makes sense.* She replayed the conversation with the officer over and over, searching for any logical thread, but everything seemed to unravel the more she thought about it.

The pressure in her chest, held at bay for so long, finally broke. Tears surged from her eyes, hot and unstoppable, spilling down her cheeks. She fumbled around the car for a tissue, but her vision blurred with the flood. She shouted and slammed her fists into the steering wheel.

The sound echoed in the small space, but it did nothing to quell the fury now bubbling up inside her. Days of fear, confusion, and helplessness churned in her gut, rising fast, the sorrow morphing into something sharper. *I'm done being scared.* She tugged her sleeve across her face, wiping away the remnants of her tears. *I need to find Gwen and we're getting out of here.*

Her mind buzzed as she reached for her keys, a sudden thought piercing through the chaos: *Officer Lambert.* Why hadn't he filed the report on Liam McGregor? And why would the officer in the station say Lambert was off duty? Sarah's fingers hovered over the ignition, her heart pounding faster. *Why would he lie about that?*

The key clicked into place, and the car roared to life, vibrating beneath her. Sarah wiped her eyes again, snatching a couple of tissues from the console before shifting the car into gear. But just as she lifted her foot to press the gas, a knock on the window made her jump.

Sarah stared through the glass at the familiar short figure. *What now?* She thought as she rolled down the window.

"Miss Jensen, right?" the officer asked, leaning in slightly. Her voice was softer now, and there was a glimmer of something like concern in her eyes. Sarah nodded stiffly, unsure how to feel about this sudden shift in tone.

"I'm sorry to bother you, but I had a quick question. Are you sure Officer Lambert was the one who responded to your call the other day?"

"Yep." Sarah's response was clipped, her emotions still raw.

"Officer Clark Lambert?" The officer's expression tightened, her brow creasing with concern.

"I don't remember his first name. Could've been Clark… but really, how many Lamberts could you have on your force?"

The officer gave a small nod, acknowledging the point. "Well," she began, her tone even more careful now, "we just got a call from his wife. She hasn't seen him in a couple of days – says she's been trying to reach him, but he's not responding. You wouldn't happen to know anything about that, would you?"

Sarah's eyes widened in disbelief. *Lambert's missing?* "Officer," she said, her voice steady but laced with bitterness. "All I know is what I told you inside. Maybe you should tell her to call back after seventy-two hours."

The remark hung in the air between them. For a moment, the officer didn't respond, her expression unreadable as she processed Sarah's words.

"Listen. My name is Officer Bradford. Clark Lambert's wife is a friend of mine. If you see him, would you please call me?" She handed Sarah a small business card, her eyes pleading. "She's really worried. It's probably nothing but I'd appreciate it."

Sarah stared at the card, her mind spinning with even more unanswered questions. *What the heck is going on?* A pang of guilt tugged at Sarah's chest. She swallowed hard, pushing back her initial reluctance. "Okay… I'll let you know," she muttered, her voice softening.

"Thank you, I appreciate it," Officer Bradford said with a kind smile. "And I need to apologize for earlier… I'm not having the best day."

Sarah nodded, a new tear threatening to go down her cheek.

"Listen, we're reaching out to Officer Cooper, Lambert's partner. Once we get ahold of him, we'll see if he can visit the address you gave us. I'm sure your friend is alright, but he'll be happy to assist you."

A wave of relief washed over Sarah, her tight shoulders loosening ever so slightly. As the tension ebbed, the single tear slipped down her cheek. She wiped it away, her voice trembling as she spoke. "Thank you…"

Officer Bradford touched her arm. "Everything is going to be fine."

Sarah drove away from the station, her simple plan still in her sights. She was going find Gwen and get them both home.

After refueling her car and scarfing down a disgusting gas station hot dog, Sarah sped back down the small two-lane highway, back to her aunt and uncle's house, back to look for her best friend, back to the creature that seemed set on hunting her.

24

Rumors

22 November 1710

Elizabeth picked up a bolt of fabric and held it against her chest, casting a glance toward Martha, seeking her approval. Martha wrinkled her nose and tilted her head thoughtfully. "I think red might suit you better," she said, selecting a deep crimson fabric from the nearby table.

Alexander followed behind them, feeling content. The town bustled with activity, vendors and shopkeepers tending to their stands as people moved in and out of the small shops. When Elizabeth turned toward him, presenting both fabrics, he nodded his approval for both, smiling. The fresh air invigorated him after weeks spent indoors managing his late father's affairs, alongside his mother. The chance to be out in the open air again was a welcome reprieve.

"And what do you say to this?" Elizabeth asked, draping a gold-colored cloth over her shoulder.

"I do not believe there exists a color that would not flatter you."

She cast him a glance that made his heart quicken, her reddish-blonde hair catching the light, and those emerald eyes – how they took his breath away each time she looked his way.

"You are too much the charmer, Alexander. Perhaps I'll keep your mother's opinion over yours."

But he knew it to be true. Elizabeth was more beautiful than she realized. As he looked about, he noticed the other men – young and old alike – watching her, their gazes lingering longer than propriety suggested. There was something undeniably special about her. Despite her striking beauty, she possessed a kind, innocent demeanor that seemed to captivate everyone around her.

Since his painful break with Margaret, his feelings for Elizabeth had kindled into something more. He had known her as a dear friend for so long, but now, it was clear to him that his feelings for her had always been more than mere friendship. They had blossomed into more over the months. Margaret had never ceased her attempts to rebuild their relationship, and he had a deep bond with her. Despite this, he knew that they would never be free of the dark practices that her family – and now she – devoted themselves to. It pained him to think about her, and he had to often push her from his thoughts.

"Son." Martha's voice broke interrupted. "I must see the baker. Will you and Elizabeth tend to the purchase of salt and the other spices?"

"It would be my pleasure, Mother." He winked and then put his arm in the air with flourish. "Will you accompany me, my lady?"

Elizabeth gave a playful nod and a curtsy before extending

her delicate hand as though inviting him to lead her in a dance. They wandered through the bustling market, pausing at each vendor's table, taking their time as they looked for what Martha had requested.

"So? Do you have an answer for me?"

"Answer? To which question, my Dove?"

"Have you decided yet? Will you be joining us on our journey south the week after next?"

"Ah. Well that likely depends."

"On what?"

"On whether your father would approve of us traveling abroad without him."

Elizabeth laughed softly. "My father likes you, Alex. At times, I believe he holds you in higher regard than he does me. I believe he wishes I were a boy like you."

"Aye, you speak the truth." Alexander said wryly.

Elizabeth knitted her brows together in mock offense and gave him a soft shove. "So, will you join us?"

"Yes, my Dove. I shall join you and your mother, though I must attend to a few matters before we depart."

They continued their leisurely stroll, but the bustling of the market grew louder as they rounded the next corner. The press of people increased, forcing them to weave in and out of the crowd. As they neared their normal spice merchant, Alexander's attention was drawn by the mention of a name that still caused him pain. His heart tightened as he pulled Elizabeth gently to a halt, motioning for her to listen.

Two shopkeepers sat near one another, their conversation turning to dark rumors. "I swear it, by my mother's grave, God rest her soul – I saw it with mine own eyes. Those Vikars are naught but trouble," said one man, his voice low and conspiratorial.

"Oh, come now," the taller man beside him said, shaking his head. "Should not make such accusations without proof. 'Tis not right."

"But I tell you, I saw it! Agatha – one of the twins, sure as I stand here. There's wickedness in that one, I swear it upon my very name."

A woman nearby, overhearing their exchange, nodded grimly. "Aye, wicked, indeed. There is no doubt in my mind that they dabble in dark arts. I know their kind when I see it."

"Tomfoolery and poppycock. Strange they may be, but followers of the devil? Nay, thou wilt need more than idle words to convince me of such."

Alexander's heart sank as the conversation continued. He felt Elizabeth's hand tighten around his, and when he looked at her, her brow was furrowed in concern.

"Alex, are they referring to the Vikars near your home?"

He nodded slightly; his expression grim. "The Vikars have long been whispered about, by such rumors… not all of it necessarily without reason."

"Does it trouble you? This talk – does it weigh on you?"

"Margaret… she was never what the rumors say. While she has become quite attached to the practice recently, rarely involved herself in the dark business. But others in the family… they are entangled in something I cannot understand, and I don't agree with. To my knowledge, they've never harmed anyone, and I promised them I wouldn't share their family practices. I intend to hold that secret close to my chest as long as I am able."

Elizabeth nodded slowly, her gaze lingering on his face. "I

167

understand."

"Thank you, my Dove. It's not something I like discussing. Perhaps I will share the details with you when it is less painful."

They shared a glance and made an unspoken decision to move on to an alternate vendor.

From behind them, Alexander heard a loud voice. "'Tis true, just ask him – he lives just over the hill from the Vikars!"

Alexander's back stiffened at the realization that he was the target of the conversation. In that fleeting moment, he decided to ignore the reference, quickening his pace to avoid confrontation. But the man was insistent, raising his voice even louder.

"Alexander McGregor!" the man shouted, his tone carrying a note of challenge.

Elizabeth turned her head, glancing back toward the speaker before Alexander could urge her to keep moving. He stopped, reluctantly, his shoulders tight with frustration, and slowly turned to face the man, unwilling to be drawn into this unwelcome discussion.

"Yes?" Alexander's voice was flat, his patience already worn thin.

The man waved his pipe toward him, grinning as though he'd won some small victory. "Pray, settle something for us, would you?"

"We haven't the time—" Alexander began, but the man interrupted, raising his voice again, drawing the attention of more onlookers.

With a sigh, Alexander realized there was no avoiding the encounter now. He cast a quick glance to Elizabeth, then turned and walked back toward the man, the crowd parting slightly to make room for them.

"What is it that you require of me? We have much to do."

The man leaned forward; his eyes gleaming with malicious curiosity. "We've long suspected there's something odd about thy neighbors – the Vikars. That they may be dabbling in… darker matters, if thou catch my meaning."

"I am certain I do not, and if you would excuse us, we must be on our way."

"Oh, come now. Thou meanest to say you have never noticed anything strange? No peculiarities? You live just over the hill from them. Surely you have seen something."

"I make it a habit not to pry into my neighbors' personal matters. I would know nothing of their affairs."

The man's eyes narrowed, his tone turning accusatory. "You mean to say, after spending all that time with the Vikar family – being in an understanding with their daughter, what was her name? Margaret – that thou sawest nothing amiss? Nothing that would lead you to believe they're in league with the devil?"

At the mention of Margaret's name, a flush of anger rose in Alexander's cheeks. He took a step closer to the man, standing so near that the tip of his pipe was almost touching. "That, friend, is exactly what I'm saying."

Without waiting for a response, Alexander turned sharply on his heel, grabbing Elizabeth's hand and leading her away from the crowd.

As they walked away, the man's voice drifted after them, faint but unmistakable. "I know what I saw… and I'll be speaking to the constable about it."

Alexander's grip tightened on Elizabeth's hand, his mind racing with thoughts of what might come. He had tried to put the Vikars behind him, but it seemed that the past – and the rumors surrounding that family – would not let him go so easily.

25

The Woman

Gwen took a long swig from the half-full jar of milk, the cool liquid barely soothing her dry throat. She sat in the very chair she'd been tied to, now at Liam's dining table – if that's what he called it. Hours had stretched on, her initial panic turning into a grim determination as she tried to stay awake, her weapon of choice, a cast-iron pan, resting within arm's reach.

She had no idea what time it was. The house was devoid of any clocks, and every window was sealed tight, offering no hint of the outside world. Liam had made sure of that. He wasn't just keeping people out – he was trapping her in.

Her gut told her it had been at least three hours, but without a watch, she could only guess. Exhaustion finally settled in, and with her adrenaline depleted, Gwen had decided on a plan of action: she would snoop through Liam's personal belongings. If she was going to survive this, she figured she needed to know who Liam McGregor really was. She had already done a thorough search for a way out and there was simply no escape.

Now, scattered across the table, were bundles of papers she'd discovered under Liam's bed. The same key that opened the basement had unlocked his room – Gwen smirked to herself. *What an idiot.*

The papers were mostly old black-and-white photos, probably family. One newer photo, in color, showed a young boy with reddish-blonde hair. Curtis McGregor, it read on the back. His son, maybe? *Who in their right mind would marry a monster like Liam?*

One bundle contained a newspaper clipping, an obituary confirming her suspicion. Curtis McGregor had died suddenly, leaving Liam as the surviving parent. There were no details about a wife or a mother. She flipped through the rest, searching for any details on how the boy had died, but there was nothing.

A loud creak echoed through the house, freezing Gwen mid-motion. She grabbed the skillet, gripping its cool handle tightly as she strained to listen. After a moment, when the house remained silent, she exhaled. *Just old building noises,* she thought to herself, though she kept an eye on the door.

She turned her attention to a small cardboard box on the table and lifted the lid, her breath catching as she peered inside. Her hand trembled as she pulled out a handwritten list of names. Dozens of women, each one scrawled in messy handwriting. *Liam's?*

"Mary, Anne, Clara, Charlotte…" Her voice wavered as she read the names aloud. Anger, fear, and a deep, nauseating dread churned in her gut. The list was long, way too long – each name more damning than the last.

Morbid curiosity kept her from tearing the paper apart. Instead, she folded it carefully, slipping it into her pocket.

Evidence. *I need proof on this sick jerk.*

Just as she folded the list, her eyes snagged on one name at the bottom: Elizabeth Wrenkle. A cold realization washed over her. She knew that name. But from where? It gnawed at her, tugging at some distant memory she couldn't quite place.

Determined, she dove deeper into the box. The rest of the contents made her stomach turn – newspaper clippings, one after another, detailing unexplained deaths, all matching the women on the list. She flipped through the yellowed pages, her pulse quickening as the articles stretched back decades.

How long had the sick old man been doing this?

Gwen's mind raced as she took in the scope of it all. This wasn't just a deranged man – he was a serial predator.

And then it hit her – the name 'Gwen' would be added next.

A fresh wave of dread washed over her, chilling her to the bone. She thought of the last time she and Sarah had spoken. By now, she would be awake, probably worried sick. Gwen felt a knot of nausea twist in her stomach. *She doesn't know McGregor did this.* The realization hit hard. *Is that where he went? Perhaps to get Sarah?* Her pulse quickened as her mind raced.

Gwen squeezed her eyes shut, cringing at the mental image of him breaking into that cabin again, creeping in while Sarah slept. She could almost hear the floorboards creaking under his weight and see his shadow looming over her friend's bed. *No. No.* She shook her head violently, as if the motion could dispel the thought.

She tried to hold onto hope, clinging to the idea that maybe Sarah had sensed something was wrong and gone for help. Maybe the authorities were already on their way. *Maybe.*

Her hands trembled as she began returning the newspaper clippings to the box, but a couple of dates snagged her attention. One, from 1974, detailed the disappearance of a woman missing for several months. The clipping described her family's desperate pleas for any information on her whereabouts. Gwen's heart raced as she stared at the grainy photo of Isabel. She was again astonished by the notion that Liam could be a seasoned serial killer, at large all these years.

She continued sifting through the papers, each article worse than the last. Then, her fingers brushed something different – older. She pulled out a brittle, yellowed sheet of paper, so worn it was nearly translucent. It looked like a missing person poster, but ancient. *No, this definitely doesn't add up. This would make Liam's age over a hundred years...*

Her breath caught in her throat as her eyes landed on the name: *Elizabeth Wrenkle.*

The name seemed to glow on the page, pulling Gwen's thoughts toward it. *Elizabeth Wrenkle...* that name again, like a word forgotten that lingers at the edge of memory. She wracked her brain, trying to place it. "Why do I know that name?" she said to herself, eyes closed, and her nose wrinkled. She squinted to read the small print. It appeared that the authorities were on the lookout for Elizabeth Wrenkle McGregor rather than citing her as a missing person.

She folded the paper and placed it carefully back into the box. Several others remained, their edges yellowed and brittle with age. One, a piece of parchment that appeared to be a newspaper clipping from the year 1727, caught her eye. It bore a single, ominous headline: 'The Ship of the Damned.'

Gwen's pulse quickened as she scanned the faded text. The article recounted the harrowing voyage of a ship that had crossed the Atlantic from England to the British Colonies. A tragic crossing – men and women perishing under mysterious circumstances, only a handful of crew and passengers surviving. Her breath caught as two names leaped from the page: McGregor and Wrenkle. Her fingers tightened around the parchment, and she pushed it against the table, trying to flatten and make it more legible.

A sudden bang from outside shattered her focus. The popping sound echoed like a gunshot, but the rumble that followed brought her to a far more disturbing realization: *Liam was home.* She let out a loud expletive. She dropped the paper back onto the table before getting a chance to completely read it.

Panic gripped her, and her limbs refused to obey as she fumbled to gather the papers into a messy pile. She snatched the heavy skillet from the table, barely managing to cradle the papers in one arm, the skillet in the other. She hastily shoved the crumpled bundle under Liam's bed. Moments later, she was back in the front room, breath shallow, waiting.

The rumble of the truck grew louder, the sound of tires crunching over gravel triggering a wave of nausea in her gut. *Stay calm.* She forced the plan back into her mind – *hit Liam, hit him hard, and keep hitting him.*

But doubt crept in like an unwelcome guest. She remembered how effortlessly Liam had overpowered her before. *He's too strong...What if he doesn't go down?* Her hands trembled. The fear simmered in her stomach, turning into a boil as the moments ticked by. She took her position, gripping the skillet with both hands, ready for the ambush.

The locks rattled as they always did, but this time, it took longer. *What's taking so flipping long?* she thought, teeth clenched, her entire body tense. A tiny whimper escaped her throat, unbidden, as the pressure became unbearable.

Finally, the last lock clicked, and the door swung open. With a guttural cry, she swung the heavy skillet down, aiming for his head.

Thud.

The sound was muffled, deadened. Her eyes flew open, filled with disbelief.

Liam stood there; hand wrapped around the iron skillet like it weighed nothing. His grip was firm, unyielding, stopping her full-force strike in its tracks. His cold eyes met hers, and before she could react, he wrenched the skillet from her hands and shoved her, hard. The force sent her sprawling several feet across the floor.

"You little firecracker," He spat, examining his hand. "That hurt."

Gwen twisted to face Liam, her mind scrambling to process what had just happened. But the sight froze her in place, rooting her to the floor. Liam shut the door behind him with a slow, deliberate push, as if he hadn't just disarmed her with terrifying ease.

But that wasn't what made her go cold.

Liam was cradling a woman in his other arm. She lay limp against him, her head resting on his shoulder, a cascade of long, red hair partially covering her face. Her skin, pale and bare, seemed to glow faintly in the dim light.

Gwen's throat constricted. She couldn't look away, her chest tightening as her breath caught. The woman wasn't moving, but her half-open eyes – bright, green – stared blankly out from behind her red hair. Gwen's heart thudded violently in her chest. *I know those eyes or at least eyes like the*

176

ones in that picture. She thought about the picture next to Elizabeth's on the stairs. *Elizabeth! That's where I know that name. Elizabeth Wrenkle McGregor!* The woman before her was the woman in the picture next to Elizabeth, Gwen would swear on it.

"You're a murderer."

Liam turned toward her, his face as emotionless as ever, though a certain heaviness hung around his features. His eyes, devoid of warmth, swept over Gwen before he carried the woman past her, heading toward the kitchen. His footsteps echoed, slow and unhurried, while Gwen's entire world seemed to stop.

The shock hit her all at once, like ice water rushing through her veins. *It didn't make sense.* She couldn't believe what she was seeing. But there was no denying those eyes – their brilliance seared into her mind. It had to be her, but the woman looked the same age as in the photo and while the picture was more modern, it looked to be at least thirty years old. Her stomach lurched as fear gripped her again.

Without thinking, she shot to her feet, her movements frantic, her limbs finally obeying. Her hand reached for the door, the cold metal of the handle sending a jolt through her body. *Just get out. Just run.*

Behind her, Liam's steps descended into the basement. And then – a scream. High-pitched, it pierced through the house, filling every corner with horror.

"No, please!" The woman's voice was desperate, broken. "No, not in there! Not again please!"

The door rattled under Gwen's hand. She hesitated, her breath coming in shallow gasps, her heart pounding in her ears. Could she really leave? Could she abandon this woman to that monster?

Another scream echoed from below, tearing at Gwen's resolve. Tears spilled down her cheeks, but her body moved on its own – it had to.

With trembling hands, she yanked open the door. She could barely think to herself over the woman's sobbing cries. *If I stay... neither of us will survive. If I leave, we both have a chance.*

26

Inquiry

13 December 1710

Three loud knocks echoed through the house. Elizabeth was busy helping Martha roll out dough for supper. The two exchanged amused glances as Martha's arms were covered in flour up to her elbows.

"I shall receive whomever has called at the door," Elizabeth said, swiftly pulling off her apron. "It is likely more folk seeking work on the farm. I shan't be but a moment."

Another three knocks sounded as she approached. Drying her hands on a cloth, she lifted the metal latch and opened the door.

Two men stood at the threshold, dressed in dark black suits with brass buttons and flat-brimmed hats. Far behind them, Elizabeth noticed a short man awkwardly holding his hat in his hands, looking rather uneasy. She recognized him at once – it was the spice merchant who had been so vocal at the market about the Vikars.

"May I be of service, gentlemen?" Elizabeth asked, her voice

179

warm but measured.

"Good afternoon, miss," said the taller of the two, a man with a kind face and a thick black mustache. He bowed slightly as he spoke. "We are constables in the district. Might we inquire if the owners of this estate are at home?"

"I am but a friend of the family. However, the mistress of the house is indeed present. Shall I fetch her for you? Would you care to step inside?"

"No, no, thank you, miss," the constable replied with a polite wave of his hand. "We are quite comfortable here. We would be much obliged, however, if you might summon the lady of the house."

Martha stepped forward from behind Elizabeth, smiling as she dried her hands. "Good day to you, gentlemen. How may I be of assistance?"

"Good day, ma'am," the taller constable replied. "As I was telling your companion, we are officers of the law, and we do beg your pardon for the intrusion. We simply have a few questions we hope you may answer."

"Think nothing of it, officers. I shall answer what I am able," Martha said kindly, though there was a certain firmness in her voice. "Might I inquire as to the identity of the gentleman standing behind you? And perhaps the purpose of his visit as well?"

The constable glanced over his shoulder as if he had quite forgotten the man's presence. "Oh, do not trouble yourself with him, ma'am. He is here merely to assist us."

Elizabeth eyed the the short man again scrutinizing him. *What is it you've been up to Mr. Arnall?* she thought as she watched him. He seemed to squirm under her gaze and quickly looked away.

"Very well then, ask what you will," Martha stated, confidently.

"Thank you, ma'am. We shan't take much of your time. We have come to inquire about a neighboring family – the Vikars, to be precise." The constable paused after his sentence as if looking for a reaction. Martha gave him none.

"Ahem... Would you happen to know the family of which I inquire?"

"Yes, we are acquainted with the Vikar family."

The constable nodded and cleared his throat, glancing briefly at his companion. "To put it plainly, ma'am, we have received reports suggesting that they may be involved in practices of a nature... how should I put it... less than Christian, if you take my meaning."

"Officer, I pray I do not know what you imply. Could you put it more plainly?"

"Ahem... well, we speak of matters that have troubled this district before. Dark matters, if you will, that are not unfamiliar in certain circles."

"I apologize, constable, but I am afraid I am not familiar with the 'dark matters' of which you speak. Now please, just be out with it."

At this, the shorter constable, who had been silent until now, stepped forward with a more severe expression. "Ma'am, we refer to witchcraft. We are investigating its presence in this region, and we have reason to believe the Vikar family may be involved."

Elizabeth flushed at the implied connection between the Vikars and the term 'witchcraft.' Alexander had shared a few of his experiences at the Margaret's home but for the most part had been fairly guarded on the topic. In any event, there was no question in her mind that the Vikars were involved to some degree. The smaller man's eyes flickered to hers, seeming to detect her reaction. He opened his mouth to ask a question, but Martha interrupted him by letting out a soft chuckle that quickly grew into a hearty laugh.

"Witchcraft, is it? Gentlemen, I fear you jest! Surely you don't mean to say you're investigating the Vikars for such nonsense? Why, witchcraft is but the stuff of old wives' tales is it not?" The man switched his attention back to Martha.

"Ma'am, we do not debate the merits of that claim. We are simply tasked with determining whether it is being practiced by your neighbors."

"Gentlemen, the Vikar family has been nothing but kind to my own. That they are perhaps unconventional in their ways, I will not deny. But witchcraft? I've never witnessed anything of the sort. Surely you have been misinformed."

Before the constables could respond, a voice came from behind them.

"Gentlemen."

They turned to see Alexander approaching, an axe resting on his shoulder. "Is there something I might assist you with?" he asked, his eyes narrowing at the sight of the spice merchant. "Mr. Arnall, I believe? Good to see you again."

"Good day," the taller constable greeted him. "We were just inquiring about your neighbors in relation to... certain suspicions of dark practices."

"Ah yes, the matter of witchcraft," Alexander said, stepping between the constables and walking over to his mother and Elizabeth, planting a kiss on each of their cheeks. "I thought we had settled this matter with Mr. Arnall."

Mr. Arnall opened his mouth, but the taller man spoke.

"Well, we simply hoped you might provide some clarity on the subject."

"Are you not satisfied with my mother's responses thus far? If so, I assure you mine will be no different."

"Well… Yes… But—"

"Gentlemen," Alexander interrupted, his voice firm. "I have had the distinct honor of spending the most time of any of us with the Vikar family, and I have no doubt that Mr. Arnall has made you aware of my past understanding with Miss Margaret Vikar." He shot Mr. Arnall a sharp glance. "While I do not know what he imagines he has seen, I can tell you plainly that in all my time with the Vikars, I have witnessed nothing that would help you in your inquiry. Now, unless you intend to stay for supper, I must kindly ask you to excuse us. I fear I am quite famished."

The taller constable smiled and tipped his hat. "Of course, we apologize for the disturbance and thank you all for your time."

Alexander offered a slight bow in return, then gently closed the door. From outside, they could hear Mr. Arnall's high-pitched voice, continuing his accusations.

Martha looked at her son, a question in her eyes. Alexander simply smiled.

"Mother, as I've said before, I promised not to expose their practices. It is a matter of honor and best left alone."

Martha opened her mouth to argue but stopped herself and simply smiled and walked into the kitchen.

"Alex. Are you not concerned by the possible connection between the Vikars and you? Does this not put you and your family in danger?"

"No, my Dove." He turned to her and pulled her into his

183

arms. "To my knowledge, the Vikar family has done nothing wrong. Thus by extension, we have done nothing wrong." He planted a kiss on her cheek and smiled.

"This is quite concerning Alex. Are you not afraid of the possible misunderstanding? I've heard of others that have become mixed up in these trials and have also been tried in connection."

He kissed her again. "Nothing is going to go amiss, my Dove. I promise." He released her and they walked together into the kitchen to join his mother.

His words were reassuring but Elizabeth felt a small knot form in her stomach. She wanted to help Alexander put Margaret and the Vikars in his past but there was an undeniable feeling that told her this issue was far from over.

27

The Friendly Officer

The crowbar finally found its purchase, and the door popped open, vibrating as it swung inward with a hollow creaking noise. Clark stepped back a couple of feet, his heart racing, as he dropped the crowbar and put a hand on his firearm. Officer Cooper stood behind him, mirroring his tense stance.

"Back up, Liam!" Clark yelled, his voice echoing in the stillness as he pushed his way into the dimly lit house.

Liam put his hands up, palms facing them, his face flushed and sweat-soaked from shouting about how he had become trapped in his own home. He obliged, backing into the shadowy confines of his front living space.

"Close the door, Coop," Clark said over his shoulder, his eyes scanning the room for any sign of danger. Officer Cooper peered out at the police cruiser, gave Gwen a thumbs-up, then waved before shutting the door with a resounding thud that reverberated through the silence.

"Sit, Liam. Right there."

Liam complied.

The officers cleared the knife and a few other dangerous items from the cluttered table before stepping back.

Clark relaxed slightly, taking his hand from the hilt of his pistol. He took a seat across from Liam and then shook his head, an exasperated look on his face.

"Tell me what you're thinking, Liam. I thought we had come to an understanding when we discussed your little break in at the Moore house, yet here you are, getting in my way again."

"Lad, you don't know what you're into. This is not mere children's play."

"We told you to stay out of the way, and what do you do? You keep interfering." Clark leaned forward, his expression sharp, the tension in the room crackling like static.

"So what's your plan? You let it out and let it take that poor girl? Is that what they're paying you for?"

A flicker of guilt crossed Clark's face before he grinned, the smile not reaching his eyes. "Something like that. So, what do we need to do to keep you out of the way?"

"Clark, can I speak with you?" Officer Cooper called from the other side of the room. He was still standing ready, but he now had a puzzled expression on his face.

Clark waved him off, his focus locked on Liam.

"Clark, I need a minute."

"Not now, Coop!" Clark yelled but didn't look his way.

"Hey, I don't remember some of this being part of the deal, Clark. I need a minute!" Officer Cooper insisted, the tension in his voice mirroring the atmosphere.

Resigned, Clark stood and pulled his partner to the corner, their voices hushed but urgent. "Listen, we talked about this, you don't need to worry. I have this completely under control."

186

"Yeah? Why does it sound like someone's going to be killed?" His whisper grew louder, and Clark motioned for him to be quieter, eyes darting to Liam.

"Listen, man. They told me the girl won't be killed. It's more like an abduction, like a kidnapping. They said she'd be fine, so don't worry about it, okay?" He paused, waiting for his partner to respond but there was doubt still. "I have this completely under control, Andy. I promise. You just need to trust me."

Andy lowered his head, but the frown on his face deepened. "Okay, whatever you say. This is just getting really odd, big money or not, I won't be an accomplice to murder, Clark."

Clark nodded reassuringly, though his own anxiety seeped through. "This will be over soon, I promise. For now, this is what I want you to do: take the girl, Gwen, back home." Officer Cooper opened his mouth to object, but Clark continued, his tone firm. "Tell her we found the evidence and that we're taking Liam in, locking him up."

Andy titled his head, still obviously shaken.

"Just do it… we don't have time for this. And tell her we didn't find any woman here. Go, I'm right behind you."

Officer Cooper slowly nodded, the gravity of the situation settling heavily on his shoulders. He shot a quick glance at Liam. "The girl's looking for her pack, you have it by chance?" Liam didn't look up but merely gave a small nod and motioned toward outside. Officer Cooper looked out at the truck and back at Liam once more before leaving through the door, closing it behind him with a finality that echoed in the stillness.

Clark turned back to Liam and un-holstered his firearm, the metallic click slicing through the tension in the room.

"All right, get up. This way." He pointed his gun toward a small archway, the atmosphere thick with foreboding.

Liam sighed, resignation washing over him, as he allowed himself to be guided into the kitchen and down the steps, the wooden stairs creaking beneath their weight.

"I'm not going to let you get in the way any longer, Liam. We've been nice to you. We've pleaded with you. We even said we'd include you in the payout," Clark's voice was steady, but the undercurrent of menace was unmistakable. "But it's clear to me now that you've made up your mind on the matter. Well, now you're going to help me release that thing."

Liam walked down the stairs, arms raised, but didn't respond, the darkness closing in around them. Clark guided him to the edge of the well. Its large wooden cover loomed ominously, a metal bar lying across the top, secured with a padlock that seemed to glisten mockingly in the dim light.

"All right, unlock it," Clark commanded, gun pointed at Liam's head. "Right now, Liam."

"No, lad. You don't want me to do that."

"Right now! I am not messing around here!"

"Lad, you don't want that lid open right now. You're going to have to do it yourself." Liam looked down, backing into the room. Clark kept the gun trained on him and reached over to the padlock, yanking on it.

"Stop playing with me, old man!"

Liam shook his head, backing up another foot. Satisfied with the distance, Clark brought his firearm around and pointed it at the lock. He closed his eyes and pulled the trigger. A loud bang echoed through the room, reverberating off the walls, followed by the clank of the destroyed lock hitting the ground. Clark grinned triumphantly at Liam, who began to move to the side.

"Not another inch, Liam."

Clark reached down and tried to heft the iron bar off the lid, but it didn't budge. He eyed Liam warily. He then placed the gun on the wooden lid. With both hands, he lifted the bar and pushed it aside, where it fell to the floor with a loud thud, the sound hanging in the air like a warning.

A woman's voice echoed from deep within the well, her muffled cries piercing the silence. The sudden sound startled Clark, causing him to stagger backward in disbelief. Instinctively, he shook off the shock and forced himself to step forward, his heart racing as he grabbed his gun, but it was too late. A sudden flash of pain exploded in his skull as something struck the back of his head, making his legs nearly buckle beneath him.

Liam swung the long coat rack rod again, a look of wild determination in his eyes. Clark raised one arm in a feeble attempt to shield himself, but a second blow landed with a sickening thud, sending him sprawling over the small bed. He felt warm blood trickle down his face, the metallic taste mingling with shock. Liam advanced toward him, his expression a mixture of fury and desperation, but Clark managed to raise his gun awkwardly, his vision blurred. Liam's blurry figure could be seen reaching for the gun, causing Clark to fire a round wildly in the air. Over the ringing in his ears, he heard footsteps quickly retreating up the stairs. The room around Clark began to darken, the edges of his vision fading as dizziness overcame him.

Minutes later, he came back to consciousness, vertigo slowly subsiding, but his head throbbed, the pain radiating. A low curse escaped his lips as the thought of Liam flickered through his mind. *The next time I see that man...*

He pushed himself up, only to fall back onto the bed, his body still sluggish and uncooperative. The incident replayed in his mind, each detail sharp and haunting. He closed his eyes, trying to regain his strength, when he was jolted back to reality by a sound that stopped him short.

It was a slow, creaking noise – like wood straining under an unseen pressure. At once, the realization hit him. *The woman!* In the chaos, he had forgotten her. He attempted to push himself up again, but the room swayed violently, and his head slammed back to the pillow. He wouldn't be going anywhere for a while.

Lying there, he forced his gaze toward the wooden lid of the pit. For several agonizing minutes, silence enveloped him, thick and suffocating. Then, with a deliberate slowness, the lid began to shift. One side popped up, then fell back down with a dull thud. Clark held his breath, watching in dread. It popped up again, this time remaining aloft a few inches from the well's surface. A fragile-looking arm emerged, holding the lid open, trembling as if it had a mind of its own.

He stared, transfixed, as the scene unfolded like a macabre tableau from one of those horror movies his wife had insisted they watch. The ones where the victim, paralyzed by fear, could do nothing but await their impending doom.

The arm slipped over the well's edge, followed by the woman's head, which pushed the lid upward with agonizing slowness. She maneuvered her body fully out of the well, then dropped to the floor, just beyond his line of sight. Then, she stood, unsteady at first, her movements almost inhuman.

Clark tried again to push himself up, but his body had not yet caught up with his mind. He collapsed back onto the bed, heart pounding loudly in his ears. The woman's face, illuminated by the dim light of the room, looked just as he remembered it from the well when he'd let her out, but now it was different. In the light, she seemed almost ordinary – beautiful red hair cascading down her shoulders, deep, piercing green eyes that locked onto his, wide and unblinking.

As he watched, a chill swept through the room, causing his breath to mist. The temperature plummeted, and he felt a numbing sensation creeping into his bones. The woman began to walk toward him, her steps slow and mechanical, like a marionette pulled by invisible strings. As she approached, her eyes shifted, and Clark swore he saw pain reflected in their depths, a single tear streaming down her cheek.

In a panic, he wriggled, forcing himself to fall onto the floor farthest from her, escaping the impending confrontation. The mattress creaked ominously as the woman crawled over it in a slow by stead pace. He stared petrified as the mattress ebbed and flowed under her wriggling movements. Slowly, her head appeared and then her eyes, her gaze unyielding, staring down at him like a predator eyeing its prey.

"Please..." he managed to choke out, the word barely escaping his lips as her cold, unblinking eyes bore into him. Her face contorted as if caught in a silent scream, teeth clinched and tears dripping from her eyes, leaving a glistening trail of despair.

The room had turned into a freezer, and he shivered violently as frost crept along the walls and the edges of the mattress.

Then her mouth dropped open. A gurgling noise escaped. It sounded like she was trying to say something, but the words were unintelligible. Fingers grabbed at the mattress on either side of her face. She drew in a raspy breath and then shrieked "Run!" There was anguish in her voice. He shook his head in disbelief, his eyes wide, glued open in horror.

Then in a single moment, it happened. Her body began to change, the shadows swirling around her like smoke rising from a dying fire. Her skin shifted, mottling with black and purple veins that pulsed beneath the surface. The fingernails transformed into long claws, tearing the bedding as they trembled violently. She began to speak again, but her words faltered, swallowed by the dark transformation.

Clark squeezed his eyes shut, the icy grip of fear tightening around his chest. The inevitability of the situation sunk in as he began to accept his fate.

In an instant, there was a piercing noise from above him and the mattress flew up as if exploding. It pinned him against the wall before it crashed back down onto the frame with a loud thud. The loud noise turned into a bitter scream that filled the room. Items could be heard clattering off the walls, and then the rapid, frantic footsteps echoed through the room, rushing up the stairs. There was a sound of someone racing across the upstairs floor, then then out the front door, leaving an ominous silence in its wake.

Clark lay on the floor, his chest still heaving as the room's temperature slowly returned to normal. Lights danced across his face as a light bulb overhead swung back and forth, the only reminder of the chaos that had just ensued.

28

The Reunion

Sarah brought the white coupe to a stop in front of the large, familiar cabin. She stared up at the darkened windows, one by one, dread tightening her chest. Her eyes never left the front door as she stepped out of the car. *Is the creature inside?* She half expected it to leap from the house at any moment. The fear gnawed at her, but another, more pressing need won out. She had to pee badly. *Perfect timing.*

Sarah knelt by the loose stone near the door, reaching for the hidden key – *but it was gone.* She took a quick breath. *Gwen?*

For a moment, hope stirred. Maybe Gwen was still here. Maybe she was safe. Her trembling hand found the doorknob, and, to her surprise, it turned easily and creaked open.

"Gwen?" she whispered, barely audible, not wanting to alert unwanted visitors in the silence. Her breath hitched as she stepped inside. Each shadow seemed to hold a threat, every corner hiding something sinister.

Her pulse quickened when she noticed the letter she'd left was gone.

That sliver of hope pushed her forward, her steps slow but determined. She moved cautiously, scanning each room for any sign of her friend. Rounding the corner into the kitchen, Sarah froze. The back door's window that had been broken was now hastily patched with plastic and tape.

Before she could process what it meant, a voice rang out. "Monkey?"

Her heart leaped at the sound of Gwen's voice. She barely had time to react before she felt the familiar embrace – Gwen was here, alive, holding her tight, her sobs filling the room. Sarah hugged her back, relief flooding her system, her arms tightening around Gwen as if she might disappear again.

They held each other for what felt like forever, neither speaking, just soaking in the moment. When they finally pulled away, both were smiling through tears, disbelief etched on their faces.

Sarah broke the silence first, her expression turning serious. "Gwen… I need to use the bathroom and then we need to get out of here. Now."

"No, it's okay. I – I have so much to tell you, but… it's over. He's gone."

"Gwen, we don't have time," she said, heading into the bathroom at the end of the hall. "Pack your stuff, we're leaving before dark," she said, through the door.

"Okay, fine, yes, we should leave. But seriously, Sarah, he's gone. Liam is gone. I need to tell you everything."

Sarah finished up and then hastily yanked the bathroom door open. Anxiety was already beginning to build in her chest and her mind was still screaming for them to flee. Gwen's face was a canvas of confusion and hurt all mixed in one portrait. "You aren't going to move until you tell me your story are you? Very well Gwen, make it quick." she said as she walked past Gwen who followed her into the family room. With loud sigh, Sarah flopped down onto the sofa with a loud sigh. "Tell me everything." Despite her anxiety, her body really did need a rest.

Without a pause, Gwen launched into her story, starting from the moment she'd left Clark's cruiser. Her voice was still breathless with disbelief as she recounted how she'd accidentally stumbled upon Liam's cabin in the course of searching for her lost belongings.

"Why on earth would you go near that place?" Sarah asked from under her partially closed eyelids. The comfort of the soft couch had easily lulled her into a relaxed state.

Gwen held up a finger, grinning sheepishly. "I got lost and... I don't know, I thought maybe I could find a phone or get directions. Big mistake. Anyway..."

Sarah listened as Gwen described her ordeal – how Liam had overpowered her, held her captive, and the terrible things she'd uncovered. Each detail made Sarah's skin crawl, her mind racing to fill in the blanks. The things Sarah had gone through over the last twenty-four hours were horrendous and she struggled to find a place for these in her mind. Then something Gwen said piqued her interest, catching her off guard. She stiffened and sat upright.

"Wait. There was a woman?"

Gwen nodded quickly, signaling that she wasn't done yet. "Yeah, a woman. It was... strange, she actually sort of looked like you or like one of your relatives... I'll show you in a minute... but let me finish."

As Gwen went on, explaining how she'd managed to trap Liam using his own locks before fleeing, Sarah felt some of her anxiety slowly subside – if only a little. The way Gwen smiled, triumphant and proud, gave her a sense of relief she hadn't felt since this nightmare had begun.

Gwen giggled softly. "What's good for the goose, right? I locked him in and got the heck out."

"And then what happened?"

"Well, then I found Officer Cooper on the road, patrolling. I flagged him down and here is where it gets good."

Gwen leaned back slightly, still beaming from her recount. "At first, he didn't believe me. He said Liam didn't seem the type. But I insisted, and eventually, he called Officer Lambert, and he met up with us and followed us back to Liam's place."

"Wait, you saw Officer Lambert? The same officer we met the other morning?"

"Yes, the same cute guy you were drooling over. Now don't change the subject."

"Gwen, are you sure?"

"Yes, why?" Gwen responded, she was getting frustrated at the interruptions.

Sarah considered her response for a moment. *Did I get the name wrong? Didn't that woman officer tell me he had gone missing and that his family was looking for him?* Her thought was interrupted by Gwen who was snapping her fingers. "Earth to Sarah... you there?"

"Sorry, I was just thinking about that officer... I think his family is looking for him. I wonder if it's a different person."

"It's got to be. He didn't let on that he was missing... just seemed to be on duty."

Confusion flooded her mind. *The missing officer... and why would they take Gwen back to a crime scene? This story makes no sense.* "You went back there? Back to where you were being held?"

"Right? Crazy! Now listen, the officers used a crowbar to break in. Liam was shouting through the door about being trapped or something. I could hear him from inside the cruiser. He was livid." Gwen let out another small chuckle, clearly still relishing the moment.

"What did they find?"

Gwen held up a finger for Sarah to hold questions. "They searched the house, his truck too. They found my pack in the cab and inside the house, the ropes tied to the chair; enough proof to at least give them – what did he tell me, *probable cause*? – that he'd kept me there. And then, under his bed…" Gwen's eyes gleamed, her voice dropping to a near whisper. "Officer Cooper said they found the papers. All those incriminating lists I told you and them about. Cooper then brought me back here. Said they were taking Liam into custody."

"So, they've got him. That's good news… but, what about the woman? Is she okay?"

"That's the strangest part. He told me there was no sign of the woman, but they were still looking."

"What? But you said you saw her. You said she was there, with him."

"I know right? I know I saw her, Sarah. That red hair, those green eyes. Anyway, I told him about the well, and I bet they've found her by now. Clark actually stayed behind, I bet to keep searching."

Gwen bit her lip and paused for a moment. "I can't stop thinking about her though, Sarah. Something's a bit off about her. That woman looked exactly like the picture on the wall by the stairs over there." Gwen pointed over her shoulder.

"But it couldn't be her, that picture is at least thirty years old. The woman I saw, at least as much as I could see, looked nearly the same age. So, it must have been a coincidence."

Sarah nodded, passively. Her mind was still hung up on several details in Gwen's story and then among her swirling thoughts, it surfaced again, *the creature.* Everything else seemed to disappear from her mind as she remembered her experience from the previous night. This despite a very strong urge to share what she had witnessed. They simply didn't have the time. "Gwen, I really appreciate what you're telling me and I'm glad you're okay, but we really do need to leave right now. Liam isn't the only threat up here."

Gwen's eyes narrowed in confusion and then darted to the broken door as if she'd forgotten something. "Oh yeah, tell me what happened here? Took me a good thirty minutes to cover that door and clean up the place. Looks like a bear came through it and ran through the house."

Sarah wavered for a split second. She needed to tell her about the creature and all that had happened, but her anxiety finally got the better of her. She stood and was already headed up the stairs. She felt her body seeming to move on its own; it had a sense of purpose that drove her to hurry.

"Are you listening?" Gwen called from behind.

"It wasn't a bear, Gwen. We're out of here. I'll tell you everything… but on the road. We need to be gone in twenty minutes." She made a motion to look at her phone and then remembered its damaged state.

"Why? Liam isn't a threat anymore, right?" Her words echoed from the bottom of the stairs. There were other things she said but they were now muffled. Gwen's footsteps could be heard running up the stairs. "Sarah! What's going on? Will you at least tell me what you're talking about?"

Sarah stopped tossing items in her bag and looked out the door. "Gwen... I saw it. It was here. And it tried to kill me. Right where you are standing as a matter of fact. And Gwen, it's strong. Strong enough to throw me down the stairs like I was nothing. It's what caused all the damage downstairs. Luckily for me, someone saved me."

Gwen's breath hitched. "The books and other items on the floor of the library..."

"Exactly, it's not safe here." Sarah turned back to packing, her hands working frantically. *We're out of here and she's coming with me. That thing isn't getting another chance at us.* She finished the thought with a hard zip of her suitcase. "We need to go, now! Hurry!"

Gwen hesitated, then backed slowly to her room. "Okay... I'll pack. But are you sure it wasn't Liam? He'd been gone for a while. Maybe he—"

Sarah froze mid-motion and stared down the hallway at her. "This wasn't Liam," she said, her voice low and certain. "And it wasn't a figment of my imagination. Whatever it was... it's not going to give up... and I'm not going to give it or anyone else another chance at us."

Gwen nodded slowly and quickly got to work.

29

Warning

05 January 1711

Alexander felt the sun warm his body as he sat by the lake's edge, fishing rod in hand, its string sagging lazily in the water. The scene was immediately familiar – it was his and Margaret's favorite fishing spot, the place where they had spent both their first and last day together. Leaning back against the old fallen log, he felt an overwhelming sense of comfort, as though the weight of months of heartache had lifted from him.

This must be a dream, he thought to himself, though he relished the moment. It had been so long since he had known such peace. He had made the conscious decision to break things off with the love of his life and the choice had brought serious consequences. He drew in a long breath and continued to enjoy the quiet.

The wind blew softly, carrying the scent of wildflowers, and he sighed contentedly, watching the water ripple beneath the gentle breeze.

A dull thud sounded behind him, followed by the light tread of footsteps. The sound didn't alarm him, but he tipped his head back curiously. Instead of the grassy field that should have been there, a small white cottage stood in its place, surrounded by a neat picket fence. A slim figure approached him along a stone path, her hair as black as a raven's wing.

"What brings you here?" he asked, his voice touched with mild alarm.

The woman continued toward him, her steps slow, deliberate. Her face was even more beautiful than he recalled, though paler, almost porcelain-like. Her lips were red as apples, and when she smiled, her white teeth gleamed in the sunlight. His heart quickened at her presence. *You always were lovely to look at*, he thought.

"Well, I thank you. And you always were a flatterer."

He blinked, startled that she had responded to his unspoken thoughts, then remembered – this was, after all, a dream. "This is but a dream, Margaret. How can you be here?"

"That is a question for you to answer. If I am not truly here, why then do you dream of me?" She knelt and then lay down next to him, resting her head upon his chest.

The familiar scent of her hair flooded his senses, and the comfort of her nearness washed over him like a wave. This was a dream, but he felt her by him – the warmth, her weight, it was so real. A sting of pain filled his chest at the memory of the last day with her. "I cannot remain here with you. I must wake up."

"And who, pray, says you cannot?" She leaned in and kissed him softly on the lips.

"Margaret, I… I should not be here. This is not right."

She paid no heed to his words, settling her head once more

201

on his chest. "Alexander, why did you forsake me? Why did you forsake us?"

"You know well why, my Raven… Margaret. I cannot be with one who is… a witch."

"But can you not see we are meant for one another? Can you not?"

"I had long hoped so… but it is not to be."

She brought her head up again, her eyes touched by a desperate yearning. "You wounded me. Come back to me. I beg of you."

"Margaret, please…" His voice cracked beneath the weight of his emotion. "I'm with another now. I'm with Elizabeth. Please release me."

"With another…" She rasped, a harsh whisper that sounded like broken glass. The wind, once warm and gentle, turned cold, whipping across his skin. The sun dimmed, clouds amassing swiftly overhead. Panic rose in his chest. "Margaret! What is happening?" He strained to move, but he found himself rooted in place.

He looked down at her again, and dread overcame him. Margaret's black hair had turned brittle, her face contorting into something darker. Her eyes, once familiar, now burned with an unnatural fire, and her mouth twisted into an angry snarl.

He tried to break free, to turn his head, but his body betrayed him.

"You promised me, Alexander. You said we would be together forever. Was that some sort of farce?"

In one swift movement, she swung her leg over him, straddling his body. He lay frozen in terror, utterly powerless to resist.

"You think I shall let you break your vow so easily?"

Her voice deepened, becoming a menacing growl. He shook his head vigorously as the world darkened, the air growing frigid. Margaret drew her face closer, her breath filling his nostrils. He clenched his teeth, shutting his eyes tightly, bracing for the horror to come but nothing happened.

When he dared to open his eyes, her face had returned to its normal beauty, but her eyes were now sad, full of tears.

And then, as quickly as it had begun, it was over. The sky was blue again, the warm breeze returned, and the lake shimmered beneath the sunlight. She planted a kiss on his lips. She and the dream then began to fade, her and the landscape dissolving into the air until nothing remained but the dim light of his darkened bedroom. "You said we'd be together forever. Come back to me." Her voice faded into the blackness of the room.

His heart pounded in his chest as he sat up, gasping for breath. The cold wind of January swept through the room, and he realized with a start that his window stood wide open. From outside, he heard the faint sound of footsteps fading into the distance.

He leaped to the cold floor and moved swiftly around his bed to peer out into the darkness. A thin figure was fleeing into the night, its shape barely discernible in the gloom. He quickly shut the window, engaging the latch with trembling hands. His chest heaved as he sought to regain his breath. The room still carried her faint scent, stirring a mixture of anger and sorrow within him. How had she come to him again and why?

Clenching his jaw, he bristled at the intrusion. He had been violated, haunted in his very chambers by her presence. He drew in a long breath and sighed loudly.

Settling into the chair by his bedside, he fumbled with the tinder box and lit a candle. The flickering light cast long shadows across the room as he opened the drawer of his desk. Inside, a small box lay nestled beside a black velvet pouch. He lifted both items, feeling the weight of them in his hands. After a moment's hesitation, he let the pouch fall back into the drawer and closed it with a soft thud.

He carried the candle and the box back to his bed, the flame casting a dim glow as he seated himself and pulled his blanket over his legs. Placing the candle on the nearby table, he opened the box with a soft creak. Inside lay a golden ring, delicate in its design. A single diamond sparkled in the center, flanked by smaller rubies. He took it between his fingers, holding it up to the candlelight, watching as the gem flickered in the glow.

He sighed deeply; his heart heavy. *What could have been,* he thought bitterly. The ring had once held so much promise – yet now it was little more than a reminder of all that was lost.

With a weary breath, he returned the ring to its box, snapping it shut with finality. He lay back upon the bed, pulling the covers over him once more, attempting to rid his mind of the dream and the lingering feelings for Margaret that stubbornly refused to leave him.

30

The Attempt

The tension in Sarah's shoulders continued to relax as they got farther from the cabin, but not by much. The dark woods still pressed in around them, and every bend in the road seemed to hide another threat. Gwen was going to drive her car but found that her keys had been missing from her pack. After a bit of arguing about options and an ultimatum from Sarah, Gwen had agreed to leave her car until they could arrange something.

Sarah swerved in and out of turns, the car bouncing and skidding as they hit potholes and loose gravel. They had passed several of the turn-offs from the main road and she scanned each one, peering up or down each. She was watching for something. Looking for signs of the creature, half-expecting it to show up and halt their escape.

The car's rear wheels slid as they went around a tight corner and Sarah was going much faster than normal when Gwen's voice shot up in pitch as she pointed at something ahead in the road.

"Watch out!"

The large object was now in view and Sarah slammed on the brakes. The tires screeched, gravel scattering as the car skidded out of control. For a breathless moment, they were sliding helplessly, and then the car hit something with a bone-jarring crash.

Sarah blinked, her mind reeling, as the windshield slowly came back into focus. The airbag in front of her had deployed, now hanging limp and deflating.

"You okay, Gwen?" she managed, her voice hoarse. She turned to see Gwen struggling to react, still dazed by the impact.

"Yeah, I think so… nothing feels broken." Gwen unbuckled her seatbelt and shoved the loose items from the back seat away. "Man, I thought you were going to stop in time, but we just kept sliding… that was crazy. It was like slow motion!" she added, her voice unsteady but relieved.

"How about you? Other than your poor car and the tree we hit, you okay?"

Sarah gave her a thumbs-up sign. The various scrapes and bruises all over her body screamed in pain as she said this. She'd never put her body through this much torture it was letting her know. After a long pause, Sarah sighed and let out a small giggle. "Gwen… You know what? I've had enough of this vacation."

That sent Gwen into a giggling fit, which quickly turned into a loud, breathless laugh. "Right? What's next on the agenda?!" The absurdity of the situation hit them both, and for a few minutes, they laughed until tears stung their eyes.

But the laughter faded as reality came crashing back in. Sarah tried the ignition. Nothing. "Let's see what the damage is," she muttered, pushing her door open and stepping out.

The car had slammed into a tree that lay across the road, its massive trunk creating a blockade. The sight of it made Sarah's stomach drop and she stared at the spectacle in disbelief. She ran her hand along the rough bark, noticing how it propped up slightly against the trees on the other side of the road.

Gwen joined her outside, also staring at the tree. "How do you think this happened? Wait… look at this." She pointed toward the base of the tree. "It's been cut… recently. Doesn't it look like a chainsaw, or an axe made those marks?"

"For sure, and this tree wasn't here when I drove up this road earlier today. Definitely wasn't an accident and happened not long ago."

The two stared at each other, the implication of the moment floating in the air. "Why would someone cut a tree like this? Probably Liam… think it was him?"

"I don't want to find out, Gwen. Grab what you need. We're leaving."

Gwen, shaken but compliant, started pulling her small suitcase from the back seat. "You think we can make it back to the cabin before midnight? It's gotta be at least five miles."

"No, not the cabin. We keep going down the mountain."

"Wait, what? Keep going? Seriously? We're just going to walk?"

Sarah listened but wouldn't meet her gaze as she rummaged through her own suitcase, pulling out clean clothes and tossing aside her dirty ones. "I told you, Gwen. I can't stay here. I can't go back there. Not unless it's our only choice… And even then." She said this while tossing clothing onto the road. "And you're coming with me." She started changing right there, her fingers fumbling slightly as she

207

dressed in the open air. The urgency continued to build inside her stomach, and she couldn't seem to move nearly fast enough.

Sarah saw Gwen pause as if to argue but then seemed to mirror her actions. She opened her suitcase and started pulling out her own clothes. "How far do you think the town is?"

"It's pretty far, but we've gotta be close to the main road. If we can make it there, someone's bound to see us, and we'll catch a ride."

The forest loomed silently around them as they packed their bags, the threat of whatever – or whoever – had cut the tree still in their minds.

Both girls were now dressed in fresh clothes, their packs slung over their shoulders, armed only with what they could carry. Silently, they exchanged a glance and nodded, the agreement unspoken but clear – they had to move. Together, they scrambled over the massive tree that blocked the road, clambering and helping one another.

Sarah looked back up the road, relief flooding through her momentarily. They were leaving, finally, even if only on foot. "Ready?" she asked, her voice quieter now.

Gwen nodded, offering a small but warm smile.

Sarah's heart swelled, feeding off Gwen's optimism. *How does she stay so hopeful?* she wondered. But the warmth quickly vanished.

Sarah froze mid-thought. The blood drained from her face and a familiar feeling boiled up from her stomach. Down the road, only a few hundred feet away, a dark figure stood. Motionless, foreboding, its presence unmistakable.

"No." The word escaped Sarah's lips, barely audible at first, then louder. "No!" she screamed, her voice trembling with fear. "Why?" Her cry was full of anguish, her eyes wide with terror.

"Is that who attacked you, Sarah?"

Sarah heard Gwen speak but she was unable to respond. Something inside her, something primal, drove her actions and she scrambled away.

"Stay away from us!" Gwen shouted, though her voice wavered, betraying her fear. "I'm armed, you know!"

Sarah frantically clambered back over the tree, abandoning her pack without a second thought. She fell hard on the other side, scraping her hands on the rough bark on the way down. Panic surged through her as she began to run.

"Sarah!" Gwen screamed from behind. "Help me over!" But Sarah's brain was still trapped in survival mode, every memory of the creature flooding through the fresh cracks in her mind – the terrifying whispers, the cold presence. *Sarah...* the voice echoed in her head.

A distant sound snapped her out of her trance. The rumble of a truck, loud and approaching fast. She glanced down the road, spotting the dust clouds rising around the bend.

But then Gwen's voice pierced through the air again, this time more desperate. Sarah whipped her head around and saw Gwen stuck, crawling under the tree instead of over it. Her eyes, wide with panic, locked onto Sarah's.

"Oh Gwen! Sorry! No! You gotta go over, not under!"

It was too late. From behind Gwen, Sarah saw the figure approaching – close now, only a dozen feet away – it's dark silhouette moved unnaturally, and wisps of black smoke seemed to seep from its form, coming under and over the massive log.

Demon... Sarah's mind screamed.

Sarah ran back to the log and latched onto Gwen's arms, pulling with all her strength. "Ow, ow, ow!" Gwen yelped in pain; her body pinned beneath the tree.

Sarah's heart pounded as the creature drew nearer, the horrible crackling noise she'd heard before echoing behind Gwen. The air grew cold – unnaturally cold. Frost crawled over the log, moving in every direction. Desperation fueled Sarah's next pull, and with a sudden lurch, Gwen's body came free from the tree. She scrambled forward, wriggling slowly out from the narrow space.

Just as Gwen gained some ground, a powerful force yanked her backward and she let out a guttural scream. "Sarah!"

The cold, suffocating presence surged through Sarah's arms. She could feel it – the creature's touch, its icy pull. She gritted her teeth and kept pulling, refusing to let go, but it was like pulling against a mountain.

Gwen continued screaming, her eyes locked on Sarah. "Help me! It hurts!" she yelled before going silent, her eyes rolling back into her head.

Suddenly, from behind, the sound of heavy footsteps broke through the chaos. Sarah didn't turn, but the force on Gwen's body seemed to slacken.

Then, a melody – a soft, haunting tune – floated through the air. The strange music cut through the tension like a knife, and suddenly Gwen was free. She tumbled forward, Sarah falling backward onto the gravel with a hard thud.

She didn't waste any time, dragging Gwen's slack body back several feet, her breath ragged with exhaustion. She finally fell to the ground next to Gwen, who had a dazed look on her face.

The music continued. Sarah's gaze flicked upward and saw a figure moving over the log – Liam. He navigated the barrier with ease, a small pan flute pressed to his lips. He played the strange melody, stopping only briefly to adjust his position as he climbed.

"Wha... What is it?" Gwen asked, her voice weak, shivering from both fear and the unnatural cold that lingered in her body. Sarah pulled her closer, feeling how cold Gwen's skin had become. "What is that creature?"

"I don't know, but whatever it is, it doesn't like that music."

Gwen's shivers became more violent, her body rippling with uncontrollable tremors. Her eyes kept rolling back into their sockets before refocusing as she mumbled. "I felt it... I heard it. It showed me things, Sarah. It keeps showing me things! It... she... It's a she and she wants you. She wants to kill you... No, wants to get you. To keep you." Gwen's breath was labored, her chest rising and falling as if each breath pained her. "Sarah, it's real... It's really real."

Gwen whimpered, her voice raspy from screaming. She raised a trembling hand, pointing toward Liam.

Sarah's gaze followed, and her breath caught in her throat. Liam was clambering back over the fallen tree, but he moved more slowly now, burdened. Draped over his shoulder was a woman. Bare legs dangled limply from beneath a jacket, and her long red hair spilled over his back.

Liam staggered onto their side of the tree and met Sarah's eyes briefly, his expression hard to read. Without a word, he continued toward the truck, carefully laying the woman's still body in the bed, covering her with a blanket and a tarp.

"I don't understand," Sarah muttered under her breath. *None of this makes sense. Was he the one who rescued me? And*

211

why?

But as Liam's broad figure loomed over the truck, something clicked into place for Sarah. She turned to Gwen before she could voice her panic. "I know what you're thinking, but... I don't think he's what we thought. He's been protecting us – at least, it feels like it. Whatever this is, he saved me from it."

"No, Sarah!" Gwen weakly yelled. "He's a very bad man..."

"You need to trust me, Gwen. She's the threat and I think Liam wants to help us."

Liam slammed the truck bed shut and turned; his breathing ragged. "Long fortnight," he muttered as if that explained anything. He met Sarah's eyes again, grim and resolute. "You'll want to come with me. There's more danger ahead. Bring that firecracker with ya."

He didn't wait for a response. He flung open the driver's door and climbed in. Sarah, hesitant but knowing they had little choice, reached down and pulled Gwen to her feet. "Come on, we need to go."

Gwen opened her mouth to argue but she was too exhausted to fight. She tumbled forward, falling into Sarah's open arms.

They stumbled toward the truck and awkwardly climbed into the cab beside Liam. Sarah carefully pulled Gwen's pack off and tossed it on the floor. The engine then roared to life, and gravel scattered under the tires as the truck whipped around. They weren't headed down the mountain – they were speeding back up.

Gwen rested her head against Sarah's shoulder, her body still cold and weak. Sarah glanced nervously at Liam, the tension in the air thickening as they hurtled forward.

"It's asleep... for now. But not for long."

"It?"

Liam didn't answer. His jaw tightened as he expertly maneuvered the truck through the winding mountain roads. Dust swirled in their wake, the forest closing in around them. Sarah's mind raced, trying to piece together the fractured events of the past week. None of it fit. None of it made sense. She thought about what Gwen had told her, about the missing woman. Her suspicions of Liam still haunted her but now they were clouded with doubt.

Her eyes flickered to his neck, catching sight of the instrument he'd been playing. It was the pan flute, worn on a leather cord. Next to it, a strip of red cloth, also tied to leather.

As the truck barreled down the road, the family cabin flashed by. Sarah flinched at the sight, memories of the horrors within flickering in her mind.

"We're taking the back road," Liam muttered, glancing at the cabin as it disappeared behind them.

Sarah only nodded, feeling Gwen's cold forehead as her friend's breathing began to slow, her exhaustion overtaking her fear.

The truck sped past several other cabins nestled deep in the woods, their windows dark and foreboding. Sarah felt a knot in her stomach, wondering which one was Liam's house.

She kept silent, not wanting to wake Gwen, other questions continuing to gnaw at her. She felt her eyelids flutter and then close but her drowsiness was cut short by the abrupt slowing of the truck. The engine's sudden quiet brought an uneasy calm, and Gwen woke with a jolt.

Ahead of them, a police cruiser was blocking the road, its lights off but its presence unmistakable. A black-haired

213

officer stood in front of it, legs apart in a strong stance, left arm extended while his right hand hovered dangerously near his sidearm.

Liam cursed under his breath, eyes flicking nervously to the rearview mirror, then craning his neck as if looking for another way out. But there was none. The truck came to a full stop.

The officer began approaching the driver's side, and Sarah's tension eased briefly. She recognized him – it was Officer Lambert's partner, the same man who'd helped them once before. His familiar, friendly smile disarmed her for a moment. But the tension quickly returned when she saw Liam's face. Something wasn't right.

A sharp knock on the window startled them all. The officer, brandishing a large black flashlight, motioned for Liam to roll down the window. Liam hesitated but eventually complied.

"You can be quite slippery when you need to be, Liam" the officer said with a polite nod, tipping his hat towards Sarah and Gwen. "You put my partner in quite a bit of danger earlier."

Liam grunted, eyes still fixed ahead, clearly avoiding the officer's gaze.

The officer glanced at Sarah and Gwen, moderate concern flickering across his face. "Gwen, girls, is everything okay here?" His tone was friendly, but his posture tense.

Sarah began to explain, "We're fine. Liam was just giving us a—"

The officer cut her off, his tone sharper than before. "I thought you and Liam weren't on good terms. Change your mind?" His eyes flicked between Sarah and Liam. His question was obviously rhetorical and he left little time for any explanation. "Liam, mind if I take a look around?"

Before anyone could protest, the officer switched on his flashlight and moved toward the truck bed, inspecting it. Liam shot Sarah a long, meaningful look, his face a mix of frustration and warning. Slowly he shook his head. Sarah heard the tarp being moved around in the bed and then the sound of footsteps on gravel as the officer came back to the window.

"Okay, Liam, let's have you step out of the vehicle."

"Officer Cooper... you don't need to do this, lad. You've got a wife, a child... You don't want to be part of this."

"Liam, I said step out of the vehicle."

Liam shot Sarah another brief glance. She thought she noted a small tinge of concern in his eyes. With a sudden jerk, the officer pulled the driver's door open, raising his voice. "Liam—"

Liam raised his hands for a moment but the compliance was short-lived. "Have it your way, lad." Suddenly, his hand darted toward the gear shift, and, with a roar, the truck shot forward, its tires screeching as the truck slammed directly into the front side of the police cruiser. The officer's face was a mask of shock and he didn't have time to react before Liam threw the truck into reverse, backing up at full speed.

Gwen screamed, clutching Sarah as the truck jolted violently. Sarah tried to stay upright, but both girls swung to the side with Gwen hitting her head against the side window.

"Freeze!" The officer's voice stopped abruptly, his gun raised just as the open driver's door swung back, slamming into him and knocking him to the ground. Liam didn't pause. He floored the gas pedal, sending the truck spinning as he reversed at breakneck speed down the narrow road.

Liam turned the wheel hard to the right, causing the truck to spin sideways. For a second, it stopped but the moment he got the truck in drive, it violently shuddered and started moving forward, slowly picking up speed.

Gunshots rang out. Loud pops echoed in the cab, and the back window exploded, shards of glass raining down around Sarah. One of the bullets had come terrifyingly close, making a pinging noise nearby. She hunched down instinctively, her pulse hammering in her ears. More shots followed as they sped away, but the distance between them and the officer grew, leaving the young policeman far behind.

31

Pretense

28 January 1711

The small carriage rolled steadily along the narrow road. Alexander cast a glance toward Elizabeth, giving her a quick wink. She nestled closer to him, her cheeks flushed by the biting cold.

"Rather cold for a carriage ride, Alex," she said, shuddering mildly.

He chuckled, drawing the thick woolen blanket further over her shoulders. "Nonsense, my dear, 'tis quite warm for January," he replied, his breath forming visible wisps in the crisp air. He smiled at her again, pulling her more tightly against him. "Though I confess, it may be a trifle chilly for a ride, I could scarce endure another day without the sight of you."

"You saw me but yesterday."

"Aye, and therein lies the very heart of the matter, my Dove. Yesterday was too long ago."

Elizabeth returned his warm gaze, her cheeks reddening

slightly at the comment. She leaned in to kiss him, but her attention soon wavered as something ahead caught her eye. "What do you suppose that is?" she asked, pointing toward a dark object near the side of the road.

Alexander followed her gesture and saw the form of a small, dark figure crouching by the roadside. Just as his eyes settled upon it, the figure rose and began to run slowly along the road. "It appears to be a young girl."

She was slight, and her dark hair trailed behind her as she ran. His recognition was immediate. It was the youngest Vikar girl. "Alice! Alice, it's me, Alexander."

The young girl turned to look but began running quickly as if to escape. He unwrapped his scarf from around his neck and let it fall to his chest to better reveal his face. "Alice, it's me, Alexander McGregor! Do not be afraid."

Alice turned, her face red and tear streaked. "Alexander! Oh Alexander, I… I was—" She faltered, her breath too short to continue.

He halted the carriage and swiftly descended, placing a steady arm around her shoulders. "No need to rush, child. Take a moment and breathe."

"I was coming to find you just now. I… I didn't know where else to go."

"Alice, what has happened?" He guided her toward the carriage and then lifted her into the seat beside Elizabeth, who immediately wrapped the blankets around the trembling girl.

Alice continued to sob and had a difficult time talking. After a few minutes she had regained her breath and wiped some of her tears away. "They came… They took her! The constables came and took her away."

"The constables? Took who, Alice?"

She began to cry again making her words wet and difficult to understand. "Agatha… They took her to a witch's trial."

"And where might your father and mother? Your sisters?"

"Father is away and Mother and Claire are in bed, ill. You need to help her… They are sure to burn her Alexander… please!"

"And Margaret, where is she?"

Alice continued to sob, her small frame shaking as she pressed her tear-streaked face into Elizabeth's shoulder. Her voice was muffled but she responded. "She's with Agatha, they took her as well… I believe as a witness or something. They took them both."

Alexander and Elizabeth shared a long look before she finally nodded.

"Do not fret, Alice," he said. He climbed swiftly into the carriage, and with a snap of the reins, they were off, speeding in the direction of his home. "I shall see that you are placed in Elizabeth's care, and then I will do all that can be done."

"No, Alex, I wish to come with you." Elizabeth said, a small note of fear tugging at her eyes.

"Elizabeth, I would rather you not be there. It's not likely to be safe for you." He shot her a glance and after a moment she merely nodded.

The carriage soon reached his home, and Elizabeth helped Alice down. "Be careful, Alex," she whispered. There was concern in her voice and she looked as though she was going to say more.

Alexander nodded curtly. "I love you, Dove. I'll return as soon as is possible." He flicked the reins, and the horse galloped forward, leaving the cottage far behind. As he raced along the country road, his thoughts turned to the Vikar family and their strange practices. He had never seen them cause direct harm to anyone, yet he had felt the power they wielded – unmistakable, potent, and dangerous.

If not for Margaret, would I care so deeply about aiding them? Their arts and dealings were an affront to all he believed, a shadow that threatened the core of his principles, his values. He had bent the truth on their behalf more than once already – could he do so again? And, if he did, how long before his own family would find themselves imperiled by the mob mentality that so often accompanied witchcraft? He shoved the thoughts aside and raced on. He then thought about Margaret and pictured her sitting with her sister in some prison cell, afraid. He decided there, he'd do anything in his power to help her and the Vikars. Even now, he still felt a great deal of love for her and would do what he must.

He pulled the reins, slowing the horse as the town came into view. The hall, where the prisoner would surely be held, was already surrounded by a throng of people, their faces grim, their voices murmuring with tension. There was no space to stop the carriage closer, so he dismounted and made his way on foot, drawn to the noise and torch lights.

As he pushed through the crowd, the jeers and questions grew louder, the mob restless. He shouldered his way through the throng, all the while hearing snippets of fear and suspicion woven into the murmurs. The words 'witch' and 'evil' rose above all other noise.

Near the entrance, he found his path blocked by a constable, the man standing firm. "Hold back!" the officer barked, pressing his hands against Alexander's chest to halt his advance. "No one's to see the prisoner!"

Alexander straightened his coat and tie, and adopted a composed demeanor, determined to present himself as every inch the gentleman. "You have me wrong, I'm familiar with the one you've captured."

"What of it? None are to be let near the prisoner. Now, back away!"

"My good man. I have matters to attend to here. Please allow me a moment with your captain." Alexander reapplied the best of his charm, but the man was ready to yell again before he was interrupted.

"Who is that?" came a voice from nearer the door. Alexander turned to see another constable, taller, one whose face he recognized from a recent visit to his home.

"It is I. Alexander McGregor," he said, tilting his head to ensure the officer had a clear view of him. "We met not long ago at my home."

"Aye, Alexander." There was a trace of regret in the man's posture. "Apologies master, you've come all this way for naught. Many have clamored to see the prisoner, we are permitting none inside."

The officer's words began to drown in the growing clamor of the crowd, and Alexander found himself being jostled backward. Desperation flared within him. "Officer, I come to provide witness to guilt!" he declared, the lie heavy on his tongue but necessary. His chest stung at the fallacy. He'd already lied several times for Margaret, but the guilt never seemed to soften.

The taller officer paused, his eyes narrowing in scrutiny. Then, with a swift motion, he called out, "Let him through!"

With a push from the crowd and a pull from the guards, Alexander found himself whisked through the doors and into the building's darkened hall. *Now what have you gotten yourself into, Alexander?* He thought as the last light of the day disappeared behind him.

The offensive odor hit his nostrils like a stone, a thick stench that clung to the damp, oppressive air of the prison. He brought his hand to his nose, but it was of little use. The dampness seemed to choke his senses as he followed a younger guard down a narrow, fire-lit hallway. His boots echoed off the stone floor, and from the cells lining the hall, prisoners' eyes followed him, cold and accusing from behind the iron bars.

"This way," the young guard called, motioning to a large metal door at the end of the corridor. With a creak, the door swung open to reveal a wider room, where several armed guards were stationed, pacing restlessly. The oppressive air of judgment and despair seemed to grow thicker here.

Alexander's eyes scanned each person until his heart leaped as he spotted Margaret sitting on a bench in the far corner, her head bowed, her eyes swollen from what must have been hours of weeping. She looked as if she hadn't slept in days, and she had irons clapped on each of her delicate wrists. Alexander winced at the sight. As though sensing his presence, her gaze lifted, and their eyes locked. The look of anguish and hopelessness she gave him sent a sharp pain through his chest.

"Margaret." His mouth whispered the word without permission. Seeing her like this, broken and forlorn, was nearly unbearable. His chest seemed to seize momentarily.

Their silent connection lasted only a moment before Alexander forced himself to look away.

"Are you here to bear witness?" a man sitting at a small

desk asked, breaking the painful silence.

He felt Margaret's eyes boring into him, but Alexander kept his composure as he answered.

"Yes, officer. I have come to do just that."

The man nodded, pointing toward a small group of people gathered by the side. Alexander recognized one of them – Mr. Arnall, his face drawn and tired, his disheveled appearance mirroring his frayed nerves. Begrudgingly, Alexander moved to stand beside him.

"Young McGregor," Mr. Arnall said, surprise evident in his voice. "You have had a change of heart?"

Alexander said nothing, his expression hard and unyielding, his eyes cold with disdain. Mr. Arnall faltered under the icy gaze, shrinking back slightly.

Another guard approached, sensing the tension. "Alexander," he said, a note of familiarity in his voice, "what has brought you here to this damp and terrible business?"

For the first time since he'd entered the prison, Alexander forced a smile. "Oliver! I did not think I would see a familiar face here."

Oliver, the guard, grinned wearily and gestured to the captain's badge on his overcoat. "Not a good day to be in charge, I am afraid. What brings you here tonight?"

"I came to see what I could do to help in this matter." He kept his tone light. "I am under the impression that you are holding a member of the Vikar family? On suspicion of what is it... witchcraft?"

"'Tis so. A nasty business, but the law is the law unfortunately. I would be grateful for any help you might bring, though I do not comprehend how you may," Oliver said with a weary frown.

"You came to witness her guilt, did you not?" Mr. Arnall interrupted from behind.

Alexander shot him a sharp glance and pictured himself strangling the little man. "I've had more than enough from you, Mr. Arnall," he said, through gritted teeth. He then relaxed his expression and returned his attention to Oliver. "Apologies, Oliver. Yes, if there is guilt to witness, I will gladly testify. But first, I need more information on the matter."

"What more do you need? She's a witch plain as day!" murmured Mr. Arnall.

Oliver waved Mr. Arnall away, his patience fading. "I have also had enough from you, Robert! Pipe down, you've had your say. One more word and I'll put you in there with her!" He then turned back to Alexander with a sigh. "Anything you can add to help us determine guilt?"

"What can you tell me about the charge?" Alexander asked, struggling to keep his voice calm. His heart raced, knowing any false move could ruin his credibility – and risk his and Margaret's family's safety.

"Yes, well, we are holding Agatha Vikar, charged with practicing witchcraft. We plan to transport her to Lancashire for a formal trial tomorrow. Robert Arnall's testimony was the strongest against her, though honestly, I believe it to be mostly hearsay. I could use your help on this. Do you have anything to say on the matter?"

"Witnesses… have any of them provided evidence to support the claim?" Alexander pressed, keeping his tone neutral.

"No, not necessarily. Just Arnall's word and support from a few others. I don't like it, but as you saw outside, the town's been whipped into a frenzy, small thanks to Robert's abnormally large mouth. Messy business, like I said."

"I understand. And I believe I can be of some assistance to you in your quest for truth."

He stole a glance at Margaret, her face frozen, her eyes pleading. His resolve wavered, but he forced himself to continue, clearing his throat.

"Oliver, I have spent a great deal of time with the Vikar family. As you likely know, I had a close understanding with one of the Vikar women."

Oliver's eyes flickered to Margaret as he said this.

"In all my visits, I have never witnessed anything resembling witchcraft, with the exception of peculiar eccentricities."

"Peculiar eccentricities! Pssh!" Robert spat from behind him.

"Robert, shut that mouth!" Oliver yelled, his gloved finger pointing at the little man.

Alexander ignored the interruption. "As for Agatha Vikar... while I haven't seen her practicing witchcraft, I do believe she's capable of it. She has implied as much to me on more than one occasion. I've always cast it off as whimsical but under these circumstances, I believe it's damning evidence."

He heard Margaret's breath hitch from behind him, but Alexander pressed on, ignoring her quiet sobbing. He took a deep breath before proceeding.

Oliver nodded gravely, taking Alexander's words seriously. "Your word carries weight, Alexander. What do you propose?"

"Thank you Oliver. Before I provide you an answer, could you humor me? I would like to see the prisoner and confirm her identity," he said, his voice calm despite the chaos in his mind.

Oliver gave him a curious glance but nodded. "She hasn't denied her name, but you may do as you wish."

"Thank you again, Oliver." Alexander slowly walked the long stone path to the barred cell door. Inside, kneeling on the cold stone floor, was a woman, her black hair greasy, and her clothes soiled. Her hands were bound in heavy chains. She lifted her head slowly, revealing a mischievous smile beneath her tangled hair. Her eyes, wild. It was Agatha – no doubt about it.

She bore her teeth at him, staring him down. The hate in her dark eyes was evident as she stared into his. "You will pay for this…" she said in a low whisper that only he could hear. She glared at him, seeming to expect a certain response but to her surprise, he shot her a quick wink. Her head cocked back. He stifled the snicker in his throat as he reflected upon the one and only time he'd managed to confuse the devious woman. He steadied himself and then drew in a deep breath before letting out a loud laugh that seemed to fill the cavernous room.

He shot Agatha another wink and then turned to look upon the dozen confused individuals before turning to Oliver. "I hate to be the bearer of poor news, Oliver."

"Poor news?"

"Aye. I'm sorry but it could be good news depending on how you look at it. I may have saved you a trip to Lancashire after all."

Oliver's eyes widened at the prospect but then narrowed again. "And pray tell me how you've achieved such a feat?"

"Well, I'm afraid you have the wrong Vikar in your cell. It is as plain as that."

Oliver's expression shifted to confusion and then immediately to shock. "Pardon? That's Agatha Vikar. I'm absolutely certain of it."

"Certain? I say nay, Oliver. That is her twin sister, Claire Vikar. I'd wager my favorite horse on it."

Oliver stared at him, dumbfounded. "How is it, you can be certain?"

"Well, as I and others have observed, I have come to know the Vikars for quite some time. I am acquainted with each and every one of them. However, you may ask Margaret – she is their closest sister, after all. Simply inquire of her if you or others doubt the truth of my account." He spoke with feigned confidence. He felt the heavy anxiety of the lie pushing his limits and looked away and held his breath, trying to maintain his smile.

Oliver turned to Margaret, whose tear-filled eyes were cast downward. "Margaret, is this true? Do we have Claire Vikar, your sister, in custody?"

Margaret hesitated, her whole body trembling. Slowly, she nodded.

Oliver's face fell. "You should've told us sooner, ma'am," he muttered, shaking his head. "We could have avoided all this. Instead this honest man had to come down here and provide clarity on this matter. I swear some of you are thick as thieves, letting your sister carry a punishment that wasn't hers to carry."

Oliver turned to Alexander and shook his hand. "Thank you, Alexander. I thank you for your character." He paused for a moment, remembering something. "I also hear congratulations are in order on your recent engagement. Well done. You and Elizabeth make a fine match. Very well done."

Alexander smiled but his eyes flickered to the dark silhouette sitting in the corner. He then shot Robert Arnall a stern look. The small man's mouth sagged open as the men around the captain stood ready to review orders. His mouth then snapped shut and he backed up, his eyes downcast in resignation.

Oliver then signaled the guards. "Unchain the prisoner and take her and her sister out the backdoor. Give them rides home. Also have the guards out front dismiss the crowd, we don't have a witch in our midst, at least not today."

"And the witch Agatha? Should we retrieve her?" One of the guards asked.

Oliver paused for a moment before answering. It was clear that he was relieved that all of this was over. "Not tonight. We'll retrieve her when there is much less activity in the town."

The man nodded and pulled a set of keys from his belt. As the guards moved to release Agatha, Alexander and Margaret exchanged one final look – hers now filled with a mixture of relief and sorrow.

The choice to sacrifice Claire's character to save Agatha today would surely be an unwelcome if not unforgivable action but he had found no other way to protect the Vikars as well as his own family. Had he plead directly for her innocence, there would have been a deeper inquiry into the McGregor family as well as others in the area. *No, this was the only way. The Vikars will very likely never forgive me. Margaret most of all. She now knows the truth about Elizabeth. It's better this way.* He would now be able to close this chapter of his life. He hoped Margaret would be able to as well. He turned away, led from the room, leaving Margaret behind forever.

32

The Anxious

Officer Bradford sat at her cluttered desk, peering through a pair of oversize reading glasses. The sound of the soft clacking of her fingers on the keyboard filled the quiet room, punctuated by occasional murmurs from the other officers around her. Some were on the phone, while others rifled through papers or leaned back in their chairs, lost in thought. It was a rare calm night at the station.

The front door chimed, its familiar ring slicing through the stillness. Bradford sighed, pushing her glasses up to the top of her head. She stood, her chair creaking as she moved to the front desk.

"Mel! What are you doing all the way down here?" she asked, spotting Melanie Lambert in the doorway. Melanie's eyes were tired, and her expression gave Bradford pause. Beside her stood a shorter woman, cradling a baby in her arms, her face equally weary.

"Hey, Sandy, have you by chance heard from Clark? He still hasn't come home, and I haven't heard anything. Has he called in?"

"Umm... No, Mel. He hasn't called in following the voicemail I left him. I was actually going to call you tonight. I hadn't heard from you, so I thought you had already heard from him." There was obvious concern written across both of the women's faces and Sandy, while feeling her own worry, decided she needed to give them confidence rather than add to their anxiety. "I'm sure he and Coop are probably out fishing. You know how they are – no cell service in half the spots they go. Typical men. I don't think you need to worry."

Melanie shifted uncomfortably, clearly unconvinced. Anne began to rock her baby and then spoke up. "We don't think they went fishing."

"I'm sorry, I've seen you around before, but I don't think we've officially met. I'm Sandy Bradford." She offered her best smile, though her concern deepened as she took in Anne's worried expression. "Let's head to an office for some privacy, and we can talk this through. Don't worry, we'll get this sorted out."

Sandy led them to a small room in the back of the station and closed the door behind them. She sat at the desk, gesturing for Melanie and Anne to sit across from her. The tension from the two seemed to follow them and it filled the small space quickly.

"So, you don't think they're fishing? Let's start there. What makes you believe that?"

Anne hesitated, glancing at Melanie before speaking. "Well... for one, neither of them took their rods. Or any of their usual gear. I mean, we just bought Clark a new, very expensive rod because his old one broke on the last trip. He's been bursting at the seams, wanting to try it out."

"Okay, that's unusual... but maybe they've got some equipment you don't know about?"

"No, Sandy, honestly, they've both been acting strange. Every year, without fail, those two spend weeks planning that fishing trip. Not only that, but they also usually include their pal Rusty. This year? Nothing. No talk, no prep, and Rusty told me they didn't include him. They took their leave; told us they were going fishing and are just... gone."

Tears welled in her eyes, and she wiped at her cheek. Sandy reached across the desk, squeezing her friend's hand. "Mel... Anne, I know you're worried. What you've told me is odd, but do you really think something's wrong? Is it at all possible that they're taking a break, blowing off steam, down at the casinos? Maybe they didn't want to tell you?"

Melanie raised her eyebrow considering the possibility, but Anne shook her head, her voice trembling. "Andy never goes a day without calling me. And ever since this little guy came along, he calls twice a day." As if on cue, the baby boy let out a little whimper. Anne looked at Melanie with a meaningful look before speaking again. "And... I found this hidden in our house."

She reached into her bag and pulled out a small, rectangular object wrapped in brown paper. She placed it with a thud on the desk, carefully unwrapping it to reveal three stacks of hundred-dollar bills.

Bradford's eyes widened and pulled the stacks closer. "That's... at least thirty thousand dollars. Where did you—"

"Hidden in his closet, poorly at that," Anne interrupted. Her voice broke as she rocked her baby, tears slipping down her nose. "Please, Sandy. Andy doesn't keep secrets like this from me. I think he's in real trouble."

"And Sandy," Melanie added, "I got worried when Anne told me… did my own searching… Clark has an even larger stash just like this one… Idiot hid it in his tackle box."

Sandy stared at the money, her thoughts racing. The signs were there, and they were not good. Her mouth went dry as she tried to formulate a response, her mind flashing back to similar cases she'd seen before. But never had she expected it to involve police officers… *not in this town.*

Sandy's voice softened. "Okay. I'll look into this. Don't worry… There's got to be a reasonable explanation." She pushed the money back to Anne. "Don't spend that until we know where it's from." She then turned to Melanie. "Do you remember what I told you yesterday? About that woman who came in and mentioned seeing Clark?"

Melanie nodded slowly.

"I think that might be a good place to start," Sandy said, squeezing Melanie's hand again. "But in the meantime, I'll keep trying to raise Clark and Andy on the radio. You should both head home and try to rest. I'll let you know the moment I hear anything. Everything's going to be okay."

The two women reluctantly agreed, seeming exhausted and defeated. Melanie wiped at her tears, and Anne clutched her baby tighter as they said their goodbyes, thanking Sandy.

Once they were gone, Bradford sat back in her chair, thinking about the officers and the nicely wrapped cash that had been on her desk. Her stomach churned. She knew deep down that something was wrong. *Very wrong.* And whatever Clark and Coop were involved in, it was likely more dangerous than either of their wives realized.

She pondered for a minute and then picked up the phone, dialing a detective's number. "Hey Mike, it's Sandy," she said, her voice low. "I think our boys on leave are into something bad. I think we better find them, and fast."

33

Wedding

15 April 1711

The large wooden doors burst open releasing loud cheers and allowing the newlyweds to step out onto the stone steps of the grand church for the first time as man and wife. A crowd of smiling attendees swelled along the pathway, cheering as the handsome couple slowly descended toward the waiting carriage. A loud cheer erupted as they paused to kiss and wave at the crowd. Rice flew from every direction, pelting the couple and those nearby in joyous celebration.

Elizabeth turned, she could see herself in the glass of the coach, her tall, slender figure accentuated by the high-waisted white dress. Spotting her small group of bridesmaids, she turned in the customary fashion and tossed her bouquet overhead towards them with a wide smile.

Alexander stood nearby and could be heard shouting and tossing coins to the large group of attendees. Elizabeth flinched at a large cloud of rice that formed above her and descended quickly before being blocked by Alexander's shielding arm.

"Ready my love?" he said as more hails of rice rained down on them amongst the cheers of the group.

Elizabeth waved to the crowd, which included her family, and then nodded to him. She felt herself lifted from the ground as he picked her up in his arms and kissed her once more, then moved with her into the open carriage to another round of applause. They laughed together, brushing off flecks of rice and confetti. Alexander then tossed another few rounds of coins into the crowd and closed the door.

"Mrs. Elizabeth McGregor," he said with playful formality, his eyes gleaming. "Are you ready for our honeymoon?"

Elizabeth leaned back into the plush velvet seat and nodded. She felt her cheeks flush with excitement at the mention of her new surname. "Can you believe this day has finally arrived? It feels like a dream from which I should ne'er wish to wake."

"I am indeed the most fortunate of men," he said before signaling to the driver. The carriage began to move, and she could hear the crowd walking behind, following them on foot. Slowly the sounds died down as they left the cobblestones of the town.

She held up her left hand to admire the large wedding ring glittering in the sunlight. The diamond and rubies reflected rays inside the cab. "'Tis beautiful, Alexander. I thank you for this, and for everything."

"A mere set of stones compared to your beauty. I am one very fortunate man, and I shall ever be by thy side, my Dove, forevermore."

The carriage bounced as it continued its journey, rocking gently from side to side. They had agreed to spend their first week as husband and wife in the south, near Corbridge, not far from her grandparents. Elizabeth looked out the window, the sunlight filtering through the trees as they moved farther into the countryside.

"Alex, are you certain we are on the right road? It seems as though we are heading back toward home."

"Aye, I had the driver take us past the house. Our luggage awaits us there. It will not delay us long."

"Of course, ever one step ahead of me. I would have had us set off on our honeymoon without so much as a stitch of clothing."

"The very same thought crossed my mind, my dear. I am most pleased we are of one accord," he said with a wink.

She felt her face flush and could feel butterflies fluttering in her stomach. She settled back into her seat again and opened her mouth in mock surprise. "Why, Mr. McGregor, wouldst thou speak so unto thy mother? She doth believe thee to be a perfect gentleman."

At this he sat up straight and put his hand on his heart. "So I shall be, madam. I intend to be the model of gentleman and husband." He then leaned in and gave her a long and sensual kiss, then smiled broadly. "Whether we are clothed or not."

She pulled him in for another long kiss. "Perhaps not the perfect gentleman," she said in a soft whisper, and then went in for a longer kiss, leaning into him. He then put up one finger, stopping her advance.

"But not at this moment, my Dove."

"And why not? Are you worried the driver will discover us in the act?"

He kissed her quickly on the nose and then grinned. "No, my Dove. We are here." At that the coach slowed and

Elizabeth recognized her surroundings. They were near the McGregor home. She smiled at him and slumped back into her seat. She felt her heart thud wildly in her chest.

"Very well. I'll certainly allow an abeyance sir," she said. This time it was her turn to shoot him a wink.

She looked out the window to admire the countryside, and, as she did, something caught her eye. On the low hill ahead of the house, she spied three figures coming down to the plain.

As the coach continued, Elizabeth could see them more clearly. They were three women, their long black hair swaying as they moved, walking to intercept the coach. Elizabeth's stomach knotted as she recognized them. Margaret, in the middle, flanked by her two twin sisters, Agatha and Claire.

Elizabeth leaned back again; her pulse quickened by the sight. The Vikars, especially Margaret – Alexander's first love – made her uncomfortable. The thought of facing them chilled her blood and she felt her face flush. And the sisters, she had heard enough stories about the Vikar girls, especially Agatha, to feel an unease she could not shake. The constables had been looking for her, if only casually, but she was a person of interest in the region. It had been enough to lead to wild speculation among everyone. She'd also heard, first-hand, the dark, unsettling tales Alexander had shared with her in hushed tones late at night – tales she had long wished to dismiss as mere superstition yet could never quite forget.

She risked another glance. The three women were nearer now, their cold stares locked upon her through the carriage window. Elizabeth felt her breath quicken. She did not wish to face them. What could she possibly say? *I beg your pardon, Margaret. I have but married the man who scorned you and confirmed your sister's guilt to the law. It's a pleasure to make your acquaintance.* The thought made her laugh nervously.

The carriage came to a stop, and before she could speak, Alexander kissed her on her cheek and left. "I shall not be long, my Dove," he said, disappearing through the front door of the house. She reached toward him, her mouth wide open. She had meant to tell him something that would allow her to come inside with him, but that moment had passed and now she felt stuck, prey caught in a trap, the inevitable encounter with the predators just seconds away. She leaned toward the open door, ready to slide toward it.

A soft tap upon the window startled her, and she froze mid-move before slowly turning back. *Caught in a snare.* Claire stood just outside the window. Instead of the harsh glare Elizabeth had expected, Claire smiled. She looked pleasant enough, but Elizabeth did note something unsettling in her eyes. *She's a very beautiful woman but there is something wicked there.* Elizabeth took a deep breath and forced herself to open the door near her.

"Good day," she managed, stepping out onto the ground.

Claire studied her closely, her eyes lingering upon the wedding ring. "Mrs. McGregor, I presume," she said, with a sly smile. "Congratulations are in order."

"I thank you. Pardon me, but I do not recall your name."

"My name is Claire. It's a pleasure to meet you. And across the way, that other stunning beauty is Agatha."

Elizabeth nodded and waved awkwardly at the twin standing across the road.

"And I am certain you remember our younger sister, Margaret."

"Yes, hello, Margaret," Elizabeth said, looking at the smaller woman but Margaret's face remained cold, her eyes blank behind long black lashes. "Alex has spoken much of her."

"Alex, what a charming little moniker. I do hope he has not told you too much." Claire's smile remained but her eyes grew more mischievous, a look that was impossible to ignore.

"Pardon?"

"I jest. We came not to delay you, but merely to offer our felicitations to the happy couple."

"Of… of course. I am grateful, Claire. Very nice to make your acquaintance and I thank you. We are just about to leave, but perhaps, upon our return, we might sup together."

A loud thud came from above as the driver packed the luggage. "That would be most agreeable," Claire said, though the warmth in her voice seemed to fade. "Yet I suspect you will have other priorities."

Another thud from the carriage roof caused Elizabeth to glance up. The tension had begun to mount and there was an awkward pause as Claire stood staring at her. Elizabeth opened her mouth, hoping to break the silence but Alexander's voice interrupted from above.

"What do you want with us, Claire?"

"Alexander! I did hope to see you before you headed south! Surely you have time for a brief farewell?"

"Amusing, I don't recall telling you we were headed south."

"Oh, just a guess on my part. You know I'm very good at guessing, my dear."

Alexander dropped down from the top of the carriage, his face tight with frustration. "Claire, you and your sisters should not be here."

"Be not so unkind. After all that has passed between us, surely there is no need for enmity."

A muffled sob came from across the road. Elizabeth looked

at Margaret and she was hunched over. She felt a tinge of compassion for the poor girl and thought about going over to comfort her but immediately thought better of it.

"Especially considering how you did save Agatha," Claire added, her voice now laced with mockery. "Were it not for your cunning, Alexander, she would be standing trial for witchcraft."

"Good day, Claire," Alexander said curtly, beginning to move to his side of the carriage.

Claire's voice rose behind him. To Elizabeth the pitch was akin to a songbirds. "We are fugitives now. Thanks to your little ruse, we are no longer welcome in town. You might take greater care with your pretense in the future. Otherwise my entire family might find the noose!"

At this he turned on her. "As you did say, I did save Agatha. Perchance, you and your kin might take greater care in concealing your family's pastime!"

Claire's smile only widened at this, and she took a step toward him. "Take heed. That pastime, as you call it, might well come to visit you, Alexander."

Almost unconsciously, Elizabeth felt herself move toward Claire. "Claire, he only meant to help your sister. Do you not understand that?" But her words were ignored and she thought she saw Claire tug something long and thin from her pocket. She kept it concealed from Alexander's view. *Is that a wand?* The thought made her feel giddy. It was almost comical, but she felt the fear it invoked. She went to stand by Alexander, but he put up a hand.

"It's okay, Elizabeth," he said, giving her a kind look. "Just return to the carriage."

"But she…"

"It's fine Dove."

Hesitantly, she backed up to the door and did as he said, shutting it. More words were said but they were muffled. It sounded something like Alexander not wanting any trouble and that the families should just avoid each other. A higher pitched voice could be heard from across the road, presumably Margaret's, but it was too muffled to make out. It sounded pleading and Alexander seemed to ignore it because he turned to walk around the carriage.

He hopped into his side and then slammed the door shut. He wore an indignant look on his face and he roughly knocked twice upon the carriage roof, signaling to the driver. The carriage jerked forward, rolling away from the three sisters. Elizabeth looked back and the three seemed to be walking behind them as the coach slowly turned, making a wide circle. One of them, presumably Claire, was pointing something into the air. The carriage would inevitably need to drive back up the road and would bring them very close to the Vikar sisters.

Alexander rapped on the ceiling again to signal the driver to go faster as the retreating coach started toward the three.

"What are they doing? Why are they standing in our way?"

"They'll move," Alexander replied, his voice cold.

Something white and blue seemed to arc through the coach and a few of the glass panes on both doors shattered, sending shards flying many directions. More electrical arcs sparked about the cabin.

Elizabeth felt pieces of the glass ping off her body and head. The small volleys of sparks sizzled her hair roots, and she could feel them go through her body. Instinctively she looked toward the girls as the coach rolled past them, but she felt her body being pulled to the other side of the cabin. Alexander had yanked her onto his lap and his arms covered her face, as more sparks could be heard sizzling overhead.

"Faster!" Alexander barked but the coach was already speeding forward, the loud whine of the horses could be heard, their fear driving them much too fast down the road. A loud clatter came from the roof, items shifting and likely falling to the road.

In the distance and over the loudness of the carriage, Elizabeth thought she heard Margaret's somehow booming voice yelling the name of her new husband as they rode away. "Alexander, you said we'd be together forever! This is not over!"

Dark clouds miraculously formed in the sky, and it began to rain. Elizabeth could now see that the blue arcs were small bolts of lightning, as several more hit the ground nearby. The coach kept racing down the road, into the now black storm.

34

The Collateral

Officer Andy Cooper's head smacked the ground as the truck door clipped him, knocking him off his feet. The wheels spun violently, kicking up dirt that filled his eyes and mouth. He lay there, stunned, for a moment before rolling over onto his chest, spitting the grit from his mouth.

He desperately fumbled for his gun. He finally secured the weapon in his hand, eyes darting toward the truck that had spun sideways violently in the distance. The engine roared as it shifted forward, dust obscuring it as it sped into the darkness.

Blinking rapidly to clear the dirt from his eyes, he lifted his gun and aimed toward the retreating truck. His vision blurred as he pulled the trigger, the loud crack of gunfire cutting through the night. Metal and glass sounds pinged in the distance, but the truck didn't slow down, although its tailgate fell as it raced off, dropping items on the road before disappearing around a corner.

Panting heavily, he rolled onto his back, his mind racing.

Had he hit Liam? Or anyone else? He cursed under his breath. Shooting someone wasn't something he ever thought he'd do, and now he was left wondering if he'd just made a terrible mistake.

A sharp pain radiated up from his leg, pulling his attention to it. His right knee throbbed, and as he shifted to inspect it, he saw the tear in his pants and blood seeping from the cut. *Did that lunatic run me over?* he thought, wincing as he tried to move.

The sound of static filled the air, and he realized it was coming from the cruiser. It was his radio. Gritting his teeth, he pulled himself to his feet, careful not to put too much weight on his injured leg. The pain stabbed at him with each step as he limped toward the car.

"Coop! Come in, Coop! Where are you, man?"

The radio was full of static, but he recognized Clark's frantic tone. He leaned through the shattered window and grabbed the radio from the seat.

"This is Cooper, over."

"Hey, where've you been? I've been calling for ages!"

"Sorry man, I was being detained by our friend Liam."

"Yeah, what happened?"

"He came my way. Liam had the girls in his truck. Let's just say, we had a little run-in. They're headed back your direction, towards the first barricade – over."

"A run-in? What does that mean?"

"I'll explain when you get here – I'm going to need a lift."

"I'm headed your way now, but I'm still at least an hour out. It looks like one of them crashed their car into the tree." There was another short pause. "Wait, why do you need me to give you a lift?"

"On account of my car being wrecked. Old Liam decided to use it as a crash test."

The radio was silent for several long seconds and then Clark's voice could be heard, a loud curse. "Copy that. Wait – we'll need to figure that out... maybe tow it down..." Another pause. "Oh hey Coop, HQ's radioing, it's Sandy, I might need to take this. I've been ignoring their calls, but it sounds like I better take it... it sounds like we have a problem."

"Come again, Clark. Did you just say we might have a problem? Like what kind? I thought we were on radio silence. Why would Sandy want us?"

"It's fine, Coop. Let me see what they want, and I'll let you know."

"Okay, man. You've got me worried though. We're supposed to be fishing but I haven't talked to Anne in days... think she is looking for me? I'll bet you money, she found my fishing gear... I told you we should have taken all our stuff."

"Hey, relax. Like I said, let me find out. I'll call you back."

Andy let out a long sigh then tossed the small radio onto the roof of the car. *As far as I'm concerned this deal is done.* He hobbled to the trunk, retrieving the first aid kit. Lowering himself painfully into the passenger seat, he cut away the fabric around his knee with scissors. The gash wasn't too deep, but it was messy, and the tire marks on his leg told him that he had indeed been run over, if only lightly. "Liam, I've had enough of you... I've had enough of this whole thing," he muttered to himself as he tore the rest of the fabric away.

At first, this job had been too good to be true. Andy's part was almost laughably easy. All he needed to do was help Clark intercept any calls coming in from headquarters via an operator that Clark had apparently made a deal with. Andy didn't know much about that part of the deal but sure as Clark had said, a call had come in about a disturbance at the Moore house from the Jensen girl. They had responded to the call like any other incident. Where it started to get strange is when Clark had told the girl they would take Liam in but instead of doing that, Clark had just yelled at the old man at his home and then just let him go.

Andy paused at this. *We should have just taken him in. We had a breaking and entering charge on him. Why just let him go? Sure, we were supposed to be fishing but couldn't we have just had him detained?* His mind swam through the questions, trying to make sense of them. *Then we see that girl on the road... What was her name? Gwen? And we take her back to Liam's, something I did not agree with.* He sighed at this thought. He had worried that his partner was going to actually kill Liam and that definitely didn't sit right with Andy, regardless of what Liam was involved in. *To be honest, I almost did the jig when I saw the old man pull up to the barricade. Didn't realize the lunatic was going to run me over and wreck my cruiser when I found that woman in his truck bed.*

The thoughts all swirled together and there were too many gaps to make sense of. Clark had just been extremely secretive about all of it. But frankly Andy didn't care. He didn't want to know the rest of the details. He was out and he was going to tell his partner this fact the moment he showed up. *Even if I have to give the cash back.*

He pulled some gauze pads, alcohol wipes, and some bandages out of the kit. He looked at the wound again and considered using thread and needle instead.

A noise drew his attention away from his leg, faint but distinct – a sound like plastic flapping in the wind. He glanced around, his gaze falling on something blue down the road. At first glance, it looked like a tarp, maybe debris tossed by the wind, but the air around him was dead still. He squinted, trying to bring the object into focus.

His heart lurched as he recognized the shape. *No, that can't be can it?* The body of the woman from Liam's truck. His skin prickled recalling what Clark had told him, how she'd been kept in that deep well. It was one of the reasons he went along with the whole thing. They'd eventually turn the old man in and save the woman. *I mean, he was obviously into the sick stuff to have her in some sort of wet hole in the ground.*

"Poor woman," he muttered, reaching for the needle and thread. He really hadn't understood her part in all of this, yet another detail he didn't want to know. But when he saw her body in the back of the truck, his instincts of a police officer had kicked in. *If she wasn't dead then, she probably is now.*

"Coop, come in!"

He reached for the radio above him on the roof, distractedly fumbling with the kit.

"Yeah, I'm here. You headed this way? What did HQ want?"

"Gonna be a bit. You okay?"

"Minor injury, no problem. Again, what did HQ want?"

"It's not a problem, Coop. I'll tell you when I get there."

"No partner, why don't you tell me now?"

"I told you it's no problem and I have this under control."

"Yeah, you've been saying that for the last few days. What's going on?"

"It's our wives... they're worried and looking for us. Like I said, not a problem. I told Sandy we've been in a service dead zone."

Andy let out a loud sigh and slammed the small radio

247

against the seat of the car. "What do you mean, not a problem? I told you we should have grabbed our gear. This isn't going to look like a fishing trip, man. How do you intend to cover this up?"

"Andy! I have a plan... Relax! I promise everything will be fine."

"I hope you're right, partner. This deal that seemed too good to be true now feels like we didn't get paid nearly enough."

"Don't worry. By tomorrow, you'll be thanking me. I'm heading your way. Are you still okay, man?"

"Other than I have to sew up my leg and figure out how to fix my car, just peachy. How about you?"

"Funny you ask. I still have a splitting headache from our mutual friend when he did that number on me in the basement with that creepy woman. Feels like I got hit in the head with a coat rack."

"Oh, speaking of which... Clark, there is something else odd here."

"Yeah? What's going on now?"

"Speaking of that creepy woman in the well..."

There was a long pause on the line. "Yes. What about her?"

"Well, she was in the back of Liam's truck. Red hair just as you described. He had her under a tarp or something. I think she was dead."

Clark's response was quick, almost interrupting. "You get a chance to see her eyes?"

"Checked them myself... the greenest eyes I've ever seen."

A low crackling noise came from the radio but no response. "Anyways, I'm not sure but I think Liam left her body here in the commotion... I think she's in the road here under a pile of tarps, but I can't be sure."

Clark's voice abruptly came to life on the line, it was loud and to the point. "Andy, listen to me man. You need to get yourself out of there! If she's there – please get out of there!"

"Come again, Clark. Did you say get out of here?"

Clark's voice started to stutter and slur as he responded. "Coop, there are things I haven't told you. Figured you wouldn't want to know…"

"What? Why? What's going on?"

Clark's voice turned frantic. "I'll tell you later! For now, whatever you need to do, just get as far from her as possible – now. I don't care if you need to crawl, you find a place to hide."

"Is this another prank, Clark? I'm not falling for that one again. And this is not the time, man." He mumbled a curse and clipped the radio to his pocket to free up his other hand to work on the wound. Clark's voice continued to crackle over the radio.

Andy halted, his gaze snapping to the figure in the distance. The tarp had come up from the ground and had slipped away, revealing the woman. Her red hair draped down her back, her pale skin glowing in the low light. She stood there, motionless, staring right back at him.

Andy froze as he took in the woman. The logical part of his mind couldn't make sense nor reconcile this with his many hours of police training and experience. "Ma'am? Are you okay?" He called out, his voice unsure. He couldn't fathom how she was even standing. She was bound to have injuries.

There was no response. She just stared, her eyes burning into him from a distance. Slowly, deliberately, she began walking toward him, her step a limp at first but then turned fluid, yet unnatural.

Andy wavered, about ready to tell her to stop and to lie down, but instead his hand instinctively moved to his sidearm, fingers curling around the grip. The kit and its contents fell to the ground as he pushed himself to his feet. *You've got to be kidding me!*

He snatched his radio from his pocket. "Clark, that woman... she's alive," he muttered into the radio, eyes locked on her. "I think she needs assistance or something."

The radio cut in and out. "I'm not... messing... you! Get the... outta..."

"Ma'am, stay where you are."

Her eyes continued staring cold at him, her face expressionless, devoid of anything human. He could feel the fear tightening his chest, his breathing shallow and quick.

"Coop! Get out of there! I'm still far away... run!" Clark was screaming now; the loud engine of the cruiser could be heard in the background over the radio.

"Ma'am..." His voice cracked as he raised his gun, aiming it at her. But she kept walking, her gaze never wavering, the distance between them shrinking with each unnatural step.

She didn't look dangerous. Small, with a slight frame and pale skin, she almost seemed fragile – except for those eyes. They hadn't blinked once, remaining locked on him with an emotionless intensity that raised goose pimples on his arms.

"Ma'am... I'm warning you. Stay where you are."

Andy leaned against the car door, keeping his gun trained on her. The tension in the air was thick, there was a sense of wrongness that had settled in the pit of his stomach. His desire to help her had entirely evaporated and he now felt threatened.

Then, something shifted. Her eyes began to blink rapidly, almost unnaturally so. Her mouth, which had hung open in a vacant expression, contorted, revealing clenched teeth as if she was in pain. There was an obvious internal battle happening and she faltered momentarily. Then her expression went blank again and the eyes that were green, were now pitch black and large.

A sudden coldness crept over him, starting at his feet and rapidly climbing through his body. It wasn't just a chill – it felt like something alive, reaching out, wrapping around him. He glanced down, confused, but saw nothing. *What is this?!*

When he looked back up, his visible breath caught in his throat. The woman – no, the *thing* – had changed. Before him now stood a shadowy figure, pitch black and shifting like smoke. Wisps of darkness curled away from it, disappearing into the night air. His feet slipped slightly as the ground now suddenly had frost covering it.

"How?" he whispered, the word barely audible, his mind struggling to comprehend what he was seeing. It wasn't possible. This couldn't be real.

His instincts took over, and he squeezed the trigger three times in quick succession. Each bullet struck the creature, but it had no effect. The shots vanished into the swirling mass of darkness, swallowed whole.

He cursed loudly, panic rising in his throat. He unloaded the last few bullets into the void, the final pull ending with a clicking noise, but it was useless. The few shots had disappeared, offering no resistance, no sign that they'd even made contact.

Before he could process what was happening, the creature was suddenly in front of him. It had moved so quickly, faster than his eyes could track, closing the gap in a single blink.

A long, misshapen arm shot out from the darkness, its fingers like claws curling around his throat. The grip was ice cold, colder than anything Andy had ever felt. It wasn't just physical – it felt like the cold was seeping into his soul, pulling him into the void.

His gun fell from his hand, clattering to the ground as his feet left the icy dirt. The creature had lifted him effortlessly, its grip tightening around his neck.

"What... What are you?" he croaked, the words barely escaping his lips. But the sound came out garbled, the pressure on his throat cutting off his breath.

In the final moments, as his vision began to fade, one last thought flickered in his mind. His wife and his newborn son. All he wanted now was to see them again.

Then the creature slammed him into the side of the cruiser, and everything went black.

35

Storm

16 April 1711

Robert Arnall closed the last cabinet in his small street store, the final clasp clicking into place with a metallic snap. He tugged at the latch to ensure it was secure and murmured to himself, "That'll do." The town around him had grown quiet, all the stores shuttered for the evening. As usual, Robert was the last to leave.

He glanced around the deserted street before pulling a small leather purse from his pocket. His fingers worked the stitching loose, revealing a mix of copper and silver coins. He thumbed through them, counting with satisfaction. Business had been good today. For the first time in weeks, he'd felt the weight of his past involvement in the witch accusations lifting. The suspicions that had tarnished his reputation were fading, though many still crossed the street to avoid him.

With a sigh, he tied the purse shut and stuffed it back into his coat pocket. The evening was cooling fast. The wind had picked up, whipping dust and loose debris down the empty road. He looked up, expecting heavy clouds, but the sky remained oddly clear. A few drops of rain splattered onto his bald head as a gust of wind tore his hat from his scalp.

"Dash it!" he cursed, watching the hat spiral down the street, carried far out of reach. He hesitated, then gave up the chase, his mood darkening as the wind pressed against him. The streets, now almost deserted, felt hostile, as if the town itself wanted to push him away. He pressed on, walking down the long street toward his home.

The wind howled, slamming shutters and forcing many of the last few lingering townsfolk to scurry inside. As he walked, he caught sight of a woman in a rocking chair on her porch – one of his old customers. When she noticed him, she quickly rose and retreated into her house, the door closing with a thud behind her.

"After all I've done for this town…"

He continued walking, hunched against the storm that continued to build. A quick gust of wind slammed into him and his balance faltered. Then a second blast hit him and knocked him down to one knee, and with a loud groan, his coin purse and several important papers tumbled from his pocket, scattering across the cobbled street. The coins rolled in all directions, and the documents fluttered like dying birds in the wind.

"Dash it all!" he spat, scrambling on his knees to recover his belongings. A man passed by, and Robert called out, "Excuse me! Could you lend a hand?" But the man gave no sign of hearing, disappearing into the swirling dust.

Robert cursed under his breath, clutching at the coins with arthritic fingers, his knees screaming in protest. He retrieved the last of them, shoved them back into the purse, and stood with a pained grunt. His back groaned, and he arched to stretch it.

He was about to leave when a shadow caught his eye – a figure walking slowly down the center of the street. Robert squinted, but the wind-driven dust blurred the figure's form. The dark shape, obscured by the storm, continued to move toward him.

He turned toward his house, deciding to ignore the person. His legs were aching, and the evening chill was settling into his bones. He pressed on.

"Afternoon, Mrs. Percy!" he called to a neighbor through her window. She scowled at him, then yanked the window shut with a snap. His shoulders slumped, the rejection stinging more than he cared to admit.

The small figure behind him seemed to close the distance so he quickened his pace. There was something peculiar about the person, something unnatural as it walked quickly in the distance.

"Mr. Arnall..." The voice drifted on the wind, a woman's voice, but distorted and though there was still distance between them, it sounded close. His skin prickled, and he rubbed his ear, trying to shake the feeling.

He limped faster, taking a side street toward his house. The wind shrieked through the narrow alley, and the ache in his right knee flared with each step. When he reached the corner, he glanced behind him – the figure was gone. He relaxed slightly, and he exhaled in relief. He bent over and put his hands on his knees. That tumble he'd taken had hurt him more than he'd thought, and the pain continued to surge up his leg as he rested.

His house loomed ahead, a modest home with a weathered

door. He hobbled the last few yards before resting briefly once more. He reached for the key in his vest pocket – only to find it gone.

"Where is it?" he muttered, slapping at his pockets in a frantic search. His mind raced back to the moment when the wind had knocked him down. The key must have fallen then. His gut twisted. He didn't relish the idea of retracing his steps.

He looked back down the street toward the alley but before he could make a decision, a soft creak reached his ears – the unmistakable sound of his front door opening.

His eyes flickered ahead; the door stood ajar. Robert gaped in unbelief, dread pooling in his stomach. He never left without locking up. His hands trembled as he pushed the door open wider, stepped in, and then bolted the door behind him.

The house was still, dark, and silent except for the sound of the rain starting to patter against the windows. He did a quick, pained search of the main area, everything seemed in order – no drawers disturbed, no valuables missing. But something felt wrong. It felt colder than normal. He looked at the wood pile considering a fire. *That should raise my spirits.*

The patter of footsteps echoed from the floor above, startling him from his thought.

"Who's there?!" he called, his voice shaky with a mix of anger and fear. His gaze darted around for something to defend himself with. His eyes landed on the iron fire poker by the hearth. Grabbing it with trembling hands, he hefted it in front of him.

"If you leave now, no harm will come to you! I can have the authorities here in minutes!"

The rain intensified, drumming loudly against the roof, accentuating the silence of the house. With the poker in one hand and a candle in the other, he edged toward the stairs and then slowly up them. His leg screamed in pain, and he considered stopping but pride urged him farther. As he nearly reached the upper landing, a loud creaking noise came from one of the rooms.

"I warn you! I am very well armed!" he yelled, but a laugh, a high-pitched cackle echoed down the hall in response. Robert froze, his blood turning to ice. A face flashed across his mind, pale and menacing. He knew that laugh. It had to be Agatha Vikar; the woman he'd helped condemn. He'd said so many things about her... so many horrible things. Many of the things he'd said were embellished to build his case against her. He gulped hard. *And many of the things I told people weren't true. I was afraid people wouldn't believe me.* And now he had to face her. He'd heard that menacing laugh when she was being questioned by the constable. That wicked and malevolent laugh. Regret filled his bowels and he began to back up.

"Robert..." A voice rang out, drawn out, sinister and playful.

Panic gripped him and he attempted to back up again, dropping the candle. It hit the steps with a loud clatter. He turned to flee but lost his footing, tumbling down in a tangle of brittle limbs. He heard loud crunches as he bounced down each stair and then an audible crack came from his shoulder as he finally stopped. Pain shot through his body, and he let out a pitiful cry.

Moments passed, and he lay there, gasping for air, blood pooling in his mouth from a broken tooth.

"Robert..." The voice came again, obviously closer now. The sound of footsteps descending the stairs sent a fresh wave of terror through him. He tried to crane his neck to look but only managed to add more pain to the already strained muscles.

"Please!" he bellowed.

The slow, methodical footsteps finally stopped, and a shadow loomed over him. She let out a low mirthless laugh before stepping over him. He felt a strong hand grab his collar and neck hair as he was yanked across the floor, dragging him like a rag doll. His broken limbs straightened, causing more damage as he was pulled around furniture at difficult angles.

"I'll do anything! I'll tell them I lied! Please! I was wrong, Agatha... please... I can make this right."

But all he heard in reply was that soft, menacing laugh.

He watched the ceiling above slowly go by and then felt himself stop near the fireplace. She laid his head on the hearth with a thud. He let out a low whimper. She then came into view, her face mostly shrouded in darkness, framed by long, black hair that swayed as she leaned over him. Her eyes gleamed with malice as she jammed her foot down on his chest. He tried to scream as he felt several of his ribs crack. He gasped, trying to breathe. His eyes widened in disbelief as she drew closer to his face. He opened his mouth and tried to speak but nothing came.

"You think she needs your help? Do you think any of my family need your help?" she purred, her smile sharp and cruel. "I need only one thing from you, Mr. Arnall... and you're about to do it very well."

Her laugh rang out, mingling with the storm outside. The rain beat harder, drowning out his screams that echoed long into the night.

36

The Return

The old truck lumbered onto the long gravel driveway, groaning as it came to a squeaking halt in front of Sarah's relatives' cabin. White smoke billowed from under the hood, accompanied by a sharp, menacing hiss.

Sarah tightened the makeshift bandages she had fashioned from her torn sleeve. A bullet had punched through the truck's cabin and had continued clean through Liam's shoulder.

"Of all places, you could have gone, you bring us back here?" she snapped, her gaze darting to the all-too-familiar house. Reaching over, she grabbed Liam's hand and pressed it firmly over the cloth covering his wound. "Hold this, it's not staying on."

Liam didn't respond, his teeth clenched in pain as he leaned forward over the steering wheel. With a grimace, he twisted the ignition key, silencing the truck.

"Sarah, what can I do?" Gwen's voice trembled from the passenger seat, her face pale and drawn. Her wide eyes were fixed on the dark stain spreading across Liam's jacket.

"Go to his side – we need to get him inside the house."

"I'm fine, lass," Liam interjected through gritted teeth. "Just need a moment." He leaned back in his seat, giving Gwen a weak grin. "What happened to you? Looks like a goose laid an egg on your head."

Gwen reflexively touched the bruise on the side of her forehead, wincing. "I... don't even remember that happening."

"And you, lass? That cop manage to put a hole in you?"

Sarah shook her head as she reapplied the bandage, now nearly saturated with blood. "No, but he hit just about everything else in here."

Liam sat up abruptly, urgency flashing in his eyes. His movements were deliberate, despite his injury. Glancing at the rearview mirror, then toward the house, he pointed to the cab floor. "Lass, I've got the wound. Grab my tools from down there – we need to move."

Sarah followed his gaze and spotted the gray tool bag; its contents were spilled across the floor. She sighed and then leaned over awkwardly, shoving the scattered items back into the bag.

He paused and winced again. "And you, Firecracker." Liam addressed Gwen, who was inspecting her reflection in the cracked passenger-side mirror. She turned to him with a wary look. "You'll help me move the payload around back."

"Payload? Oh, you mean that horrible creature?" Gwen's voice climbed as she shook her head vehemently. "Absolutely not. I'm not going near—" Her protest was cut short as she glanced through the shattered rear window. Her face went pale. "It's... gone."

"What?" Liam's eyes widened. His reaction was immediate. Kicking the door open, he scrambled out of the truck and peered into the empty bed. He muttered a curse, slamming his uninjured hand against the rusted metal. "Well, that complicates things. The gate must have fallen open in the ruckus... it does that sometimes."

Seems to be the story of my week, Sarah thought as she zipped the tool bag closed. "So, what's the plan? You really need to get inside and deal with those wounds."

Liam reappeared at the driver's side. "We need to hide this old bucket first."

A siren wailed faintly in the distance. The sound was low, but unmistakable. All three froze. Liam was the first to move, launching back into the driver's seat with surprising speed.

"Firecracker, open the glovebox!"

Gwen hesitated, wide-eyed.

"Now!" Liam barked, motioning sharply.

Her fingers fumbled for the small button. With a push, the compartment popped open, spilling its contents onto the floor near the tool bag. Gwen reached for the two items but then recoiled.

"Hand it to me!" Liam's voice was sharp and commanding.

After a few moments, Sarah sighed and grabbed the large silver revolver. She hesitated only a moment before handing it to Liam, who checked the cylinder with practiced efficiency.

"Gather that box of ammo too."

The siren grew louder; a menacing crescendo.

Liam slammed the driver's door shut while simultaneously closing the revolver cylinder with one hand. It was a move so proficient it looked like a scene from a movie. "Get down, you two. Get out of sight!"

Sarah and Gwen slouched as best they could in the cramped truck cab.

Liam leaned back slightly but kept his body twisted, one eye fixed on the driveway behind them.

"Shouldn't we turn ourselves in?" Gwen asked, her voice cracking. Her hands trembled as she wiped at the tears pooling in her eyes. "I mean, that sounds like the police coming."

"Quiet!" Liam snapped; his tone sharp. The rising wail of the siren reached its peak before gradually fading, the sound moving past the property. Liam's body stiffened; his breath caught as his eyes followed the fading noise.

Sarah sat upright, pulling the red bandage from her lap and tossing it at Liam. "We're not moving until we get some answers," she said, arms folding across her chest. "Like Gwen said, don't you think we should turn ourselves in or something?"

"Lass…"

"Don't," Sarah cut him off, her voice firm. "We just ran over a man – a police officer. And now what? Are you planning to shoot one? I'm not going anywhere until you explain." She turned away, staring resolutely at the truck's dashboard, her jaw tight.

Liam let out a long, weary sigh, his eyes forward. "We need to get out of sight, lass," he said, his voice calmer but still urgent. "Those men – at least Officer Lambert – aren't what they seem. I know it's hard to believe, but they can't be trusted. We've got to get you inside before they or… she comes back."

At the mention of the creature, both girls froze. Gwen's hand touched Sarah, and they exchanged a glance. None of this was making sense. Before today, Sarah's biggest fear had been the dark figure hunting her, but corrupt officers and

Liam's cryptic warnings added a new layer of dread.

She glanced at Liam's jacket, picturing the blood-soaked wound beneath. "Fine," she said at last. "If we go inside, you tell me everything."

"Lass, you don't want to know everything…"

"That's the deal. Take it or leave it."

"Fine," he relented, his shoulders slumping. "Once we're safe in the basement and I'm patched up, I'll tell you what I can."

Sarah hesitated, studying him, then nodded.

"Good. Hand me the bag."

She hefted the tool bag onto his lap, and he quickly unzipped it, rummaging through the contents. Sarah watched as he pushed aside tools and supplies, searching for something specific. Finally, he pulled out a rusted chain, a padlock and key dangling from its end.

"Here, Firecracker." He offered the chain toward them.

Sarah frowned, reluctant, but took the cold, grimy metal and passed it to Gwen.

"And what's this for?" Gwen asked, holding the chain as though it might bite her. "Last time, you used rope. Think this will hold me?"

Liam smirked faintly beneath his beard, then tossed the truck keys onto Sarah's lap. "I need you to hide the truck. Hand those to Gwen."

"Why me?"

"Because I asked you," he barked. Then, catching himself, he softened. "Please, Firecracker. I know you don't trust me, and I can't blame you for that. But I'm in no shape to do it, and we can't risk the cops finding it here."

Gwen lowered her head, her lips trembling. "Okay," she

263

whispered. "Where should I take it?"

"About a mile down the road, there's a break in the trees. Drive it as far in as you can and follow the river back through the forest to the back yard."

"The forest?" Gwen's voice rose. "You want me to go into the forest – where that thing is?"

"Yes," Liam said firmly. "And lock the shop in the backyard with the chain before you come in. Use the back door and the hidden basement entrance. We'll leave it open."

Sarah shot him a sharp look. *How does he know about the hidden door?*

"The forest, though?" Gwen pressed. "Why not just follow the road back?"

"We don't have time," Liam snapped. "That cop will be back sooner than you think, and we can't risk him spotting you. There's a trail by the river – hard to miss. Keep to it."

Gwen's fear was evident, her knuckles white as she clutched the chain.

"I'll go," Sarah said, snatching the keys. "Gwen can help you inside."

"No," Liam interjected, grimacing. "It has to be her."

"Why?"

"Because it's after you, lass," he said, his tone cold. Reaching up, he tugged something from around his neck and handed it to Sarah – a strip of leather with a piece of red fabric tied to it. "And put this on. Don't ask questions."

Sarah hesitated but slipped it over her head.

Liam turned to Gwen, rummaging again in the bag. This time, he withdrew an old pocket watch. His hand lingered on it before passing it to her. "Keep this in your pocket," he said. "It'll protect you."

264

"What does it do?" Gwen asked, her voice faint.

"No time," Liam replied. "Just go." And with that he grabbed the bag and left the truck. "Sarah, let's go!"

37

Fire

16 September 1712

Elizabeth gently rubbed her rounded stomach, a faint smile on her lips. Her first child stirred within her, its tiny kicks a constant reminder of the life growing inside. Alexander was convinced it would be a boy, but she quietly favored the idea of a little girl.

Her smile faded as a sudden realization dawned on her – she recognized the feeling instantly. She was dreaming again, almost the same dream she'd had many times before. Her midwife had assured her that strange dreams were common among expecting mothers, urging her not to worry. Still, this one lingered with a peculiar intensity.

The small dark room had candles as well as wooden chairs lined up neatly along its perimeter. She vaguely knew what would happen next; she'd had this same dream before and it always ended the same way with her waking up before its apparent ending. The candles around the room cast a dim, flickering glow, their gentle warmth soothing her nerves. She exhaled slowly, allowing the dream to unfold as it always did.

Without fail, one of the doors in the room creaked open. A figure entered – a person in a brown hooded cloak, their face obscured, though strands of black hair peeked out from beneath. Her stomach tightened as the name *Margaret* flashed through her mind. The thought unsettled her, draining the comfort from the familiar scene.

She tried to wake herself but couldn't. The dream had its hold on her, pulling her deeper. The figure continued to walk across the room, silent and deliberate, before settling into one of the three circles etched into the wooden floor.

Elizabeth's heart quickened. She rose from her seat, her curiosity stronger than her discomfort. The figure looked up, but the hood still concealed their face. Just then, a sound came from the opposite side of the room, low and previously unnoticed. A second hooded figure had stood and now took their place on the other side of the circle.

Her breath caught. She leaned forward, trying to discern who this second figure was, but the shadows concealed their identity. Both figures sat motionless, shrouded in mystery.

Suddenly, an irresistible pull gripped her. She felt the overwhelming urge to sit in the last spot in the circle, as though it was meant for her all along. Her unease melted into a strange calm. She wasn't afraid anymore – just drawn.

Without hesitation, she crossed the room, stepping into the last spot. She sat down, completing the trio.

As if her presence had triggered something, Margaret slowly reached up and pulled back her hood. Elizabeth's heart leaped into her throat. It was alright but there was something different about her face. It was gaunt and drawn and her eyes bore dark circles.

Margaret smiled – an unsettling, knowing smile – and turned her gaze across the circle. The other figure also unhooded themselves.

Elizabeth's breath caught again. Alexander sat across from her, his face twisted in agony. She tried to call out to him, but no sound escaped her lips. His eyes were wild, darting around as he tried to speak, but he was just as mute as she was. There was a silent desperation there that she couldn't shake.

She tried to push herself to stand but her body was numb and wouldn't budge. She looked around the room, concentrating on waking up as she had done before in her other dreams. However this time, nothing happened. Instead she noticed others had joined the room. In the chairs around her, it seemed that all the Vikar women were present, including the twins. They all bore smiles but to Elizabeth's surprise, there was also fear there. In fact, all the Vikars seemed uncomfortable.

Then, from the center of the room, tendrils of black smoke began to rise. The wisps snaked outward, creeping closer with a terrible deliberation. They licked at the floor, circling each of them in their place, the cold tendrils brushing Elizabeth's skin like the touch of death.

Panic surged through her. She tried to push herself out of the circle, but her body refused to move. She looked over at Alexander – he, too, was struggling, his hands clenched into fists as he fought against some unseen force holding him down. His mouth moved, trying to form words, but still, no sound.

Her gaze snapped back to Margaret, who was now grinning with malicious glee. That smile, one that she'd seen come from Claire before, chilled Elizabeth to her very core.

The smoke in the center of the room coalesced, twisting and thickening into a dark shape. Limbs emerged – elongated, grotesque, each finger tipped with sharp claws. A dark creature rose, towering over them, its black skin gleaming like polished stone. It looked around, its eyes wide but vacant, as if unaware of its surroundings.

Then it screamed. It too seemed to want to escape.

The sound was like nothing Elizabeth had ever heard. A high-pitched wail that shook the room, piercing her ears and leaving her head throbbing. The creature thrashed, its long arms and legs pulling against the heavy black chains that bound it to the floor. Each movement sent a jarring rattle through the room as the chains clanged violently under the stress.

Elizabeth's terror mounted. She tried again to scream, but still nothing came out. The smoke around the creature thickened, swirling violently. It spread outward, enveloping her, Alexander, and Margaret in its dark cloud.

The air turned freezing as it filled her lungs, suffocating her. The stench was unbearable, like rotting flesh and decay. She gasped for breath, choking on the foulness of it. Her body trembled, eyes stinging as she tried to escape the smoke suffocating her.

Through the smoky haze, Elizabeth's eyes locked on the chains slithering like serpents across the floor. They coiled around Margaret with an unnatural precision, tightening with every second. The wicked smile Margaret wore moments earlier vanished, replaced by a desperate panic. Her body twisted and strained against the unyielding bonds as her screams pierced the thickening air. The chains writhed, pulling her closer to the demon, inch by inch, until the two collided in a burst of searing light. Green flames erupted from the impact, flickering hungrily and growing with each passing moment.

Elizabeth struggled to free herself, her heart pounding like a war drum in her chest. Summoning all her strength, she pushed herself out of the circle, stumbling to safety. The room around her dissolved into chaos. Flames surged and devoured everything in their path, their glow casting shadows through the smoke and on the walls. The Vikar women ran frantically, their faces contorted with terror as the fire pursued them like a living entity.

Thick, acrid smoke billowed through the room, stinging Elizabeth's eyes and clawing at her throat. Each breath felt heavier than the last, her lungs filling with the suffocating haze. She fell to her knees, coughing violently, her vision blurring as the inferno raged on around her.

Then, with a deafening crack, the world snapped.

She jolted awake, her body drenched in sweat. The room was dark and quiet, but a loud wooden creak reverberated from outside the room, echoing in the silence.

Her breath came in ragged gasps as she tried to shake off the lingering terror of the nightmare. Her skin was slick with sweat, her night clothes clinging uncomfortably to her. Her heart pounded so fiercely it felt like it might break through her chest. She rubbed her belly, the baby stirring and kicking as if sensing her distress.

This time, the dream had been different and more vivid, more ominous and one she couldn't seem to escape. She replayed fragments of it in her mind, trying to make sense of the smoke, the figures, and the creature that had felt so real. The presence of Alexander in the dream haunted her. She shuddered, pushing the quilt off her legs and sitting up in their bed.

She reached for the glass of water by her bedside, her hand trembling slightly as she drained it. The cool water offered little comfort as she wiped the sweat from her brow. She felt hot, almost feverish. Her hand returned to her belly, the baby's kicks grounding her in reality, reminding her that despite the darkness of her dream, life was growing within her.

She glanced around the room. Alex's side of the bed was empty, neatly made, as usual. He'd left early – he always did, handling tasks on the owner's land with his brother. Normally, she would have risen shortly after him, but her pregnancy had kept her in bed longer lately, her body too tired to keep its usual rhythm.

A strange noise interrupted her thoughts, coming from outside the door. Her body flinched instinctively. She pushed herself up, every movement weighed down by lingering dread from the dream, and went to investigate.

Their bedroom doors led to a hallway balcony overlooking the foyer and dining area. Sunlight streamed through the windows, casting a golden glow on the floor below. For a moment, the warm light seemed to calm her.

But then she saw him.

"Alex!" Below, he was on his hands and knees, his body covered in black stains that resembled ash or soot. His chest heaved as he coughed uncontrollably, his face pale and streaked with dirt. He put his head down on the floor, his body convulsing as silent sobs wracked him.

"What is it?" She rushed down the stairs and kneeled beside

271

him and put her hands on his back. He looked up at her, but his eyes were distant, glazed over with shock. He shook his head, unable to speak, and pressed his face back against the floor again.

Heavy footsteps approached from the open doors at the front of the house. Elizabeth turned her head and saw the strange, dark smoke still hanging in the distance. Over the hill, a massive plume of black smoke rose into the sky.

Benjamin walked through the doorway, his shoulders slumped, his eyes cast down at his feet. He moved slowly; each step heavy with the weight of what had happened. Without a word, he collapsed into a wooden chair near Alexander, his face ashen.

"How does he fare?"

Elizabeth shook her head. "He hasn't spoken yet. What has happened?"

He paused for several moments before speaking. "Alexander and I were returning from town when we saw the fire... And we went to it." He shifted in his seat, rubbing his hands on his knees, as if trying to wipe away the memory. "The Vikar place, it's gone, Elizabeth. There was a fire, and it consumed everything."

Elizabeth fell back onto the floor, tears welling in her eyes. "Delaney, the girls?"

Alexander pushed himself up, sitting beside her, his hands shaking. His eyes were red, his face streaked with ash and tears. He wiped his face, smearing the soot. "We searched the place. We found none alive. We do not know who... who succumbed, but... we found remains."

Elizabeth's tears spilled over, her mind reeling in disbelief. "Madilyn... little Alice?" She choked, shaking her head at the thought. "Delaney... Mr. Vikar... the twins... Margaret?"

At the mention of Margaret, Alexander's face darkened. He wiped his face again, harder this time, and stood abruptly. He pulled Elizabeth to her feet and wrapped her in a tight embrace, his voice low but firm. "Listen, Ben and I must ride into town to inform the local authorities. I want you to remain with my mother while we are away. You'll be safe there."

He pulled away and hurried up the stairs, disappearing into the master bedroom. Elizabeth watched him go, her heart aching for him, for the people lost in the fire. Moments later, he reappeared, dressed in a clean shirt and pants. He crossed the room and took her hand gently. "Come, Dove. I'll escort you." He then nodded at Benjamin, who had already stood. The three left the guest house and headed toward Martha's house.

Elizabeth thought again about the dream... the nightmare she'd had. She couldn't help but wonder about the similarities between her dream and this nightmarish reality she was witnessing. She thought again about each of the Vikars one by one. Though she and Alexander hadn't gotten along with some of them recently, none of them deserve the fate they'd been given. More tears formed in her eyes, and she pulled herself tightly to Alexander as they continued their journey.

38

The Trail

The truck shuddered forward, sputtering to a stall for the second time. Gwen let out a nervous laugh, giddy at the absurdity of the situation. "Oh, come on!" she said, smacking the steering wheel. She hadn't remembered the truck being a manual transmission – probably because she had never driven one in her life. She'd only received some light reading material on it in her Driver's Education class in high school.

She jammed the clutch down again with a little too much enthusiasm. "Here we go!" she yelled, as if she had an audience in the empty cab. She inspected the ridiculously long gear shift like it was some kind of alien technology, making sure it was set firmly in the '1' position. A fit of nervous giggles erupted from her. "Okay, Gwen. You got this!" Slowly, she pressed down on the gas.

The engine growled – a bit too much – and she pulled her foot back nervously. "Whoa there, boy," she coaxed, as if talking to a skittish horse. Gently, she eased off the clutch, and this time, miraculously, the old yellow truck started to move. "Yes!" she yelled triumphantly, pumping a fist in the air. She had absolutely no idea how she'd managed to back out of the driveway. Gravity, maybe? Divine intervention? Either way, this was progress.

"Oh crap!" she yelped, jerking the wheel to the right, narrowly avoiding a tree that had materialized out of nowhere. The truck lurched forward awkwardly, like a newborn calf learning the walk.

"Okay, okay," she whispered, trying to calm herself down. Clutch in again, pull the stick – easy does it. She slid the shifter into second gear. Somehow, this worked, and the ride smoothed out instantly. "Oh! So this is how older people drive," she mused, feeling very accomplished. *I should always start in second gear,* she thought, mentally adding this groundbreaking insight to her nonexistent driving manual.

Steam began to rise from the hood, accompanied by an alarming sizzling sound. "Uh oh," Gwen muttered, her nervous grin fading. *What had Liam said?* Something about a notch? A hitch? *No, a break,* she remembered. But where was that supposed to be again?

Her face scrunched in concentration, and she slowed the truck down, trying to remember how far he'd said it was. She squinted at the road ahead, hoping for some magical landmark. Nope. Just trees and more trees. Her concern deepened, brows knitting together. She did not want to walk all the way back. Definitely not this close to those officers and their barricade. *Guns. They had guns. Oh boy.*

But just as she began to panic, the roadside widened, and the forest opened up, just like Liam had promised. She pumped the clutch and turned, more or less gracefully, into the indentation. The path sloped downward, and she

275

carefully navigated the truck through the trees, her tongue poking out in concentration. Finally, the tree line grew too dense. She stopped the truck, turned off the engine, and mashed the circular switch to kill the headlights. She leaned back in the seat, grinning. "Nailed it!"

With the chain and lock slung over her shoulder, Gwen slammed the truck door shut and shivered slightly in the cool night air. *Man this thing is heavy. Why didn't I leave it at the cabin?* "Okay, road, cabin. Cabin... Where are you?" she muttered, spinning herself in a circle like she was about to perform some kind of dance. Thirty feet behind her, the road was still visible, but that didn't help much. "Guess we're walking," she said aloud, setting off in what she *hoped* was the right direction.

Before long, a trail appeared, one that looked familiar – like the path she and Sarah had taken before. If this was the same trail, it would lead her to the cabin's backyard where her and Sarah had found it. Gwen allowed herself a small smile but then focused again. The trees loomed large around her, casting long shadows that made everything seem almost foggy in the dim light. It was unsettlingly quiet. Even her boots made unnatural, echoing sounds on the ground as she walked.

Despite the eerie quiet, the trail felt like it was heading in the right direction, and Gwen's confidence grew. Inside the thick trees, away from the road, she felt a small sense of safety that carried her forward.

To the right, she heard the faint sound of running water, like a small stream nearby. She tried to recall if they had crossed one before but pushed the thought aside. Liam's instruction was to follow the river, and this added to her confidence. She walked for several minutes before, suddenly, there was a new sound – quick splashes in the water, like someone wading through it.

Her body tensed, every muscle on high alert. The splashes stopped, and then she heard faint footsteps, the sound of someone walking on dirt. Gwen's heart raced, her eyes searching the darkness for any movement. Could it be a deer, like the ones she had seen the first day on her way up the mountain? She clung to that thought, but it didn't stop her from quickening her pace.

A sharp crack rang out, like a branch snapping, and Gwen froze. Her comforting thoughts of deer vanished, replaced by the image of the dark figure that had nearly gotten her earlier. A shiver ran through her, the forest suddenly feeling far more dangerous. In the distance, she thought she could hear the shrill laughing of a woman. *Wait, was that real or did I imagine it?* The thought seemed to hit her square in the chest, and she stopped walking and looked in the apparent direction of the sounds.

She finally took a step back, moving off the trail, her breath quickening. From one of her ankles she felt pain. It felt like a cut or a blister that had been aggravated by rubbing against something. She looked down, pulling her pant leg up. In the dark she couldn't see anything, but the pain was there and seemed to go all the way around her ankle. She wondered if it was a remnant of that creature's tight grasp on her legs before. She then heard more noises, quiet but there. It sounded like something or someone breathing several feet away.

She backed up another step, uncertain how to proceed. Then like a spark, she remembered it, the item Liam had given her. She felt it dangling against her chest and quickly gripped it in her hands, clutching at it. She listened intently but silence pressed in, the weight of it almost unbearable.

Another snap, closer this time and more of the loud breathing. Gwen held her own breath and pulled the pocket watch over her head, holding it in front of her like a shield. The silence stretched on, broken only by the occasional rustle in the distance. Finally, she heard it – another branch breaking, more hurried footsteps, and then the retreating sound of splashing in the water, growing fainter by the second. Whatever it was, seems to have been scared away.

She exhaled sharply, realizing only then how long she'd been holding her breath. The thought of a startled deer returned to her mind, and she forced herself to believe it, pushing away the darker thoughts.

Looking back along the trail, she was startled to see what looked like the cabin, not far down the path. Relief washed over her. *Another small victory for me.*

Finally crossing the familiar yard, she approached the shop, its exterior looking ominous in the darkness. She now understood why Sarah had been so unnerved by it. The dark windows and wide-open doors sent a fresh wave of unease through her. It looked like something out of a murder mystery.

Gwen shook off the feeling and pulled the chain from her shoulder, threading it through the metal handles of the now closed shop doors. With a click, the padlock secured the chain, completing the circuit, and locking the door tightly.

Satisfied, she turned and headed toward the back door of the cabin, carefully avoiding the shattered glass scattered on the ground. She pulled the door shut and secured it as well as she could.

39

Vikar

31 October 1712

A cold wind blew through the open barn, swirling bits of hay in the air before they drifted back down. Alexander glanced up at the night sky, noticing for the first time how late it had become. He grabbed his jacket from a peg and slipped it on, the fabric stiff with the cold.

He stepped back, inspecting the small crib. It wasn't quite finished, but another glance at the darkening sky told him it could wait another day. The rough rag he had used to clean the wood was tossed into a long wooden toolbox, and he began putting his tools away with slow, careful care.

Footsteps crunched on the gravel outside. Benjamin's familiar silhouette appeared in the doorway; a large sack of grain slung over his shoulder. He dropped it onto the growing pile with a grunt, brushing his hands on his trousers.

He smiled, his eyes catching sight of the crib. "Aye, fine craftsmanship, little brother. It should keep your new daughter well."

Alexander smirked. "Son," he teased back, wiping his hands on his chest. He felt the rough grain of sawdust still clinging to his skin. "Though, I'd not mind a daughter, either." He glanced back at the crib, pride swelling briefly before the night's chill settled deeper into his bones. "I'm late for supper. Will you be joining us?"

"My thanks, but I'm late myself. Best get home lest Mary scold me again." Benjamin chuckled, but as he turned to leave, his expression sobered. He stared at Alexander, seeming to attempt to assess his thoughts. Alexander had seen this look many times in the last months.

Alexander forced a smile, though his throat tightened. "I'm well, Ben. Truly."

Ben nodded, a tentative smile on his lips. "Please, do let me know if you ever feel the need to speak of it. We've not spoken of the fire since that day."

He forced the knot in his stomach back down as the thought of that terrible day returned to his mind. He could still see the burned house and charred remains of the Vikar bodies in his mind. A memory of Margaret's sweet face flashed in his head adding salt to the wound, but he pressed it down.

"I am well, brother."

Benjamin's eyes lingered for a moment before he nodded. "Give my regards to Elizabeth – and to Mother."

"I shall." He used his sleeve to wipe a tear from his eyes and then tugged a thick blanket over the crib, securing it before locking up the barn.

The wind picked up, carrying with it the first whispers of an oncoming storm. He pulled his jacket tighter as he walked toward the house. Above, the stars twinkled against the inky sky, indifferent to the fading unease in his gut.

The large metal handle of the door clunked as he lifted it, and the door swung open with a heavy thud. "Forgive me for being late!" he called into the house. Silence answered. He frowned, glancing toward the dimly lit kitchen. Candles flickered on the table, set for supper, but no one was there.

His brow furrowed as he walked through the hall, checking the parlor and the stairs leading up to the bedrooms – no light, no sound.

"Elizabeth?" he called, more softly now.

Something was wrong.

His pulse quickened as he moved toward the back of the house. The back door was slightly ajar, swaying gently in the breeze. He froze as he turned the corner.

There, on the kitchen floor, lay a body.

"Mother!" he gasped, dropping to his knees beside her. Her form had been twisted unnaturally, her face contorted in a rictus of pain, her eyes wide open and unseeing. There was a meat cleaver near her outstretched hand.

His voice cracked as he cried, panic rising in his throat. He tried to rouse her, shaking her gently, but the truth settled in, cold and final. His mind spun violently until it settled. *Where is my Elizabeth?*

Reluctantly, he staggered to his feet, backing out of the kitchen and bolting up the stairs two at a time. He tore through the bedrooms, checking every space, every corner. They were empty. The sheets on the beds were untouched, the attic silent.

He leaned over the banister, gasping for breath, his eyes drawn back to the open door.

"Elizabeth!" he shouted into the night as he ran outside, his feet pounding across the field toward the guest house.

"Please Lord, no…"

He stumbled, his foot catching on a stone, sending him sprawling face-first into the dirt, his head barely missing a larger rock. A sharp pain shot through his chest as he scrambled back to his feet, his pulse pounding in his ears.

The guest house loomed ahead, dimly lit and eerily still.

He flung the door open, his breath coming in ragged gasps. The room was in chaos – furniture overturned, glass shattered, plates broken and strewn about the floor. A suffocating sense of dread clawed at his throat as he surveyed the mess.

"Elizabeth! Are you here?!"

He gingerly walked around the mess, deeper into the large foyer. Then, he felt it – a presence. His eyes darted to the far side of the room, where a lone chair sat facing away from him. In it, a figure sat, long black hair spilling over the back of the chair and nearly touching the floor.

His fists clenched, his breath shallow with rage.

"It is about time you arrived," said the figure, calmly.

"Agatha?" he asked, a fresh flood of emotions filling his chest. His head spun, feeling conflicted between surprise, fear, and anger. "Is that you? But how did…"

The figure interjected, laughing; a cold, mirthless sound that made his skin crawl. "Oh, Alexander. Still unable to tell us Vikars apart. Or is that more pretense?"

The thought of his mother's dead body rekindled his anger, and he took a step toward her. "Where is she? Where's Elizabeth?"

She stood then and began walking toward him, her movements unnaturally smooth, the chair scraping across the floor as she dragged it behind her. Her bare feet made no sound as she stepped toward him, her grin widening into something grotesque, something not of this world.

He stepped back at the sight. The dim candlelight flickered, casting long shadows across her face, revealing it to him.

"No! How?"

He stumbled back over a broken chair, crashing to the ground. His head slammed against the floor, and stars flickered in his sight. His eyes widened as the shock began to overtake him. She was then above him, the chair still in her hands.

"Margaret," he stammered, and then began to get up. With inhuman speed, she slammed the chair down onto his chest, the force knocking him back to the ground and the wind out of him. A sharp jolt of pain shot through his ribs as he gasped, struggling to breathe. She straddled the chair, pinning him to the cold, unforgiving floor. She leaned down, her face hovering several inches above his, her breath hot and seeping into his senses like poison. This wasn't the beautiful and delicate woman he'd fallen in love with, this was something else.

"Surprised to see me, my love?"

"What have you done?" he managed to get out. The shock was still there, a tangible mass that seemed to sit in his chest, stepping on his heart. He stared at her face, still with many of the beautiful features that he'd loved, but now her countenance was changed, as if all happiness had been supplanted by something malevolent.

"I've done what you couldn't. I've made it so you may keep your promise. You are quite welcome."

Alexander felt a fresh batch of pain lurch through his body as the chair pressed on his ribs. "What have you done with

Elizabeth?"

She slammed a fist against the chair, adding to the pain. "Would you like to know, Alexander?" He lay aghast at the sight of her grotesque mouth as it stretched into a wide vicious smile. It reminded him of something. It was the same smile that he'd come to recognize Agatha by. He shuddered at the thought.

"Should I tell you where your sweet Elizabeth is?"

He groaned, muscles quivering as he pushed against the chair. It didn't budge. Something freakish was holding him in place – her strength, her presence, felt monstrous, beyond human. Spittle dripped long and disturbingly from her mouth and landed on his face.

He tried to speak but nothing came.

She let out a long malevolent laugh. "She is here with me, Alexander. I have her and here she will stay."

"Lies!" he managed to croak.

She laughed again, savoring every moment until she closed her eyes and then opened them again. Elizabeth's familiar green eyes stared back at him – unmistakable, beautiful, but entirely wrong.

"No… Please, Margaret… What must I do to undo this?"

"There is no undoing this, Alexander! You caused this! You broke your promise! I warned you yet you did it despite yourself! "

"No," he managed to say, air rasping as he choked out each word. "I did nothing… It was you, Raven. It was you… who left us."

She flinched at the nickname. It seemed to cut deep within her, slicing away layers of the unholy force that had possessed her. It was a token of their love, bringing her back. Her face, moments before twisted into a devilish form, now looked youthful. Her beautiful brown eyes fluttered and she looked into his. Alexander saw the longing there – saw the desperate love that she once had for him. He saw the red color return to her lips, and they pouted and quivered as a tear fell from her eyes. "Alexander... I love you... why did you betray me?"

He stared into her eyes, a bittersweet pang in his heart, mourning for the woman that he'd lost. "What is it that you've done, Margaret? This is not you."

Another tear fell down her cheek. "Alexander... stay with me? I'm scared."

"No, Margaret. That time has passed. I love... Elizabeth," he said through clenched teeth.

She screamed and the evil facade slowly returned, and she sprayed more hot spit on his face as she yelled. "Then you are no better than a liar! You will pay for this, Alexander." She pointed a finger at his head.

His mind fractured, reeling with the weight of her power. In his mind's eye, a vision of Margaret and her sisters completing the ritual that sealed the powerful curse. He recognized the large circle from Claire's room. He saw a dark demon being pulled from a dark portal. It fought as if iron chains pulled it slowly to Margaret and eventually bound it to her. She screamed in agony as it got closer to her. She had obviously not intended for this to happen, and the creature bound itself to her, easily overpowering her. A bright green flame sprang from the dark passage that quickly engulfed the bedroom. The Vikars struggled to escape but it quickly devoured all there. The vision began to fade and the last thing he saw was Margaret, naked and untouched by the flames as it fed on the rest of the home. His eyes flickered open to

Margaret now standing over him.

With unnatural ease, she ripped the chair from his chest and tossed it aside as though it were nothing more than a feather. It exploded into kindling on the far wall. He gasped, but before he could catch his breath, her hands were on him. She seized his jacket, lifting him as if he weighed no more than a child. Her grip was iron – unyielding, suffocating. He struggled, but it was futile, like being trapped in the jaws of a beast.

In one brutal motion, she hurled him across the room. His body slammed into the dining table, the wood splintering beneath him as he crashed through it, sending shards flying in all directions. Pain exploded in his back and ribs; his vision blurred as he gasped for breath.

She stalked toward him, slow and deliberate, savoring his agony. Her smile was gone, replaced by a dark hunger in her eyes. As she loomed over him, she reached down and grabbed him again, her grip like iron. She lifted him effortlessly high above her head, her face twisting into something more monstrous than before. Her eyes gleamed with a demonic light, her features warping with malevolence.

There was a gruesome look on her face, and Alexander braced for further impact. But she did nothing. Her expression was frozen.

Her eyes were drawn to something dangling from his vest pocket. The small, brass pocket watch – the one she had given him long ago – swung gently, glinting in the dim light. It slipped from its place and looped around her head and neck like a necklace.

Her expression contorted into a mixture of rage and fear. A shrill scream tore from her throat, piercing the air. She dropped him back into the rubble, clutching her head and chest in agony. Her body began to tremble, her movements erratic. Her flesh at her chest sizzled, black smoke curling from her skin as if she were burning from the inside out.

Alexander, dazed and aching, scrambled backward over the broken table and watched in horror as Margaret's form writhed, the smoke thickening, swirling around her in a suffocating cloud. Her screams became garbled, unnatural, echoing with an otherworldly resonance. Her form changed within the smoke into what looked like a large grotesque monster and then seemed to shrink again.

And then, as suddenly as it began, the smoke collapsed, slapping against the floor with a deafening silence. It dissipated into nothingness, leaving behind only the faint scent of ash and something darker.

The candles nearby flickered out, plunging the room into a cold, heavy darkness. The wind blew through the broken windows, chilling him. He continued to stay still for a moment, his breath ragged.

Was it over?

Wincing at the sharp pain that shot through his battered body, he finally stood. The room was too dark to see clearly, but there was no sign of Margaret. She was gone.

And then he heard it – a soft, trembling whimper. It had come from the spot where Margaret had been.

His heart lurched and he scrambled forward, tripping over the ruin. He continued crawling toward the small form until he was close enough to see her.

"Elizabeth!"

She was sprawled on the floor, her face pale and tear-streaked, her body trembling. He pulled her into his arms, cradling her against his chest. Tears streamed from his eyes as he cradled her. She slowly came to, putting her arms around him.

"I thought I lost you, Dove," he cried, pulling her closer.

For a moment, the world around them fell silent, the horrors of the night retreating into the shadows as they clung to one another. Then, a small glint of light caught his eye – a faint shimmer around her neck. Margaret's watch. It seared her skin, sending a faint wisp of smoke into the air. Elizabeth stirred weakly, a faint moan of pain escaping her lips. Without hesitation, he tore it from her neck and flung it far into the darkness.

Elizabeth let out a long, trembling sigh and went limp in his arms, her weight heavy against him. He pulled her closer again, burying his face in her hair. He listened to her labored breathing as she slept. Then softly, unexpectedly – he felt it. A faint, rhythmic thump against his leg.

His breath caught and then he remembered. Disbelieving, he lowered a trembling hand to her rounded belly. Another gentle flutter met his touch, fragile yet full of life. His chest tightened, and a sob broke free. Tears streamed down his face, falling onto hers. Against all odds and Margaret's wrath, their child had survived.

40

The Decision

Clark finished the long drive to the second barricade, threw the gear into park, and kicked open the door of his cruiser. The creak of the door seemed unnaturally loud in the oppressive silence, and his nerves were already raw. Stepping out, he instinctively drew both his flashlight and service weapon. His hands shook slightly as the beam of the flashlight swept over the wreckage in front of him – the cruiser's front side was smashed in, the metal crumpled like foil.

The headache he'd been nursing returned with a vengeance and a wave of nausea hit him as he took in the sight. He had hoped, maybe foolishly, that the wreck wouldn't be here, that somehow Andy had driven off and would be safe. But seeing it now, mangled and abandoned, only deepened the fear he felt deep in his gut.

He swallowed hard and inched closer to the vehicle, his heart pounding against his ribs. His mind flashed back to the conversation he'd had with Steve, Melissa's husband – Sarah's aunt and uncle. The temptation of easy money had driven him to make the worst decision of his life. He hadn't believed them fully, not at first, about the creature. But the money... the allure of it had clouded his judgment, and he had convinced himself it was just a job. A job he needed, or so he had told himself.

But deep down, he knew now it was greed that had driven his decision. Greed and the deep desire to hide his large gambling debts and other addictions.

He remembered that night vividly. Steve had told him the plan: break into the house, release the woman from the well, and keep Liam at bay but on the mountain; that was basically it minus a few minor instructions. Simple. And when he had asked why, Steve had brushed it off, telling him he didn't want to know. *And I wish I'd left it at that.* Steve had finally told him nearly everything after some heavy coaxing. *In retrospect, I should have taken his advice.*

The basement had been easy to find in Liam's house, just as Steve described. Removing the boards sealing the door? Even easier. The hardest part had been when he reached the well. The stench was unforgettable. As soon as he lifted the wooden cover, the foul odor of death and decay hit him, nearly making him vomit. And then there was the weeping. It sounded like a woman, fragile and vulnerable.

He, ignoring Steve's orders, had looked inside the hole. The woman had been down there, staring up at him, her face helpless and in pain. In that moment, something inside him had wavered. He had almost called it off, almost walked away from the job. No amount of money was worth this.

But then the woman changed. One blink and she was no longer human. Her delicate features twisted, morphing into something monstrous. He had bolted, not looking back once, fear taking over. Since then, he hadn't been able to sleep, haunted by the strangeness of the woman. Then his fear had been verified when he witnessed the transformation later in that very basement. He'd almost lost his life when that crazy old man hit him with a coat rack. He had been lucky that the creature left without attacking him. Now he worried that his best friend had taken his place and hadn't been so lucky.

His flashlight swept the interior of Andy's wrecked vehicle, the beam reflecting off shards of glass and landing on splotches of dried blood speckled across the dash. "No... Coop," he muttered, his breath catching in his throat.

Andy hadn't wanted to be part of this. Clark had manipulated him, convincing him it was a quick, easy payday. He'd even used Steve's same trick, playing on Andy's concerns. It was too easy; he just used his newborn son and dangled the promise of college money in front of him. And now his best friend was missing, or worse.

Tears welled up in Clark's eyes as he clutched the flashlight tighter. He'd betrayed Andy and he'd betrayed his family.

"Please be alive. Please please please..."

He circled the car, calling Andy's name into the cold night air. "Andy!" His fear of the creature gnawed at the edges of his voice, but he shouted anyway.

Suddenly, a glimmer of hope sparked. He pulled out the two-way radio he and Andy had been using. "Come in, Cooper. You there, pal?" He waited, but silence answered. He pressed the button again. This time, he heard a faint beep, echoing from somewhere nearby.

Clark followed the sound, his flashlight swinging across the trees until it caught a glint of yellow. His pulse quickened, and he rushed over, hoping to find Andy there. But it was just the radio, lying near a tree. His stomach twisted into knots.

Then, a sound. A faint, rhythmic dripping.

He swept his flashlight towards it, and his heart stopped. Blood – dark, viscous – was pooling at the base of the tree. Clark's light traced the source, slowly revealing the body hanging above. Andy's lifeless form was tangled in the branches, his unblinking eyes staring down.

Clark stared at his partner's lifeless body, trying to make sense of it. His head spun as he considered the consequences. The weight of everything – his betrayal, the money, the death – sank into him like a heavy stone. How could he possibly explain this to anyone? His friend at the station already suspected something, and the phone call earlier had rattled him with too many pointed questions. *What do I even do now? Sandy was already asking too many questions.* He slammed his fist into his leg and swore loudly.

"Do you kiss your mother with that mouth?" It was a woman's voice, and it came from the direction of his police cruiser. He raised his flashlight, his hand trembling toward the car, the beam of light cutting through the dark. Silence. But the voice had certainly been real. His breathing quickened, his senses on high alert.

As Clark edged toward the car, a small shiver ran through his body. His grip tightened around the gun.

A woman was now perched on the hood of his cruiser.

His heart fluttered and he thought about the woman he'd encountered before. But she wasn't the creature he remembered from the well. That woman had wild, red curls and bright green eyes. This one had sleek, straight black hair, and dark eyes, her expression was different – almost playful.

She sat casually, dressed only in Coop's police jacket. The realization hit him like a punch to the gut. *Coop's jacket.*

Reading his thoughts, she smirked. "Well, it's cold out in the forest. Thought I'd try it on, you like it?" Her voice was smooth, almost teasing. He recoiled, taking a cautious step back.

"Oh, don't run away from me, officer," she purred, her voice dripping with a dangerous edge. "I'm not going to bite you."

Everything about this screamed wrong. His instincts yelled at him to run, to fight, to do anything but stand there. He raised his gun.

"Oh, are you going to shoot me now? No, I don't think you will."

The eerie smile twisted into something darker as her tone shifted.

"What do you want?" Clark stammered, trying to sound commanding but hearing the fear in his own voice.

"You know what I want. Stop playing the fool!"

Her sudden fury made him flinch, and he took another step back. But just as quickly, her smile returned, sinister and full of malice.

"You have a decision to make," she said, sliding off the hood with fluid grace. He noticed her legs were wet and her bare feet, covered in dark mud. She circled him, predatory, her eyes never leaving his. "You can die here, like your friend…" She glanced toward the tree where Andy's body hung lifeless. "Or you can help me get that brat away from that McGregor. You do that, and maybe… just maybe, you'll live. You might even get to go back to your family and clean this mess up."

His mind raced. *How did I get here and what do I do?*

"You'll find a way," she continued, stepping aside to reveal the open door of his cruiser. "Your choice, officer. Help me, or I'll kill you and everyone that cares about you."

Her sneer cut through him like a knife. His heart hammered in his chest as he quickly weighed his options. Could he really go through with this? Sarah would certainly be killed. She made that evident on his partner. Or could he simply walk away and try to leave town with his family? The reality of the choice loomed over him like a shadow, dark and heavy.

"If I do this, you'll let me live?"

The woman's smile widened, becoming even more wicked. "Do you really have a choice, officer?"

Finally, Clark's resistance crumbled. He lowered his head in defeat and shook his head. His hand trembled as he holstered his sidearm. He didn't have a choice. Slowly, almost mechanically, he walked back to his cruiser, giving the woman – *the creature* – a wide berth. Each step felt like he was moving through thick mud, his heart sinking deeper into despair.

Sliding into the driver's seat, he gripped the steering wheel, trying to shake off the overwhelming sense of dread that clung to him. He couldn't escape it. *It's over.*

As he pushed the key into the ignition, he dared to look at her one last time. The playful, human-like facade had vanished. She had already slipped the jacket off, tossing it carelessly through the open car window. "Didn't fit me anyway," she said with a mocking smile. "Isolate the girl and I'll do the rest." Her voice echoed with that same dark playfulness, but her form was now changing.

His eyes widened in horror as the familiar grotesque transformation began. Her pale skin darkened, elongating and twisting until the woman was no longer recognizable.

She was the creature once more, its eyes black and barely visible, full of malice and triumph. The creature then leaped and sprinted into the forest, much faster than humanly possible.

He watched it disappear and then turned his gaze away, his hands tightening on the steering wheel, fighting the hopelessness. There was no running now. He'd made his choice.

He was hers.

The car engine roared to life, and without looking back, he drove into the darkness, his mind swirling with regret and fear.

41

Poetry

15 July 1714

Her scream tore through the quiet, yanking Alexander from his sleep, as it had so many nights before. He reached out in the dark, his fingers brushing against her trembling form. Elizabeth's body was soaked through with sweat, her frail frame rocking back and forth uncontrollably beneath the covers.

"Elizabeth. My Dove. Wake up," he whispered, his voice soft but edged with exhaustion. He shook her gently, as if afraid she might break. Her rocking slowed, but soon her quiet sobs filled the room, muffled by the pillow.

He gathered her to him, wrapping an arm around her clammy skin. He pulled the damp blankets away and wiped her brow with his sleeve. His hand fumbled in the darkness for the glass of water on the bedside table, pressing the cool glass to her fevered cheek.

Her hand trembled as she took the cup. "More, please?" Her voice was ragged, barely above a whisper. The cup rattled slightly as he took it from her.

"Of course, my love." He kissed her forehead, but her skin was already slick with sweat again. He lit a candle, its small flame flickering against the oppressive dark. The wavering light cast shadows across her face, pale and gaunt. Her eyes, once bright and sharp, now appeared sunken.

"Hurry back."

"I'll be but a few moments, love."

Night after night, the terrors had come for her, more frequently, more violently. Downstairs, he refilled the cup, swallowing down his own thirst as he closed his eyes to steady himself. Since that cursed night with Margaret, Elizabeth had begun to gradually change – her quick wit dulled, her memory fractured. But it was more than that; strange behaviors had begun to surface, ones that filled him with an unnamed dread. Today, he'd found her standing at the sink, her hand frozen inside a glass, unmoving, as if suspended in time. He had called her name twice before she blinked back to life as though nothing had happened. He shook his head at the memory.

He climbed the stairs again, each step heavier than the last. A terrible memory flashed in his mind: Margaret's twisted smile on that night. He forced it down, focusing on the task at hand. He quickly checked on their daughter, who was still fast asleep, and then continued on to their room. When he re-entered the bedroom he immediately froze.

Black eyes stared back at him.

The candlelight flickered revealing Margaret's face. Long black hair, that playful smile – a nightmare made flesh. She leaned back against the wall and shot him a playful, almost seductive smile. She raised a hand and slowly beckoned him to come. She then patted the bed next to her.

Dumbstruck, he stepped backwards, his elbow hitting the doorframe, knocking the candle to the floor. The room went dark. Eyes wide with shock, he tried to peer through the nearly pitch black room. There was no sound except for his own quick breathing. After a minute, he fumbled around, righting the candle and getting it lit.

As the light filled the room, standing inches from him was Margaret, those black eyes, wide and seeming to stare through him. Before he could fully react, she began to speak in an eerily monotone voice. It was something like a poem, dark and twisted. He tried to make sense of it but the blank stare on her face was too much to allow him to focus. When she finally finished, the candle blew out and the room was dark again.

He then heard Elizabeth's voice. "Is that you, Alex?" He let out a loud sigh and leaned over clutching at his knee with his free hand. He worked to relax his shoulders and felt his legs go weak. He steadied himself and then slowly shuffled to the bed until she clutched his arm with icy fingers and took what was left of the water from him. "I don't like it when you have to leave me at night. I hate the dark. I have horrible dreams, Alex."

She drank quickly, hands still shaking, before thrusting the cup back at him. He barely had time to set it down before she pulled him into the bed, clutching him as though afraid he might vanish.

He felt himself shaking as he recalled what had just happened. He could feel her body, it was cold now. He pulled her close. "I'm here, love. No need to be afraid. It was just a dream."

A small whimper escaped her lips. "They don't feel like dreams. They feel real."

He swallowed hard. "Are they still the same ones?"

"Always the same." Her voice faded as she began to drift off again. "She was there tonight… she wants me to do things… horrible things…" She twitched suddenly, jerking awake for a moment. "But those dreams aren't the worst. It's the ones with him. The dark thing… He hurts me, Alex…" Her voice trailed off again as sleep overtook her.

He lay awake, staring into the pitch-black void of the ceiling, the weight of the night's events pressing heavily upon him. Beside him, her soft breathing steadied, a reminder of her presence. He turned over, willing himself to sleep, yet his thoughts refused to relent. This wasn't the first time he'd seen Margaret in Elizabeth's features. Over the past few months, there had been fleeting gestures, subtle inflections, and faint glimpses that stirred memories of her. He had tried to dismiss them as tricks of his mind, desperate to believe they were nothing more. But tonight had changed everything. He was certain now – Margaret lingered within Elizabeth, hidden somewhere beneath the surface.

Fragments of the dark poem played over and over in his mind and despite the missing pieces, he kept trying to fill in the gaps. Hours passed and he would see sunlight before he would finally find sleep.

42

The Curse

L iam winced and grunted as Sarah worked on sewing the hole shut on the back of his right shoulder. He'd remarked more than once how lucky he'd been that the bullet had gone all the way through rather than getting lodged.

She wasn't much of a seamstress, and every push of the needle made her grimace. "I'm making a mess back here."

"Nonsense. You're doing fine," he said, taking another swig from the flask in his bag. "I've always had to do it myself with a hot iron. Hell with that."

Her hands shook, but not because of the wound. When Liam had pulled out the thread, needle, and alcohol, she'd thought it was bad enough. But nothing prepared her for the sight when he removed his shirt. The gunshot wounds seemed like scratches compared to the map of scars spread across his torso. She'd asked him what they were from, but he simply waved her off and mumbled what sounded like a name under his breath. *Margery? Or was it Margaret?*

"What did you call these again?" He held up a couple of

bright orange corn chips, his words starting to slur.

"Serious? You've really never had them before?"

"Delicious," Liam belched, clearly feeling the effects of the alcohol.

With the last stitch in place, Sarah sighed in relief. She grabbed a wet rag and wiped the dried blood as gently as she could. "All done you old sailor."

Liam grunted again and stuffed another chip into his mouth. Sarah packed the bloody tools, rolled up the rag, and shoved everything into the large bag. She pulled her chair around to face him, arms crossed, eyes locked. Her expression was expectant.

Liam tossed the bowl of chips aside and looked at her. "What? You want a tip?" He let out a low belch again.

Sarah didn't respond, her silence pressing him.

"Fine then," he muttered. "I've told this story a few times. Might as well tell you too."

Sarah leaned back, putting her feet up on the coffee table.

He stared at the table, his mind somewhere far away. "One of my ancestors was named Alexander McGregor, from Scotland or, eh, England... one of those. He married a woman named Elizabeth Wrenkle, beautiful and kind, so the family stories say. It was during a time of witch hunts – witchcraft hysteria as you may have read about. People were obsessed with it. Many women were falsely accused, including poor Elizabeth." He paused, taking another swig from his flask, his eyes clouded with memories. "Something did happen *to* her but not *by* her as far as I know. One day she was normal, and the next... Something had changed. According to Alexander's journals, she started having nightmares, falling into trances. It wasn't long before people whispered that she was in fact a witch or something else. They were terrified of her. Used to call her 'The Wrenkle.' To protect his wife, Alexander eventually moved them out to the highlands, away from the rumors and away from as many humans as possible."

Sarah nodded, her fingers gripping the armrests of her chair.

"They had a family, lived fairly quietly. But eventually, people moved in around them again, it was like they were drawn to her. Then folks, mostly women, started disappearing, and the old accusations came back." Liam leaned forward; his tone grim. "But this time... the accusations weren't just rumors. Elizabeth had changed. Alexander had learned of her... err... condition and tried to help her, tried to protect her, even as he learned the truth."

"The truth?" Sarah asked, leaning forward.

He stopped, listening to heavy footsteps from above. Both of them froze. He grabbed the gun at his side.

"Officers?" Sarah whispered.

After a moment, he shook his head. "Too loud. I think our little Firecracker is back." He relaxed, placing the gun back on the couch.

The basement door slammed, and Sarah let out a startled yelp. Loud, heavy footsteps descended the stairs.

"Can someone help me, please?" Gwen's voice was muffled behind a pile of supplies, her entrance both alarming and comical.

"Welcome back. Think the entire county heard you? Head back up and make sure," Liam said with a smirk.

Gwen set down her load and grinned unapologetically. "Very funny, Liam."

"Is that... sandwiches and fruit?" Sarah asked, incredulous.

"From the refrigerator? We can't have lights on, Gwen!"

"I was starving, and I needed the good stuff. You know I get cranky without the good stuff."

Liam's frown deepened, but he reached for a sandwich. "Hand one over." He paused and then saw the object around her neck. "What did I tell you? Put that in your pocket, out of sight."

Gwen tossed him a sandwich and then pulled the pocket watch from her neck and stuffed it in her pocket, rolling her eyes. Then she turned to Sarah. "Your aunt is tiny. I could barely find anything that fits." She threw a clean set of clothes into Sarah's lap. "Liam, I found this for you." She tossed him an oversized Hawaiian print shirt. On the left pocket of the shirt, it said 'Black Coast Insurance.'

Liam grunted and tossed the shirt aside, focusing back on the conversation. They ate in relative silence, Sarah catching Gwen up on the story.

"So… Elizabeth's curse," Sarah ventured once they were finished, "does that explain the creature?"

Liam paused, nodding. "Yes. You see, witchcraft isn't an old wives' tale as modern science would claim… but in this case Elizabeth wasn't the witch. She was an unfortunate pawn in someone else's plan. In fact, according to Alexander's journals, there were several people he discovered being caught up in the devilry. And the Wrenkle curse, as the villagers coined it, was real, it affected both families: McGregor and Wrenkle.

"Are those chips?"

Sarah slid the bowl to Gwen, but her eyes never left Liam. "How does it work?"

"Well, according to the stories and writings, there are three parts to it. Elizabeth's part is to walk the earth forever, never aging, unable to pass on. To others, she appears to be human but she's something else, undead or immortal. And bound to her is a demon – insatiable, filled with an eternal hunger to consume others, causing them to share a similar fate to Elizabeth. His part, surprisingly enough, is no different than hers; he doesn't want to be here and hates the one that put him there."

"How on earth do you know that?"

Liam looked at Gwen and shuddered. "That is a tale for another time, Firecracker."

"And… my mother… did she know about this?"

Liam looked back at Sarah, his voice barely above a whisper. "Your mother was consumed by the Wrenkle. She didn't die in that fire like you were told. She was taken, fed to the beast by your aunt – a selfish act to save her own soul and feed Steve and Melissa's dark schemes. I'm sorry, lass, it's the truth."

Sarah froze, trying to absorb his words. Tears stung her eyes as reality settled in. It was starting to fit together. The ongoing dreams, the vision of the women she'd seen. The beast she'd seen chained to the floor. That black-haired woman in the chair.

"You mentioned the one that put them there. Do you mean the person that created the curse? Who are you referring to?"

"I don't really like to say her name, but I'll tell you. Alexander mentions her name a lot in his writings and findings. Her name is Margaret."

"Margaret, that one that gave you all those scars?"

"You need not worry about her, lass. She's been bound and locked up deep inside the depths of the demon for many years." His eyes flickered to the bulge in Gwen's pocket. "I've met her many times. Best to not talk about her," he said, while rubbing an old scar on his face.

Sarah shifted in her seat, she still had too many questions. "Why my mother? Why me?"

"Oh that's the simple part. You and your mother are of the Wrenkle line, or I should say, you have the Wrenkle bloodline. The demon feeds on any female souls that share that bloodline."

"Feeds?" Gwen said, spitting out her drink. "What does that mean?"

Liam snatched up one of the chips in front of her and tossed it in his mouth. "Not like that. The best way I can describe it is that they are sort of absorbed and are imprisoned somewhere inside." He grabbed another chip and put it in his mouth. "I witnessed it once. I think you have some experience with this, lass. The creature, that demon, emits some sort of cold black smoke that envelops its victims. When the smoke clears, the person is gone, body and all."

Sarah's breath hitched. "So… my mother is inside that creature?"

Liam sighed, anticipating her next line of questioning. "Lass, there's no way to save her. Believe me, people have tried. I have tried. None know how. It always ends in more deaths."

Sarah leaned forward in her chair to press the issue, but he shook his head.

"I've tried."

Sarah slumped back into her chair and looked at her feet.

"And how are you involved? You said the McGregors are also part of this?" Gwen asked, breaking the silence.

Liam looked at her, his smile bittersweet. "Yes, the Mc-

Gregors share the curse. We're bound to protect those with Wrenkle bloodlines, bound to care for each one even though we know we'll have to watch as each one is consumed. We're simply drawn to it. I can't really explain it. We care for each Wrenkle, and we are forced to endure as the curse takes them one after another."

A single tear fell down his cheek and he turned to Sarah. "Your grandfather, a very good man, was my friend. He kept you safe as long as he could. That was his part. He did a pretty good job of it too."

Sarah reached out, holding his hand as tears filled his eyes. "So... we're family."

"Aye," Liam whispered, his voice thick with emotion. "Once or twice removed. You used to call me Uncle in fact. You probably don't recall. Used to check in on you and your Grandfather Jensen... make sure you were okay." He paused, staring at nothing and then reached over and yanked the clean shirt next to him. He then awkwardly pulled it over his head and Gwen tugged the right side over his injured arm. "Thanks, Firecracker." He then let out a loud yawn.

"Girls, I haven't slept for days. I think that's enough for tonight. We should get some sleep. We'll need to take shifts to watch the door."

"I'll go first," Gwen said, brightly, the tension in the room easing slightly. "Couple of questions, though. What do I do if I hear something?"

"I'm a light sleeper, just wake me."

"And, what about these objects you gave us? What are they and should we try to use them if that... creature... thing comes in?"

"They're powerful and no you shouldn't have to use them.

I'll tell you about them in the morning." His eyes were closed now but one of them popped open. "However, that one," he pointed to a circular bulge in her pocket. "We use it when all else fails and only then."

With another loud yawn, he pushed the pistol with his foot to her and closed both his eyes again. It wasn't more than a few minutes and the sounds of snoring rumbled from his chest.

"Well, that was a lot to take in," Gwen whispered, her forehead puckering as she glanced at Sarah. "You gonna be alright?"

Sarah nodded, though her gaze remained fixed on the table. "It's a lot to think about, but I'm too tired to make sense of it right now."

"Not me... I'm weirdly jazzed for some reason. That walk through the forest was scary... but oddly satisfying. Once I even thought I heard something following me but with old rusty, I felt safe." She patted the pocket watch in her pocket.

"The watch? Must be like this." Sarah said, pointing to the red fabric on the table.

Gwen began fiddling with the pistol, her eyes focused down the sights as she practiced aiming it.

"Point that thing away from me," Liam grumbled, his one eye open again.

"Oops, sorry! Never held one before."

"Hmph, city girls. Get some sleep, Sarah, you're up next for the shift."

Sarah nodded, watching as his breathing slowed, and he drifted into sleep once more. She lingered there, studying his face, her thoughts swirling. Not even a week ago, she had harbored doubts about him, questioning his motives and fearing he might be dangerous. But now, as she sat in the quiet, everything had changed.

He was no predator – he was something far more complicated, far more human. His life had been hard, his body and soul bearing scars of pain she could only begin to imagine. She wondered if he had ever known the softness of childhood, or if the curse had stolen that from him too.

Tears welled up in her eyes again, the weight of unspoken emotions settling deep within her chest. A smile tugged at her lips, fragile and bittersweet. *I have another family member. A good one,* she thought. For the first time in what felt like ages, the word *family* didn't seem so foreign.

She stayed there, watching him, as the moments slipped away into the stillness of the night, before her own exhaustion took over and she dozed off, a quiet sense of peace settling over her.

43

Cruelty

10 March 1725

"Leave her be, Charlie!" came a sharp yell from behind Lucy. She recognized the voice faintly but couldn't be certain. It sounded like one of the Edisbury sisters who often walked this way after school. Lucy hesitated but kept her head down, focusing on the dirt path ahead. She preferred the main road home, where she could glance at the lake and let her mind drift, but lately, even that small comfort wasn't worth the risk. Charlie and his friends had made sure of that, with their taunts, shoves, and unkind laughter.

Her friends – if they could still be called that – had begun to ignore her over the past few weeks. Some joined the mocking, while others stayed silent, leaving her to fend for herself.

A tear slipped down her cheek, but she kept her chin high, determined not to give Charlie the satisfaction. Still, she couldn't ignore the sound of approaching footsteps and hushed giggles behind her. They were following her today. She quickened her pace, but the group matched it easily.

"And why should I, eh? Just having a bit of fun!" Charlie's voice rang out, louder now. "Besides, she deserves it, don't you, Wrenkle."

Something flew past her head, grazing one of her braids. Lucy flinched involuntarily, her head tilting as though the dirt clod had struck her. The reaction drew a roar of laughter from the group.

Her chest tightened as more tears spilled over. She didn't dare look back. She didn't need to; she already knew some of the laughter and which of her friends it likely belonged to. Betrayal stung more than any insult Charlie could hurl.

"Charlie Banks!" the voice rang out again, angrier this time. "You put that rock down!" This time, Lucy recognized the speaker for certain: Dorothy Edisbury.

"Yeah? And what are you going to do about it? Fetch the constables, eh? Witch lover?" Charlie sneered.

"She's no witch, and she's no Wrenkle! She's Lucy McGregor, and you've no right, Charlie. No right at all! I'll be talking to your father about this if you even think of—"

A sickening thud silenced Dorothy's words. Lucy spun around just in time to see Dorothy collapse to the ground, clutching her face.

"Dorothy!" Lucy cried, rushing to her side. She knelt, gently cradling Dorothy's head. Blood dripped between Dorothy's fingers now clasping her damaged nose.

The crowd stood frozen; their laughter replaced by uneasy murmurs. Lucy's stomach twisted as she spotted three of her former friends among them, their wide-eyed stares betraying their guilt.

"You all saw it!" Charlie's voice cracked with an edge of desperation. "She stepped into the way! I didn't mean to hit her!" His protest hung in the air, unanswered. Charlie's face darkened. "You've seen how true my aim is! She bewitched me – cast a spell, she did! Made the rock hit poor Dorothy. You all saw it!"

Lucy's hands trembled as she wiped tears from her cheeks. "Charlie, you're naught but a poor excuse for a lad. That's utter rubbish, and you know it!"

His shock was evident, but it quickly twisted into rage. His gaze darted to the silent mob, seeking support, but found only averted eyes. "You won't put no hexes on me, Wrenkle!" he spat.

Before Lucy could react, he lunged. The force of his weight sent her sprawling onto her back. Dorothy's head hit the ground with a sickening thud as Lucy's hands were wrenched away.

"Get off me!" Lucy shouted, struggling beneath him.

"Not until you admit it!" Charlie yelled, his knees pinning her arms down. His face hovered above hers, red with fury.

Lucy's anger boiled over. "Admit what? That you're a coward who can't fight fair?"

Her defiance only seemed to enrage him further and he raised his arm up in the air as if to strike her. This caused Lucy to flinch, closing her eyes.

"You and your family are nothing but filthy witches! The whole town knows it – my mother said so," Charlie sneered, his voice laced with contempt.

"Take that back, you freckled bittor!" Lucy shot back, her words sharp and defiant. She clenched her fists, her fear melting into a simmering rage. The mention of her family had struck a nerve, igniting something deep within her.

The slap came swift and stinging, snapping her head to

the side. The sharp crack echoed in the air, followed by a collective gasp from the crowd lingering just out of sight behind Charlie.

He raised his hand again, his expression unrelenting. Instinctively, Lucy turned her head aside and closed her eyes in anticipation of the second blow. But it never came. Instead, she felt Charlie's weight leave her arms and chest in one swift motion. When she opened her eyes, she saw her cousin Jack holding Charlie up by his jacket, his feet dangling above the ground.

Jack's eyes were wild with anger, and without hesitation, he tossed the smaller boy to the ground. "Think yourself a man, picking on a little girl?" Jack spat, already pursuing Charlie, who scrambled away in a desperate attempt to escape. But Jack was far too fast. He caught up to Charlie in an instant, pinning him to the ground just as Charlie had done to Lucy.

The crowd, which had been eerily silent, now erupted with shouts, closing in as Jack began pounding Charlie's face and chest. Charlie's screams and desperate wriggling filled the air as he struggled to break free from the beating.

Lucy scrambled to her feet and pushed through the crowd. When she reached the boys, she was met with the sight of Charlie, his face bruised and bleeding. Part of her hated him, thinking he deserved every blow. But she couldn't bear the thought of Jack getting in trouble on her behalf. "Jack! Stop! Jack, that's quite enough!" But the punches continued, fueled by the few Charlie had managed to land in retaliation. "Jack!" Lucy cried again, her tears flowing freely now, her voice pleading.

Then, someone pushed through the crowd and yanked Jack away from Charlie. Jack fought against the figure for a moment, but his resistance quickly faded. His breath came in ragged gasps, his fists still clenched and red from the blows. Charlie, on the other hand, remained curled in a ball on the ground, his hands covering his head and neck, whimpering softly.

"Continue on your way. Break this mob up at once. Continue on your way I said," a woman's voice called, firm and commanding, though muffled under a hooded cloak. She kept her arms tightly around Jack, who was still breathing heavily. After a few moments, she released him, and he sank to the ground, sitting beside his book bag. The crowd, either running or walking swiftly, dispersed quickly, clearing the path.

"Lucy. Please see if that girl requires assistance," the woman called. Lucy turned to find Dorothy standing, a wad of cloth pressed against her nose to staunch the bleeding.

"Let me take a look," Lucy said, softly, pulling back the blood-soaked cloth. Dorothy's nose was bruised blue and red from the rock that had struck her. "You should have your mother inspect this when you get home. I am no doctor."

Dorothy nodded; her eyes still wet with tears. "Thank you, Lucy."

"I am the one that ought to thank you. I wish the rock would have struck me in your place."

"He was treating you very poorly. Charlie is and always has been quite a foot and somebody needed to stand up to him."

"I thank you, Dorothy, just the same."

The woman who had intervened was now kneeling beside Charlie, inspecting his neck and head. She pulled back her hood, revealing the blackest hair Lucy had ever seen, almost as dark as a raven's wing.

As if sensing Lucy's gaze, the woman turned to her. Her skin was fair, and her lips, a striking shade of red, caught Lucy's attention. "Lucy, you should be on your way. Take her with you and see that she arrives home safely."

"Ma'am, how is it that you know my name?" Lucy asked, curiosity getting the better of her.

"I'm an acquaintance of your mother and father. And my students address me as Miss Vikar, but you may call me Alice." She was already pulling Charlie to his feet, dusting him off before helping Jack up and handing him his bag.

"Vikar, as in the witches?" Charlie asked, his dazed voice tinged with alarm.

At this, Alice smiled. "Witches do not exist, lad. Now, let's get you on your way. Jack, you ought to be going as well. Get your cousin and friend home, and I'll finish up here, perhaps finish what you started," she said, giving Jack a wink and a smile.

"Yes ma'am. Come Lucy and Dorothy."

The three of them followed her instructions and continued their walk home. On the way, Lucy couldn't help but wonder who this woman was and how she knew her parents. What had Charlie meant when he spoke of the Vikar witches? Lucy had heard plenty of stories about the Vikars and the house fire, but never anything about witchcraft. She also puzzled over why Charlie had started calling her Wrenkle and being so horrible to her. There were many questions and no answers.

The three rounded the last corner before the trail reconnected to the main road. Lucy looked across the flat plain, hoping to catch a glimpse of the old Vikar home before the hill obstructed her view, but it was too far to see the ruin. She'd seen it up close a few times on their way to church when

Uncle Ben had taken them, but beyond a few stories, she really hadn't known the details. There had been a family that once lived in a home there, which now appeared as nothing but a pile of charred wood and brick. Why had they not seen fit to rebuild the house? And might the woman, Alice, whom we had just met, be one of the Vikars who once dwelled there?

"Jack, thank you for coming to my aid," Lucy called ahead to her cousin, who was several steps ahead of them. She and Jack had never been very close, and the fact that he helped her today was nearly as surprising as the other strange things she'd heard this week. She'd had many opportunities to see and get to know Uncle Ben and Aunt Mary, but for some reason, they very seldom brought their four children with them. Outside of school and infrequent dinners, they didn't come around.

Jack turned his head and looked back. "Think naught of it. I've long wished to have a scrap with Charlie, and you merely gave me the occasion." He raised one fist in the air and shook it once before dropping it. "Besides, I know you couldst have bested him, had he not fought so foully. Charlie is naught but a coward."

"I thank you, nonetheless. Perhaps you will stop by my home so I might reward you with a slice of apple pie my mother baked?"

He seemed to ponder this for a moment before shaking his head and offering her a courteous smile. "I've chores to tend ere supper. I'd best see to them. Fret not about Dorothy. I'll see her safely home – it lies not far out of my way."

Lucy's thoughts returned to Alice and what had been said. She considered bringing it up to Jack but didn't know if it would be prudent with Dorothy in their company. But, as if

315

on cue, Dorothy pulled the rag from her nose. "Think Alice is the same as she who dwelt in the Vikar home when it was consumed by flames?"

Jack looked back again and nodded. "Aye, I do believe she is one and the same. She visited our home on occasion. I reckon she's one of the few to have survived the fire."

"And what of the words Charlie used in speaking of the Vikars? He called them witches," Lucy asked, but Jack merely shrugged.

"I've heard the same tales. 'Tis said they were entangled in the witch trials of some years past. My parents have shared a few of the stories with me, but I put no stock in such nonsense," Dorothy said, putting the rag back to her nose, which had begun to bleed again.

Lucy considered this for a few moments before building enough courage to ask her question. "Dorothy, do any of the tales your parents recount make mention of my family?"

Dorothy averted her eyes at the question, at least confirming Lucy's thoughts. She decided not to press further, but Dorothy spoke up.

"They call it The Wrenkle. I have heard it spoken of by my own parents and by others too. They say your mother, and all the Wrenkle women besides, are witches." She looked back up at Lucy and gave her a wistful smile.

"I have also heard the same tales," Jack said, without looking back. "My father says the stories are merely rumors and that we should not speak of them. Don't place any weight on them, Lucy."

Lucy felt her stomach churn at the mention of the rumors. The unfairness of it was unbearable. It was true that her own mother, Elizabeth, had always been special, as her father put it, but a witch? The thought had never crossed her mind. Her stomach lurched again, and a fresh wave of tears began to form in her eyes as her emotions overwhelmed her. Without another word, she began to run, pushing past Jack, who called after her. Heavy sobs broke out as she ran the rest of the way, unable to stop until she reached the barn at the edge of their property. She slid inside the large door and dove into a pile of hay, where she wept bitterly.

The mere fact that these rumors had reached her schoolmates was bad enough; knowing that others in town were also passing them around made her stomach cramp even harder. She clutched at it as she cried, her sobs muffled by the hay.

A soft knock came from nearby, startling her into holding her breath. She wasn't ready to speak to anyone, least of all her father. She buried her face deeper into the hay, hoping to disappear entirely.

Footsteps approached, light and deliberate, before someone settled beside her.

"I did not mean to cause you any pain."

The familiar voice caused her embarrassment to subside just slightly. Slowly, she lifted her tear-streaked face, bits of hay clinging to her damp cheeks. She brushed them away hastily, her gaze falling on Jack, lying casually nearby with his hands clasped over his chest.

"I thought you meant to see Dorothy home?"

"She'll manage," Jack replied, without looking at her.

Lucy wiped her face again, brushing at the stubborn strands of hay tangled in her hair. She rolled over and sat up, her voice quieter now. "Do you believe there to be any truth to the rumors? The ones about my mother – and my family –

being witches?"

Jack turned his head to look at her for a moment, his brow furrowed, before shaking his head firmly. "Lucy, I am but a lad. Yet, I have known the Wrenkle family for some time. Ne'er have I met kinder folk. Nay, save for their fair looks and those strange green eyes that you all have. Nay, none are witches."

Lucy's shoulders sagged with relief, but the threat of more tears loomed as she spoke again. "Then why do people speak it? Why my mother, of all the folk?"

Jack shrugged, his gaze drifting upward once more. "As I've said, my father has told me many tales of old. Perhaps 'tis time you ask your own father. He may shed light on the matter."

He stood then, brushing hay from his clothes, and extended a hand to her. She hesitated for a moment before taking it, letting him pull her to her feet. Jack smiled and started toward the barn door. Then he paused and looked back.

"Meet you here early tomorrow," he said, with a casual tone. "Methinks 'tis time we walk to school together."

Lucy felt another swell of emotion rising but held it back this time. "Thank you, Jack."

He grinned, his smile faintly mischievous. "Think naught of it. Besides, how else shall I get another go at Charlie?"

And with that, he was gone, leaving Lucy standing in the barn. For the first time that day, a faint flicker of hope kindled within her, and she needed her father to fill in the gaps in her mind.

44

The Betrayal

"Excuse me." A woman's voice broke through the bustle of the casino as she bumped into Steve from behind. His glass tipped against the marble table, spilling its contents onto his lap. He stifled a curse, offering her a tight smile she never saw. "No problem," he muttered, dabbing at the damp spot on his trousers with a cocktail napkin.

The dealer declared Steve's hand a loser, sweeping away his bet. Steve barely noticed. The flashing lights and clamor of voices in the packed casino felt oppressive, the noise merging into a headache pounding at the base of his skull. He spotted Melissa across the room, waving a bucket of coins triumphantly from her slot machine. She flashed a smile, oblivious, her laughter lost amid the whirl of electronic beeps.

Steve raised a hand, signaling he'd be back, and slipped out of the casino. The air in the corridor was cooler, quieter, but the dim lighting still affected his eyes. He needed some aspirin. The gift shop wasn't far – he grabbed a small sleeve of headache pills, signed the bill, and was about to head back when –

"Mr. Moore?" A voice echoed down the corridor.

He turned to see a man waving, approaching with brisk steps. Steve furrowed his brow. "Yes, I'm Steve Moore."

"I'm terribly sorry to interrupt your evening, sir," the man said, slowing his pace as he neared, "but I've been searching for you. There's an emergency call." He held out a silver tray, a sleek black phone perched atop it. "We don't typically take calls at sea, but the gentleman insisted and said it was urgent."

"Did he give a name?"

"Yes, sir. Clark. Shall I escort you to a private room?"

Steve hesitated for only a second and then nodded.

After signing off on the ludicrous cost, Steve followed the man to a small, nondescript office. The door slid closed to a small crack, mostly sealing him off from the hum of the ship. He picked up the phone, bracing himself.

"This better be important."

"Steve, can you hear me?"

"I'm in the middle of the Pacific. What is it?"

Clark's response came quickly, panicked. "Steve, we need to cancel the whole thing. It's gone too far."

"What are you talking about? You want to give me a reason?"

"She killed Andy, Steve. My partner's dead."

Steve closed his eyes trying to absorb what he was hearing. The pain in his head began pulsing even harder.

"Did you hear me? She killed him."

Steve pressed a hand to his forehead, exhaling sharply. "I'm sorry to hear that, but what do you expect me to do from the middle of the ocean?"

"Did you not hear me? My office is on me, non-stop. They're suspicious. This whole operation is about to blow up in our faces!"

Steve stood, pacing the small room as the tension in Clark's voice stacked brick upon brick on his headache. "Alright, calm down. There's no need to panic. We can fix this."

Two passengers strolled past the office window, pausing to glance as his voice rose. He reached over and slammed the sliding glass door shut and turned back to the phone, his heart racing.

"Clark, are you still there?"

"Yeah, where would I go?"

"Good. Let's start with Andy. Is there any way to... clean that up?"

A silence stretched over the line, thick and uncomfortable. Clark finally spoke, his voice barely above a whisper. "I have a plan. I'll make it look like an accident. The lake – it could work."

"Okay, that's a start. Handle it." He paused and let out a long sigh. "Sorry Clark... sorry about your partner. I know he was important to you."

"Steve... this thing, this woman – she's threatening me. She basically said she'd go after my family."

"Wait a minute, Clark. She spoke to you? Threatened you?"

"Oh yeah. And she wasn't subtle about it. Creepy little minx if you ask me."

A soft knock interrupted Steve's thoughts. Melissa stepped into the room, her smile faltering when she saw his face. She mouthed "What's going on?" as she sat beside him, her expression shifting from curiosity to concern.

Steve placed the phone on speaker. "Clark, describe her. What did she look like?"

"What? What does that matter?"

"Just answer the question," Steve insisted, exchanging a glance with Melissa, who had gone pale.

"Small, dark hair... evil black eyes."

Steve's grip tightened on the phone, his stomach knotting.

Melissa leaned forward, her hand covering her mouth. Her pail of coins fell to the floor and the color drained from her face.

"Clark, listen to me carefully. What do you need from us?"

"Well, for starters, Liam's helping them. They're still out there, somewhere on the road. We've blocked both exits but I can't find them."

Steve's fingers drummed nervously on the desk. "What about my house? Could they still be there?"

"I checked. No sign of them. No vehicles either."

Steve exchanged a grim look with Melissa. "Alright, Clark. Give me an hour to figure things out. I'll call you back."

Clark sighed, weary. "Alright. But make it quick."

Steve ended the call.

Melissa stared at him, her eyes wide with fear. "Could it be Margaret?"

"There's no way. Liam would never... let her out. I don't even think he has that old watch anymore." Steve waved the suggestion off, but the name stuck in his mind like a thorn. His expression tightened, betraying the doubt he tried to hide. "Still... we may need to go to Plan B." He saw the protest forming on her lips and raised a hand. "But let's see how this plays out first. We've got a few options left."

Melissa leaned forward, resting her hands on her knees as if trying to ground herself. "Okay, I hope we can figure this out, Steve. We didn't make out so well on that last one and we really needed this payout."

"I'm fully aware, dear."

"Fine. I have a headache. I'm going to lie down in our room for a while."

"Good idea. I have one too," Steve muttered, his mind elsewhere. "I need to make sure this call wasn't recorded by the ship's system and make a couple phone calls. I'll be right up."

They shared a brief, tense kiss, more out of habit than affection, before parting ways. Melissa walked out, kicking the bucket on the floor out of the way without another word, her heels clicking softly against the polished floor. Steve lingered for a moment, staring at the phone in his hand. The luxurious surroundings suddenly felt too quiet, too stifling, as if the weight of everything Clark had said was pressing down on him.

As he headed toward the ship's communications office, Steve couldn't shake the uneasy feeling that their carefully laid plans were slipping beyond his control. He pulled his wallet out of his jacket and searched it. Out came a small card with dark raised letters on it that said 'Black Coast Insurance.' He dialed some numbers into the ship's phone as he walked to the bridge.

45

Alice

19 July 1725

Alexander's Journal

I ne'er thought we should face so dire a choice. My family hath tended this land longer than I have drawn breath, and I had believed my sons would follow in my stead. Yet, the rumors that have gathered these many years past have grown beyond bearing for me and mine. Elizabeth and I have had no recourse but to keep our children from the school. The unkindly treatment toward them, as well as toward all the McGregors, hath become impossible to overlook.

To make matters worse, many in the town have taken to speaking openly of their mistrust toward my poor wife, as well as toward other women of her family. Never hath our honor been called into question before, yet now, we can scarcely enter town without being mocked or interrogated.

Benjamin and I have begun to deliberate upon the prospect of selling our claim to the land and seeking refuge in a place less hostile. It grieves us to entertain the thought of migrating, yet we believe it may be the only means by which our families might find peace.

22 July 1725

Alexander's Journal

Our family had a most unexpected visitor this week – Alice Vikar, one of the few survivors of the fire of the year 1712. I was astonished when our own daughter, Lucy, spoke of seeing her after school, but ne'er did I imagine she would appear on our doorstep. We had known of her survival for some time, yet it hath been many years since I last laid mine eyes upon her. She hath grown into a comely young woman, her countenance much resembling that of her elder sister.

It did sadden me to hear that, not only doth she attend, but also doth she instruct at the secret school where the other Vikar sisters did once study. I had nearly made up mine mind to send her away from our abode, yet she did share with me that she hath forsaken that practice and now seeks a new calling. Given that she hath no kin, we have welcomed her to stay in our guest house for as long as need be.

Alice and I have had many good opportunities to catch up on matters of old. I was able to share with her many things concerning her family that she was not privy to, seeing as she was but a child when they did pass away. Our family hath spent many a late night in the joy of her company.

2 August 1725

Alexander's Journal

Alice and I have begun to discourse upon the strange affliction that hath beset my poor wife. Given her practiced experience in witchcraft as a teacher, she did reveal the truth of the matter. She confessed to not knowing the full particulars, yet she disclosed that it is, in truth, multiple curses that have fastened themselves upon Elizabeth. She recalls being present when her mother and Margaret did exercise the curse, though she remembers but few details, for she was but a child at the time. However, she hath given me much hope, and together we have commenced seeking ways to better understand, and God willing, break this curse. This, more than any other thing, hath brought my wife and I hope.

4 August 1725

Alice pushed the book closer to Alexander so he could better see what she was reading. He squinted at the small, cramped text, then brought the candle nearer to illuminate the page.

"My eyesight fares not as it once did," he muttered, following her slender finger to the passage she had indicated.

When he read the section, he felt a little uneasy. He hadn't been keen on her bringing books or items of witchcraft into their home; such things had always felt foreign, even dangerous. And though his church congregation had politely asked them to no longer attend the meetings, he was still a very religious man. Yet, his attitude on the dark arts had softened since they began unraveling the curse together. In truth, he had grown engrossed in the topic – though he would never admit it aloud – and found himself strangely captivated by the intricacies of magic. "This speaks of charmed tokens.

Are you suggesting the brass pocket watch is one of these tokens?"

"That is precisely what it is," Alice replied, her tone steady, though her expression bore a trace of reluctance. "I shall not bore you with every detail, but enchanting such a token is an arduous and costly endeavor. It exacts a heavy toll upon those who forge it – physical, emotional, even spiritual. I have no doubt my sister suffered greatly in its creation."

"Is that why it harmed her when it touched her skin?" Alexander asked, his voice low, mindful of those of his family that had retired for bed.

Alice shook her head, her face lit softly by the candlelight. "The token was fashioned to shield you from any magic wrought by those bound to it. As you've recounted, that would include Agatha – and Margaret."

Reaching into the small, black pouch, Alice carefully drew out the brass pocket watch. It gleamed as it caught the flickering light, spinning lazily as she held the chain between two fingers. "The reason this brought my sister pain is that it happens to be an object of great meaning to her. Though she gave it to you, she is ever mindful it was hers, and thus it has become a potent thing, both commanding and drawing her in equal measure. It is a clear reminder of her prior mortality."

Alexander reached out, his fingers closing around the watch. He had not touched it, nor even removed it from the bag, since retrieving it after that grim night in the guest house. The weight of it in his palm felt heavier than he remembered. "Do you mean to tell me," he began cautiously, "that this object could serve to bring Margaret back?"

Alice's gaze hardened, and she leaned forward slightly. "Have you ever shown it to Elizabeth?"

"Nay," Alexander replied at once. "The watch has not left its place in greater than ten years."

"Good," Alice said, her voice edged with urgency. "It should be returned to its place within the sack. Even the mere act of showing it to Elizabeth could provoke any number of unforeseen events, and such matters are not to be taken lightly. It is no mere trifle and should be treated with the utmost respect and care."

She held the pouch open for him, her eyes fixed on his, as though testing his resolve. Without a word, Alexander tossed the watch back into the pouch and Alice drew the strings tightly. She then handed it to him, her eyes still looking into his. He took the pouch and stuffed it into his pocket.

Alexander leaned back in his chair, stretching his arms above his head. The lateness of the hour was beginning to weigh on him, and the thought of an early morning loomed. "Alice, we should continue this discourse tomorrow evening," he said with a yawn. "I believe it time I turn in for the night."

Alice paused for a moment and then nodded, her hands moving to close the various books spread across the table. For a moment, she worked in silence, her movements efficient and deliberate. But then her pace slowed, her fingers hesitating as though something had just struck her. Her brow furrowed slightly, and instead of rising, she sat back down, her gaze distant.

"I heard a tale once," she began, her voice quieter than before. "Whilst I was attending my sisterhood." Her eyes flicked toward Alexander at the mention of the school, gauging his reaction. He stiffened slightly – her connection to the witches' circle always left him uneasy – but he remained silent, waiting for her to continue.

"We did study the case of a witch who had wrought a dual curse – one set upon the other. The first was fashioned to disarm, to confound, but the second…" She paused, her gaze shifting to the flickering candle as her thoughts momentarily drifted. "The second curse was of a far more sinister nature. It did draw upon the power of demons themselves."

Her words trailed off; her sentence left unfinished, as though she were grappling with something unspoken. Alexander leaned forward, the lateness of the hour momentarily forgotten. "What did happen next?" he asked, his voice steady but laced with apprehension.

Alice's lips parted, but for a moment, no words came. She looked as though she were weighing what to reveal. Finally, she began stacking the books again, her movements slower now. "The one who summoned the spirit…" She hesitated. "Was overtaken. As I comprehend the tale, meddlin' with such dark forces ever beareth the peril of the demon escapin' its prison – and bindin' itself to human flesh."

As she dropped the last book into a wooden chest by the table, her brow creased with thought. "I know not whether the tale be true or naught but an old fable. Yet, given what we've seen – and what you have shared with me – I fear there be a chance it befell Margaret."

Alexander froze, her words dragging him back to the horrors of that night years ago. His hands trembled as memories surfaced – Margaret's disappearance, the fleeting glimpse of a creature in the darkness. He had dismissed it as a trick of the mind, a product of grief, but now…

Alice moved closer, clutching his hand. "What is it? I didn't mean to trouble you."

"Nay," he murmured, shaking his head. "It's not of you.

It's..." He hesitated, then exhaled sharply. "I do recall something from that night – something I've sought to banish from my mind. It was dark, yet I saw it, Alice. A creature. And now... I fear you may be right." At this his hand tightened on hers and he felt a sudden desperation surge from his gut.

"Alice, if this is true – if Elizabeth is bound to such a creature – is there aught that can be done to break the curse?"

Alice stared at him, startled by his sudden intensity. She shook her head quickly. "I... I know not," she stammered. "I have not studied such magic. I've always avoided it."

He blinked at her answer and then let out a loud sigh. "I am so weary. I have not slept soundly these many months, and I am desperate – desperate to save my wife and to free my family from this accursed life."

Alice moved to his side, her voice soft with resolve. She put an arm around, a consoling gesture. "I understand. I swore I would forsake the craft, but if there be a chance to aid you – to aid her – I shall find a way to learn what is required."

Before Alexander could respond, a voice cut through the silence. "Aid? Why would I need any aid?" The words sounded dark and playful.

Both Alexander and Alice whipped around, startled. Elizabeth stood at the bottom of the stairs, her expression dark. Alice immediately withdrew from his side.

"My dear," Alexander said, moving toward her. "What are you doing awake?"

"I might ask you the same, dear," Elizabeth replied, her tone sharp.

He reached out to touch her shoulder, but she pulled away.

"Elizabeth, my Dove. Have you had another nightmare? What may I do for you?"

Her voice rose, taking on an edge that sent a shiver through him. "I require my husband to retire at a proper hour. That is what I require!"

The tone was wrong – too forceful, too unlike her. Alexander stiffened, a memory stirring unbidden: Margaret's voice, Margaret's anger. "Of course, my love," he said carefully. "Allow me to escort you."

"The two of you have grown rather familiar, have ye not?" she snapped, her eyes narrowing. "Is there something I ought to know, Alexander? Alice!"

Alice stepped back; her hands raised in a gesture of innocence. "Elizabeth, I... I only wish to offer help."

Elizabeth advanced on her, her face twisting into something unrecognizable. For a fleeting moment, Alexander saw it – Margaret's malevolent expression etched onto his poor wife's face.

"Elizabeth!" he exclaimed, stepping between them, his arms raised in defense. Before he could reach her, she let out a piercing scream. The sound seemed to carry an unnatural force, snuffing out every light in the room, plunging them into darkness.

"Elizabeth!" Alexander called again, his hands fumbling in the pitch black. He found her trembling form and pulled her into his arms. Something fell to the floor with a dull thud. She slumped against him, weeping uncontrollably.

He guided her to his chair and eased her into it, then fumbled for the single candle on the table. After a few tense moments, its flame flickered to life, illuminating the room once more.

Elizabeth looked normal again, her face streaked with tears but free of the anger – or whatever had taken hold of her. She blinked up at him, dazed. "I am most sorry," she murmured. "I must have nodded off. Is it time for bed already?"

Alexander and Alice exchanged a tense glance. He forced a smile as he knelt beside his wife. "All is well, my love. Yes, it is now time for bed. Allow me to escort you."

With a weary sigh, he rose and helped her to her feet. As they ascended the stairs, he glanced back at Alice, who stood frozen by the table, the black pouch containing the brass pocket watch clutched tightly in her hand. Her wide eyes met his, and she gave a subtle nod – confirmation that she, too, had seen Margaret.

Alexander turned back to Elizabeth, his jaw tightening. Whatever had happened tonight hadn't been for the first time and it wouldn't be the last.

46

The Last Shift

Sarah woke with a start, her heart pounding hard in her chest. The bright lights in the room stung her eyes, forcing her to blink rapidly until her vision adjusted. The injuries her body had sustained seemed to have festered, and multiple points of pain registered immediately. She shifted in the leather recliner, reaching for the long lever at the side. With a click, the chair snapped forward, and she pushed herself into a sitting position. Rubbing her eyes, she tried to bring the room into focus.

A ripple of unease crept into her chest when she realized the couch where Liam had been lying was now empty. She blinked again, her mind sluggish from exhaustion. To her right, Gwen lay sprawled on the floor, sound asleep, the silver pistol tucked into her pants. *Jazzed? Wasn't that the word she used when volunteering for the first watch?* Sarah thought with a tired grin.

Feeling the pressure of her bladder, she stood, her sore body protesting with every movement. The room swayed slightly as she stretched, her equilibrium struggling to catch up.

Carefully, she maneuvered past Gwen, but just before she was able to get to the bathroom, a noise stopped her cold.

"Psst."

Sarah spun toward the sound and saw Liam, silhouetted in the dark and hunched as he pushed himself up from a folding chair near the basement stairs. He moved cautiously across the room; his footsteps deliberate and quiet. His tired eyes were visible as he came into the light.

"Hey, Liam—" she began. He quickly put a finger to his lips, his expression serious. His eyes flicked upward, and she immediately understood.

Moments passed in heavy silence, and then Sarah heard it – a slow creaking from above. Footsteps pacing across the floor above them. She felt alarmed, but Liam remained calm, signaling to her to stay quiet. He pulled a small notepad and pencil from his bag, scribbling something down before handing it to her.

I think it's the police. Sounds like one of them. Been here for an hour.

Sarah swallowed hard and nodded, her fear spiking. Liam took the pad back, quickly jotting another note.

If you can't hold it, do not flush.

Liam handed the pad and pencil to Sarah and quietly shuffled back to his post at the bottom of the stairs. Sarah watched him as he moved, noting how tired and worn he looked. Her heart sank a little – this man had lived a vastly different life from the one she had. He'd also been instrumental to her safety.

Liam settled into the folding chair again, his shoulders sagging under an invisible burden. Sarah couldn't ignore the exhaustion etched into his face. It was her turn to take over. He needed to get more sleep, and she couldn't let him shoulder this alone. *Right after I take care of my bladder.*

She crept into the bathroom, careful not to disturb Gwen. In the dim light, she caught a glimpse of herself in the mirror and froze. The face staring back at her was a stranger – gaunt, dirty, bruised. Her hair was a tangled mess, and dark circles clung under her eyes. She did her best to fix what she could, but the lack of any real supplies made it a losing battle. The cuts and scrapes dotting her skin told a story of survival. She flexed her aching limbs, each movement a reminder of what she'd been through.

Finishing up, she slipped out of the bathroom. Liam had returned to the couch, leaning back with closed eyes.

"Whoever it was is gone," he muttered. "I heard them leave through the front door and drive away."

"Are you sure?"

Liam nodded. He absently dumped a few pills into his hand from a bottle of painkillers. He popped a few in his mouth, grimacing slightly, and then chewed them.

"Good. You should sleep. I'll take over now."

Liam didn't argue, just nodded and settled deeper into the couch.

As Sarah began to move, something gnawed at her. She hesitated, then turned back toward him.

"Liam... Earlier, you mentioned women being consumed by the creature. The woman you put in the truck bed. Who was she?"

Liam's eyes opened to narrow slits, considering her question. "Sarah," he began, his voice quiet but firm, "it's a complicated business. You don't need to know all the details."

"Was it my–" she started, but Liam cut her off.

"The woman you saw this afternoon was your grandmother, Clara. But you shouldn't think of her like that."

Sarah's breath caught. *Grandmother?* She stared at Liam, her mind reeling.

"I like to think she's still in there somewhere, fighting against the demon," he continued, his voice softer now, "but it's in control most of the time."

"Is it always her?" Sarah asked, barely able to form the words.

"Yes and no." He sighed, rubbing his eyes. "I can make others appear if I want to. But your grandmother… she's more subdued, easier to manage."

Liam leaned forward, picking up a small wooden flute from the table. "This was your grandmother's. For some reason, when I play it, it causes the demon pain – brings the human side back, just for a little while."

"And when you use it, only she comes back?"

Liam smiled faintly and nodded. "My family calls them tokens – powerful tools in this family business."

Sarah's gaze fell on the red cloth on the table. "And this? What does it do?"

"That belonged to your great-aunt Ruth. It's useful too."

Sarah's heart raced. *Do you have one for my mother?* she wanted to ask, but Liam seemed to read her thoughts.

"We had all of them, including one for your mother, but many were lost years ago."

Her shoulders slumped in disappointment. Liam pointed at Gwen. "She has one too, but we're not using that. You don't want to meet the woman that belonged to."

He tossed the flute back onto the table with a finality that told Sarah not to press any further.

"Thanks, Uncle. Good night," Sarah whispered, slipping quietly into the shadowed corners of the room. Her hands fumbled for the chair as her eyes adjusted to the gloom. She finally found it and sat down. It was hard and uncomfortable – nothing like the recliner she'd been sitting in earlier.

Her thoughts churned in the quiet darkness. Liam's words lingered with her: the curse, their lineage, the weight of a hidden family legacy that had caused so much suffering. A familiar ache filled her chest as she thought about her mother. She had been so young when she died. Sarah's memories of her were foggy at best, reduced to vague images and a few faded photos her grandfather had once shared. Did her mother know about all of this? Had she been burdened with the same painful knowledge, or had she died in blissful ignorance? *And what about me?* she thought. It was impossible to drown the thoughts about the curse and how it had certainly impacted her own life. She wondered how it likely guided, even molded, her life and how things may have been otherwise.

The floorboards creaked above her, jerking her from her thoughts. Her body tensed, heart racing. She held her breath, listening for more. Liam's heavy breathing rumbled steadily from across the room. After a minute of silence, she released the breath she'd been holding. *House noises*, she told herself. Still, every sound now felt like a potential threat.

"Keeping watch is a lot more boring than I thought," she muttered softly. Sitting in the chair felt pointless – her muscles ached from inactivity, screaming for movement. She stood up, stretching stiff limbs. Her body protested with familiar soreness, a reminder of the injuries she had endured in the past week.

She decided to pace the basement, each step slow and cautious, not wanting to wake Liam or Gwen. As she moved, her gaze fell on the walls, on old family photos and decorations she had already scanned earlier. There was nothing new to distract her from the whirlwind of thoughts in her mind.

After what felt like an hour of pacing, her feet finally carried her back to the office door – the same office she had hurriedly explored before. The weight of its mysteries still hung in the air, but tonight the tension was different, more manageable. Curiosity pulled her forward. She gripped the cold knob and twisted, pulling the door open with a faint creak.

The small lamp on the desk was still on, casting a faint glow across the room. It felt almost welcoming. She stepped inside and softly closed the door behind her, flicking on the main light. The office came to life with a warm yellow light. The large family tree murals on the wall stared back at her, just as they had before.

She turned to the old color photo from the sixties, the one of the woman who haunted her thoughts. Her heart skipped. The fiery red afro and piercing green eyes felt familiar, too familiar. *Grandma?* Sarah's mind whirred, trying to piece together fragments of memory, dreams, and what she'd learned tonight.

Taking a deep breath, she sat down at the desk. The genealogy chart she had examined before loomed above her, its lines and names weaving an intricate web of her family's past. Her eyes traced it, scanning for the photograph that she had seen before. It stood out like a beacon, calling to her.

On the branches beneath the photograph, two placeholders

sat, representing Sarah's parents. Her father's name was reduced to a single word: *Jensen*, while her mother's name, *Gloria McGregor*, was listed clearly. Tears welled up in her eyes. Seeing their names in this context made them feel more real than they had in years, almost as if their presence was palpable in the room.

She let her eyes roam the other names etched into the branches, quickly spotting her aunt and uncle. Her heart tugged as she moved down the tree, scanning through generations: *Mary, Charlotte, Isabel, Lily* – some with the McGregor name, others with married names. However, each had writing next to them in red that said 'Wrenkle.' Also most names had a checkmark and others had an 'X.' *I wonder if that means they were taken by the curse or not.* She continued down the tree, reading each name and note as she went. Finally, her gaze settled at the base, where it all began: *Alexander McGregor* and *Elizabeth Wrenkle.*

"This is my family tree," Sarah whispered, the words feeling heavier than she'd expected. These weren't just names; they were the lifeblood of her legacy – people she'd never met but whose choices shaped the path she now walked.

The quiet snap of the door behind her jolted her upright. She swiveled quickly in her chair, her heart hammering. Liam stood there, his face tired, eyes surveying the room.

"So, you found your relatives' special room. Yes, that's the McGregor line. As you can see, you and I come from Thomas McGregor, the youngest son of Alexander and Elizabeth."

"Wow, Uncle, you scared the devil out of me!"

Liam didn't respond immediately but stepped toward the wall, his fingers tracing the edges of the photo before pulling it off. He studied the image in silence for a moment. "I haven't seen a picture of your grandmother in many years," he said, his voice soft, almost reverent. After a few seconds, he carefully tacked the picture back into place. "I wonder what other possessions your aunt and uncle have of mine."

"You should be sleeping, Uncle."

He ignored the comment and walked around the room. "Have ya seen the rest of these?"

"I saw them, but I haven't looked at them closely. What are they for?"

"Your aunt and uncle figured out that the curse doesn't just claim the McGregor family in our line. They discovered what your sixth-great-grandfather knew and documented. That the powerful curse not only bound itself to Alexander and Elizabeth but to all McGregors and Wrenkles born during that time."

Sarah felt some of the puzzle pieces fall into place in her mind. "So these family trees are other McGregor and Wrenkle families?"

With a nod he walked to the chart nearest to him and pointed. "Yes, you see, here's Benjamin McGregor and his tree. He was one of Alexander's brothers." He walked to the next one. "And this one, this is Amelia Wrenkle. I've seen her name in many of Alexander's journal entries."

"So all of these people are cursed?" Sarah said, her eyes wide as she tried counting the many charts.

"Yes, lass. In one way or another. Now I can't tell you I understand exactly how it works with the McGregors, and a great deal of what Alexander wrote has been lost, but it seems your aunt and uncle have figured it out and are using it in some dark way to benefit and protect them."

Sarah felt a small pain in her stomach at the mention of

340

her aunt and uncle's involvement in all of this. "Well, Uncle, maybe the answer is in here somewhere?"

"Maybe, lass. But we don't have any time to find out. It's five in the morning. Gwen's up and looking for you. Also, I think our officer friend is back. I think it's time we talk about getting you two out of here. Don't take too long and lock the door when you come out." He turned to leave. He put his hand on the picture of her Grandmother Clara and then walked out.

47

Exodus

10 November 1725

Alexander's Journal

I write near the end of our long journey, putting thoughts to paper though the travel has hindered my ability to compose as I had wished. Yet, I feel that documenting these events remains of paramount importance. Thus, I press on with my entries today, determined to record all I can before we reach our final destination.

It has come to pass – quicker than we could have imagined – that we shall settle far to the north, in Scotland. Alas, I regret to say that we have learned from many who once counted themselves as our friends, that we are no longer welcome in those parts. Even as we took our leave of our former home, a mob of angry townsfolk saw us off with none of the kindness I had hoped for. The venom of their fear and anger was chiefly directed toward my dear wife, as well as the other women, those of the Wrenkle and McGregor lines. To my dismay, the old talk of witch trials was raised, even as we made our departure.

Yet, we found favor in the most unexpected of places. My friend, the constable's captain, came to our aid in a moment of great need. He, with the support of his men, reminded the crowd that the days of witch trials were no longer, that the rulers of England had cast away such practices in favor of reason. His words quelled the mob's fury and gave us precious respite. For this, I will be eternally grateful to Oliver, who saw us safely along with protection from the growing hostility. His kindness will never be forgotten.

Accompanying us on this journey is my brother, Benjamin, along with his family. His assistance has been invaluable in securing our new home. He, with his wit and persistence, negotiated with Lord North, the nobleman who owns the land. To our great fortune, Lord North showed sympathy toward our plight. He offered not only his support but also his assistance in securing our future. He helped us find a secluded estate in Scotland, on one of his own properties. We are to work the land for him, much as we would have in our previous life, and we are grateful for this generous arrangement.

Alice hath also joined us and shall remain with us as though she were a daughter. We have spent much time together these past months, and our affection for her hath grown considerably. She and I continue our search for a means to break the curse, one that hath affected not only my wife but also the McGregors and the Wrenkle family. Alice's knowledge of witchcraft hath proved invaluable, and we continue to document many of the intricacies of the curse in a separate book which we both keep. We now know that there be not one, but three curses or charms upon our households, and we learn more each passing day. Alice hath brought many of her volumes with her, including those that delve into the darker magics now understood to be entwined with the curse Margaret did cast.

We hold hope for the future. We expect to reach our new home, high in the mountains, within a fortnight. The cold hath become more intense, so I beg thee to continue thy prayers, that we may arrive swiftly and safely. To my utter surprise, Elizabeth doth seem to have moments of clearer thought, more so than in times past. At times, she hath nearly returned to her former sharp wit, and in many cases, her good humor doth reappear. The journey is indeed arduous, yet we continue to press forward, ever with hope in our hearts.

Alexander pushed the book to the side of his makeshift desk, frustration weighing on him. His mother had always praised his penmanship, but in these conditions – tents, rain, cold, and the creeping weariness from his accelerated aging – his handwriting now looked like chicken scratch. With a sigh, he glanced at Elizabeth who lay fast asleep beside him. She was as beautiful as ever, as serene as the day they first married. In fact, to his and others' observations, it seemed she had literally not aged a single day. This was becoming more and more difficult to explain.

Alice had uncovered something troubling in her books. After conducting a series of tests, she had confirmed there was not one or two, but a third curse – or 'charm' as she called it – upon them. Alice believed Margaret had hastily added it, likely in an attempt to prolong or enhance her beauty, woven into one of the many incantations she had dabbled with. The thought sent a dull ache through Alexander's chest. Alice had also remarked on how dark and depressed Margaret had become, and Alexander couldn't help but feel responsible. He hadn't intended to hurt her but knew now that his breaking their relations off had been at least partially to blame for her irrational behavior.

He leaned over, pulled another blanket over Elizabeth and then closed his journal, reassured that the ink had dried. Rising, he moved to the adjoining tent to check on his children – Lucy, Martha, Rose, and little Thomas. Each child received an extra blanket, and Alexander stoked the coals, adding more to keep the tent warm through the night. He kissed each one on the cheek, and as he turned to leave, something caught his attention.

Through the tent's opening, he could see that the front of his own tent was now wide open. He distinctly remembered securing it before. He secured his children's tent and then returned to his. He stepped inside, and to his surprise, Elizabeth was gone. The bed where she had lain just a half-hour earlier was empty. A gust of wind blew through the short opening of the room, flickering the candle on his desk. Alexander moved deeper into the tent but stopped. Something was different.

On the bed lay a small, soft black pouch. He kneeled to grab it, expecting to feel the familiar object inside but it was empty. His eyebrows knitted together – how had the pouch gotten here? Had Elizabeth seen it, touched it? The various scenarios began to pile up in his mind.

From outside, he heard footsteps. He rushed out of the tent, hoping to see Elizabeth. Instead he was met by a woman's loud scream in the distance. It was sharp and shrill, rising above the wind. As the noise grew, shouts filled the air – men's voices, mixed with the cries of other women. Faint lights flickered in the distance, signaling the source of the chaos.

Without a second thought, Alexander sprinted toward the commotion. The rain had stopped, but the ground was still slippery with mud, making it difficult to run. His boots became heavy as he ran, and he slid several times as he tried to navigate the camp.

As he neared the source, the front of a tent burst open, and a man was hurled out of its front. His body cleared a nearby fire pit before hitting a tree with a sickening thud. Alexander changed direction and started toward him, but a second scream from the tent froze his momentum and he slid to a stop.

His gut wrenched as he took in the sight. The nightmare resurfaced from his consciousness as if it were just yesterday. His heart began to thump hard in his chest as if picking up where it left off from years ago. There, amidst the collapsing tent, stood what appeared to be Margaret – or at least, her twisted form. Billowing black smoke swirled around her as she emerged from the wreckage, seemingly searching for her next victim.

She paused only momentarily to look at him. Their eyes locked, and through the haze he saw a wicked smile stretch across her face. The memories of that night came back with a vengeance, and he knew immediately what she was capable of. He also recalled the only way to stop her was through a token like had happened before. However the whereabouts of the pocket watch was now unknown. *How had she learned to manage it? How had she been able to touch it?* This was beyond his reckoning.

She took one step toward him, but a loud crack split the air as something snapped over the creature's head, stopping it temporarily. It was Benjamin, wielding a thick branch. He brought it back up for a second blow, but the creature swatted him aside effortlessly. He landed unconscious on the newly collapsed tent.

The creature turned its gaze upon Alexander once more. Despite every warning sounding in his mind, he charged forward, his footing uncertain as an unnatural frost coated the ground beneath him. The air thickened, biting at his skin, but he pressed on.

He leaped, fists clenched, aiming to strike – but before he could make contact, a clawed hand shot from the swirling black mass, seizing him by the throat. The grip lifted him effortlessly, cold seeping into his flesh, the icy tendrils creeping through his veins and sinew. His muscles locked, frozen stiff, his breath coming in ragged gasps.

A guttural laugh rumbled from the shifting dark. "Greetings, my love," came the voice – familiar, yet twisted with malice. A smile flickered across the creature's shadowed face before, with a flick of its wrist, it released him. He crumpled to the ground, his body still numb, unable to move. The earth beneath him was both wet and unyielding.

Around him, the chaos raged on. Men barked orders at each other and women and children could be heard screaming. He tried to lift himself, but his limbs refused to obey. The burn on his neck from the creature's touch radiated outward, but the rest of him remained lifeless and numb.

Then he felt it. A warmth spread through him. It began at his back and blossomed outward, his fingers tingling as feeling returned. He gasped, his chest heaving as his breath returned. Turning, he found Alice kneeling beside him, her eyes shut, lips moving in hurried whispers. Her face was pale, and she had a pained expression.

Moments later, she exhaled sharply, her eyes fluttering open. Relief flashed across her face. "You live!" Her voice was hoarse, and she wiped at her damp eyes with a trembling sleeve.

He pushed himself upright, flexing his fingers, testing his strength. "I had thought you had forsaken magic," he murmured, offering a faint, grateful smile.

She returned it, but the moment was fleeting. She reached down, grasping something from the ground. More screams rang out in the distance.

As they ran, she lifted the object for him to see – Elizabeth's wooden fiddle.

His breath hitched. "Do you believe it to be her token?"

"I know not for certain," she panted. "But I have suspected it, and—"

They rounded the corner – and froze.

The creature loomed ahead, its form hunched over the trembling body of Hannah Wrenkle, Amelia's younger sister. The poor woman's eyes were wide, her mouth parted in a silent scream as tendrils of black smoke coiled around her, draining the life from her trembling frame. Her husband lay unconscious nearby.

Before Alexander or Alice could act, the darkness swallowed Hannah whole. The last glimpse of her features twisted in agony before the void claimed her completely.

"Margaret, no!" Alice cried, thrusting the fiddle high.

The creature snarled, recoiling as though stung. But in an instant, it lunged. The force of its attack sent Alice hurtling backward into Alexander. The two crashed onto the cold, muddy ground. His head struck something hard and pain exploded behind his eyes. His vision filled with sparks and stars.

"Alice..." he groaned, blinking against the blur.

She lay motionless beside him, her fingers slack, the fiddle now streaked with mud. He reached for it, his grasp weak, vision splitting as he struggled to focus. He could hear the creature's slow, deliberate steps drawing near.

With a final surge of effort, he yanked the fiddle up. *This is folly*, he thought and squeezed his eyes shut, bracing for the end. But no blow came.

Daring to look, he saw Alice rising unsteadily, one hand clutching her ribs. "Was it successful?" she rasped.

"I know not..." He turned, scanning the surroundings. The creature was gone – but the battle was not yet won. Agonized cries echoed from beyond the trees.

Alice coughed, dark blood speckling her lips. Her knees buckled, but she caught herself. "Go," she whispered, nodding toward the fiddle.

Alexander hesitated until more cries came from the distance. "I shall not be long."

Wiping the mud from the fiddle, he pushed forward, his steps unsteady. His legs threatened to fail him, but he pushed forward.

He didn't need to go far before he found it – the creature, standing over the contorted form of a fallen man. His axe lay abandoned, shattered at his side.

"Margaret!" Alexander called, echoing Alice's earlier cry.

The reaction was instant. The creature convulsed, its form flickering as it recoiled. It staggered backward, limbs trembling, smoke unraveling at its edges.

With little thought, Alexander advanced, brandishing the fiddle like a torch. "Where are you headed, my Raven?" he taunted.

The thing flinched, its body writhing as though struggling to hold itself together. It stumbled, crashing into trees, knocking aside debris in its frantic retreat. Each step seemed to draw more and more energy from it, and it slowed.

And then, with a final, anguished shriek, the beast collapsed. The darkness around it surged upward, a great black cloud expanding, enveloping everything in its path.

Alexander shielded his face, staggering as the darkness swallowed him whole. The air turned thick, suffocating, the world reduced to a howling void.

He waited. And waited.

Then, the blackness thinned.

A shape emerged, shrouded in shadow. Huge. Unmoving.

Alexander stumbled forward, tears burning his eyes, his breath coming in desperate gasps.

"Elizabeth?" he whispered.

Then he saw it.

48

The Wrenkle

The three of them sat huddled around the small coffee table, the tension from earlier still lingering in the air. They had waited in silence, listening for the intruder upstairs to leave, and only now, with the house quiet, had they dared make any noise. Gwen had spread out the last of their provisions, and they each grabbed a small portion, making the most of their makeshift breakfast.

Liam leaned back against the sofa, which had doubled as his bed, and pulled his large bag onto his lap. He yanked hard on the metal zipper and rummaged, his hands disappearing into its depths. Sarah and Gwen watched him, curious but silent. After a few moments, he produced a small, familiar key chain.

"Hey! Those are mine!" Gwen exclaimed, her face lighting up as she reached for the keys.

"Yep. Found 'em on the floor of my truck. Must've fallen out of your backpack."

He shoved his hand back into the bag and this time pulled out a semi-wrinkled, laminated map. Spreading it out on the table, he began tracing the faded lines with his finger. "The barricades we ran into last night."

"Literally," quipped Gwen.

Liam nodded and gave her a slight grin. "Those were set up by Clark and Cooper to keep you from leaving, they're likely still up. These are the two main roads that'll take you down the mountain to the highway."

Sarah leaned in, squinting at the worn map. The folds had almost worn through the paper, and the faded ink made it hard to read.

"This is where we are now, and this is the road we took last night." His finger traced a winding route. "Everyone knows those are the only ways off the mountain." He paused, frowning thoughtfully. "But there's another way. A narrow trail that leads up over the ridge, then down a steep path. It connects to this road – after the barricades."

"That's the hiking trail I used earlier…"

"Yep, Firecracker. Same trail. I use it now and then when I need to avoid… complications. The problem is, I don't know if your little car can handle that terrain. It's a tough road, and if they've set up a third barricade at the other end…" He trailed off, rubbing his chin in thought. "But I don't think you two have a better option."

"Wait, you keep saying 'you two.' Uncle, aren't you coming with us?" Sarah asked, confusion clouding her mind. "You're in danger too."

Liam shook his head slowly, avoiding her gaze.

"That makes no sense!"

He reached out and touched her arm. "Listen, I can't leave – not easily. It's… complicated."

She shoved his hand away, leaning back into the sofa, her

arms folded. "Then I'm not leaving either."

"Lass, please. I can't come with you."

"Oh yeah? Why not?!"

Liam exhaled heavily. "Because... where I go, she follows. You'll never be safe if I'm with you. I'm cursed. It's drawn to me – always knows where I am and seems bound to my general vicinity. I don't know how far she can range but she... the creature has never been able to leave, not without me."

"I'm cursed too you know."

"Yes, lass, you are, and you will always feel compelled to come back. Drawn to the Wrenkle. You'll always feel it calling to you. You'll be drawn to it; you'll continue to have the dreams – always feel something missing. But no matter what you do, lass, you cannot, for any reason, come back. You get off this mountain and you stay as far away as possible!"

"But why you? Aren't there any other McGregors who can take your place? Are you the only one that can play that role? You've been doing this for – who knows how long."

"And I'll keep doing it until I die." Liam's voice broke, his eyes filling with tears. "There's no one left – no one who can take this from me anymore." He wiped his face roughly, then turned back to the map. "Now... The old trail is your only chance. If it's not blocked..." Liam stopped immediately, his eyes now fixed on something across the room.

"What if it's blocked?" Gwen asked, absentmindedly nibbling at a pastry.

"Oh, don't worry about that. I cleared it this morning. But you won't be leaving that way," said a voice from the stairs.

Startled, Sarah and Gwen turned to see Clark standing on the other side of the room, disheveled, a pistol in his right hand, and an iPad in his left. His uniform was wrinkled, his shirt partially untucked, and a long tear running down his pants.

"Raise your hands where I can see them!"

"Clark."

"Shut your mouth, old man! I don't want to hear a word from you!"

"Please, listen to me, Clark…" Liam was pleading. It was a strange contrast to his normal monotone voice.

"Not another word, or I swear I'll put a bullet in you!" Clark's face twisted.

Liam leaned back, raising both hands in surrender, watching Clark with a mix of sorrow and resignation.

Clark's gaze swept the room, his gun still pointed at Liam. "Back up!" he barked at Gwen, who quickly moved aside, fear etched across her face. Using his heel, he slid Liam's pistol out of Gwen's reach.

"Aren't you going to call this in?" Sarah asked, her voice tinged with indignation. "Is this how you normally arrest suspects?"

"Not this time." Clark muttered, his lips curling into an unsettling smile. His eyes darted wildly between them. "Now move… over here." He waved his gun, forcing them into a corner. They obeyed; hands still raised.

"Why are you doing this?"

Clark ignored her. He kicked the gun on the ground toward the sofa and began rifling through the items on the table.

"You three have caused me more trouble than you're worth. But it's going to be fine. I've cleaned up the mess, and now I'm going to fulfill my part of the deal." He glanced at the iPad in his hand and waved it in the air. "By the way, I reviewed the footage on this thing, it led me right to you." He tossed the iPad at their feet. "Your uncle was very pleased that his surveillance system came in so handy."

Sarah winced at this, the pain of betrayal sizzling in her chest at the implication.

"Clark, please… this won't end well for you," Liam said softly, his voice almost a whisper.

"What did I say, Liam? You want to get shot?" Clark's eyes flared and he stormed toward them, moving a few feet. He stood motionless, daring Liam to speak again. "Alright then," he muttered after a few moments and then lowered the gun slightly. "Here's what's going to happen, and I don't want to hear a word from any of you."

Chirp chirp! The iPad lit up. Then more chirps came in quick succession. They all stared at the device. Clark shot them all another warning look and pointed at Liam. Just then, a loud noise echoed nearby – a metallic bang, like a heavy door slamming shut. Sarah and Gwen exchanged fearful glances before turning back to Clark.

"You two, with me. Ms. Jensen, you get to stay." He raised the gun again, gesturing wildly, directing Gwen and Liam like an unhinged traffic officer. "Upstairs! Both of you!"

Gwen began sobbing uncontrollably as she moved, tears streaming down her face as she reached for Sarah.

Suddenly, a metallic thud reverberated from inside the office, the sound louder than before. The noise echoed through the basement, startling even Clark. Sarah saw fear flash in his eyes as he edged closer.

"Upstairs, now! I won't tell you again!" His voice cracked, his bravado fading. His captives weren't looking at him anymore – they were staring at the office door.

There was another thud, followed by a low, unsettling vibration. Whatever was trying to break through had come through the secret passage through the shop and had successfully broken through the outer door and was now in the office. Clark instinctively turned; his gun aimed in that direction.

"Get upstairs," he commanded again, his voice barely above a whisper now, retreating toward the stairs. Fear seemed to ripple through him as his gun jerked from left to right, uncertainty clouding his face.

A softer, more deliberate thump sounded at the door, and Sarah's heart pounded fiercely. She moved with Gwen and Liam toward the stairs, the metallic sounds growing louder behind them.

"Liam… you have the little girl in there?" The voice was cold, raspy, eerily upbeat. Something about it sounded different – more human, clearer than ragged whispers Sarah had heard before. The voice let out a low, bone-chilling cackle that sent shivers through her body.

"You stay right there!" Clark screamed; his gun now aimed directly at Sarah. His face twisted into a grimace, a blend of madness and terror.

"Get the flute!" Liam's voice was a hoarse whisper, filled with urgency and terror. His eyes were wild as they darted from the office door to something across the room.

Clark swung the gun toward him, shaking his head. Liam's eyes flickered desperately between the door and an object in the corner. "The Moores ordered that you were not to be harmed, Liam, but I promise you, we're beyond that now."

"Clark, please! You don't want this – you don't know who's on the other side of that door!" Liam's voice cracked with desperation. His eyes darted to the watch in Gwen's pocket and then to Sarah. He mouthed the name "Margaret." and for the first time Sarah saw true fear there in his eyes.

"That's right, Liam… You tell em." The voice behind the door sounded almost playful.

Clark looked at the door and hesitated, his eyes wide with uncertainty. For just a moment, regret flashed across his face.

A booming laugh erupted from behind the door, followed by another thunderous slam, rattling the door frame.

As if on cue, Liam didn't wait – he lunged toward the coffee table, his eyes set on the pan flute, but a deafening crack split the air that halted his movement immediately.

Sarah blinked and in an instant, Liam's body lay motionless on the ground.

"No!" she wailed, her voice cracking in anguish. Clark stood frozen, staring at the gun still smoking in his hand. His fingers trembled as he lowered the weapon to his side, the reality of what he'd done sinking in.

"Run… Sarah." Liam's voice was faint, muffled by the gurgling sound of blood in his throat.

The office door burst open with a thunderous crash, the hinges snapping as it fell forward, landing with a thud on the carpet. Clark stumbled back, barely dodging the door as it slammed down at his feet.

From the billowing smoke, the creature emerged, a dark silhouette in the choking blackness. Clark's wide-eyed terror was palpable as he scrambled away, but the thing was too fast, only pausing for a brief moment to look at Liam's body on the floor. It lunged at Clark with terrifying speed, and in a split second, his body was engulfed in a swirling mass of darkness.

A sickening crunch followed by Clark's bloodcurdling

scream echoed through the room.

Primal instinct took over Sarah. She grabbed Gwen, her limbs shaking, as she hauled her up the stairs, each step a clumsy scramble for survival. Gwen was in shock, barely moving, her eyes glassy with fear. Sarah nearly dragged her up, her muscles burning from the effort.

"Gwen! Come on!" Sarah's voice was desperate, cracking with panic. Clark's tortured cries mixed with the monster's feminine, angry laughter echoed from below, sending another jolt of fear through her. Gwen collapsed onto the floor, curling into a fetal position as Sarah struggled to pull her away from the basement door.

Slamming the heavy door shut, Sarah knew it wouldn't hold back the demon, but in her frantic state, it was the only thing she could think of doing. She could hear her heart hammering in her chest, the adrenaline pounding in her veins as she hooked her arms under Gwen's and dragged her toward the garage.

"Come on, Gwen! We have to move!" With one final heave, she yanked Gwen through the garage door and down the cement steps. They tumbled onto the cold garage floor, Sarah gasping for breath, her mind racing. Clark's screams had stopped, and an eerie silence filled the house.

Sarah's body trembled with the fear of what might come next. Her mind scrambled for a plan.

"Gwen, you have to get up. You have to help me." Gwen's blank, wide-eyed stare remained fixed, her mind seemingly shattered by the horrors of what they'd just witnessed.

Tears blurred Sarah's vision as panic clawed at her. "Keys!" she yelled frantically. Her hands fumbled through Gwen's pockets, spilling their contents onto the cold concrete – coins, wrappers, an old piece of paper with scribbled names on it, and the old pocket watch – but no keys. *Hadn't he given them to her?*

"Please, please…" she muttered to herself, her voice rising in desperation as she checked the pockets again. Nothing. The dread in her chest deepened. With Gwen in shock and no way to escape, the creature would find them. They were trapped, and Sarah knew, deep down, that they wouldn't survive much longer.

49

Isolation

15 January 1726

Alexander's Journal

We have endured grievous days. The McGregor and Wrenkle company did reach our destined settlement in late November of the year 1725. Yet, twelve souls were lost upon the journey, with but one claimed by natural cause. The curse that now afflicts our small communion did manifest in most dreadful fashion when Margaret did contrive a means to overcome Elizabeth by use of the pocket watch. How this came to pass is yet beyond our knowing, yet I have since retrieved the token and secreted it where she shall never lay claim to it again.

Margaret – or rather, the fiend that hath taken her form – did consume four women of the Wrenkle line, whilst seven men did forfeit their lives in the vain attempt to thwart the creature, among them both McGregors and Wrenkles. This calamity hath left a deep scar upon our settlement, and great strife doth now fester among our number. Many have embraced the name once ascribed to the curse – *The Wrenkle* – and most unfortunate it is, for it hath sown division betwixt the families. The McGregors whisper accusation of witchcraft against the Wrenkles, whilst the Wrenkles themselves cast blame upon Elizabeth. By providence, the estate wherein we now abide is vast and well appointed, such that those whose discord is most grievous may be housed apart. My own family is the most estranged, for those who bore witness to the horror are yet shaken, having beheld Elizabeth in the wake of the fiend's banishment.

We do rejoice that Alice yet liveth. Though sorely wounded – her ribs broken by the hand of her own sister – she hath been mercifully preserved. By what means she doth yet draw breath, I cannot say, save that the very magic which did restore my own strength hath, in some wise, aided in the mending of her grievous hurts. 'Tis a thing I scarce can reckon with, for witchcraft doth set my soul in unease, yet in these two instances, I must needs offer my gratitude for its effects.

Alice and I do continue in our endeavors to break the curse. Much of mine own days art spent in labor to build our new life, yet at night we toil long hours, poring o'er ancient tomes and testing such means as may rid our company of the hexes that do plague us still.

We do keep many documents in support of our work, and whilst I shall not write them here, there be several matters of great import that we have together uncovered in our study of Alice's books and the scattered notes of her schooling. We now perceive there be more than three curses and charms entangled in this foul work. Alice hath said oft that such be the reason it is so grievous a task to undo. Of these, we have discerned four with certainty. The first is the *Vitae Perpetuum*, which in Latin signifieth Perpetual Life. A spell most difficult and perilous, it doth perform as its name would suggest, though not without dire consequence. Next, we have found knowledge of a charm called The Soul's Lantern, which doth allow Margaret to know the whereabouts of any she seeketh. We believe she did inherit this enchantment from Claire, having bewitched a lock of mine own hair. With this, we do suspect she employed a further charm known as Woven Affection, which bindeth a soul with unbreakable devotion to the one who hath cast it. Of these workings, we have gained some understanding, and Alice doth surmise that Margaret, in her desperation, did cast them in reckless succession, thinking to regain mine affections.

Yet most troubling of all, we know she did at last invoke Sanguis Pactum; the Blood Pact. We cannot yet fathom what did drive her to perform so foul a rite. All who practice witchcraft have heard the dread warnings of this curse, and none do dare attempt it. The spell is said to grant great power, but little else is known save that it doth call forth a demon into the realm of the living, if but for a fleeting moment. We continue our search for the other curses or charms, for one among them must needs be the seal that bound these spells to more than but a few. Margaret, being yet unskilled in the craft, must have wrought them amiss, for the curse did bind itself not only to three souls, but to entire lines of descent.

At length, I would record a strange occurrence which we have lately witnessed. We do now believe we have uncovered how Margaret doth at times manifest herself in our world. Some weeks past, she did appear before Alice and me as we studied in the late hours. Unlike before, she seemed possessed of her full faculties and held herself with greater command. We were afeared, yet when we saw she meant us no harm, we did put questions to her ere Elizabeth should reclaim herself. Margaret did then confess that all who are taken remain in a dark place, deep within Elizabeth. She herself doth not fully comprehend it but likens it to dwelling behind a shadowed veil, which at times doth part, allowing her brief glimpses into the waking world. She spake further of the demon, who is ever among them, whispering to them, bending their wills to his own purpose. She described a cruel order in which they must abide – Elizabeth seated foremost, followed by Margaret, and then the demon himself.

Yet beyond this, Margaret would say no more. A sudden wrath overtook her, and she would answer us no further. Still, we did glean one grim certainty – whensoever Margaret doth return, the demon shall ever follow. This knowledge doth shed new light upon many questions, for though Elizabeth hath before spoken of the dark place, she doth but recall it dimly upon waking from troubled dreams.

In sum, we are yet no nearer to a cure for this most wicked affliction. I do continue to age, now nigh unto six and thirty years, whilst mine own wife remaineth unchanged, fixed in the bloom of her nineteenth year. By reason of this, and of many things besides, I am grown most desperate to find a remedy. I have e'en considered loosing Margaret from her prison, that she might yield some wisdom in how we might break the curse. Alice doth stand firm against this course, and she doth warn me most fervently that Margaret is yet enthralled by the demon, and that we should be hard-pressed to wrest any command from her.

I do pray and hold great faith that a cure shall be found in due time. I believe God doth guide our endeavors, and despite our manifold woes, we do yet live in a measure of contentment, removed from the scornful gaze of those who once stood in judgment against us.

50

The Clever

What am I doing? she thought, her pulse throbbing in her limbs. She knew the creature could be anywhere, waiting to strike. But there was no choice. *I need those keys.*

Sarah descended the basement stairs, holding her breath, listening for any trace of the demon, Margaret. The house had gone deathly silent. The wood steps creaked underfoot; every squeak magnified in the stillness. Each sound reverberated through her, but she couldn't afford to stop.

Her hand, trembling, gripped the dangling pocket watch, its chain swinging gently with each step. She'd managed to flip the basement light switch, casting a weak yellow glow over the scene, but it did little to dispel the shadows.

At the last stair, Sarah halted, straining to see around the wall. Her stomach churned as she peeked, expecting to see the dark woman lurking.

Her breath caught at the sight of Clark Lambert's body, twisted unnaturally on the floor. His face. His eyes, frozen in terror, stared wide and blank at her, and his mouth gaped open in a soundless scream. His body was misshapen, the angles all wrong, as if every bone had been broken and reformed in the wrong way.

Her knees threatened to give out, her free hand slapping over her mouth to stifle the scream rising in her throat. *He was furious only moments ago, now... gone.* She had seen death, but nothing like this. Slowly, carefully, she edged around his body, keeping her distance from the horror, her eyes scanning desperately for the keys.

But they were nowhere to be found. She continued to search the large room. She glanced toward the dark tunnel. The shop passage had a broken door that yawned open, dark, until the end where light could be seen illuminating the ladder. *Had the creature used it to escape? Was it outside now, waiting?* Light flickered faintly at the tunnel's end as loose wooden debris swung at the opening. She took a long step past the room as her nerves got the best of her.

Then a soft sound, barely audible, snapped her focus back to the room. Her heart leaped into her throat as she turned. *Liam.* He lay against the couch in a contorted heap, one leg propped awkwardly on the table. Without thinking, she rushed to him, dropping to her knees beside his broken body.

His face, peaceful, despite the blood smeared across his beard, seemed too calm for the chaos around them. A fresh gunshot wound gaped at his side, but in his right hand, he held something tightly. *The red cloth token.* He had used it. *He must have scared the demon away.*

"Liam..." Sarah's voice cracked, and her throat tightened as tears poured freely down her cheeks. She grabbed his hand, clutching it as though her touch could keep him here. For a moment, it felt safe, just being next to him.

His eyes fluttered open, and he coughed weakly, blood staining his lips. "I... I knew you'd come back, lass." His voice was wet with blood, his chest heaving with effort.

She choked on a sob and wrapped her arms around him, her face buried in his chest. "I'm so sorry, I'm so sorry!"

Liam's eyes closed again for a moment, but his hand shifted toward her, palm opening to reveal a bloodied set of car keys. He'd never had the chance to give them to Gwen. "Here... Take these... Go." She stared at the keys, realization flooding her mind.

"No. You're coming with me. I'll bring the car around. I can help you—"

Liam's weak, defeated smile cut her off. "No, lass. I'm staying here."

"Liam, please, don't do this! I can't leave you here, I can't—"

"I was never leaving. Not alive." He coughed violently, blood spraying from his mouth. "Lass, this is peace for me. Please let me go."

Her heart shattered and she dropped her head onto his chest, her tears soaking his shirt. *How many times had he saved her?* And now, when it mattered most, she couldn't save him. At least not in the way she wanted.

Liam's hand weakly stroked her hair. "Love you, lass. Go." His voice was barely a whisper.

Argument after argument came and went from her mind but she finally relented and backed away. "I love you too, Uncle." She lifted his head, placing a pillow beneath it gently. *He deserves peace.* His head lolled to the side, his breathing slowing, a small smile pulling at the corner of his mouth.

As the quiet overtook them once again, reality snapped back. *Gwen.* She wiped her face, shoving the keys into her pocket next to the pocket watch. *I have to get out. I have to save Gwen.* She gently pulled the red cloth from his other hand which had entirely relaxed now. She then took one more look at him, his face was peaceful, and she could no longer hear his breathing. She kissed her hand and touched his forehead and stepped back around the coffee table.

That's when she saw it.

She'd missed it on the way in, her focus fixed on the open office door. She had walked within inches of it without realizing. Now, near Clark's grotesquely twisted body on the far side of the room, the door to one of the previously empty rooms stood shattered, its wooden frame splintered inward.

But that wasn't what froze her in place.

On the floor, a long black arm extended from the doorway, its fingers curling and flexing slowly, deliberately.

Sarah's breath hitched, stopping entirely as her body locked in place, one foot hovering mid-step. Normally, she might have called it something she'd never seen before – but she *had* seen it. She recognized the hideous claw from her dreams. Memories surged back, vivid and sharp, of the grotesque demon chained to the floor in her nightmares. The clarity was almost unbearable, a visceral jolt that made her want to scream. Fear alone kept her silent.

The arm moved again, withdrawing slowly back into the room until it disappeared from view.

Her primal instincts took over, her mind racing in panicked loops. *Run? Scream and run? Just run?* The absurdity of her thoughts swirled, each option worse than the last, as though she'd spun a game show wheel where every prize was a nightmare.

Moments passed, stretching unbearably in the silence. Finally, her body moved, unbidden. Tiptoeing through the room, she traced a wide arc to avoid the ominous doorway, her every step as careful as a breath.

Then it was there.

The creature sprawled across the carpet; its massive, hulking form larger than anything she could have imagined. A grotesque tail – or limb – stretched across the room, its sheer size defying reason. *What could possibly have happened here?* Her mind spun with the lack of information. *Liam spoke of the tokens but mentioned nothing of the demon. How did this come to be?*

Her eyes widened, impossibly so, as she took it all in.

Holding her breath, she edged forward, her head turning, neck craning to keep the beast in view. Just as it was nearly out of sight, she caught it: a single, glowing yellow eye staring straight at her. Watching her.

The scream escaped before she could stop it, sharp and piercing, only to be muffled hastily by her own fist. It was too late. The demon stirred.

It began to move, dragging itself out of the room with sharp, jerking motions. Its claws tore into the carpet, ripping it apart as it crawled forward. Its enormous head lolled from side to side, as though struggling to shake off its own sluggishness – a struggle that was quickly fading. With every motion, it grew faster, stronger, more deliberate.

Sarah couldn't look away, her body frozen as terror rooted her to the spot. She backed up until her heels hit the wall behind her, then the corner. Her instincts screamed for her to curl into a ball and disappear, but sheer panic drove her to keep moving, sliding along the wall toward the stairs.

The creature snarled; its yellow eyes locked on her. The anger and hunger in its gaze were palpable, an animalistic drive pushing it forward. Its legs twitched, then jerked to life, until finally it managed to push itself into a low crouch. It was nearly fully mobile now.

Sarah broke. She bolted toward the stairs, heart hammering wildly, her flight taking her dangerously close to the creature. Its massive form loomed, claws reaching as she darted past. She sprinted along the wall, her focus solely on escape – until her foot caught on something.

She fell, tumbling head over heels into the far wall, landing with a jarring thud. Pain flared through her body, but she twisted around instantly, her leg caught in the very chair they'd used the night before.

The demon was coming. It was still sluggish, but its movements had quickened and now was just feet away.

Sarah yanked her leg free from the chair, her hands trembling as she shoved it away with her other foot. The metal frame skidded across the floor toward the creature, but it reacted instantly, swatting the chair aside with terrifying ease. The crash echoed through the room as the demon let out a deafening bellow, a sound so powerful it seemed to shake the walls and pierce her eardrums.

In that moment, amidst the chaos and fear, a thought emerged from the recesses of her mind – simple, almost absurd in its clarity. She had forgotten it in her panic, but now it was undeniable: she was holding something.

Her fingers opened, and there it was – the red fabric crumpled in her fist.

Heart pounding, she merely turned her palm upward, the wad of scarlet unfurling like a flower in bloom. The fabric

369

seemed to move of its own accord, its vibrant hue stark against the dim room, opening like a time-lapse of petals reaching for the sun.

Time seemed to slow.

The creature crouched, its massive form tensing as it launched itself through the air. For a brief, horrifying moment, she doubted. *Did this token actually hold any power?*

The answer came with breathtaking certainty.

Mid-leap, the demon froze, its massive body suspended unnaturally. Then, with a sickening crash, it plummeted to the floor, the impact shaking the ground beneath her.

Its blackened skin began to crack, thin fissures spreading like a spiderweb. Chunks of its body splintered and fell away, each fragment dissolving into plumes of dark smoke before disappearing entirely.

Sarah kept the fabric held high, her other arm shielding her face as the room filled with the acrid black haze. The air turned cold, a familiar chill rushing past her, carrying the last remnants of the creature's disintegration.

When the smoke finally cleared, the monster was gone.

In its place lay a small, red-haired woman curled on the floor. She writhed in apparent pain, clawing and pushing herself backward, as if recoiling from the scarlet token still in Sarah's hand.

Their eyes met for the briefest of moments, those bright green eyes, before the woman scrambled to her feet and bolted toward the open office door.

"Ruth!" Sarah yelled. Instinct had taken over and the idea of meeting her great-aunt, even if possessed, momentarily made her forget fear. The woman paused and looked back over her shoulder. Those beautiful green eyes showed sadness that cut through Sarah's heart. All Sarah wanted was a chance to be with her, a chance to ask her questions. A desperate desire to know her family, if only her aunt. Unconsciously, she reached a hand toward her.

"Sarah run... I can't hold it... Go now... Run." Her voice seemed pained as she spoke through clenched teeth. She then turned again and ran through the open office door.

Sarah could hear the frantic patter of her footsteps fading into the distance, growing quieter until they disappeared entirely.

She let her body slacken and she fell to the floor. Tears streamed down her cheeks as she tried to make sense of what just happened but there was nothing. Her mind seemed to have shut down. She lay there staring at the ceiling. The voice of her great-aunt replayed over again in her head.

Then a noise came faintly from the main floor, snapping her out of her trance. *Gwen! We've gotta get out of here.*

With a renewed sense of urgency, she rolled over and got to her feet before rushing up the stairs. As she approached the garage door, she heard Gwen's voice, faint but present. "It's okay, Ralph... It's going to be okay."

She burst through the door to find Gwen sitting up, holding the cat. Relief flooded Sarah's chest. "Gwen! You're back!"

Gwen smiled, though her eyes still looked distant. Sarah didn't waste any time. She slammed her hand on the garage opener, the large door creaking as it slowly rose. "Come on, Gwen, let's get you on your feet."

She led Gwen out to the car, dropping Ralph into her lap and hastily finding the right key. The engine roared to life. *Finally.* As they backed down the driveway, she glanced at the cabin, half-expecting to see a dark figure in the window or in the yard. But the house stood silent, shrouded in shadow and the yard empty as ever.

Is this really it? The thought came and then she pushed it aside.

Gwen seemed to be thinking the same thing. "Did we make it?" she asked, her voice soft but hopeful as she petted Ralph's head.

"We're about to find out." Sarah pressed the gas pedal down hard.

Dust swirled behind them as the cabin and the forest slowly shrank into the distance. Clark had spoken the truth; the wrecked cruiser was gone. *Freedom!* Sarah's heart soared as they sped down the curved paths and switchbacks. Each mile passed by until they eventually crossed from the dirt road to asphalt. The smooth surface under the tires felt like salvation. She let out a joyful scream, startling Ralph, but Gwen was laughing, grabbing her hand.

"We're going to make it! We're finally going to make it! Did you hear that, Ralph?"

"We are," Sarah agreed, a wide grin breaking across her face. "And we're never going back. Not for a million dollars."

More miles and minutes passed, warming Sarah's heart as they passed road sign after road sign. She looked at her friend and they exchanged giddy smiles. It was over, they had survived. They hadn't begun to understand how to put the nightmare behind them fully, but they were safe. *Can we celebrate yet? Did we actually make it from the curse?* The thought sat in her head, her days of fear keeping her from mentioning it.

Gwen seemed to be thinking the same thing but broke the silence in a way that only she could. "Hey... I know we don't want to stop until we're farther away from that mountain but I'm starving. I've got the best idea."

"Aren't all of your ideas the best?"

"Well, this one is. Two words, ice and cream!"

Sarah shot her a grin and raised her eyebrows. "You know, you've got a deal! Actually, I can't believe how hungry I am. That is a great idea."

They laughed together before Gwen went quiet. "Hey Sarah, how do we explain this when we're home? What do we say happened while we were here? I mean, the things we've seen this week... the things we've learned... How do we even begin to explain it?"

Sarah considered it but there was still way too much to unpack. "I have no idea... I'm too excited to think about that right now," she said, but in reality, she couldn't even begin to bring herself to face those dark facts yet. She really didn't want to think about any of it. She didn't want to think about the cabin nor her aunt and uncle or the part they played in this week. That one stung a bit. *Note to self, cancel the thank you gift to Aunt Melissa and Uncle Steve.* She didn't want to think about Officer Lambert. Her heart fell as she thought about Liam, sitting there against the couch, and his final words to her. She bit her lip as the memory made her eyes tear up.

She reached up and wiped her eyes. She wanted to put it all behind her: the curse, the truth about witchcraft, and the demon that had consumed so many of her ancestors before her and tried to do the same to her. She smiled at Gwen, hiding the thoughts that would haunt her for the rest of her life.

Gwen giggled. "As it turns out, Monkey, I guess I'm not as good at fixing things as I thought I was." She jerked her thumb over her shoulder with a sheepish grin. Sarah turned her head and saw something out of the corner of her eye. The green oxidized trunk lid was raising and lowering in the wind as they went down the highway.

"Well, nobody's perfect," she said, reaching over and holding Gwen's hand again. They both giggled. "We'll take a look at it when we stop for that ice cream."

The trunk continued to bob up and down during their journey home. It was sort of mesmerizing, distracting Sarah each time it popped up and then back down out of sight. She tried focusing on the open road until the trunk lid popped up once more and then didn't go back down.

Sarah couldn't help but look through the rear view mirror. A familiar feeling surged inside her chest. The very last thing she saw before she lost control of the car and went careening off the road, was her great-aunt Ruth's green eyes, wreathed in black billowing smoke, staring at her through the small space under the open trunk lid.

51

Opportunity

16 March 1727

Alexander's Journal

I am afraid I can write but little, and I believe this may be the last time I am able for many months hence. The tribulations of these past months have rendered it most difficult to find leisure, and the growing disquiet of our company hath demanded that I spend much of mine hours tending to Elizabeth in her present state.

Alice and I do hold it to be the work of some charm, yet for all our strivings, many of the Wrenkle and McGregor kin do persist in drawing near to our dwelling, as though drawn unto Elizabeth as moths be drawn to flame. Among them are those who stand with us against this accursed craft, yet others have traveled from far lands, undertaking long and wearisome journeys to settle within our once humble community. The nearness of so many who bear the Wrenkle blood hath wrought a dire change in Elizabeth, and alas, she doth now comport herself in a manner most akin to Margaret. There have been disappearances – Wrenkle women lost without trace. I have not beheld it with mine own eyes, yet in mine heart, I fear my poor wife is, in some hapless way, the cause of it.

The murmurings of witchery amongst these new folk have been stirred anew, and I can endure it no longer. I have resolved that a small number of us shall quit this land. Ere long, we shall set forth upon a ship bound across the vast ocean to the British American Colonies. There, I do hope, we shall find a place so remote that no soul of Wrenkle blood shall ever chance upon us.

Alexander closed the journal with a snap. He gazed upon his young wife, fast asleep in the nearby bed. She had held reservations about the long journey and the thought of leaving their homeland, yet she knew it was necessary. He had observed how those feelings had grown stronger the further south they traveled. Yet, her mood had lightened notably when they had visited her former home on their way. As the journey continued, she became ever more lucid, growing ever more like the wife he once knew.

Suddenly, loud noises echoed from outside. Alexander rose and stretched before moving toward the window, peering out at the port. He saw men working tirelessly into the night, large bundles of luggage and provisions being hauled up the gangplank, while others descended to fetch more.

He had never set foot upon a ship, nor had his family. The sight filled him with excitement, and a smile crept onto his face. His children would surely share in his wonder at the sight. Thomas had asked him about it each day, and Alexander had even crafted a small toy vessel for his son.

He yawned and stretched again. For the first time in many months, his heart warmed at the thought of their future.

Hope felt present in their lives, and though it worried him to entertain such a notion, each day he allowed himself to give in to it. He cast one last look at the bustling port and then to the dark sky above. Afterward, he pulled the curtains closed.

He turned but was met with a surprise. His body convulsed momentarily before the shock wore off. Elizabeth stood before him, gazing at him in the dark. This was not an uncommon turn of events, for she often suffered from bad dreams, sometimes rising silently from the bed. He reached out to guide her back to bed, but she merely giggled.

"Did I frighten you, my husband? I did not mean to alarm you."

He paused for a moment, somewhat in shock. "Aye, I did not hear you rise. What troubles you?"

"Is it a requirement that something be amiss? I awoke only to search for my missing husband," she said, a smile dancing on her lips.

He gazed at her in astonishment. It had been years since he had heard her laugh. It sounded like a bell in his ear, and it nearly broke him, causing his lip to quiver as he fought to contain his emotions. She stared into his eyes and laughed again.

"Do not be troubled, Alexander," she said with a knowing expression. "I do feel my strength growing with each passing day. I believe this change does strengthen me, preparing me to fight it."

He stumbled again slightly, astonished at her recognition of the burden they had borne together for so many years. The only time she had spoken of it before had been in rare moments of lucidity, following one of her dreams. A tear trailed down his cheek. Had it been this way all along?

Was the solution as simple as removing themselves from the Wrenkle family? He dared to hope again, and it stung in his chest. It felt entirely too good to be true and yet, the pain lingered after all this time.

She drew closer and enfolded him in her slender arms. Then she leaned in and pressed a kiss to his lips. "Come to bed. We leave early, and you will need your strength for the long day ahead."

He pulled her in a tight embrace and then picked her up into his arms. She laughed again, this time loudly. He grinned widely and allowed himself a hopeful chuckle before returning to bed with her.

52

The Deal

March 15, 2018

Steve sat up with a start, the book on his chest falling to the wood floor with a loud thud. The iPad's chirping noise had brought him out of an unplanned nap. He looked around the room, his eyes fluttering.

He rubbed his eyes and then grabbed his wallet, a folder that held airline and cruise tickets, and the tablet from the nightstand. "Hey, you ready yet!" he called to a closed door in front of him. The door opened to a crack and Melissa put up five fingers. She had a toothbrush in her mouth. He nodded. "Okay, I'm going to take these bags downstairs. Remember our flight leaves in a few hours. We don't want to miss our cruise this time."

He turned his iPad over and looked, there were two new alerts from his security system. He absently pressed a thumb to the notification and the surveillance software loaded. His eyebrows furrowed at pictures it displayed. Then he understood. He sat on his bed and moved to the camera playback section of the application. This was password protected, and he quickly put the five-digit code in.

His fear was confirmed as he reviewed the two videos. The first had captured the shadowy movements of the dark creature moving across his backyard and then entering his shop. He gulped and played the second video, showing the creature climbing the wall and quickly crawling into the attic access with inhuman grace.

He paused for a moment and then exhaled. He then nodded and opened his nightstand, grabbing two items: a small keychain, and a beaded bracelet.

"Mel, our officer friend, was a little too efficient and let our guest loose early. I'm going to finish preparations." The bathroom door came open and she stared at him wide-eyed, a brush in her hand. "It's okay, just as we planned... She's just here a day early. I'll take care of it – you stay here. We'll be gone and on our way to our cruise in no time." He put the iPad back in its charger. He picked up the book off the floor and tossed it to the nightstand on his way out the door. "Oh and make sure to get the letter written for your niece. Remind her to feed Ralph while we're gone." He walked down the stairs while Melissa yelled something. Something about how she'd already taken care of it.

He yanked the shop door open just enough to slip inside, scanning the dim room with cautious eyes. His gaze flickered upwards, settling on the small attic opening he had pried open a week ago. He lingered there, tension creeping into his limbs.

"I saw you on my cameras. I know you're here." His voice betrayed more fear than authority. His hand, still buried in his pocket, clenched around the bracelet. "I see he managed to free you – that's good news." He knelt down and quickly unlocked a door on the floor of the shop and then stood back up.

The final words barely escaped his throat as a thick plume of smoke began curling out from the attic. He flinched and felt the unease in his stomach. *I'll never get used to this thing.*

From the shadows above, clawed hands gripped the edge of the opening, and slowly, the creature's head emerged. Steve recoiled instinctively, nearly stumbling backward, but forced himself to hold his ground.

"Right, well... Everything's ready. Just like our other... arrangements." Steve's voice cracked as cold air settled around him, sharp as ice against his skin. He pulled the small, beaded bracelet from his pocket and held it out like a shield, the name 'Gloria' etched into the worn beads.

The creature halted its slow descent, retreating with a screech that echoed through the hollow attic space. A few moments of tense silence followed, punctuated only by the sound of Melissa's hand creaking the door open behind him. She peeked through, curiosity and fear mingling on her face.

"I told you to stay upstairs during this," Steve hissed, not daring to lower the bracelet, the beads dangling precariously in front of him.

She gave a half-hearted nod but didn't leave, her eyes glued to the attic. With the talisman in hand, his bravado returned. "We'll be gone for a few weeks. Everything's set as usual. You've been freed and, well... a suitable offering is on its way. You should have plenty of time to... do... what you do."

The creature stirred again. Its voice, jagged and inhuman, seeped through the darkness.

"Who..."

Steve stiffened, confused. "Who? What do you…?"

"I know what she's asking," Melissa interjected softly, a knowing smirk tugging at her lips. She stepped closer, her voice cold and clear. "It's your daughter."

He whipped his head toward her, eyes wide with anger and panic. "Don't!" he barked. "Don't provoke it." He didn't wait for the creature's response and without another word, he backed away, pushing her along and exiting through the door as fast as he could manage.

From inside, they heard a pitiful, guttural sob echo through the shop. The sound followed them as Steve slammed the door shut, locking it with trembling hands.

Melissa turned to him, unbothered by the creature's wails. "I'm hungry. Want to grab something to eat before the airport?"

Steve grunted, turning his back on the creature's cries. "Yeah. Let's go. I'll call Davis on the way. He'll be pleased we have another life insurance deal for him." They both grabbed their luggage and left out the front door, locking it behind them.

"Oh remember to put the key under the rock for… what's her name?" Steve said, his forehead creasing at the thought.

"Sarah."

"Oh, that's right, Sarah. I really hope it doesn't make a mess this time. That last one was pretty nauseating."

"Food, Steve."

"Okay, I'm right behind you, dear."

53

The Aftermath

O fficer Sandy Bradford sat on her porch, the cold condensation of her drink chilling her fingers as she absently sprayed water over the plants. The gentle hum of the hose, along with the buzz of distant lawnmowers and neighborhood chatter, should've been calming. Instead, the peaceful suburban backdrop felt too quiet – like it was holding its breath.

"Hey, Silvia!" She forced a smile as her neighbor walked her dog, trying to keep up some semblance of normalcy. Her son's voice broke through the air from deep within the house.

"Mom!"

"I'm out here!" She watched the shimmering arc of water soak the flower bed, trying to suppress the gnawing feeling in her gut.

"Mom!"

"I'm out here!"

The front door creaked open, and her son stepped out, phone in hand. "It's for you." The look on his face told her all she needed to know – something was wrong.

Her heart sank as she reached for the phone. "Hand it over."

She stared at the screen for a moment. *Mike.* She took a deep breath and pressed it to her ear. "Hello?"

"Sandy." There was a pause, too long for comfort. "I'm sorry to call on a Saturday, but... it's bad."

"Spit it out, Mike."

"I found Clark and Coop. They're both dead, Sandy. I'm so sorry."

Her world froze. The cold drink slipped from her grasp, crashing to the porch floor. The soda seeped into the cracks, unnoticed. "Mike..."

The words hit her like a sledgehammer. She gripped the armrest of the chair, knuckles white, as her body went numb. "What – what happened? Do we know?"

Mike's voice was heavy, filled with the weight of things he couldn't yet explain. "We don't know yet. Andy was found early this morning, Clark just a bit ago. It's not... normal, Sandy. The coroner will make the final call, but it looks like they were attacked. Something mauled them – badly. But it didn't eat them. It just..." He trailed off, the unspoken horror settling into the static on the phone.

Sandy squeezed her eyes shut, forcing the bile back down her throat. "I can't believe this, Mike. Nothing about this makes sense." Her voice cracked. "Could it be gang-related? Mob?"

"Not out here, Sandy. That's not what this is." His tone was flat, certain. "We found Clark in the basement of the Moore house. Not a pretty sight."

Sandy's breath caught. "The Moore house... Sarah – Mike, did you see anyone else?"

"No, there was no one else there. But it's funny you mention

Sarah. We found her license at the scene of a wreck nearby. There was one survivor in the car, she's barely alive, they flew her and her cat up to Miller Memorial, but they haven't found Sarah's body. It's like she just… disappeared. They say her friend was saying her name over and over again."

"Sarah… No body?" Her mind raced, trying to fit the pieces together, but they slipped like sand through her fingers.

"Yeah. Lincoln from patrol said the wreck was bad, but no sign of her." There was a brief pause on the line as she heard the voices of people talking to Mike. "Good reminder," he said to someone. "We also found Miss Jensen's car down the road, wrecked and abandoned. We're getting it towed as we speak."

The phone trembled in Sandy's hand as she thought of the interaction she'd had with Sarah. She stood up from the chair, pacing the porch. "Mike, I think Sarah's involved in this. I don't know how, but something's not right. I feel it." She paused. "What about Liam? She mentioned him when she came in."

Mike sighed. "Hold on, Sandy," There was muffled talking in the background for a couple minutes. "Never mind, we just found him too. The old guy is actually alive, barely. He was in the Moore house, in a pool of his own blood, found him in the basement bathroom. Apparently the guys missed him until the clean-up crew showed up. Found him behind the door."

Sandy blinked, trying to process. "Liam? If he was there, he'd know something."

"Yep, I'll talk to him once the doctors clear it. I'm also going to follow up with the Moores when they're back home. There are a lot of unanswered questions on this one."

"Sounds good, Mike. I'll let you get back to it. Thank you for letting me know. I need to prepare myself. I have no idea how I'm going to let Melanie and Coop's wife know. With the chief out of town, I feel I should probably do it."

"Thanks, Sandy, I'll let you know what else we find." The call disconnected and Sandy stared at the ground. Tears welled up in her eyes as she thought about the two men and their families.

"Mom, what's wrong?"

"Oh nothing, buddy. Mommy just hates her job sometimes."

54

The End

Liam awkwardly tightened the last screw into the large metal plate. With a final twist, the door was repaired. He grunted as he stood from the small stool, his back protesting with a sharp ache. Dropping the screwdriver into his tool bag, he kicked it aside and pushed the heavy door shut, testing it. It slammed home with a satisfying thud. The sound echoed through the empty cabin.

He locked one of the bolts with a dull *clunk* and stood there for a moment, listening to the silence. The air in the room felt heavy, like the quiet after a storm. It wasn't as nice as the Moore home, but it was his.

He grabbed the stool and hung it on a fat peg on the wall, the wood creaking under the weight. Then, he went about straightening up the room. It had become cluttered over the last month thanks to the visitors and the mess they'd left behind. He winced, the memory of those encounters bringing a flicker of pain to his side. Even after all this time, some of his wounds hadn't fully healed. His arm, stiff from the damage, still hadn't regained its former strength. He'd spent time at the hospital as well as at the rehabilitation center.

The broom swished against the floor as he swept, clearing dust and dirt, the sound almost soothing in the stillness. After making his bed, he knelt and pulled a few boxes from beneath it. Placing one on the mattress, he opened the lid, revealing a jumble of papers. He smirked to himself. *That little snoop, Gwen. Always poking around.*

Reaching into his pocket, he retrieved a crumpled newspaper clipping. The headline detailed the case of a missing woman – Sarah Jensen. A recent photo of her smiled out from the page, alongside the faces of her worried aunt and uncle, their reward for any information displayed in bold letters. He scoffed softly and smoothed the paper before tucking it into the box with the others.

Steve and Melissa Moore's behavior had long ceased to surprise Liam. They'd been playing their little scam for years, deceiving one victim after another, betraying family and committing insurance fraud with every turn. In the past, their actions had made him sick to his stomach, but now, after witnessing their true colors countless times, he no longer flinched. He had once made a great effort to repel them, even considered leaving entirely, but he knew that Melissa would be drawn to the Wrenkle Curse, and she would follow him wherever he went. At one point, he'd even entertained the idea of helping the creature reach her – but that thought was quickly abandoned. Some part of him, whether moral decency or the lingering grip of the curse, rejected that path. Instead, he had resigned himself to merely tolerating them, and so, they coexisted on the mountain in their uneasy truce, while the Moores continued to carry out their vile agenda.

However, recently, to his amazement, the Moores had up

and vanished. One day they were repairing their heavily damaged home, the next the house was essentially empty. Perhaps the ongoing investigation by the police got a little too risky for them. In any event, it was a welcome turn of events for Liam.

He closed and shoved the box back under the bed and then reached for a small piece of metal on the windowsill. With practiced movements, he pried up a loose set of floorboards. A shaft of pale light from the window spilled into the cavity below, revealing a collection of hidden objects. He pulled a shattered cell phone from his pocket, its screen spiderwebbed with cracks. For a moment, he stared at it, feeling the weight of everything it represented. Then, he placed it next to an old pocket watch and a small brown fiddle. Carefully, he replaced the boards, sealing them from view.

In the kitchen, he started preparing breakfast. The gas burner clicked as it lit up, flames licking the underside of the cast-iron pan. Butter sizzled as it hit the heat, the sound filling the small space. He moved methodically, adding ingredients to the pan and cooking them slowly. The scent of food mingled with the musty air. When it was done, he spooned the meal onto a thick blue plate, placing it on a wooden tray alongside a glass of milk and silverware.

Unlocking the basement door, he hung the key back on its hook. The stairs creaked under his weight as he descended, the dim light from above growing weaker with each step.

"Good morning, lass. Hope you slept better last night."

Sarah sat at the edge of the small bed; her thin fingers clasped together in her lap. She stared blankly at an old black-and-white show on the television. When she turned to look at him, her gaunt face twisted into a faint smile before she returned her gaze to the flickering screen.

"Time to eat. I hope you're hungry today." He put the food next to her dinner plate that was nearly untouched.

She nodded absently, her motions slow and mechanical, like a marionette with tangled strings. He set the tray down on the table and sat across from her.

"I had more dreams. The dark lady… She was there again."

"Aye? And what did she say today?"

"She wants me to leave… To find others like me. But I told her I wasn't supposed to and that I wouldn't."

She turned to him again, her hollow smile creeping back, as though seeking his approval.

"Good, lass. You did the right thing."

Her smile wavered, her expression darkening. "It's not the dark lady I mind. It's him… The dark demon." Her voice trembled, and a tear slipped down her hollow cheek. "He hurts me."

Liam clenched his fists, his chest tightening. He couldn't bear to see her like this – thin, bruised, a shell of who she once was. "I'm sorry, lass."

"It's okay." Her hand brushed his knee in a gesture so fragile, it made him ache more. "You're so nice to me. It's him I don't like… He wants me to do bad things. He wants me to kill you."

Liam tensed, watching her carefully. His hand slid to the pan flute hidden beneath his shirt. He knew the signs. He waited.

She blinked, and the blankness lifted. The smile returned, hollow and vacant. "But I won't. Mother tells me I shouldn't."

He exhaled, relief mingling with sorrow as he pushed the flute back into place.

Standing, Sarah shuffled to the television and turned it off before sinking back onto the bed. "Uncle Liam. Tell me again what my name is. I can't seem to remember."

He let out a short sigh. "Your name is Sarah Jensen. Your mother's name is Gloria. Your best friend is Gwen, and I call her Firecracker."

"Gwen. Yes, I remember her. I miss her. When can we go see her, Uncle?"

"I'm not sure, lass. We can't leave these mountains. It's not safe."

His words lingered in the still air, heavy as a shadow, pressing down on the room. The faint hum of the television filled the silence once more, a dull backdrop to the uneasy quiet between them.

She settled back onto the bed, her brow furrowing, a flicker of unease in her otherwise vacant eyes. "Uncle, do I have to go into the dark hole tonight?"

Liam held her gaze for a moment, the pain in his expression raw and undeniable. He hesitated, his eyes flickering toward the television, as if searching for some reprieve in its soft glow. "We'll see, lass."

"I don't like it in there – it scares me."

His breath hitched, and for a moment, he couldn't find the words. He turned his head, swallowing the knot of sorrow that had risen in his throat. "I know, lass. It scares me too."

www.ingramcontent.com/pod-product-compliance
Lightning Source LLC
Chambersburg PA
CBHW060146260626
47160CB00001B/149